TERRY ANDREWS is the pseudonym of a well-known author of children's books who lives in New York City.

THE STORY
OF HAROLD

TERRY ANDREWS

 A BARD BOOK/PUBLISHED BY AVON BOOKS

AVON BOOKS
A division of
The Hearst Corporation
959 Eighth Avenue
New York, New York 10019

First Equinox Printing, November, 1975.
First Bard Printing, April, 1980.

Printed in the U.S.A.

To my living friends—who will know who you are

THE STORY
OF HAROLD

October 1, 1968

Again last night, for a little while, I was able not to be alive. I was only the life of two people whom I do not know, people perfectly anonymous. I died, was nothing except what they shared: no heart, brain, body, soul, sex—nothing left, apart from their idea of me. The bliss that derives from oblivion is not a simple thing. I live only for such incidents. And soon not even them.

The telephone at nine o'clock; and its ring always makes immediate the remote and still unknown. A man's voice: "Is Terry Andrews there?"

Unfamiliar to me. The unknown came closer. "Yes. This is me."

"We got your number from Connie and Max."

And instantly, in the fire of possibility I was burning alive. I live—mostly truly live—in wallets or in pocket books: other people's address books, not mine: a name and a telephone number, nothing more, exchanged at a party with a recommendation. "They're great."

"They say you're pretty good too."

"Yeah, but they're really great!" A little low-class slang, for effect. The theater of—

"They say you dig a lot of things."

"They're right."

"Like what?"

"Like men and women." —the absurd! The Impossible.

"And everything?"

"If you show me something new, I'll find a new way to be grateful."

"My name's Tony. And my wife is Irene."

"Hi, Tony. Is your wife understanding?"

"Oh yeah. She likes to watch."

"She'll be part of it too, though—"

"Sure. You do dig cunt too—?"

"Your wife'll be able to answer that when I leave." That's vanity, but sadly true.

"When then?"

"As soon as possible."

"Tonight?"

"Just tell me where!" He gave me an address in Brooklyn. "I'm halfway out the door!"

"Oh hey." Before he hung up. "Our kids love Harold."

"Do they?" Children! More and more! The most remote of all human beings.

"Their favorite."

"Tony—are we okay there? I mean, with the kids?"

"They'll be asleep. And I've got a thing: I tie their door shut."

That lambent madness, Saint Christopher's fire—to bathe in it and not be consumed! "I'll see you in half an hour."

The voyage to Brooklyn was a climbing flight to Paradise. I love the train when it finally emerges out of the tunnel and starts its skimming above an infinitude of little houses, perfect square back yards. The thrilling sense of myriad ordinariness, spread out for miles on every side, and utterly visible, has always been one of the great sensations New York has to give. And the common stops—DeKalb Avenue and Nevins Street—ring to me with strangeness of ancient cities.

I got off where he had told me to and walked the blocks to their house: ideal, since it was identical with all the others on that street. In the yard an overturned tricycle, on the stoop a broken doll. The debris of daily experience, but as precious to me as the Mycenaean masks or pre-Columbian jewelry. I rang the bell, and the worn buzzer under my thumb felt as round and firm and valuable as a star sapphire.

He was dark, Italian, and his wife dark too, the man swarthy and overweight, his wife trim, slender, I would guess five years younger. The lights in the living room were already lowered to the proper degree. I was glad of that, since I wanted not to see them too clearly—to preserve the purity of their being utterly unfamiliar.

We had the obligatory social drink, and talked about Connie and Max and others of the group I know—

"Frank got promoted."

"Did he? Great!"

"Anita's so proud." Names, bodies, nothing more, these are.

—But not sex talk yet, only praising them as friends. This deceit is delightful: the delay while you sail on the surface of a situation, while the knowledge of what's to come churns beneath.

But the critical pause occurred, and he pulled her on his lap. The rules of this couple came clear: he strips his wife and plays with her—proprietorship—then he and the second man get undressed together.

Their bodies were utterly indistinguishable from hundreds of others—and another craving was satisfied. And apparently they were pleased with mine. The wife, Irene, gave a little kitten-like murmur. (Thank God I've worked out in a gym so long!)

"We stay down here," said Tony. He took cushions off an open-out couch. (Like mine! Another gift.)

"Swell. But you're sure—about your kids—"

"Come here." I was led to the foot of the stairs. Above, two doorknobs were tied together. "They can't get out. Feel better?"

And behind those doors—children! "Yes." The most inaccessible and difficult souls. Damn them!

On the couch, again to show his authority—his wife, his house—he gently lowered my head to his lap. I was glad to oblige, to his wife's canny-eyed delight. And then to her even more greedy satisfaction, he reciprocated the courtesy. And after that, initiation complete, I could start.

They sensed my excitement, and like almost all of these people, they let me mold them into positions, the physical combinations that give me most pleasure. Within a few minutes the two of them became perfectly plastic, melted down by a desire that they hoped was stronger than theirs, and I got that glorious sense of creation: creation in living material. It's much more than making love, although there's a special thrill to be felt when a husband, of his own accord, slips a rubber over your dick and then waits to watch you fuck his wife. But the true beauty of it is the cracked, patched

3

sidewalk outside the front door. The beauty is the street light showing through the living room blinds. The beauty is faded slipcovers, the secondhand Chevy you sense in the driveway. The whole beauty of it all is the ordinary Impossible world in which the symbolic sex is embedded.

"Now, Tony, lift up your legs. Okay. You go for that, don't you?"

Skeptically—"Sometimes."

"And Irene, crouch over his mouth. Face me. I want to kiss your lips. It's a circle I like."

The moment arrived: I was nothing except the circuit through which their love, desire, their whole marriage perhaps—whatever bound these two people together—raced round and round and round, obliterating me. But then orgasm—the only true beast of prey—rushed out of the jungle of nothingness. I was killed back into life again. And identity—absence, loss—seeped back.

"Oh wow!"

"You okay, Tony?"

"Yeah!"

"Irene?"

"M-*hmm!*"

The melodramatic middle-class moans of sexual satisfaction: they're very endearing, when murmured so self-consciously. These were decent people. I started to like them, and the estrangement of knowing two genuine human beings crept in.

"Can you come again, Terry?"

"Try me."

"In her this time."

"You want my tail?" Difficult—but possible. In the time I have left.

"No. I want to jack off and watch."

I came, and—*noblesse oblige*—faked even more enthusiasm for the woman than the man. But the world was close, and getting closer. We had a little erotic lolling, and then, fatal gesture, I swung my legs over the edge of the couch.

As we dressed, Irene said, "Can we call you again?"

"Any time. Day or night." I have a lie—a girl in town—all prepared to put them off.

At the door, to mend the madness, perhaps restore his dignity,

4

I extended my hand. "You're great, man. Very special people."

He flushed like a boy scout receiving a merit badge. Affection swelled and I had to leave. A friend's cheek-kiss to Irene—but she held me at the door.

"Oh wait! You've got to sign your book."

I hadn't noticed it, hidden under magazines on a table beside the accomplice couch. She picked it up and read the title: *The Story of Harold.* Then opened it and read the first sentence of Chapter One. " 'Harold woke up one morning, and as usual his first thought was that something was wrong.' That's so cute!"

"What are your kids' names?"

"Like us: Tony and Irene."

In the flyleaf I wrote: "For Tony and Irene. And for Mom and Pop too. The very best! Terry Andrews." And said, "Good night." . . .

You see, my unknown witnesses—*whom I now summon urgently* —I inherited a little money, but I make a living—or rather I support myself: it isn't what you'd call a life—by writing children's books.

October 2

Yes, it is time for the creation of *you.* (My hand is quaking deliciously as I approach this notebook. But there's no point in postponement now. The process has started. I'm flying on fear and euphoria.) And I think you're myriad. Not legion. I don't need to be possessed by devils: I've got plenty of my own . . .

A drink now. (My tipple: Scotch.) I do need a *bit* more fortification . . .

> Yes—myriad souls I force to be!
> Oh myriad souls I force to see.
> You myriad souls who will judge me . . .

At least one of you I saw at the Met, standing at that hideous "soipentine" bar. (I have a friend who works at the Met and smuggles me into the management standing room. He has nothing to do with my death, and you won't hear anything more of him.) I was there alone, and not, as usual—

Not yet—oh, not yet . . . When I can, I will, I promise you . . . but not yet.

It was a performance of *Die Frau Ohne Schatten*—the second I'd seen—and you reminded me of that selfish, elegant empress in the opera. And I do remember that night very well. Because Jackie Onassis was there! Do you remember how gorgeous she was in the days of her glamorous widowhood? (If she knew what she was losing, she goofed.) She glanced, from a box, very naturally—a great glance!—at the audience enthralled beneath her. A deity of sweet sadness—blithe, smiling, blinding mere mortals with legends of pain—still gowned in the aura of gorgeous disaster: an effigy of lovely grief . . . Well, I hope I never meet her. She too must be a human being. And as in the case of all swans, beneath that graceful gliding there must be a pair of madly paddling flat feet.

> Brightness falls from the air,
> Queens have died, young and fair,
> An' Jackie just married a Greek millionaire! . . .

Now stop it now, Terry! Get back to your purpose, and stop this life-giving procrastination. Remember: you too are one of your witnesses! . . . Still, there you were at that cramped and snake-like bar. And you'd just had champagne. You were twirling the slender stem of the glass in that gorgeous—God, gorgeous—device of yours: five fingers articulate beyond any animal's ambition—evolution's chef-d'oeuvre—a woman's hand . . . And your face, when I was able to unfix my eyes, was commensurate with your hands. If Spinoza was right and God's hobby really is making watches, he made one of his loveliest in your face. Much more elegant than—no. Not yet.

You seemed as cool and distant and intimate as time itself. That's what your husband, there beside you—a wedding ring—cannot resist. His torso—bull's strength, pants nicely filled out, granite neck—bent toward you in docile obedience. (But your husband is not like my master at all.) *You,* lady, are the aristocrat. Indifference is your mastery. You wield it—as he does over me—like a whip, an insubstantial lash: the casual glance of an Indian dancer whose eyes flash soft and ambiguous shafts of sensuous irony . . . There's a phrase in Aeschylus, in all his majestic genius, when he characterizes Helen of Troy, as "the blossom of love that gnaws on the heart"! How like him—

Stop it! You *cannot* avoid the inevitable by quoting great poetry! Right, lad. But if it had been *you,* any beautiful lady, instead of another, I wonder if I might have made it all the way to my life. No, certainly not. At least not if you had loved *me.*

(Odd, that that couple at the Met should remind me of Jim and Anne . . . But of course! In your arrogant beauty, lady, you're Jim. And your consort, in his decent humanity, Anne.)

Two thirds of my life. . . . And damn all those I love!

But as for all the rest of you—ya fuck yas!—you are Black Militants, White Militants—Militant Hobbits—Jews—especially yentas who gaze out your windows all summer long, leaning on your "looking cushions"—you are bartenders and used-car salesmen from the Bronx—I like you guys especially for the size of your swinging dicks and the slow, banked, inextinguishable fires of your ordinary lusts. (But don't get me wrong: I don't like to get fucked.) Oh and somewhere among you, sitting right next to a priest who loves Bach—oh yes, I need a priest, need to *be* a priest—there's a spinster schoolteacher—perhaps she's a librarian —who will like this journal least of all. (I'll let you in on a secret, auntie: whenever a little old lady appears in one of my kiddies' books—it's *me!* But so are the Frog Princes, and the stalwart younger sons.)

So there you all are, in your millions: the real and unreal inhabitants—remember, I'm inventing you! and quite a few of you have cancer—of this unreal but really collapsing planet. And don't dream that you're sitting in some celestial Dantesque amphitheater, or the Radio City Music Hall of my mind. I have locked you up in a narrow little abstract room. A schoolroom, I think. Yes, of course! A schoolroom with little hard-backed chairs—old-fashioned—where the children *behave!* And you're wondering why I've brought you here. God, it's gorgeous! The mood I'm in, even the weariest clichés reverberate like Scarlatti notes on a harpsichord. (God damn Richard Strauss!)

Well, my unwilling witnesses, a suicide needs to be observed . . . You deny that? What about all the lonely ones who shoot themselves in forests, alone? They think someone's watching. Believe me! I know . . . And I choose you—you have no choice—because the living friends I have, or anyone living—they do exist, and I despise them, because they're real—might somehow contrive to keep me alive. That will not happen, luckily . . . You'll help me there . . . Oh yes you will!

I turned the interior corner about a week ago. An incredible experience. Like being trapped in a forest fire: scorched by heat, and blazing branches falling all around, and then—an exit. Not just a way out, away from all the flaming trees. But through the narrow opening an Elysian prospect: green fields, a stream, and after a short and pleasant walk—why nothing, just nothing. Or say I was a sculptor, desperately kneading chaotic clay; but the next shape wouldn't come. Then suddenly—there it was: a simple elliptical form—my death. Or—an idiotic comparison, but perfectly accurate—it was like whipping cream. You thrash it and thrash it, and then, abruptly, undisciplined liquid turns solid and sweet and edible . . . Or if I was a sailor, shipwrecked and without a raft, floundering amid mountainous waves, then blissfully, from the crest of the highest one, in the farthest distance I see a shore . . .

I hear you, Black-White Militant: "Big deal! So what? Another phony takes the gas. Just jump—don't bug us. Let us *out!*"

No—no! One doesn't just jump. At least this one doesn't. I know my own mind. And death must be deserved, discovered, after a series of intricate moves. Do you remember Parcheesi? How long it seemed to take to get your pieces home? Or chess? The infinitude of possible plays before the check is mate. It's like that. My life, like a jigsaw puzzle—one of the ones with hundreds of pieces—is scattered across a table. It takes a time to fit the little things together, to find that precious last angular key. But you know all the time what the picture is: you've seen it on the cover.

It now is October—and glorious today: clear light that sweeps the city clean. But after the autumn and after the winter, sometime toward spring, the day will come. Near the last there will be a crime—the big move in the game—which will make my momentum absolutely irreversible. (I will tell you about that soon.) Then after that event has occurred—I feel it in the future like an architect's blueprint—I will dare you to judge me and judge me wrong.

For now—relax! And come with me. You have no choice: I've invited you. We will have a lot of sex. You are going to laugh a

8

great deal—people have no idea how blithe a suicide can be!—and you will meet a few human beings whom you'll have to love as much as I do . . . I will insist on that.

Then afterwards, I set you free. And leave these pages—to God, if you are correct, Father. If not God, to the garbage man. Whoever collects dead manuscripts: the confessions left by the dead to anyone.

October 8

God, I do adore New York! Especially now. I've been taking long walks. Today is Sunday, and definitely the fall: air chilling into the tilt of earth, away from summer, and the gold light clinging tenaciously to buildings that it once bathed with ease. I walked down through the streets that used to be the Washington Market, the ruins of Baja Manhattan. It's an ugly area, the vacant lots grown up in weeds, the gutters full of broken glass, the semi-derelict human beings, warehouses about to be torn down, all permeated with the poetry of helplessness. No section of this city that doesn't already feel to me blessed with the hard holiness of taking leave. It's all become vivid, living again, but with an excitement the opposite of what I felt—the novelty—the first time that I saw New York.

Then back to the Village and my apartment, and the usual spat with that damn dog: a collie, my enemy, who lives in the ground floor apartment next door. He hates me, and I cordially return the affection. He sticks his damn long collie's nose out under the partly opened window and shouts at me, "Woof!" when I walk past.

And I shout back, "Oh woof!" myself. It makes him furious to be recognized and met on his own terms. The mutt!

My apartment. The one thing in it that's beautiful is a picture above the couch, an illustration from *The Story of Harold*. But actually it's not. I wanted one of the illustrations and wrote to the artist, asking him. He's a difficult and I'd thought a fairly insensitive man, but enormously talented, and he said, quite bluntly, no: a whole set of illustrations is much more valuable when it's intact. But a month later through the mail I received this great original picture. I only wish it was in the book. It's almost a formal Victorian portrait: Harold, in his best clothes, checkered vest, that perpetual derby hat, standing with two close friends, Sylvester, the rubber plant, and Terry, a cocker spaniel, who is myself of course. But the thing is, the guy has caught my Harold exactly as I wanted him. He's frowning, naturally, with his right index finger lifted, as if he's about to deliver a lecture or a very stern rebuke. The drawing is absolutely superb. But as for the rest of the place—

Until I jelled a week ago, I used to hate it. The walls—"French gray"—have not been painted for eleven years. There's an open-out couch that's almost threadbare and radically needs recovering, a black canvas sling chair, and a desk that has had the paint worn off it by the jouncing of my typewriter. There's a bedroom only big enough for a bed and a bureau and only for sleeping: all sex of all varieties takes place on the well-worn couch. A minimal kitchen, and a standard bathroom—which, alas for you nuns and librarians, may very well figure prominently in certain episodes. Oh, and also in the living room: a usable fireplace, with a great Victorian marble mantle. Which of course I don't use.

So you see: an ideal, deadly—home! And to think, for all these years the unpainted walls, the furniture, my desk have been whispering the one terminal word. And not till last week did I hear. How patient inanimate objects are, and persistent and kind and trustworthy. Because now, as I look around, the place is transfigured, and all of its drabness only a mask for the coming inexorable. The rooms are clean—dirt bugs me, all you cleaning ladies—and that's all due to Iris Brife.

Ah, Iris—you all have to meet her now. The one great luxury in my life is my cleaning lady: Iris, as reedy and sturdy and tall as her flower, and also sporting, somewhere inside her, a baroque blossom of personality. She's sixty-eight years old, looks fifty, dresses like a Bergdorf buyer, and still has the angular unconsummated grace of an adolescent girl. Her sex life (she imparts to me in the most discreet terms) is still very active, and she loves to dance. She also loves me. She thinks *Harold* is the greatest story ever written, and stays with me out of pure faith. For four dollars she cleans my apartment once a week and refuses to take any more.

If I choose myself as a metaphor for death, then Iris must represent life. She would die, or worse: not believe in God—her trust exceeds yours, my priest—if ever she even suspected the goal that I have set myself. Another thing you have in common with Iris, Father: you both adore music. I was flicking the dial of my radio once, when Iris was here, and chanced on that moment in the Berlioz *Requiem*—the *tuba mirum spargens sonum*—when it sounds as if some glorious seraph's colossal wings were made of nothing but burning trumpets. And God, how He flies! Iris raced to turn off the vacuum cleaner, and stood transfixed till the passage ended. Then she looked at me with the radiance of someone who had just fallen in love and said, "Oh, Mr. Andrews, people who are wicked can't ever really have *heard* music, can they—?"

Goddammit! the telephone. Here I am rhapsodizing about my Iris, and the goddam telephone has to ring! . . .

A voice from the past, and not a welcome one. I stupidly let myself in for one of those kiddy scenes I hate . . .

But back to Iris: I feel a very intense inner joy in behaving quite naturally with her. I take this joy with the world as well, but since Iris somehow typifies the most enthusiastic, most optimistic acceptance—a *yes!*—of human existence that I know, I take a special pleasure in simply being in her presence—but always with my secret concealed: a crucifix, beneath my shirt, or a diamond I'm holding tight in my fist.

October 19

A curious experience. Difficult and disheartening for me . . . As all things relating to children are.

That call last week was from an old friend of mine. I met her almost six years ago at one of those half-assed Upper East Side cocktail parties. My first kids' book had just come out—it stinks and, thank God, has gone out of print—I was catapulted into anonymity—she'd just gotten divorced—her opus went out of print before mine—but she had a year-old boy, and just loved the idea that "someday he'd be reading *your* books!" I saw her several times. We never did make it to bed—she too obviously was husband-hunting—but I sort of found her fascinating—representatively speaking: as an example of the species Moderately Intelligent, Moderately Wealthy, Chic Upper East Side Divorced Female . . . Ugh!

Well, her kid *has* been reading my books—or book—and that's the problem.

As soon as she opened the door, it was as if six years had never existed: precisely the same, no aging at all. But, worryingly, I also had the same sensation I had the last time we said good-bye. I wish I could describe her to you—words are my business—*were* my business—but there isn't an essence there toward which one is challenged to penetrate. Her hair, in its natural color, seemed to come from a beauty shop; the makeup impressed you, not the face. She was like her apartment: perfectly furnished and expertly decorated, but basically a collection of gestures that had never reached the temperature necessary to be melded into a living woman. Her maiden name—resumed, as an act of hate for her husband—was Edith Willington. Smart Edith, well-bred Willington—Westchester, Vassar, Quogue, and El Paso. And there you have it . . . And damn all those—

"Terry! How marvelous to see you again!"

"Hi. Been a long time."

"Much *much* too long!"

There are some people whose very tones of voice lock you up in the unreal, the dishonest. Words only serve to keep you apart—not bonds, but rods.

"And this is your number-one fan!"

In a corner of the never-lived-in living room, in an isolated chair which I guessed he had picked himself, sat a lump of a little boy.

"*Ber*-nard, this is Mr. Andrews."

Like a gob of underdone dough, he lurched up to his feet and trudged forward. His head was lowered, like an animal overtamed, eyes strictly reserved for the neutral floor.

"Aren't you going to shake hands like a big boy?"

Immediately the hand went out: I shook five unformed fingers. "Hi, Bernard."

"*Ber*-nard—" She pronounced it, insistently: *Ber*-nard. "—simply adored your book!"

A remark which hurt: his dumb head swung away.

My standard answer: "Always glad to hear that!" I wondered how long she meant to prolong the kid's embarrassment. And mine.

"*Ber*-nard, why don't you go into your room and play? While Mr. Andrews and I have some grown-up talk."

The domesticated little beast slouched off.

When he'd shut the bedroom door behind him, Edith said, with all the connivance of adults behind a child's back—another tone of voice I loathe—"He's on his good behavior today. Because of you." That cowed obedience—good behavior. I began to wish, very vividly, that I'd gone to a whorehouse or the Turkish baths instead of coming here. "It's because of *Ber*-nard I called you, Terry. A lot's happened since I saw you last."

"Let's hear the highlights." I thought, while she talked, I could devise a scheme—a literary appointment—for getting out in half an hour.

"The highlight is a perfectly marvelous person! Frank Henderson, from Denver. Who made the same mistake I did."

"Divorced, you mean?"

"Yes. And now, I am happy to say, engaged."

"Congratulations."

Her face knitted into some very upper-class reserve. "It hasn't been without its problems."

"*Ber*-nard, I take it."

"It isn't that he dislikes Frank. I don't see how anyone *could!* And when Frank's in New York he goes out of his way—I mean, the zoo, the Statue of Liberty—*everything!*" Somewhere too in the background, I guessed, was a shrink. "It's the whole situation. He just can't cope."

Which cliché would do, I wondered. And get me *out!* "It takes time."

"Yes, but more than time too. I don't like to say it, but I honestly think that *Ber*-nard's fighting *not* to accept the situation. By the way, Frank luckily has no children." She heard what she'd said and rearranged it rather neatly. "So I mean, he *can* be a father to my little boy."

That phrase—"little boy"—she said it, and meant it. For the first time in the past ten minutes I felt a little thrust of affection for Edith Willington.

"I wouldn't admit this to many people—we've even had him in therapy."

How's that for a bull's-eye. Freud? Ah-*ha!* "Did it work?"

"Disaster. He hated the doctor. We had some scenes—" Her eyes lifted upwards and searched for relief in the very fine molding of her living room. "—I just can't tell you! I mean, smashing his favorite toys. Just awful! I took him out a month ago."

"When are you going to get married?"

"Probably not till next year sometime. Frank's changing jobs. Same company, but a much more important position! We want him to settle in—" Her lips flickered into a grin of self-acknowl-edged maturity. "—before he accepts still another position."

"But you see him—"

"As often as we can. He flies up a couple of times a month." My God, Father, that marriage will last! They're already adjusted to being apart. "The one thing in the past two months—it's why I was bold enough to call you—the one thing that *Ber*-nard's held onto is *Harold*."

"My book?"

"Your book. And I mean *literally* held onto. Even when he wasn't reading it, he wouldn't put it down."

A reaction that I have myself to a book I really dig: I like the sensation—literary osmosis—of a heavy volume in my hand transmitting its words through my skin. "That's very flattering."

"When I told him I knew you—" Her jaw went down in a caricature of admiration. "—he just gaped."

"Did he ask you to call me up?"

"No. My idea. As I remembered you, you wouldn't mind being used."

"I don't. But he didn't seem very interested. To meet me."

"He was awed. And by the way, I'm awed myself. The book's a huge success, isn't it?"

You're damn right, lady! "It's doing pretty well."

"I see it everywhere. In *all* the bookstores!"

"So what can I do to help?"

"Well, I thought—if you'd just *be* with him. Just talk to him. He obviously respects you. He must. Maybe take a walk in the park—" Oh *Jesus!* "—and just—oh I don't know. Do your thing. You must know how to deal with children. You wouldn't write children's books otherwise."

In point of fact, I don't know how to deal with children. The humble truth is—most I dislike. (Me, teacher—who up to now was your favorite kiddies' author!) A lot bore me. The ones who don't bore me intimidate me. Because they still have that capacity, in the flesh, of the unrealized, the possible.

"*Would* you take him for a walk in the park?"

"Sure. I'm afraid it can't be for too long." I glanced at a clearly threatening watch. "I've got to get down to my publishers—"

"Any time, I'd be grateful for. Ten minutes."

"All right!"

She went to *Ber*-nard's bedroom door and knocked. It opened with the methodical slowness of a door to a prison cell, and the bleak, blank, underdone face looked out.

"I have something very exciting to tell you! Mr. Andrews is going to take you for a little walk in the park!"

He looked at me quickly, with real abrupt terror, and I'm sure that my own face returned the same glance of apprehension.

"Is it chilly out, Terry?"

"A little nippy."

"I think—your camel's-hair jacket and cap. And quick now— hurry! Mr. Andrews is a busy man."

In a minute he was back, ill at ease in clothes that he somehow knew were too expensive and had to be kept too clean.

"Have fun now, you two!" At the elevator door Edith twinkled at us merrily, voice, fingers lilting us into a little adventure.

She only lived one block from Central Park, and I didn't need to talk to him as I steered him through traffic and across the street. But then we reached the uninterrupted walk on the west side of Fifth Avenue, the green and gold trees of October beside us, and not to be speaking became a growing embarrassment. I'd dropped his hand as soon as I could, when the cars were no longer threatening.

So I said, in my most uncley voice—the one I cultivate for book fairs and Author's Day at school—"Do you like stories?"

He was staring at the ground as we walked, and answered flatly,

"Yes."

"What's your favorite fairy tale?"

In the narrow path he had chosen to walk he took a few paces, then tonelessly said, "I don't know."

"You know what *my* favorite fairy tale is?"

"What?"

"*Rumpelstiltskin!* You know that one, don't you?"

"No."

"You don't?" My god, you keen teachers, *Black Bob and Scandinavian Jane* is a gas, but in your haste to keep up-to-date don't let all the great ones go by unnoticed! "It's a wonderful story! The best there is. You want to hear it?"

He shrugged, imprisoned in a grown-up's inexorable expectation. "I guess so."

"Let's sit down." *Rumpelstiltskin*—my out—would take at least fifteen minutes. And then I'd be free of the sad little brute.

So, on a bench too high for his legs to reach the sidewalk, I told him the marvelous tale . . . The poor miller with, naturally, a beautiful daughter. A little mercenary, this miller, since he confidentially reveals to the king that the beautiful daughter can spin pure gold out of straw. And the avaricious king—it's a realistic story—says, "Great! Have her up to the palace at seven o'clock." The lonely tower room—the pile of ordinary straw—and the poor girl waits and wails and weeps, since it's death in the morning if the work isn't done. And then—the fantastic apparition! Out of a trapdoor—no, out of the smoldering fireplace—all dressed in brown and forest green, with a visored hunter's hat on his head—the little demonic soul himself! The bargain struck. He does what others dream to do—and the first night's reward?—a necklace. Fine! And she does not see the smile he hides.

And the second night's reward? "This ring from my finger?" Very good!

And the third night's? His smile flares out at last. "Your firstborn child!"—since obviously the realistic king has decided to marry such a talented girl. And she heedlessly agrees. What else can she possibly do? It's death in the morning, otherwise. Was she going to be burned alive?—or is that another fairy tale? . . .

And the year elapses.

The great bedchamber scene: the king is snoring, fast asleep,

16

and the lovely young queen—for royalty becomes some common-
ers—is bent above her baby's crib, when out of the fireplace,
flaming this time, the little madman leaps. And demands what she
promised.

She offers him anything—all the wealth of the realm. And I
remembered exactly his answer to her. "No, my queen, I would
rather have some living thing than all the treasures of the world!"

But the bargain struck: three days to find his name. And the
messengers scurry across the hills, and ask and listen, and ask and
listen, scouring the kingdom for news.

The first day the names are biblical. "Is it Caspar?" the queen
asks. "Balthazar? Is it Melchior?"

"No! no! no!" the wild soul laughs.

The second day: crazy names. "Is it Cowribs? Spindleshanks?
Spiderlegs?"

"No! no! no!"

Then night—the final night. And one messenger sees the
incredible scene. (This messenger—Jim, most likely, with his
damned handsome face—has always worried me. I wish he was
more germane to the story. But after all, it *is* a klessik, isn't it?)
Concealed in dark mountains, beside a dark lake, a cottage of
wattle twigs. In the heart's woods. Before it a fire. And cooking on
the fire—sausages, certainly. And Rumpelstiltskin dancing around
it, mad with anticipation and glee. I'd forgotten his song, but
remembered enough to come up with this:

> Today my secret beer I brew.
> Tomorrow my special bread I bake.
> Next day, for the gold I spun for you,
> My queen, your tiny child I take!
> And lucky I am not a soul doth know
> That Rumpelstiltskin is my name. Ho! ho!

And the last day comes: the queen, a bit too slyly for me, begins
with ordinary names: "Is it Bob? Is it Tom?"

"No! no!" the doomed demented fool squeaks.

"Then is it, by chance—*Rumpelstiltskin?*"

His face contorts with rage and frustration. "The Devil told you
that!" Or was it God, the story said? No, the Devil, it had to be.
"The Devil told you that!" And then, in despair, he stomped his
right foot into the ground. Right up to his hip! And that made him

even angrier! So he took his left leg in both his hands and actually ripped himself in half. It wasn't an accident either. He *meant* to tear himself apart.

Ber-nard didn't look up once. Just watched his dangling feet.

"Do you like that story?"

"No."

A dull brat, as I'd suspected, as well as being crushed and unhappy. How dare he not like my favorite story! (None too secretly, as all of you have already guessed, I identify very strong with Rumpelstiltskin myself. His work—the artist's activity: ordinary straw transformed into gold. And tearing yourself apart! Wow! I do it often, and very well. Or rather I used to. Oh, God—that sudden thrust of bliss, at knowing it soon will be—)

But I did hate that child just then! . . . For a few sadistic instants, I was tempted to make up a tale about the Three-Legged-Nothing—a creature that haunts the dopey dark corners of my imagination, and one that I've never been able to narrate . . .

But uncley sanity overcame my madness, and I said, "Well, I like that story anyway." A couple of useless exchanges more, and then I would take him home. "Now you're going to tell *me*—what *is* your favorite fairy tale?"

With his head turned away, in a separate world of embarrassment, he murmured, *"Harold."*

"My *Harold?*" I was honestly taken aback: I'd been thinking of klessiks. *"The Story of Harold?"*

"Yes."

"Well—that's very nice to hear. But I meant stories like *Hansel and Gretel,* or *Snow White and the Seven Dwarfs.*

"Harold."

"Well, well!" I inhaled a breath of gratification, and as you can all imagine, began to wonder if there might not be something to this blob of a kid after all.

A word to you prisoners now—about my book, *The Story of Harold.* It started life as a simple technical exercise. I wanted to see whether I could write—whether anyone could—a contemporary fairy tale—a fairy tale *now,* in New York. Not the whole different world—Tolkien did that, and, God knows, superbly!— but the magic around the corner. My first impulse was to try to create a whole separate species of magical creatures: a parallel world that sometimes intersects ours. But it wouldn't come right. I spent a couple of miserable months. But then little by little I got taken over by this idea: one person—my Harold—who does live in New York, and in the same world with us. I saw his derby hat first, and then his colorful checkered vest, and finally I saw his face. And his friends would be everybody: human beings, teddy bears, Sylvester the rubber plant, animals, everybody. But the thing about him is, his magic is strictly limited—a finite amount and going fast. One of the leitmotifs of the book is—*"He had just enough magic to do that."* And I hope you recognize, ladies and sadists, that I worked like hell—I busted my balls, in fact!—not to overwork the line. And as for dimensions, Harold is very short: ordinarily twelve or thirteen inches, although when excited he sometimes reaches a foot and a half, and naturally, when dejected, sinks down to six or seven—

Oh my Christ! I suddenly realize—

If the teachers and librarians ever get the idea that Harold is really my—Jesus! The sales would surely plunge—

But again, that abrupt consolation. I have enough money to last six months.

Anyway, my Harold is a very uptight guy. As soon as I saw his face, I knew that. He spends his time racing around New York getting other people out of trouble and, of course, himself into it. I gave him a little jingle to sing.

> *Some*-thing wrong! *Some*-thing wrong!
> *Some*-thing been *bug*-ging me *all* day long!
> Is it a pain? Like a stomach ache?
> No.
> Is it the fear of a big earthquake?
> No.
> But *some*-thing is wrong. There's *some*-thing wrong.
> Because *some*-thing's been *bug*-ging me *all* day long!

I varied the inner lines in each chapter. Wrote twenty-one of them, to be exact. As for instance:

> Is it an overcast, rainy day?
> No.
> Is it the dumps, and they won't go away?

No.
But *some*-thing's—(Et cetera.)

Believe me, it's a lovely little book. Just ask *Ber*-nard Willington. This glum little troll in front of me only happens to think
it's the best book ever written. Well. Well!

"Since you like my book so much, I guess I'll have to tell you a
story of Harold."

And now, for the first time—life! His face swings toward me,
amazed; its emergent puffy features, striving to be a countenance,
suddenly strain into definition. "Are there *more*?"

"Of course. You didn't think those adventures in the book were
all Harold ever had, did you?"

"I—" A gasp of disbelief—at the undreamed of, brought very
close.

"Things happen to Harold every day. Just this morning, for
instance—" I paused a moment, sadistically. His face was a blank
page, pure expectation. "When Harold woke up, as usual his first
thought was—what was it?"

He leaped in breathlessly, "—his first thought was that something was wrong?"

I launched into a story I'd debated for the book but discarded
as a bit too contemporary—*Harold and the Crash-Proof Moth!*—
since I couldn't tell it totally. But I could to *Ber*-nard, disguised in
part.

Seems Harold was living in Mrs. Throttlebottom's closet—she
hadn't yet come back from Quogue—and when he woke up—*uh-
oh!*

Is it the fear of a big earthquake?
No.
Then is it—? Good Lord, it's just Jake!

Seems also in Mrs. Throttlebottom's apartment were living a
couple of other souls. Under the refrigerator an ant named Louie,
who has no problems, so let him live, and deep inside one of the
pockets of Mrs. Throttlebottom's Best Beaver Jacket—you do
capitals with a tone of voice—a moth named Jake, who has
smoked so much pot that it's addled his brains and he's crashed so
repeatedly that his lovely antennae all are broken and bent. (No, I

didn't tell *Ber*-nard that my moth smoked marijuana. I just said
that he had these kooky little cigarettes that he stowed behind his
ears, and every now and then he'd take one out and light 'er up.)
His speech has also been impaired by the weed. He called Harold
"Harolharol" and "s" became "sh." "Ish a gash, man!"—when he
crashed against the wall. And a drop-out, me suspecting that
Ber-nard was being schlepped from school to school . . . Poor
soulless little bugger, with his nothing but listening face . . . Wake
up, Jake! (Earlier Harold himself woke up with a compulsion—he
is *always* compelled—to invent the crash-proof moth.) Two bleary
eyes peer over the edge of the Best Beaver Jacket. "Whasha
matter, Harolharol?" . . . And a series of experiments begin.
First, trying to straighten the antennae out. Jake practically
de-brains himself against the fireplace. "Ish a groove!"—from a
little heap of moth wings and moth fur and dangling, hopelessly
damaged antennae.

"No! No!" Harold flings his arms up and down—his ritual
gesture of despair. "You mustn't learn to like to crash, Jake!"

"Okay, Harolharol. But you kill me, man!" . . . Another try.
With his eyes as beacons now. But—

"You look pretty glassy-eyed, Jake."

"Feel great, Harolharol! Charlsh Lin'berg! Geronimo!" . . .
And he's battered beyond belief, of course. Giggling there in the
middle of Mrs. Throttlebottom's Persian carpet . . .

Harold stamped in rage . . . But—very philosophically, with a
chin stroke and everything—"You know there's one thing I've
always liked about you, Jake."

"Whashat, Harolharol?"

"Your hair!" . . . Begins a magic incantation: Harold combs
and strokes Jake's hair. And sings, to his own hand—the sorcery
sensed in one's self—

> Oh fingers thin! Oh fingers thin!
> Let this be the right way to begin!

Right! His fingers grew thin, like the teeth of a comb. Harold
went on softly whispering—

> Oh fingers thin! Oh fingers long!
> Now let this hair be thick and strong!

Yes, *magic accompli* . . . "Hey, Harolharol—shomething'sh happenin' My hair'sh—" . . .

"Now fly, Jake! Fly right toward that wall!" . . .

The moth flew straight—and then veered off! And chanced and danced in front of my soul!

"Hey, Harol!—I can't crash! What a gash!" . . . A quick ending: so Harold invented the crash-proof moth. And flung his arms up and down. It stands for joy as well as despair. But there were many more moths. Just dozens and dozens—

And suddenly Harold got tired. He sent Jake into the Best Beaver pocket, and retired back into his closet himself . . . To think of all the young moths in New York that he'd have to make crash-proof—!

There occurred that solemn, splendid silence—a good story ended: sufficiency—that only children generate.

"And that's all," I pronounced.

He lifted his head from listening, with a smile so subtle it makes the Mona Lisa look like Martha Raye.

"I think now it's time to go home."

And we walked the blocks back. Without a word. In the lobby I said, "Can you go up in the elevator alone?"

"Oh yes." With pursed lips he affirmed, "I have for two years."

"Well, *Ber*-nard—" I began the pattern of saying good-bye to a child: it begins with unreal equality and ends with a ritualistic handshake.

But he interrupted me urgently. "Don't call me that!"

"I thought *Ber*-nard was your name—"

"It is. I don't like it."

"Would you prefer Ber-*nard?*"

"No."

His face had turned into a small chaos of flesh, and his eyes, which were hazel—like mine, I discovered antagonistically—seemed drowning in everything—the world, his mother, psycho-analysis, his own persistent wretchedness—in everything he could not comprehend. "Well—what *would* you like to be called?" I asked.

He hesitated, then risked a big question. "What would Harold call me?"

It caught me unawares. But I stared down at him quizzically for a minute—did as much of a Harold squint as I could. "I think," I began, a connoisseur of names, "I think that Harold would call you—Barney!"

That pleased. He swung his head away again and into that special dimension of absolute privacy. I pressed the elevator button. Together we waited. I didn't know whether to say good-bye. He didn't know whether to say good-bye. The elevator door went apart. In his camel's-hair coat, belt, cap with its miniature camel's-hair brim, like a wound-up toy that was set to trudge, he stepped inside. And did not look around as the doors joined shut behind him.

October 19, later, the same afternoon

The whole thing still upsets me. A great way to spend a Saturday afternoon! . . . Why should *I* be full of the misery of a hopeless little boy?

"Little boy, little boy"—the phrase tolls in my head like some kind of melodious funeral bell.

> Little boy, little boy—
> You have no home, and you have no toy.
> You just have, what you love very much: a book.
> You have no hope. You're afraid. But look—
> In Central Park, for a green gold hour,
> The fear disappeared. I had that power.

In the story of Rumpelstiltskin, it shouldn't have been "your tiny child." What the frustrated little madman surely sang was—

> Today my secret beer I brew
> Tomorrow my special bread I bake.
> Next day, for the gold I spun for you,
> My queen, your little boy I take.

Surely the queen's first child was a boy . . . And surely what Rumpelstiltskin wanted was a son.

October 19, a long time later

A few hours, that is. Time feels so slow, concerning him . . . But I need release, surcease—and sadistic peace . . . Therefore—I have called Dan Reilly. This worst and deepest third of my life—why shouldn't you meet him now?

New York was Dantesque that day. The city transfigured. About this time last year. And everything in it—human and inanimate—seemed like mortal masks put on the eternal, to make it visible. There are some things—like God, Father, like pure desire—that are, to mortals, invisible, and have to be masked to be seen. Fun City? Oh no, Mr. Lindsay. Say rather, *La Città Dolente*—the Mount of Purgatory—and eventually, for me, at midnight, even the *Paradiso.*

I left my apartment around five o'clock on a day much like this, and started to walk downtown. And on the corner of Houston Street and Hudson—a raging schizophrenic! Arms flailing like a broken windmill, he was shouting abuses and cursing Christ, himself, and nothing. The mood I am in today. Like one of those big public trash baskets that you suddenly find by itself, in flames. You round a corner, and there it is—*he* is: Dan—blazing, completely alone. What started the fire? What fuels it? Who knows? It simply burns and burns. Like that man. And myself.

A block further on—there really *are* some days when New York does feel like a boundless insane asylum—a bedraggled bum, pure filth, but with two glittering eyes imbedded in it, was stealing discarded newspapers from the ash can outside an apartment house. He saw me watching and hid what he'd taken behind his back, and his eyes—they shone like diamonds of stealth—went wild with fear: that I would read his mind and learn his secret, the innermost secret in all the world, the one he had worked so hard to solve: the infinite mystery of waste paper!

But despite the rampant lunacy, the city felt clean—rather cleansable. A strong sea wind was blowing and snatching low clouds apart. Light shattered and fell in fugitive patches. One sometimes forgets the sea in New York—that metaphor for infinity—but that day the breeze was salty and invigorating. For block after block there were shreds of paper, shreds of cloth, ripped things—the city's souls—blown hectically down purgatorial streets.

And in the West, over dirty New Jersey, where the clouds had been completely purged, there shone what Dante hoped he saw: *La gloria di colui che tutto move* . . . Ah Dante, Dante—you marvelous man! You have told the most beautiful lies that the world will ever hear . . .

(But, Father, if there really is an afterlife, I'm sure that the ancients were right, not Dante. It's a cold, dark, narrow space, where insubstantial souls slip into and out of one another, and as one of them said—much better to be a slave on earth than a king in such an emptiness. Except that I crave it!)

Eventually the sky above the city cleared too. The wind subsided. Twilight. Saturday. Indian Summer. The air felt as close and warm as silk. And the light in the sky felt like watered silk . . .

And what rippled along my skin? What was it the peace of the hour set free?

The idea of unrealized violence. Like some kind of perfume in the air, unsmelled. A subtle color, unseen. A human body, still untouched.

I turned east, to the Bowery.

In the S-M bars a few hopefuls already would be collecting, but I can't stand those places: the infantile satanism, the atmosphere of an aviary. No, if you're interested in physical pain and degradation, the place to shop is the Bowery. Of course, you may get killed yourself—but that's part of the charm.

I hadn't shopped the Bowery for—how long? Almost a year, I guess. And the last time, unsatisfactorily: I'd uncovered nothing. But the lure of the place was strong that day. Someone—*someone,* ha, ha, that's a laugh!—*that bastard*—had casually called me up and canceled a date.

I walked up Houston, turned south—and there the specialized world extended, and glowed, radiant, in the fading five o'clock sun: a moral leper colony, an outdoor hospital which all the doctors had long since abandoned, humanity's junkyard.

A sense of luck overtook me. I felt my pulse go quick: he was waiting for me in the street, somewhere among all the Bowery prey: the unbelievably young drop-outs, who have made their failures a short life's career, the ones with a sense of realized sin—my favorites—the self-consciously unfulfilled, and the purely physical specimens: the women raped and debased, the homeless in their skins, the diseased, the deserted, the defeated marine—

Oh, over these people there glows such a light of hopelessness! To walk down the Bowery—music, painting, poetry . . . But a faint screaming also. Off in the distance . . . The Three-Legged Nothing was after me.

More matter-of-factly, the inhabitants recognize aliens—and dressed as I was, clean-shaven, clean, I obviously was one—but they tolerate the sightseers of failure, and a few of them have even learned to enjoy being objects of contempt and fear and disgusted pity. He would be such a one, I thought: a victim. (Right! And so would I.)

It isn't difficult to dispense with panhandlers. The technique of rejection is simply this: one quick silent jerk of the head to the left, obliterating the bum from your sight—you deny that he exists.

About half an hour, sauntering. A little insolent, to establish a different identity from the derelicts I passed. My own dereliction —greater than theirs—I selfishly hide and preserve for myself. A few were potential, but none exact. And for that night to work, I sensed, every gesture, including my recognition, would have to be total and instantaneous.

And the world, as I'm shedding it, gave me a gift. The givenness of certain things is truly miraculous. (Grace? No. The bank's gift after a big deposit.)

He was hulked in front of a hardware store, staring at hammers, nails, a saw—I think there may even have been an animal trap in that window. (A nice touch, God, or nature, or the store owner—thanks!) He was big. Not fat, but—what word? what word?—not fleshy—*carnal*: an abundance of body. It's a type that, in men, always turns me on. And his eyes, which I saw reflected, had a dull, hollow deadness: two vessels that may, at one time, have been brimming with light, but now had been emptied utterly. And certainly Irish: every feature in his face, except those thrilling eyes, had that perky, primitive lyricism.

(A note now to all you aspiring sadists out there. If it's a masochist you're after, try to find an Irishman. Even if he, or she, has left the church, he will bring the psychological sense of abandon and damnation that is the very soul of human ownership and the special pleasure that's taken from pain. And should he still believe—why, so much the better, the luckier. His agonies afterward will prove more dense and suggestive than anything you can invent. Of course this is more true of men than women, since the sweet colleens are all brought up to expect to be beaten. Maybe I'll do a little research on that in the four or five months that are left.)

I watched the Irishman, unobserved, for a moment or two. And had my last minute of sanity for the next twelve hours. It occurred to me, very rationally, that he really was pretty big. I'm five foot eleven and I've worked out long enough to discourage most marauders, but this mick was at least six-two. And then it also passed through my mind—like a warning you've read in a subway john: VD can be cured—that there was a certain type of psychotic, the young, husky mesomorph, whose madness blooms along with his youth. And Danny Boy here was still young. About ten years younger than I am, I'd guess. (But I'll never tell!) Yet that could also be an advantage: parental authority—if we clicked.

Well, fortunately those dreary short editorials that my mind was publishing uselessly were broken off. He looked up from the window full of instruments and caught me watching him.

The risk is the thrill, as I said before. With a confident chuckle—as John Foster Dulles must have chuckled when he got us involved in Southeast Asia—I walked up to him and said, "Hi."

He grinned skeptically at being approached—a good sign: diffidence. "Hello." (His "hello" seems brilliant in retrospect. And I *do* remember all of this: one third, and the largest, too. "Hello" is so blindingly ordinary!)

"Is this the Bowery?"

The words, of course, will sound absurd. But in the beginning phase, please remember, the true conversation was altogether elsewhere. Immediate honesty cancels the game.

"It sure is the Bowery," he grinned. (Sumptuous banality!)

"I've lived in New York for ten years now—" I made my voice

fast but casual; there's a special delight to be taken from lying with ease. "—and I've never been down to the Bowery before." I looked up the street, with touristy interest.

A critical instant now occurred.

"Some dump, huh?"

"Yeah. It's a dump." I accepted his suggestion. The critical instant now was past. "Christ, why would anyone live down here?"

He laughed. "No place else to go!"

"Well, as long as I'm here, I may as well have a drink. That's what people do in the Bowery, isn't it?" My hook jiggled deliciously.

So did his. "It is when they get the chance."

"Join me?"

We went to a bar that he picked out. " 'Cause the guy there gives you an extra slosh, when he's filled the jigger."

So thus the hunt of two hours began.

I have the gift of listening. (So must you.) And it is a genuine gift, like sculpting or being able to paint. By certain specific silences, by some questions uttered and others asked only by a waiting face, you induce a human being to re-create himself. For the first half-hour I was simply a willing sucker. Besides the gift of listening, I also had the faculty of buying my Danny Boy drinks. (His name, by the way, *was* Dan—Dan Reilly: another present from pure coincidence. And he came from Boston. That was auspicious. Besides producing Kennedys, they generate a lot of usable Catholic guilt up there.) But after some fumbling appreciation, he began to seize the credulous fact that I really lived hearing him talk. I extracted lots of history: five years in the Navy—"But I couldn' stick it for another hitch"—two years of "bummin' aroun' "—his description of his roaming self—then three in the Merchant Marine. Then—then—the vague smile of failure: the Bowery: urgent aimlessness.

"An' this." He lifted his glass. "That won about a year ago."

"I'm not doing you a favor—" I signaled the bartender. "—but I'm having another drink."

"Great!" (But it's *I*, you will find, who suck liquor's tit.)

I dug for his family. In talking of Boston, childhood, he'd done the fugitive. The slow or sudden dawn of self-hatred, the sense of worthlessness, must surely have been there. Said I, lapping ice cream, "Do you have any brothers or sisters?"

"One."

"One what?"

"A sister."

"What's her first name?"

"June."

June! Beautiful! What could possibly be more banal? "That's a pretty name."

"Yeah."

"*Is* she pretty?"

"Yeah. Very."

Now right at this point, the hunter's instinct struck. Ordinarily —like now—my intuition is not so keen. In fact, most of the time it works like a Rube Goldberg machine that doesn't work. But the sensual lust of cruelty is one of the things, like hatred, love, that do sharpen the intuition. And the change that came over my Danny Boy's face—it turned downright handsome, and criminal —spoke sonnets about what he must have felt—what perhaps had happened—with regard to his sister June.

"Is she younger than you?"

He halted. "A lot."

Okay—in fact great—and as innocent as I could make it. "She must have hero-worshiped you."

The quarry tried not to exist, staring out of the branches of those dead eyes, its endless dying begun again. (Clever!) "She did."

"Well so what? No harm in that." I thought I could risk my first direct shot. "Better you, her brother, than some ass-happy stud around the block. She could have picked out some bum—"

By now our words seemed real. And especially that word: he picked it out. "She picked out a bum!"

I was hot. "Bum"—"stud"—lovely words!

(Mind you, the only thing that made this scene work was that I did, really, intend to hurt him.)

But I said nothing. I only tried to make my silence as excited and charged with disgust, disbelief, as what I gauged he felt himself. And expected me to feel.

"My own sister." He laughed to tell the tale. "You talk about somebody bein' a bum—"

Incest! As if it was all that uncommon. My God, I've known at least ten girls who got screwed by their brothers. And brothers who still are screwing their sisters! And enjoying it very much! But this lovely middle-class guilt of Danny's—the interior cross on which he would be delivered to me—it was a weapon in someone's hands.

"When I told the priest, I thought he was going to kill me. He beat the livin' shit out of me."

"He hit you? A priest?" If this was true, it was gold! A mine!

"He was our friend. We had him to dinner, once a week. It wasn't like a confession—him cold."

Oh, I blessed you, Father—what's your name? *Boyle?* God blessed you, up there in Boston! You had gone to prepare a place for me!

"You earned it, Danny. Didn't you?" It was my task now to make my witnessing vivid to him. And authoritarian, if I could. "I've met a couple of guys before who used their kid sisters—" A hit: he flinched. "—and one of them is now in jail."

"That was why I left home. I couldn't look anyone in the face anymore." His New England twang was very endearing: "any maw." "So I joined the Navy. An' got sent to fuckin' Greenland!" And low class slang—did I say it appealed?

The whole other alternative I slipped in here, being buddy-wise, only natural. "Not a hell of a lot of snatch up in Greenland."

"Shit no!"

"Course, most of the Navy guys I know—wherever they landed—found out how to lose their rocks."

"Oh yeah." Kindling, flickering eyelids. "There's always lots of ways."

"The Navy has all the bad reputation, but, Christ, I think it's the Air Force myself. That's what I was in—"

"You were? What were you?"

"A first lieutenant." A charming rank!—not *too* high, but superior. Of course I was not in the Air Force at all. I was not in anything. I've got asthma, and as soon as my draft board heard that, I was drummed straight out of my physical. But I had this history fabricated. It's been used, with success, before. "Not up in the air though. My eyes are no good." To study a flying manual to enhance one's masculinity—that really would be too much. "I was stationed in Florence, Italy. There's a big base near there. Translating stuff."

"You speak Italian?"

"Sure. Took it in college." Two points for me: an officer's rank and a college diploma. While my Danny Boy here was obviously just a drop-out. Like Barney.

"Say something in Italian."

Another chance to score:

> *Per me si va nella città dolente;*
> *Per me si va nell 'eterno dolore,*
> *Per me si va tra la perduta gente.*

I quoted the whole inscription over the Gate of Hell to him—and I did it damned well, if I do say so—and bore down hard on the thunderous last line:

> *Lasciate ogni speranza, voi ch'entrate!*

Then translated it all.

He grinned, and my liking for him, which I'd felt all along, abruptly leaped up into something like love. In cases like this, unlike the couple I told you about, it becomes absolutely necessary to define precisely the soul I'm with, to know it, locate it, and tie it to me. The sweetness of cruelty is intimacy.

"It's an easy language. You could learn it like *that!*" Snap fingers.

"Oh no—" He belittled any ability. "—I'm no good at the books."

And my smile—affectionate, paternal—was absolutely real. "I could teach you in a month."

"How long were you in Italy?"

The mere urge to chat—I hoped. And said, "A year—" the length of my scholarship "—and man, what a year on that base! They talk about you Navy guys—but the busiest spot in the whole fuckin' place was the men's john in the officers' club!"

He turned away, frowning—marvelous frown! Big bushy eyebrows! "Hell, I guess that kind of thing goes on in all the services."

(This is *not* a masturbation fantasy! It was for me then, but he'll be here in half an hour.)

His soul's fur bristled, to drop the subject: guys-gays. Mine didn't. At this point in the hunt—despite the fact that I'd been buying, despite the fact I was sightseeing him—I thought he wanted us both to be friends. And I didn't.

The first of two crises occurred—the less important one. I blanked my face—not the black mask of the executioner yet—but reportorial honesty. "Listen, Dan, I'll level with you. When I was in the Air Force, I developed a taste for fucking guys. Are you interested? If you're not—don't get mad."

"I'm not mad." Shifting gears—was I possibly a john?—"An' I'm not saying that I haven't done it. A few times, for a couple of bucks."

But oh, no john, no john, no! "I don't pay." I have me little principles too, but believe me, Pope John, they had nothing to do with that night! I had to make him crave it, for it to work for me. However, I wasn't above a little oblique bribery: "But back at my pad I've got a lot of Scotch."

He shrugged: disinterest and contempt. Then defended himself, for the last time during the night, against indignity: "What the fuck. On a Saturday night, it beats standin' aroun' on the Bowery." (Again, that accent! Words—you are my lords, my lures!)

We began the long walk home, to my apartment. I worked hard to bring back into blossom that feeling of nipped incipient friendship. Asked where he'd been in the Navy. Tangiers, as well as Greenland, and naturally he raved about the cunts he'd had there. I liked that, and in my mind I made a claylike space for him, to construct his masculinity.

By the time we reached the Village I think he believed we were peers: my edge of superiority—the first lieutenant, the college degree—offset by the fact that he knew I wanted him in the flesh. I allowed myself, in a physical cliché, the gesture of friendship, to rest my hand now and then on his shoulder, but lightly—oh lightly: an innocent weight—in a lovely inner anticipation of the opposite to come. And Danny Boy believed my hand. (No. Rather, *I* believed it.)

He liked my street. "Nice houses here."

"Last year the city designated it as a landmark area."

"I agree. I don't think they ought to go tearing down houses."

Another token of decency. Don't think that I wasn't collecting them, planning to play with them later on, at leisure, when I'd spread his humiliation out.

And my apartment—"Needs paint, Terry."

"Yeah. But I'm working on a book." It felt like the opportune moment to introduce my vocation. "And everything waits till that gets done." (It was true at that time: the apparatus had not been built.)

"You write books?"

"Yup."

"What kind?"

Surely no one is safer or more trustworthy than an author of children's stories. "For kids."

"Oh yeah?"

I showed him a copy of *Harold.* "This one's the most successful I've done."

He read the whole title—*The Story of Harold*—aloud. Which gave me a tingle I couldn't trace.

"Now sit down, Dan. Relax. We'll have us a couple of shots of Scotch."

I wished then I knew how drunk he was. My guess was—only tight. And for the high goal I had set us both he would need to be pretty looped, but still conscious enough to feel guilt, shame, remorse. As well, of course, as pain.

It had grown dark outside: a darkness charged with dying—just the year's, I thought then, and my Danny Boy's little remaining self-respect. I pulled the shades. Then made us both drinks, his twice as strong as mine.

After two more a glaze blurred his eyes, his voice, and his life. I was struck again—almost with the force of a physical blow—at the unbelievable luck I'd had: uncovering an utterly ruined human being, who still was handsome, and who still was young. (Clever!)

"Let's take off our clothes."

"Sure. Swell. Let's get it over with." He stumbled to his feet.

I unfolded the couch and watched him strip. A slave like this must strip himself, unlike someone whom you'll meet in time, and

33

whom I like to peel myself. My Danny Boy's body was just at the point of defeat. His youth was still winning, but the coming pot belly already was there. (I like a wee pot on a man, by the way. Can't stand it on women though.) And his muscular tone was still firm. But beneath that pale, marvelous Irish skin one felt that his tissues had sensed their exhaustion. He had a cross of black hair on his chest—the virile formation that turns me on—and as for equipment—you ladies—you gentlemen too, in fact—this man is a genuine loss for you! But I had no use for that, that night.

"Roll over."

Here now I extracted a joint from my leather jacket. (Too warm for leather—but *noblesse oblige!*) I started to light it. He grabbed, and appropriated, the matches from my hand. (Though I found out later he doesn't like to smoke often.)

His ass was thick and tough and big, and fleeced with the same black hair as his chest. Odd, the opposite things that excite one in women and men.

"You going to put something on?"

"Sure. Don't worry. I've got some good stuff. But why hurry? Just sip that drink of yours."

He did. And spilled a splash as he fumbled the glass to the floor.

"I'll freshen that."

"Sorry—"

"No problem, Dan. Scotch doesn't stain. There's been a lot of Scotch spilled here."

Another drink—but none for me: my altitude—the height of an angel above the earth, but with human beings still visible—was just what I craved.

"You like young chicks, Dan? Or the bosomy old gals?"

"I like them young." Words staggered out. Then, balanced, repeated themselves. "Quite young."

"How old was your sister, Dan—" This was an ordained, necessary risk.

"I don't want to talk about it." The shivering of his voice had filled the whole room with unspoken affirmations. "Fourteen." ("Fawteen." He *is* from New England, by the way. That accent he can't conceal.)

"Did you share the same bedroom?"

"No." His thick confession—voice thick, guilt thick—now

began. I made an urgent mental note to keep my own voice priestlike and clean. "We had a bathroom. Between our rooms."

"And—?"

"And—nothing. We had this bathroom between us, that's all." My momentum—even this little inch of it: a stare—was enough. "She used to come in an' watch me shave."

"You were eighteen—right?"

"Eighteen."

Just bit by bit: "Did you shave every day?"

"Oh sure. I've got this heavy black fuckin' beard." True: that Celtic electric black hair of his. It was thick and fingerable on his head, and a five o'clock shadow, desirable, on his cheeks.

"So she'd sneak in to watch you shave. When, Dan?"

"In the afternoon. I was always a lazy fuckin' slob—" It begins: he despises himself, out loud. "—so I'd shave when I got home from school. An' June always happened to be at home."

At this point I took a visionary second to focus in on this adolescent sister, June: some hot-tailed, hot-paced, half-assed little bitch, most likely. Living up there in Boston right now, and certainly married—to what? A plumber! And doesn't remotely begin to guess how lucky she was to have been seduced—if indeed he did it—by a handsome and passionate, loving brother. (I was on then. I'm on now, remembering.) Who taught her, in all probability, what fun it can be to be fucked. But that's only the truth—is it? *is* it?—and the truth was not at all useful to me for what I wanted from Danny Boy.

"Did you shave naked?"

"No!" A bit of indignation. (Promising! The foundation of all successful perversion, the energy that defines it, compels it, and makes it intense—at least in this country—is stolid middle-class morality.) "We never ran around naked in front of each other. I shaved in my shorts."

"And June was always there—" But I panted to preserve his belief that it had been his fault.

"Yeah. She'd just want to come into the bathroom an' watch. She'd sit on the john an' I'd do a big thing about latherin', puttin' the razor together, an' then shavin' myself like an expert barber—"

"—with even, long, steady strokes—" (Ah words! In the

Beginning—)

"Yeah. An' little June got the biggest kick—"

"Little June"—a lovely coarse authentic touch: I felt myself begin to swell on the strength of his simplicity.

"—out of watchin' the whole thing. An' afterwards, the after-shavin' lotion—I'd do a big thing about slappin' my cheeks—"

"—and she wanted to touch your cheeks—"

That almost went too far, too fast: the density of his reconstruction was thinned by my avaricious curiosity. "How'd you know that?"

"She'd have to want to, wouldn't she? A little sister?—who'd just seen her brother shave? New cheeks that you'd slapped the lotion on. She'd have to test them—wouldn't she?—to see if they prickled?"

"Yeah. She wanted to test them." The ease with which he had been steered back suggested that he was up himself. On his belly, I couldn't tell. But I sure as hell was! "That was the end of my shave every day. When June tested my cheeks."

"Go on."

"Go on where?"

"What happened? Finally."

"I don't want to talk about it." His shoulders heaved. (Did they heave "with Atlantean strength"? Maybe.)

"Had your parents gone away? For the day?"

"No! They were downstairs, lookin' at television!" (Yes! Reality would permit that. Yes!)

"Was there anything special? About that day?"

"No. I'd just come back from baseball practice—" Glorious! A high school athlete! "—an' I'd done lousy!" No matter. No—even better, in fact. I smelled him: sweaty, depressed, and young. "An' I started to shave."

A silence. Should I prompt him? No. On the couch, out prone, he writhed a bit. My guess: a gesture suspended between recollected desire and present remorse. "An' I started to get this hard-on. June was lookin' at my crotch."

Not too far that way, Danny Boy: you'll find out it wasn't you who did it. "But you wanted to show her, didn't you?"

"No!" He flinched against the overwhelming *yes* I felt. "I tried to hide it. I jammed myself up against the sink, with my prick going down, so she couldn't see."

"But you finished shaving—"

"I finished shaving—" Still wedged against the sink—poor trapped bastard! But my pity for his humiliation came gloved in tight expectancy. "—an' June stood up to feel my cheeks."

The second crisis came close, in his silence.

"Go on."

"An' I kissed her fingers." ("*I*" did! . . . Did he really know—?)

"You kissed them?"

"I licked them. I took her fingers inside my mouth."

We were safe! The next-to-the-last plateau had been reached. By his licking her fingers—best: taking them in his mouth—he'd committed himself to the guilt I now had in my hands like clay. I tried to disguise my own excitement as disbelief. "But Christ, Danny, didn't you know what would happen?"

"No."

"Did you screw her, right there?"

"Yes. With my mother and father downstairs."

The flatness of his voice was leveled intensity. I ventured for details. "Did you make her suck you?"

"I don't want to—"

"*Did* you—?"

"Yes. And I went down on her. We did everything."

"Get up on your knees like an animal."

Around my apartment are strategically hidden some straps, sticks, lengths of rope: the usual household necessities. From under the couch I took the wood rod I'd detached from a coat hanger. And laid it gently across his tail. It balanced there, like his doubt. (My doubt.) "Now put your shoulders down flat on the mattress."

"What are you gonna do—?"

"Just what that priest up in Boston did."

"No!"

The critical moment: he would either rear up, in a last spasm of healthy self-defense, and break my jaw—as you all may be hoping, this minute, he will—but he didn't. His guilt was large enough—it sufficed—and was circuited through him bodily. And circuited through me.

"Look—you spoiled your sister, didn't you?"

"Yes."

"You've got it coming. Don't you?"

"Yes."

"Then ask for it! Out loud."

His voice sank into a pit. "Hit me."

There! . . . There, there—oh, there. The bliss of certainty, like knowing one will die . . .

It was like an implosion: thousands and thousands of jigsaw pieces, blown apart, reversed their direction suddenly and raced back into a single shape. He had asked me—and thus had set me free . . .

One begins very gently, particularly with neophytes. Particularly with big, husky, motionless Irish neophytes, who, despite their craving to be degraded, may be shocked by a quick initial crack into jumping up and snapping your back. Slow taps on his ass—the sound not even struck flesh, as yet—one buttock after the other, that's all.

And then, in the distance of his misunderstanding—"Is that what it's like to be whipped?"—you increase. A sense of rhythm, as well as pressure, is absolutely essential here. You must know, through the body of the other soul, exactly how hard the blows are beating, and like rain, you increase it evenly. You must make it a question of pure sensation—at first, before the mind is let loose. The skin has its own possibilities. And one of them is for blood to rise, for nerve endings to do their destined work. By making the body conscious, at first, merely of what it is registering you will also render it selfless. And yours.

But momentum, once it's begun—once the body, to its own surprise, has discovered pleasure where, up to now, it has only experienced pain—momentum must be steadily quickened. You use the amazement—the amazement I felt beneath me now—to further its own increase. He had been stiff, rigid and enduring only, but at an instant—to my own relieved belief—he became the other half of an action. The time before, with the priest, it must have been all just "taking it": a bad kid's stoic acceptance of pain and a necessary prelude to this. But now, without warning, he became what I had become myself: a dancer both inside and outside of sensation.

Because there is a dance, and the steps in it are infinite. Beneath his pain—his buttocks were moving, moving now, but only in reciprocity—beneath my rage, we reached, and both of us at the same moment, an endless yet still somehow limited space: a kind of psychic dancing floor, where every gesture of violence—the great deep strokes, as well as the tiny triangle notes of pain, which he had now come to appreciate too—is met and recognized and thanked, and physical cruelty, given and taken, turns into a sort of soulless grace.

I turned out the lights. The ass of a man who is being flogged excites me for only the first five minutes.

"Now count. Out loud."

And sixty is—what? A minute? An hour? When counted according to blows, it is both. And endless time as well.

To force a soul to verbalize is another key of intensity. Especially for someone who lives in words.

It went on, in my blackened living room—a ray of light spilled in from my kitchen: enough—for two or three hours, I should guess. Periodically, in the recesses that are part of it, we refreshed ourselves with drinks, and his memories, and questions and curses and tears.

Sometime toward the end I believe he passed out. But I didn't know when, exactly. Or care.

For the rest of the night—and drunk as I was—sleep lay on me like a veil. The thought of him, lying beside me, bruised, kept snatching me back to consciousness. Oh no, not in fear! (And don't get your hopes up, you normal soul, you, for the waking—I'm here to tell the tale.) In joy! He moaned in his sleep when I touched him—even touched him tenderly, caressed him as I did, very often, and kissed him too, in that pit I had put him in.

But the unlikely morning dawned: I felt him stirring toward consciousness.

The technique of waking up with a bum that you've whipped the night before, and not getting your own bones broken, is this: you wait till he's almost wide awake, then go into the kitchen and begin, very loudly, to fix both of you drinks. I can't stand the taste of liquor when I'm hung over in the morning—but it beats a trip to the hospital.

"Hey, Dan—you awake?"

An uninterpretable mumble.

"I'm having a shot of Scotch. Want one?"

"Yeah." (The right accent. Word! It would be all right.)

And you make that first shot very strong: a pain-killer and also a promise of more. I brought the whole bottle in and set it down beside the couch. "Christ, I feel rotten!"

"*You* feel rotten—" He rolled over on his back—nice touch—so I couldn't see my handiwork.

"Here. We really got plotzed." This allows the bum, if he likes, to pretend to utter drunkenness: that it hasn't ever happened—he wasn't even there.

But all unnecessary. He reached for the bottle and winced as he moved. But made no sign of locating and blaming me, as being the cause of the pain he felt.

I took a chance on honesty. "Is your ass sore?"

"Yes."

And again—had I started him on a great career? He made it sound apologetic: as if the fact that his ass was sore was something to be ashamed of, his fault. (*Culpa? Mea? Tua?*)

"I'll get you something. Wait." I went to the bathroom and got out my trusty Solarcaine. "Roll over."

"What's that?"

"It's something they use for sunburn." (You see, I'm really the masochist's wish-fulfillment: a sadist who functions as a trained nurse too.) "It'll take out the sting. Roll over, Dan."

He did, and I rubbed a lot over his ass, the sea-rippling of welts, and finding myself in the right vicinity, I penetrated him with my index finger—

"Hey!"

"Take it easy!"

—and afterwards, when he'd spread and relaxed, with what he'd been waiting for. (I believe this is what they call adding insult to injury. I hadn't expected it, and it added a grace note to the whole episode.)

I would have blown him if he'd made any indication, but he was

40

already far along the road to pure passivity.

We made some buddy-buddy talk reminiscent of the first phase of last night—he drank more Scotch—and to get him out, I said, "Here—take the bottle."

"Thanks, Terry."

A slave who thanks you sincerely, and uses your first name like a friend!—Well, I certainly wanted to see him again. (And indeed I will!)

Which was just what he wanted, too.

He went into the bathroom and modestly closed the door, to crap me out. And then took a quick shower. Not at all like those big and pseudo-straight men—for whatever purpose you've acquired the type—that one sometimes wakes up with, hung over, next morning. They frog around in the bathroom, spitting, coughing, farting like brontosauruses. But not Danny Boy. He was fast and neat—and hung the goddam towel up!

Ah God—You do not exist—but!—whatever the allure of the gutter and aristocracy, could anything have a more mysterious appeal than the American Middle Class? No, no, it's the most occult category there is. Unbelievably lucky the demon who meets it!

But nevertheless, amazed by my fortune, when he'd dressed and stood clutching *his* great luck, my bottle, I heard him make this hesitant offer: "You serve good booze over here—" Oh yes!

"Thanks, Dan. You're welcome to more of it any time." My address—my telephone number—a handshake!—he left . . .

> Oh sad Dan Reilly, you sad little boy!
> You had no home, and you had no toy—

The buzzer—he's here . . . Come in, Dan, and we'll do the truth this time!

October 23

Crabs! . . . I've got crabs!

Did that damn Dan Reilly colonize my crotch? No. He knows I'd crucify him—and that's *not* what he wants. Quite . . .

Probably the baths last week . . . I've got to keep dosing myself with A-200.

More important, did—oh, Jesus, and Jim's got a wife! Have I given them to him? . . . Have I given them—the hell with Jim and his fucking wife!—have I given them to *Anne?* . . .

We all don't even know each other, and we're like some strangers at a cocktail party, gaily handing around a tray of crawling canapés!

Are you smiling? . . . Do you dare to laugh? Ya fuck yas! (I screw an ass on which there sits a construction worker. His only term of endearment is to call a person "ya fuck ya"! On the john once he started to read my book: " 'Fuckin' Harold woke up one fuckin' morning'—what *is* this shit?" Delightful! I like him very much.)

All right, I admit: it's ridiculous. Crabs, clap, or canker sores—they all are ridiculous. But they're worth it, to get a little love in your life.

And don't laugh too loudly, my witnesses—You! *Tua res agitur!* That's Latin. From an ode by Horace. And it means—Screw you too, gentle reader! . . . It is *you* who are discussed here!

October 28

"The name of this story is—*Harold and Miss Amanda.*"

I've allowed myself to be trapped again. Another call from Edith this morning. "What *did* you do to *Ber*-nard? He's simply been a different child!" So here we two are in the park once more. And inside it this time: this precious, protected, unreal country-side.

"Or maybe you'd rather hear a story of Rumpelstiltskin—?"

"No!" A little vigor . . . Not much.

"It just so happens that before he learned how to spin gold out of straw, Rumpelstiltskin was living right here in New York. He lived down in Greenwich Village, but he used to come up to Central Park to walk." And do a little cruising, too. "And one day—he was standing right over there—the Three-Legged Nothing came over that hill. It was running like mad, and swinging its four arms, and shouting with its two heads. 'Oh I'm hungry! I'm hungry! Find somebody for me to eat!' "

"The Three-Legged What—?"

"Forget it." (Damned demon!—where do you come from? And how can I write you, and deny you life?) *"Harold and Miss Amanda."* I arrive at that private place of his: pure listening. His head swings into emptiness. "Well, Harold woke up this morning, and naturally—'*Uh*-oh!' he said.

> Was it the zoo? Is there a sick panda?
> No.
> Then had it to do—with Miss Amanda?
> Yes.

"Harold was still living in the bottom drawer of Mrs. Throttle-bottom's bureau—no, closet, it was—and she lived on the Upper East Side, of course—but Miss Amanda lived down in Chelsea. You know where that is?"

"No—" He's into it though, and wants to know.

"Down around Twenty-third Street and Ninth Avenue. Nice houses—like houses that people live in . . . So Harold pulled on his jacket, and pulled on his coat, and pulled on his derby hat, and ran all the way down to Chelsea.

"Now Miss Amanda was seventy-five. And getting a little timid, I guess. She had come originally from—Iowa, it must have been. And she had one sister, her only living relative, who was seventy-three and was living out there. But Miss Amanda had no money, and she hadn't seen her sister for years. She had come to New York when she still was young—to be a concert pianist—but that never worked out, and she'd had to work as a cleaning lady. But now that she was old, not many people would hire her. They thought she wouldn't clean very well. And also nobody wanted the bother, if she should die on the job.

"But everyone was wrong. Because Miss Amanda was *very* clean. She lived in a little apartment—the basement rear, right next to a furnace that clanked—in a rather run-down brownstone house. But her own two rooms were spotless! They were so neat that each little thingamajig—she was very fond of thingamajigs—looked as if it was singing a song. It meant a lot of dusting, because of that damn clanking furnace!" The cuss word thrown in for Barney's delight. "But Miss Amanda didn't mind. She really sort of liked to dust. Especially thingamajigs.

"Well, Harold came tearing down to Chelsea, and he pounded on Miss Amanda's door. She opened it right away, because it sounded as if someone was trying to break it down. 'Why, Harold,' she said, 'I was just thinking of you—'

" 'I know!' said Harold breathlessly. 'Now what's *wrong?*'

" 'That rainstorm we had yesterday,' said Miss Amanda, 'and all that wind—it bent one of the struts in my pink umbrella. And I can't seem to straighten it out again.'

" 'Is that all?' said Harold glumly. After all, when you wake up every morning and you're sure that something's wrong, you want something really *big* to be wrong! 'A bent umbrella strut?'

" 'If you'd fix it, I'd be so grateful, Harold.'

" 'Oh—all right.'

"So Miss Amanda got the pink umbrella out of the closet and opened it. Just one strut was bent a little. It wouldn't even take magic to fix it. And you know, Harold never used magic for what he could do by simple work. He took off his coat, getting ready to fix the strut, and only to pass the time, he said, 'How's your sister, Alice, Miss Amanda?'

" 'She's fine, Harold,' Miss Amanda said. 'I got a letter from her yesterday. She's opened a bake shop.'

" 'Has she?' said Harold. 'Imagine—a bake shop! You bake very well yourself, Miss Amanda. I remember one pie last summer—' There was a very definite reason why Harold was harping on Miss Amanda's baking ability.

"And Miss Amanda got the point. 'Oh by the bye, Harold, I made some cupcakes yesterday with maple walnut icing. Would you like some, and a cup of coffee?'

" 'I would love some cupcakes, and a cup of coffee,' said Harold.

"While Miss Amanda was in the kitchen, they continued their conversation. 'You know, Harold, I just wish I had some money to get out to Iowa. I'd love to go into the baking business with my sister.'

" 'The Alice and Amanda Bake Shop,' said Harold. 'That has a nice ring to it.'

" 'I'm sure we could make a go of it,' said Miss Amanda. 'The two of us together.'

"Now right at this moment Harold fell into one of his moods. You remember Harold's moods—"

"Yes!" Oh, and does Barney ever remember: his head is bobbing like a cork.

"—when something begins to grow in his mind and he doesn't yet know what it is. That was happening now. Then suddenly, it was as if the pink umbrella spoke to him. You know, things *do* speak to Harold—"

"Yes! Yes."

"—and just on an instant it felt to him as if the umbrella had whispered a single word. And maybe that single word was—*'me!'* Harold looked at the pink umbrella closely. No doubt about it: it *did* have possibilities. But there'd have to be alterations. The handle was curved, for instance. Harold lifted the pink umbrella up over his head and sang to it, very softly—

> Umbrella, there's a curve in you.
> But why should Miss Amanda wait?
> I think I'll make a change or two.
> You handle—ready?—*now be straight!*

"And the handle straightened out just as nice as you might wish. But—but—

> Umbrella, you're not big enough.
> You want to be, though. Do your stuff!

"And the pink umbrella—which was really only a little old lady's parasol—grew as big as a beach umbrella!

"Right here Miss Amanda came in from the kitchen. She was carrying a tray with the cupcakes and coffee cups on it. 'Why *Harold!*' she exclaimed. 'For land's sake! What on *earth* are you doing with my umbrella?'

" 'Don't worry, Miss Amanda,' said Harold. 'It's all going to be all right.' He began to eat a cupcake. There was lots of work ahead of him, and he knew he needed all his strength. 'I'll require some tools, however.' There was much he could do just by work, you see. 'Go get hammers, nails, screwdrivers—knives and forks, if you have to! Oh, and the drain pipe from your sink. That'll have to be the exhaust pipe, I guess.'

" 'But Harold,' said Miss Amanda, 'I only wanted you to fix

that little bent strut—'

" 'Shh, Miss Amanda,' Harold soothed her. 'It's all going to be all right.'

"Miss Amanda shook her head, but she went back into the kitchen and took what tools she had from her cupboard.

"Meanwhile, Harold had started to work:

> Now—something strong to bust the wind.
> To see through too. Oh! Plexiglass.
> It isn't what you'd call a find,
> But, dammit, it will have to pass!

"A stiff cylinder of plexiglass unfurled from the tips of the umbrella struts to the floor.

> A door now . . . Where?
> Here? Here? . . . No, there!

"And a foldable door appeared in it. 'Rats!' said Harold, and snapped his fingers. But then he made a special sign with his left hand, because otherwise Miss Amanda might have had rats. 'I should have done the door with just scissors!' Wasted magic always made Harold mad.

"Miss Amanda came back with all the tools she had. There weren't very many. A hammer, and a couple of nails. A corkscrew. And some kitchen utensils. 'Is this your very favorite knife, fork, and spoon?' asked Harold sternly.

" 'I eat off them every day,' said Miss Amanda. 'But Harold, what *is* that long thing hanging from my umbrella?'

" 'Now, now,' soothed Harold, 'don't you worry about a thing, Miss Amanda. May I ask you a question though?'

" 'I guess so,' said Miss Amanda. She was sort of worried about how Harold was acting, but she trusted him anyway.

" 'Are you really seventy-five, Miss Amanda?'

" 'I'll be seventy-six tomorrow, Harold.'

" 'Well, that settles it,' Harold said. 'You'll have to ride sidesaddle.'

" 'I'm not going anywhere, Harold—' Miss Amanda began to protest.

" 'What's your favorite chair?' Harold interrupted her.

" 'Well, my *very* favorite? That big easy chair in the corner—'

" 'Too big!' Harold shook his head.

" 'But for sewing, and doing work—for concentrating—'

" 'That's it!'

" '—I like that straight-backed wooden chair.'

"Before Miss Amanda could say, 'Oh land!' Harold had grabbed the straight-backed wooden chair and knocked the legs off it. 'Harold!—you've ruined my—'

" 'Now now—now now—' Harold wiggled his index finger at her. 'You just sit back and relax, Miss Amanda.'

" 'Relax—when you've—'

"*Bang! Bang!* Harold nailed the back of the straight-backed wooden chair, and then its seat, sidesaddle, to the handle of the pink umbrella. At least he could do that by work.

" 'And to think,' Miss Amanda murmured to herself, 'all I wanted him to do was fix that little bent strut.'

"When the seat was in place, Harold muttered, 'Wheels. I need wheels. Ah!' On Miss Amanda's mantelpiece was an antique clock. Harold jumped up on a chair, and in about a half a minute the clock's insides were spread out all over the living room rug.

" 'My clock!' Miss Amanda groaned. 'My very favorite—in fact my only—'

" 'Think nothing of it!' Harold brushed her confusion away. He searched through the guts of the clock, and he found four tiny wheels. He leaned over them and sang—and you remember, when Harold was singing a spell, he sang it so softly that only the things involved could hear—"

"I remember." And Barney lives in my singing, his face reflecting mine.

"—he sang:

> Wheels! Oh wheels! You are too small.
> Grow! Just a little. *Try,* that's all!

"And the wheels grew up to the size of tricycle wheels. Harold used the four legs of the straight-backed wooden chair to nail the four wheels to the bottom of the handle of the pink umbrella. And as he did so, he said, 'Miss Amanda, do you remember that pie last summer?'

" 'I remember, Harold. It was my combination apple-and-strawberry pie.'

" 'If I were you,' said Harold—*bang! bang!*—'I would make that pie, and these maple walnut cupcakes—which I wouldn't mind another one of—the specialties of the Alice and Amanda Bake Shop. I'm sure they'll sweep Iowa.'

" 'Well, I would, Harold,' said Miss Amanda, 'if—'

" 'Something to steer by,' Harold said to himself. He looked all around the living room. And there, right in front of him, was the big hour hand from Miss Amanda's clock. He nailed it to the handle of the pink umbrella. And then sang to it softly—

> You big clock hand, you're going to steer.
> Drive safe! Be straight. You hear? You *hear?*
> The person steering must behave!
> I'm trusting you, so—Burma shave!

(That dates me—what?)

"And right away the big clock hand became a sturdy steering bar.

" 'Now—*now!*' said Harold. 'The most difficult part: the engine. Do you have a box, Miss Amanda? Any old box—?'

" 'I have a hatbox, Harold. It's twenty years old—'

" 'A twenty-year-old hatbox!' said Harold. 'Groovy!—as Jake Moth would say. Please get it for me.'

"Miss Amanda got the twenty-year-old hatbox, and Harold cut a piece out of it and then put it together again, so it went all around the handle of the pink umbrella, just below where the sidesaddle seat was located. Then, into the twenty-year-old hatbox Harold carefully placed the hammer, the corkscrew, and the knife, fork, and spoon. And also, of course, the drain from Miss Amanda's sink. And he placed them all in a circle: they touched. Then he put his head right into the hat box, and he sang very softly—

> Now listen, corkscrew—listen, hammer—
> You'll need the strength of one windjammer!
> And listen, knife, fork, spoon, and drain—
> You'll need the strength of a railroad train!
> I don't have gas, I don't have oil—
> Oh, I need such a lot of energy—!

"Harold ran into Miss Amanda's kitchen and rummaged

through her wastebasket. And he found something useful to bring back and put in the hatbox.

But here's a piece of used tinfoil!

"Then he ran to a socket in the wall and cupped his fingers under it. And what he collected, he poured down into the hatbox too.

And some leftover electricity!
I don't have any atomic power—

"In a window box on the windowsill he saw a pretty flower blooming. So he ran to it, and picked it, and threw it right into the hatbox.

" 'Harold! My favorite begonia!'

—but here's Miss Amanda's favorite flower.

"And he went on singing—

You'll be an engine for three full days.
Then back to your ordinary ways.
And don't get lost! Don't tour. Don't roam.
Straight west! And take Miss Amanda home.

"Harold stopped singing. He looked at the pink umbrella a minute. Then he sighed and said, 'Well, I guess that's it.'

" 'That's *what?*' Miss Amanda asked.

" 'Let's give 'er a try!' said Harold. Together he and Miss Amanda carried the pink umbrella out into the street in front of the run-down brownstone house. 'Now get on,' said Harold.

" 'What? Me! On that contraption—?'

" 'Get on!' commanded Harold. He was tired from all the magic and work—and also sad, at what was coming.

"Miss Amanda got on the seat, sidesaddle. 'Now what?'

" 'Oh for heaven's sake!' said Harold. 'Just use your imagination! You only have to say, "Go!" But just take 'er around the block the first time.'

"Miss Amanda made a skeptical face—but since Harold wanted her to, she said, *'Go!'* And quick as a wink, she was zipping around the block!

" 'Hooray!' shouted Harold. He flung his arms up and down. 'It

49

works! Just look at that old bat travel!' In a minute Miss Amanda was back. 'Was everything okay, Miss Amanda?'

" 'Just fine, Harold,' Miss Amanda said.

" 'The steering bar? And the engine?'

" 'It all works beautifully. Except there—that bent strut—'

" 'Oh yes!' said Harold. He stroked his chin. 'Now about that strut—' and he sang very softly—

> Tut tut—
> You strut!
> It's your turn now! Be firm and straight.
> And why should Miss Amanda wait?

"He snapped his fingers and the strut came straight. Then he sang, privately, to the whole new pink umbrella—

> And remember, all you simple things,
> Be faithful to the love she brings.
> Be steadfast, and be loyal—do!
> I've tried my best. Now it's up to you.

"And the pink umbrella seemed to say to him—'Yes!'

"Harold stood a moment silently. Then he said, 'Now please, Miss Amanda, bend over so I can reach you.'

"Miss Amanda did. And before she could say, 'My Lord!' he had lifted his arms and given her a hug, and had kissed her on the cheek. 'Good-bye, Miss Amanda,' said Harold.

" 'But Harold,' said Miss Amanda, 'What am I going to do with—'

" 'Oh, you'll think of something,' said Harold. Then he dashed up the street just as fast as he could . . . Because, you see, he'd begun to cry. And Harold, as you may remember, was a person who didn't like long good-byes."

Then absolute silence . . . *Fabula interrupta!*

Barney looks at me, cheated. "But—"

"But what?"

"What happened to Miss Amanda?"

I shrug—"Don't know"—and feign not to possess the story-teller's gift: omniscience. But then I relent, of course. "She was last seen early this afternoon. Riding up Eighth Avenue on the pink umbrella. Heading for the Lincoln Tunnel."

His eyes go huge at the sight he sees: Miss Amanda, barreling along some superhighway—the Pennsylvania Turnpike perhaps. It's a vision that I quite like myself.

"And now—we go home."

Why won't he talk to me? The silences of this unsalvageable child—my tale has drained away now: there's just emptiness—are more desperate and forlorn than any place I've ever been.

Why won't I talk to *him?* Because I echo hopelessness. I am his mirror, as we reach Fifth Avenue, in the late, fading light.

"You sure you don't want to hear about Rumpelstiltskin and the Three-Legged Nothing? They became friends, you see. It promised not to gobble him up, if Rumpelstiltskin would find people for it to eat."

"No!" I think he's found my fear of it . . .

"Why do you hate Rumpelstiltskin? *Why?*"

"I like Harold."

Well, he's right after all. One has to choose sides.

I shake my head—mock melancholy—and sigh. "I'm sorry you don't like Rumpelstiltskin."

"Anyway, he tore himself in two."

"Oh, he put himself back together again! He does it all the time." Except once. And that's the last time: now. "And he walks through New York, and he hums to himself—

> And lucky I am not a soul doth know
> That the Three-Legged Nothing is my pet. Ho! ho!

"Ho! ho!" Barney echoes, with glum, angry incredulity.

Surreptitiously, his fingers inveigle themselves in mine . . . He doesn't believe I'm the other one.

But oh, my witnesses, I am! Danny Reilly called this morning. And on Sunday he's coming by . . . And the truth he's disclosed, since a year ago, about himself—he's disclosed that much truth about me too.

November 3

"Now: tell me about your death."

Stretched out on the couch, both naked, beneath that beautiful drawing of Harold—Harold, who is all I know of magic and humanity—Dan Reilly and I were rehearsing his death, in the flattened, intense, hypnotic voices of two people who meet in a special and abstract space they've created, an area where only they exist.

"Come on, Danny—" Droning, like some kind of Eastern priest. "—tell me."

There he lies: the body, massive, not fat, and the spirit, subdued and timid, cowed. A shy giant—not glib, as he seemed, but desirable—the brute with the damaged child inside. This human being, I found, is unique: a true original among all the maniacs we exploit. It's from Danny I've learned the tremendous secret: how to live, for a while, and still not be alive. He's the only human being I know who has his death, very literally, physically, within the tissues in which he exists. At least, if a passion can ever express itself in flesh, his does. (Honesty, not a passion—on his part, at least—the unraveling of his lies, took a year.)

"Well—what do you want to hear?"

"It all."

And clever! . . . Ah, he's been clever! . . . I still don't know if that story he told me a year ago, about fucking a sister, is true or not. There are some circumstances when telling the truth takes far more skill than a simple lie. He was capable of it—or anything else, in one of those families he was farmed off among . . . My own dearest Dan!

"What color is it, Dan? Your death? Is it black?"

"No. It's red. Or orange."

Yes—someone was hooked that afternoon in the Bowery . . . But why is it that I never know whether I am the fish or the fisherman?

"Is it quick? Your death—?"

"No. No!"

He called back a week later—a very judicious week, I think—a week during which he correctly estimated the fantasies I'd entertained about the great time we'd had. And the second time it took no lengthy conversation—it took ten minutes, I recollect—before his ass was elevated and praying for pain. ("Ass elevated" —the danger of pornography is that it may turn real.)

"Then if it's not quick—?"

"It lasts."

"Go on, Danny, dig it—" My voice wooing his. "—dig your death."

Two, three, four—a hundred million times—he's come around and enlarged his possibilities for me.

"It happens—where?"

"In the cellar of my house."

One silly detail of reality here: he isn't a Bowery bum. He works for the city. In welfare! (Yes!) He was down there, five o'clock shadow and all, cruising rough trade—that means, Snow White, a bastard who fucks you and then beats you up—and what he found, lucky man, was a giddy author of children's books who, nonetheless, has the skill to kill.

"Are you clothed?"

"No. I'm naked."

He travels around from case to case—taking care of people! . . . Absolutely wonderful! . . .

And his eyes transfix me, these twelve months later. Because now—he does show them to me—there is nothing in them, just endless, endless descending space. There are some things that should remain covered, but once revealed, have an unimaginable fascination. And this man's eyes do seem to me like holes opened over an infinite abyss.

"Are you free?"

"No, I'm tied."

"With ropes?"

"Not with ropes."

"Why not ropes?"

"I might break the ropes!"

We need no lies now, he and I. The truth is sufficiently Impossible. About what he wants, at any rate.

"You think you could? Break the ropes—?"

"I might try—"

He began to reveal his past to me. And *some* of this surely must be the truth! Born of parents who both *were* bums. Farmed out like a chore that paid to a series of soulless foster homes . . . But in one of them—I believe the fourth—he did pick up some love. A man who worked as a starter for a trucking company—I remember that job, it struck me as so strange: *go! go! go!*

go!—this man apparently liked the boy and presented the alternative: life. But he died, snatched away, too soon . . . . Perhaps it was from just that man—or from God knows where—that he got the idea of welfare work.

"First though—Dan, Dannier, Danniest—" I make sure I'm always somewhat drunk when he comes. "Is there anything else you want?"

"I want your fist up my ass."

The great day! (I too was scared to death.)

This was the fourth—maybe fifth—time that he'd been around. The mask of gruff masculinity was off. He entered—I put my hand on his shoulders and pressed. I only wanted him down on his knees, face into my crotch, to get the obedience straight right away. But as always, in the past few sessions, he had gone far ahead of me. Like someone dying or passing out, with an effortless, unconscious grace—the victim, simply, of gravity—he lowered himself and twisted around, so he lay on his back in front of me, and lifted his arms above his head. If ever the shape of sacrifice materialized before my eyes, it did then. And those *eyes*—oblivion pits, into which I looked—remained open. They were locked on mine—as mine on his—but his with mastery. And he said, in a voice that lacked any accent except the purely factual, "Do anything you want to me."

"What do you want?" I automatically asked. His prisoner and he knew it.

"I want your fist up my ass."

Fist-fucking, folks . . . A clinical note now, I'm afraid, but very necessary . . .

I had thought, in my monstrous egotism, I'd been screwing him pretty well. (After the first episode, a year ago, there was no question but that he wanted that. He even convinced me that he had learned to want it from *me!* God, the craftiness of madness.) Yet, ended each session—*I* was satisfied—there seemed to be some secret he had. And lo and behold, his secret was growing right at the end of my wrist. A *dildo* I thought, perhaps, he dreamed . . . But no. My master: so far in advance of me . . . I'd heard about the practice, of course, but the idea was always frightening.

"Then you're tied—not with ropes—"

"With handcuffs. I have them!"

As if fist-fucking could frighten me now! But then it did: blood—ruptures. Yet knowledgeable Dan Reilly, with his basilisk eyes almost smiling at my innocence, just said, "It'll be okay. I've done it before. Got an enema bag?" I loathe the word "enema"— the pros all say "douche"—but a fact's a fact. And I had a bag. He disappeared into the john for a while, and came back and asked for cold cream. Which I also could provide. Quite mechanically he lifted my right hand and found the nails satisfactorily short. (A note, to detectives of anatomy: if you meet a man who keeps the nails of his right hand much shorter than those of his left—well, he may be an interesting man, that man.) Then, before my fear had time, I was wearing him like a glove.

I described this whole thing to a friend afterwards—a living friend: you won't meet him—and he asked, with the same face you now have on you, "But wasn't it just like sticking your hand in a bowl of spaghetti?" And the answer is no—oh no, not a bit! It's like putting your fingers in fold upon fold of hot, wet velvet, some fabric never felt before, that contains a living pulse within it. For you do feel the life. There are arteries, major blood vessels, along which a human existence trills. And they can be played with and plucked and bowed like the strings of a living violin.

"And what are you tied to? A rack? A pole?"

"A pipe."

"What kind of a pipe, Dan?"

"This big water pipe. It goes from the floor to the ceiling. It's strong."

"And the cuffs—"

"—are strong. I'd never be able to get away."

Whatever I did, with sticks, whips—my fists—*whatever* I did—was not enough. And this depth of human emptiness, the chaos of his need, has created a corresponding void in myself. And he knows it.

"What else is there in the cellar, Danny? Besides you. Besides me."

"Kindling wood."

That first day, when he taught me what else five fingers were good for, I thought that he only wanted a sudden lunge of my hand for his heart, or some other pretty important organ: that I'd yank it out, like an Aztec priest, and hold it up to the hungry sun. But no. The fist-fucking was bad enough—no, good enough: I've learned to enjoy it and perform it rather expertly, if I do say so myself. Not for him. Not enough. His choice is—

"And if someone would pile the wood around you—"

"And if someone would light it—then go away—"

His choice is fire . . . But how he could have chosen it!—which I still can't believe, this coming act, but know is real, as real as a match, and on which I have come to depend completely. Why, a casual accident, in his haphazard childhood . . . The most frightening thing about life is its utter arbitrariness.

"—then go away—unless he wanted to stay, and watch." . . . Who said that?—he or I?

I must tell you trapped souls now that during the course of this litany, there had been an ashtray beside my fold-out couch. In it, a lighted cigarette.

"There, Danny."

Oh also—I don't smoke. I believe what all the doctors say.

"*Ah*—" I write down "ah"—but there are no letters and there are no words to suggest the depth of pleasure in the sigh of pure satisfaction and hurt that the touch of a glowing coal gave him. "—thank you, sir."

"You'd make noise—"

"No I wouldn't, sir!"

But he would. Most appalling of all, the moans he'd make—not of pain, at first—would be the worst details of all.

"Will you touch me again with it, Terry? Please."

And I did . . .

Because, if I am important to him—the only one he's ever met who can build the final fire he seeks—by Christ alive! to me he is indispensable. I know my own moral arithmetic, the equations of my mind. And I could never kill myself unless it was justified punishment. I must murder in order to die. And a lingering sense of life—of the space individuals ought to enjoy—prevents me from intruding with death in the margin of a human being whose text does not include the wish. He too—and he knows it as well, instinctively—as I for him, is the only one I've ever met.

But it does take time. It takes time for the necessary dialectic by which the unthinkable meets the real. For a person structured in words and thoughts, as well as in passions—such a one must be reasoned to death. That's what you witnesses—and this whole damn diary—are all about. In the end, I know, you will be convinced; you'll agree with me. And then—I'll agree with myself.

You are sitting there now, in that abstract schoolroom I've fixed up, exchanging cryptic glances, and murmuring, "*Impossible! He can't*—"

But you're wrong!—I can—or rather, you're right, for a little while—I just barely still can't. But the "can't" is so tiny, so frail, compared to the "can't" I felt last October. When the idea first materialized, and fiction turned into irreversible fact.

These three things: the Impossible, the Possible, the Real. My minuscule, little soul, how they do fascinate me!

The Impossible! . . . I will show you exactly what it's like. The world, the real, with all its possibilities, is a very large encampment. It contains fields, streams, and hills, and a little bit of wilderness too, as well as the huts and the tents of men. And a high palisade surrounds it all.

Now, on the other side, just inches beyond those wooden walls, the Impossible begins. You can climb up steps, and stand on a platform, and look out into the alien world. You see there—vague shapes: enormous and tiny animals, and plants, ferns, trees, of such profusion that it makes Mesozoic Earth seem as strict and disciplined as a formal French garden. Behind you, in the encampment, you hear the mild din of humanity. There are men at anvils, men at hoes, and women washing, children fighting, playing, crying. And before you—its sounds are soft and murmuring, its figures misted and indistinct—the Impossible: a chaos of not quite living things that are straining toward creation.

Well—a person can become intrigued. He can go up that ladder again and again, and stand on that wall, alone, and watch. And he thinks he sees—but no, he's not sure. It might have been—but was it? A longing, which strangely resembles nostalgia, grows heavy in his chest: he is homesick for the Impossible.

So finally one night—and I know precisely which night it was: September twenty-fifth—on a sudden rope of certainty he lets himself over those sheltering walls and confidently slips away . . .

And the wonder—the *wonder*—of what he sees!

The beasts, and even the greatest of them—so potentially

dreadful from the wall—are all tame to his hand. They are charmed by his presence: that he should have come, and be one of them. Of course there are some that are more elusive, but they too will eat from his hand, in time. And the plants, the flowers, reach toward him their beauty, and blossom more fully the closer he comes. The soil is covered with something like moss, almost consciously tender to his feet as he walks. Sweet moisture drips from innocuous vines—the air perfumes itself—and the stars!— God, the stars. No campfires dull the tremendous multicolored lights that tempt one from the stars of the Impossible. They hang like glowing funguses a few feet above his head. Or perhaps they are brilliant burning stones, and millions and billions of light-years away. It makes no difference. They are—as all the Impossible is—exactly what he wills them to be . . . He can stroke the head of an animal. . . . As I stroked Dan Reilly's head today. And felt, beneath the black soft wave, the fur of a shy devoted beast. Which only could have been his death. While beyond us, in a farther, darker thicket—eyes bright and alive—my own death was warily watching me.

"Please touch me again, Terry—*Thank you, sir!* Now hard!"

He is covered with scars. Not many—but some—that I have put on.

"That's all."

"Once more—?"

"I *said*—" He feeds on authority. "—that's all."

"Yes—sir. You want me to get dressed now?"

"You don't have to."

"Can I lie here beside you? A while?"

"Yes."

In a pause—in that sneaky, ambitious way of his—he prepared to take another step ahead. "I've got something to show you."

"What?"

"Well, I didn't pay yet today—" Another quirk—one could call the desire to be burned alive a quirk, couldn't one?—he's one of those slaves who needs to pay: ten bucks—his choice, not mine. "—and I want you to see what I've got in my wallet."

Oh Christ! I remembered—the last time that we were together, he'd said, "Look!" He dug in his pants and opened a billfold that contained three hundred dollars—in cash.

"You're crazy, Dan!" (The redundant, sometimes, does intrude.) "You're not going to—"

"No, no—the usual ten. But I wanted you to see—I'm really getting my money out."

The subject of our discussion had been his savings: not very much, a couple of thousand—but why waste it, after all? Perhaps, in his optimistic dimness, he reasoned thus—I know I did—he was trying to turn me, from being an affectionate sadist, into a ruthless executioner. And *they* get paid—don't they? . . . Oh you Dan— poor Dan—you're too clever for me. That's how you'll get what you want. You'll outwit me into killing you.

"Look!—you're *not* to keep that money lying around your house—"

"It's okay, it's okay!" He judged how far behind him I was. "I've got a place no burglar could find. And I like to know it's there."

I understood: a pledge—that he'd made to himself, but which also, somehow, bound me—that I truly would come.

"And, Terry, you know what else I said—about someone finding your name—" He extracted a flimsy slip of paper from the wallet full of promises. "Look at this. I swear to God, that's the only place your name and your number are written down." Something lovely struck him; a spark, in those dark eyes, flashed and died. "And you can use this to start it!" he laughed.

And that laugh—halfhearted and hectic and gay, and utterly sincere—did actually occur, in this apartment, this afternoon.

I own this man. But the sensation I get most often with him, as I did at that moment, was one of powerlessness. He *will* get all that he wants from me.

"That's all." I got up.

"You mad—?"

"No. Tired. I came a couple of times. You've been here the whole afternoon."

"You could have kicked me out—"

"I didn't *want* to kick you out!"

There was one last act, before he left. Not the giving, taking, of a ten-dollar bill that's discreetly placed on a table. (Is that the way whores get paid, I wonder? This whore does.) When dressed he pauses before the door, then drops on his knees and presses his head in my belly, as trustworthy to him by now as any mother's lap. He looks up, sometimes in tears, but usually, as it had today, his face has the sadness in it of a crumpled paper bag. And he says, "I love you, Terry." (He doesn't speak much now. But what he does is worse than the porno he conned me with.)

"I know. Stand up."

"Will you come out? Soon? Just to see the place? We don't have to hurry—"

"I'll come."

"But this winter. This winter, you said."

"And this winter I meant. But it hasn't begun yet."

"I trust you."

"You can. Don't bother to look for anyone else."

"I don't. I'm lucky. I didn't think I could love the person—"

"Stop that! Go away now, Dan. I'm tired. I'll call you next week."

"You never do."

"Then you call me."

"I will."

"Good-bye."

And he went back home to his house—his little inflammable house on Long Island. He's described it to me, many times, in detail. And always has taken great care to stress the fact that it wasn't too near any other houses. "Homes," he calls his neighbors' dwellings. There was really no risk of a dangerous conflagration— "where someone might get hurt." It would be a problem only for the local fire department. And even for them, not a major blaze.

November 7

The smell of my left shoulder is death . . . So strange, what things this energy flows into. I clobbered my shoulder about a month ago at the gym—sometime in the critical period, and ever since then, on Iris's advice—to do what human beings tell me, in this unworldly state I'm in, is a secret, complex joy—I've been slathering Ben-Gay on it. Of course it doesn't do any good. (I keep re-hurting it on purpose.) But the smell—medicinal, sharp: both conviction and memory—of Ben-Gay on my shoulder is death.

And a few molecules always fly through the air and land on my tongue, and make it tingle. I like the bitterness. The taste of death should also be a tingling at the tip of one's tongue. I will put it on all winter long. Until, in the spring, an inanimate yet faithful sensation, it will remind me that the time has come.

> Behold this young author named Terry. (But he'll never tell!)
> He used to be jolly and merry. (And didn't believe in Hell.)
> But the fool fell in love,
> And now—Heavens above!—
> All he wants is to die and be—

—cremated, in point of fact. (Besides, the rhyme wasn't complete.) It's in my will. And my ashes thrown into running water: the sea, the Hudson River, even domestic Long Island Sound. But it must be into turbulence. One thing I do know, and this in my bones: that, God or not, there has to be scattering for there to be peace.

And this can be the epitaph (another narcissistic dream: the wish to write one's own epitaph, as if the world was not competent):

> Ashes scattered—
> Far the best.
> All that mattered—
> Let it rest.

November 16

I envy the physical masochists—the ones who can take it all out on their asses. They get a few hours of pleasure-pain, and then for as long as half a day, they can sit on the tingle, remembering. With me, it's my spirit that's got to be whipped.

I am in Edith Willington's living room—and don't get that cozy warm feeling, my gloppy gobblers-up! I am *not* here out of kindness! I am only here because Rumpelstiltskin knows that the easiest way to make me dance is to force me to see that kid again. You see, Rumpelstiltskin, although he started out as a freak from a medieval fairy tale, has adjusted to the times. He now sits in my subconscious at the console of an ultramodern IBM computer. And every button in front of him is another sick symptom to bring into play.

"I can't imagine why you're being so nice—" Because it hurts me, you silly bitch! "—but as long as you *are*—and I hope you'll go on—this weekend is going to be difficult."

It seems that her mild stud from Denver, Frank Henderson, is flying in this afternoon. And his imminent arrival always causes *Ber*-nard to panic. Another walk in the park—would I?

"He's just more *human* when he's talked to you."

"He doesn't talk at all. He doesn't say a single word."

"Whatever happens, he comes back happy. For a little while."

Ber-nard, by the way, has been wound up and headed into his bedroom, while we have this adult conversation.

"Well—as long as it helps—" And as long as it fucks me up.

"Oh, it does. You're a dear!" She lifts her voice melodiously. "*Ber*-nard—come back now."

And the automated thing plods in. It's already put on its coat and hat.

"Go ring for the elevator, sweet."

While the blob's in the hall, we have a bit more mature complicity. *Sotto voce,* of course. (That's one of the ways you can know you're grown-up: when you're talking behind a child's back, even when he can't hear, you do it beneath your breath.) "And talk about Frank, if you can. Just tell him—oh, I don't know— that he's nice. He *is* nice!"

That's beautiful. This big, stiff grown-up prick—who's about to barge into your life and take your mother away from you—is nice. He's *nice!* That's gorgeous, isn't it?

"Okay."

And so—to the park . . . To the zoo, this time . . . My idea, naturally. This run-down dumpling doesn't think at all. It just says, "Yes," when I ask if it wants to walk to the zoo.

I've got to make it say something!

We look at all the animals. The elephant fascinates the most.

"Do you like him?"

"Yes."

"Why?"

"I don't know."

And nothing. Not another word . . . Oh come *on!*—say *something!*

"You want to hear Harold's song to his friend the elephant?"

"Yes."

I am going to recite a pretty good poem that I wrote in college:

> An elephant looked at a bee
> And was astounded
> By the hint of immortality
> That had been compounded
>
> Of air and honey and sting,
> Unmixed of clay.
> On churning invisible wings
> The bee flew away
>
> And left the elephant there,
> Cursing his birth,
> His death, decay: the vulgar,
> Immanent earth.

Not bad for a sophomore heavily influenced by William Blake's plant and animal poems. But too subtle for Barney. So I improvise this—

> My elephant is big and strong.
> And trustworthy. He has thick skin.
> He's happy and eats all day long.
> And no one—*no one*—can get in!

He gets it: a quick semaphoric smile—safety: to become invulnerable—is flashed for an instant from his turned-down lips.

Then into the park. The preordained bench. And the story: *Harold and the Animals!* . . .

Seems that the animals in the Central Park Zoo have to be changed daily. Because Harold, who has a kinship with all caged things, sneaks into the place every night and miniaturizes all the beasts. And they stampede joyously into the park, where they live under leaves, in bushes, or make apartment houses out of abandoned old tree stumps. Harold makes them *really* tiny too! An elephant could easily tromp out and sun himself on a blade of grass. A lion could hide behind an acorn. And since the animals are all so small, and since they have known captivity, they don't quarrel a bit with one another . . .

It's a problem, however, for the city administration. They

simply don't know what to do. Since they don't want everyone in New York to know there are all these wild animals loose, they send trucks up every night to the big Bronx zoo and schlepp down fresh animals. And of course, a night later Harold sets them all free. Mayor Lindsay is in a quandary. And so is the commissioner of the Parks Department.

I sit with a sense of thrilling littleness: a secret sort of private joy at the thought of all those miniature creatures with which I've populated the park. A familiar sensation—and one I like. In the summer sometimes I'll look at a bush, and I'll know that a lot of little lizards are living inside that bush. They have big ambitions, though—they have plans. Haven't you felt that ever?—that beneath some waxy prehistoric leaves there are tiny reptiles evolving into dinosaurs? Or that somewhere in an undiscovered meadow, eohippus is playing—the tiny dawn horse, no bigger than a whippet, that danced and pranced before history.

But Barney isn't satisfied.

"You didn't like that story."

"I did."

"No you didn't. I know. Your head didn't go away, to where you would remember it."

"It didn't have anyone—special in it."

I see: a lack of protagonist. It was *all* the animals. And he's right. The criticism of children is far more valuable than what you might find in the *Partisan Review*.

"You want another?"

"*Story*—?" He can't believe his luck.

"A happy, or a sad one?"

"I don't care."

"You don't care if it's happy or sad—?"

"As long as it's Harold."

All right, you little bastard—that's a challenge! I'll tell you a story that you won't like . . . I don't—

"This is—*Harold and the Rat*.

"This morning—you know what happened:

Is it the first snow? Could it be that?
No.
Then is it my time to visit the Rat?
Yes.

64

"Now, I must tell you that once upon a time Harold received a strange letter. All it said was—'Please come and visit me.' It was signed—'The Rat.' And there was a postscript: 'P.S. I won't tell you where I live. No one knows. But if you do have any magic, you'll find me.'

"This note worried Harold. There was something doomy and gloomy about it. So he did his best to find the Rat. He walked all over New York, in fact. He walked through Brooklyn, he walked through Queens—and the Bronx—and one Sunday he took the ferry to Staten Island and walked all over there. Of course he had walked around Manhattan many times, but nowhere did he get a feeling that the Rat might live somewhere nearby.

"But one day—Jake Moth had just flown over him and shouted, 'Hi, Harolharol!' "

"When?"

His abrupt, alert interest unnerves me. "Not very long ago. About a year. Why?"

"I just wanted to know."

"Not very long ago, he was walking through Greenwich Village, and suddenly Harold felt to himself—*the Rat is near!* And he started to hum, very softly—

> Oh Rat—you Rat—I've looked and looked,
> And now you're somewhere near.
> I've used my magic—I've hooked and crooked.
> Now, finally, I'm here!

"And Harold stopped, exactly where he was: before a brownstone house with a big black fence in front of it. He went into the entry. And sure enough—beside one buzzer the name plate said, 'The Rat.' Harold rang the bell, and in a minute he got buzzed in. The nearer he got, the easier. It was three flights up and in the front. He knocked on the door.

"The Rat opened it. He was scowling. The Rat does a lot of scowling, you see. And he said to Harold, 'It took you an awfully long time!'

" 'Well, you didn't give me much to go on,' said Harold. He felt sort of awkward, standing there on the threshold, so he asked politely, 'Can I come in?'

" 'Oh, I *guess* so,' grumped the Rat gloomily.

"The Rat's apartment was really a mess. 'Needs paint,' said Harold, as he looked around.

" 'Now just don't you start criticizing!' the rat said angrily. 'Sit down.'

"Harold was going to apologize and sit down on the couch. But suddenly he couldn't move. Because over the couch he saw a picture. And it was a picture of himself. He was standing next to his friend Sylvester the rubber plant, and Terry the cocker spaniel. And his right hand was raised with one finger lifted—like this—" I demonstrate. And Barney intently memorizes. "—and it was as Harold as Harold could be. 'Why, that's *me!*' he said. 'It's me to a tee!'

" 'Of course it's you!' the Rat sulked. 'Who did you think it was?—Alice in Wonderland?'

" 'But who drew it?' said Harold. 'It's better than anything in the book.'

" 'Oh, *I* did,' the Rat admitted. He turned away."

Damned if I'd give that fink illustrator the credit!

" '*You* did—?' Harold exclaimed. 'But that's wonderful! Is that what you are—an artist?' "

Well—he can't be an author of children's stories—that's for damn sure!

" 'I draw,' the Rat shrugged. 'I paint a little. Sometimes I illustrate children's books.'

" 'That's wonderful!' said Harold.

" 'It's a living,' the Rat admitted, no more. He wouldn't let himself be praised. 'You want some coffee?'

" 'I'd love some coffee,' Harold said.

"And then, despite the fact that the Rat was a pretty nasty person, they started to be friends."

Then—what am I doing, I ask myself. In this November, in Central Park. The kid's got misery enough of his own.

But for Barney the world, disturbingly, has become my absence of speech. He pleads, like someone expecting to be defeated, "Go on—"

"So, little by little, Harold learned all about the Rat. You know, Harold was pretty good at finding out the stories of people. Sometimes, with the right kind of person, who just liked to talk, he would blurt out, 'Well, what is your *story?*' and their whole life story would come tumbling out. But with others, like the Rat, who were sort of embarrassed by everything that had happened to them, he had to be more crafty. He began by complimenting him on what a fine illustrator he was. And then, after hearing a grumpy 'Oh, I'm all right, I guess,' he went on to ask, very casually, you understand, whether anyone else in the Rat's family had been a painter, or a writer, or anything.

" 'God, no!' came the answer back, with a glum Rat laugh.

"It developed, in the course of a long afternoon—during which a lot of coffee was drunk at first, and then a lot of Scotch—that's booze—that the rat had a dreary and dismal past.

" 'He came from—' "

No. Not Philadelphia.

" '—from Ninth Avenue. And his father was—' "

No, no. Not a doctor.

" '—a garbage collector. Most rats are that, you know. It's a very respectable occupation. Promotes the general welfare. But the thing was, the Rat's Pop didn't speak to him until he was twelve years old. He was very busy collecting garbage—he loved his work, and he did it awfully well—and when he wasn't collecting garbage he was reading *The New York Times*.

" 'I wish you would talk to him,' Mom Rat would say to her husband.

" 'Too busy,' Pop Rat would answer, as he flipped a page of *The New York Times*. 'I'll talk to him when he's twelve.'

" 'He's really a great little rat,' said Mom.

" 'I'll talk to him when he's twelve.'

"But the young Rat didn't understand. 'But *why?*' he would say to his mother. 'I just don't see why Pop never talks to me.'

" 'He's awfully busy,' Mom Rat would try to explain. 'You know, with all his garbage collecting. And he does love to read *The New York Times*.'

" 'But he could say something!' the young Rat complained.

" 'Well, he will, dear. When you're twelve,' said Mom Rat. 'And don't you be unhappy now. You're the greatest little rat. Honestly, Terry, you are—' " That slips out, but I don't think Barney notices. "Mom Rat kept telling him that he was the greatest little rat in the world. And part of the time he believed he was. But the rest of the time he was sure that he must be the worst little rat in the world. Because Pop Rat wouldn't talk to him."

And between these two poles—self-adulation and pure despair—the Rat's life is discharged. How to phrase that for a seven-year-old?

"It was like being on a swing. Sometimes the Rat swung way up, in wonderful self-confidence, when he *knew* that he must be a very fine rat indeed, but then he'd fall back, in the other direction, and know, for sure, that he must be the worst little rat in the world. And he couldn't get off that swing.

"Well, the Rat's twelfth birthday finally came. And Pop Rat, who was sitting in his favorite armchair, smoking a cigar, put down *The New York Times* and said to Mom Rat, 'Okay, bring him here. We'll have to talk about his future.'

"But by then it was too late. Because the Rat had turned sulky and nasty. He hated his father—and he didn't much like his mother, either. He had decided that he *wasn't* the best little rat in the world—just the opposite, in fact—and she'd been lying all these years. But he went into the living room to see his father anyway. And he stood in front of the easy chair.

" 'Now, son,' Pop Rat began, 'I'm going to talk to you—'

" 'Big deal!' said the Rat. 'And what if I won't talk to *you?*'

"Pop Rat was very surprised. That wasn't what he had expected at all. 'I want to discuss your future,' he said. 'I think you should go into garbage collecting—'

" 'And the hell with garbage collecting!' the Rat burst out. 'I'm going to draw pictures! That's something that *I* can do—and you can't! So there! Good-bye!'

"And the Rat stamped out of his parents' rat hole, and he never went back to see them again, except sometimes on holidays. But rarely, even then. And so most of the time, when he wasn't drawing, the Rat just sat boozing and glooming out the window. Did I tell you?—he drinks, this Rat does. And they both drank a lot that afternoon—Harold and he—because far off, in the streets of New York, they heard the Three-Legged Nothing screaming, and he's what Harold and the Rat fear most—"

"I don't *want* him—!" He's remembered something. But what? I don't know myself.

"All right, all right—" And here, for the second time, it occurs to me what I'm doing. I feel as if I ought to call little Barney "doctor"—and ask him if he'd please pass some Kleenexes over to the couch. The story, after all, was supposed to be for *him* . . . I've got to smooth it out.

"So that was the story of the Rat, as Harold pieced it together over the course of the first few weeks after Harold had met him. And it didn't make Harold happy at all. One day he asked the Rat if the latter would mind if he went to visit his parents!

" 'What for?' grumped the Rat suspiciously.

" 'Well, I just thought I'd like to meet them,' said Harold.

" 'Just ordinary people, that's all.'

" 'If you wouldn't mind,' Harold asked deferentially. He didn't want to antagonize the Rat. And he knew that he was a very excitable person.

" 'Oh well—if you have to,' the Rat shrugged the whole idea away. 'I just think it's awfully silly—for a person with magic to waste his time on two ordinary rats—'

"Harold let the subject drop. But that very afternoon he went to see Mom and Pop Rat.

"They both were very glad to see him. Mom Rat's first question—a very momlike question—was 'Is he getting the right things to eat?'

"And Harold answered, sadly, 'No!' He has this thing about truth, Harold does: he just does it! 'He only eats TV dinners and Carnation Instant Breakfasts.'

" 'Oh dear,' said Mom Rat.

" 'He drinks too,' said Harold. 'Scotch.' That thing about honesty again.

" 'Oh dear, oh dear,' Mom Rat sighed sadly. 'That's what I was afraid of.'

" 'Does he have anyone to talk to?' said Pop. He was very much older now, you see, and about to retire from garbage collecting too, and he had begun to understand that it's very nice to have someone to talk to. In fact, he often said to himself, 'I wish my son would talk to me.'

" 'He doesn't have very many,' Harold had to admit. 'The thing is, the Rat doesn't really like people. A lot of people like the Rat, because the pictures he makes of people are really awfully good,

69

but he doesn't trust them. He's very suspicious.'

" 'That comes from your side of the family,' said Pop Rat to Mom.

" 'It doesn't come from *my* side!' Mom Rat defended herself testily.

" 'I don't give a damn *whose* side it comes from!' said Harold, who was starting to get pretty angry himself.

" 'Does he have a nice apartment?' said Mom.

" 'No.' Harold shook his head. 'It needs paint, and the plaster's falling off the wall.'

" 'Oh dear,' sighed Mom, in a momlike way.

" 'That's just laziness,' said Pop Rat. And he gave *The New York Times* in his lap a shake.

"Now up to now it had been Harold's big idea to bring the Rat and his parents together. But when Pop Rat shuffled his papers like that, he decided, inside himself, No. It really would be much better if Harold was only the go-between, between the three of them. So he chatted with the Rats for a while. Then he took a basket full of crumb buns that Mom Rat had fixed up—'At least tell him he should *eat!*'—and he went back to see the Rat.

" 'They worry about you,' he said.

" 'So? Let them worry!' the Rat just laughed grumpily.

"All Harold could do was become a friend of the Rat—which he did—and keep calling on Mom and Pop too."

And Barney interrupts me. Interrupts this bitter reverie. And surprises me by asking, "Didn't Harold have any magic—?"

"No, he did not! He didn't have that much magic left. I'm afraid there's no magic in the story at all. You want me to go on?"

"Yes, please"—in his emptiness.

Okay, you little creep! You've really asked for this—

"Well—this morning Harold thought of the Rat because it's getting on toward the holidays. Thanksgiving, you know, and Christmas. And holidays are bad times for the Rat." Where am I going? Let me stop before it's too late! What the hell, though. This kid won't know. "So Harold went down to Greenwich Village and buzzed the Rat's buzzer, and the Rat let him in. 'What are *you* doing here?' he demanded to know.

" 'Well, Rat, I just thought I'd come for a visit,' said Harold apologetically. He never knew how to cope with the Rat when the latter was in one of his really bad moods. As he obviously was today.

" 'Oh,' the Rat grumped glumly. 'A visit. I see. Well—sit down.'

"The first thing that Harold always did when he visited the Rat was to take a good long look, like a nice big drink of something, at that picture of himself. He thought the Rat might like a compliment, and began to say, 'That really is something special, Rat! I honestly think it's better—'

" 'Oh, now don't lose your head!' said the Rat. 'Just because it happens to be of *you!*'

"Harold sighed and sat down. It was going to be one of those days, he saw. The Rat was in his worst possible mood. He was ornery and suspicious and—just everything unpleasant. 'It's not that it's of *me,*' said Harold. 'But it's such a wonderful drawing—'

" 'Yeah, sure,' grumped the Rat. He sat down in a beat-up black sling chair and stared at nothing, in front of him.

" 'You never did tell me how you came to draw that drawing, Rat.'

"The Rat shifted uneasily in his chair. 'Oh—I heard about you. And I read your book. And I just decided to draw it, that's all. It's no big deal.'

"A very bad silence began. It felt—and tasted—like curdled milk. Usually Harold was pretty good about making conversation. But not with the Rat. There wasn't *anyone* who could. Harold started to say something—he started to *try* to say something—but all that came out was 'Um—er—'

" 'You got heartburn?' the Rat asked suspiciously.

" 'No, Rat, I'm fine.'

" 'Then stop making those nauseating noises!' demanded our friend the Rat.

" 'I'm sorry,' Harold apologized. It seemed to him he did nothing *but* apologize when he visited the Rat. He knew that he was a caretaker—that's what he was for—but taking care of the Rat was much harder than taking care of all the others. There was more sour silence. And then Harold squinched up a smile in his lips and made his voice go higher than it should, and he said, 'Say, Rat, I've been thinking about Thanksgiving—' and he didn't know what to say after that.

" 'So?' the Rat said, 'So what about Thanksgiving?'

" 'Well—' Harold's voice got gulpy and plunged. He knew that this was always a very bad subject to bring up with the Rat. 'Well I was only wondering—what *you* were going to do?'

" 'On Thanksgiving? Nothing! It's just another day,' said the Rat. 'I'll warm up a TV dinner—'

" '*No! no! no! no!*' Harold couldn't stand that. He jumped up from the couch and flung his arms up and down.

" 'What's the matter with you?' said the Rat, surprised.

" 'You can't have a TV dinner on Thanksgiving, Rat!'

" 'Well I have,' said the Rat—rather proudly, it seemed to Harold. 'And many times. And I will again.'

" 'It's just not right, Rat!' Harold was pacing back and forth.

" 'Look, if it makes you happy,' said the Rat, 'I'll make it a turkey TV dinner—'

" 'That *won't* make me happy!' said Harold. 'Now listen, Rat, I've been invited to Thanksgiving dinner, and I'm going to take—' "

Here—just here—a flicker of sanity, and perhaps my last, comes glimmering before my eyes. I stand up. And say, "Look, Barney, it's late. I can't finish this story this afternoon."

He stands up too, obediently, recognizing the quiet grown-up note of absolute authority . . . We walk through November, the graying year . . . And that silence of his—Christ—worse than the Rat's.

Defensively—to keep myself from this stillness at least—I say, "Your mother said Mr. Henderson was coming up this weekend."

Mistake! . . .

Lot's wife, or Niobe, or a troll caught suddenly in the dawn: salt, water, or stone—but something inanimate. He isn't even suffering—in no way is he alive anymore.

His petrification frightens me. "I'm sorry, Barney. That story wasn't any good. I make them up as I go along. Next time I'll—"

"I like that story. I want to know more."

It's five o'clock. The air pearl gray, and overcast . . . At least he is still alive.

"Is this Rat real?" he says, out of nothing—some intuition.

"He's real," I answer him honestly.

"Then will you tell me what happened?"

"When?"

"On the Rat's Thanksgiving."

"Oh, that's the name of the story, is it?"

"I don't know the name—" He retreats from any pretension. "*Harold—and the Rat's Thanksgiving*. Is that the name of the story?"

I've delivered myself—and he knows it. "Yes. Do you promise? To tell me?"

These little souls know well all the power they have: a promise—it's unbreakable.

"I promise. *Harold—and the Rat's Thanksgiving*!" . . .

Oh Lord—now I *will* have to go! If only so I can tell Barney a story.

November 18

> Now honesty! It's time! Now pleasure. (Or could this be pain?)
> Now doubts. Postponement. Sorrow.
> He called today. "But not today." Lightheartedly explained,
> "If not today—tomorrow."

November 19

And here he is—another third of my life—or was, last night. Two hours . . . The name, by the way, of this entry is *Rumpelstiltskin—and the Mask of Mastery*!

"There you are, you rascal!" A typical greeting of his. Since an ordinary telephoned "hello" will not suffice for Jim.

If Hermes, Mercury, for sport, had been aiming to become a fox, and in his passage through the universe had been short-circuited and ended up a human being, he would have been Jim Whittaker. The God of messages and mischief, God of thieves and also psychopompos—the conductor of the dead—but with the animal's sharp eyes, sharp nose, fine lips, and—finer still—a sly sense of the ways in which an animal survives.

"Are you at the office?" It was late afternoon.

"Yes."

And here are a few marvelously accurate descriptions, quoted from the editorial prose of Webster's Dictionary: Hermes—"an Olympian God, son of Zeus and Maia. He was herald and messenger of the gods, giver of increase to herds, guardian of boundaries and of roads and their commerce. He was further god of science and invention, of eloquence, of cunning, trickery, and theft, of luck and treasure-trove, and conductor of the dead to Hades. His attributes are the winged sandals (*talaria*), caduceus, and winged hat (*petesos*)." And under Mercury—the third definition: a heavy silver-white metallic element, the only metal that is liquid at ordinary temperatures—called also, popularly, quicksilver . . .

It's fantastic! There he is!

The son of Zeus and Maia: he once told me that his father was an overpowering bully, but his mother was an earth-nurse female

Herald and messenger of the gods: he gives the sense, at least to me, of—I don't know—*conveying* things. If not words, deeds. And he always seems to be *carrying* something—a toy, a briefcase, or his medical bag.

Giver of increase to herds: his own herds here: he's got six kids.

Guardian of boundaries and of roads: Christ yes!—he keeps the districts of his life apart.

And of their commerce: a fine American mercenary streak of greed.

He was further god of science and invention: a B.S. from Columbia.

Of eloquence: not very, as a matter of fact. He's fluent, but not deep.

Of cunning, trickery, and theft: oh boy!

Of luck and treasure-trove: he *does* find things. (Like me.) I believe the word is "serendipity"—the unlooked-for, unexpected discovery. Except, being Jim, he expects the unexpected, and demands that the unlikely happen. I envy him that faculty most of all. For me, certainty has been a curse.

And conductor of the dead to Hades: in a minute. (But he'll be mine too, though he doesn't know it.)

His attributes are the winged sandals, caduceus, and winged hat. The wings, of course, are speed. He calls and says, "Can I come over in ten minutes?" And afterwards—zip! Out the door. With that maddening "Ta ta!"

And the caduceus? He's a doctor—a surgeon, and apparently a very good one. That's the conductor of the dead as well. Some patients die—not through his fault: some patients always die. A physician yes, but not a mere medical technician. He has the kind of frictive mind struck off where the arts and sciences coincide and clash creatively. I'm sure that when he takes apart and reassembles a human physique he does it with all the skill and finesse of a first-sculptor, an artisan. He once told me—which I liked: the sentiment of an artist, not a mere mechanic—that his first impulse when he finished a complex operation was to open the patient up again and do it all over, better. I've asked him—begged him—to smuggle me into his hospital—Physicians and Surgeons—so I can watch him operate, and he's promised that he would.

As for mercury, the metal—*not capitalized,* the good book says: his quicksilver does have an inanimate quality to it: no name that would need a capital letter.

Now, here is Webster on the ordinary North American fox: "Any of certain carnivorous mammals"—that's lovely, but instead read: "humanivorous"—"smaller than the wolves, and noted for craftiness."

This fox is not small: he's six foot two. His nose is just a bit too small to go with his chin, those incredible lips—as defined as if by a palette knife—and his eyes, gray, appraising, that seem to be larger than they are. His color is high: a flush somewhere between being hectic and just good health. And that hair! Spectacular auburn fox's hair, or the world's champion Irish setter, beginning to be shot through with gray, but in such a calculated way—the calculations of nature, not Jim—it would give any hairdresser wet dreams. Indeed, in my dreams of fantasies, I have often seeded that hair myself . . . I wonder, if I got him drunk enough, if I could come in his hair some night?

"Whatcha doin'?"

"Nothing."

"Ya wanna rassle?"—with a lift in his voice on the last syllable, so it really did sound like a high school proposal.

"You hot?"

"Rah-*ther!*"—a guardsman now, and I love those subtle, swift transitions.

"Okay."

"I'll see you in fifteen minutes. Ta ta!"

The most frightening thing about the world is that it is exactly the place where you're likely to get what you ask for. I put in a request for him. (Like Eve asking for an apple.) About a year ago I called up a hairdresser friend of mine—on a night of restless indecision—and asked, not believing he would, if he knew of any handsome, husky, muscular man who'd like to get belted and fucked.

"Have I got a goil for you!" he said. (He's nice, this hairdresser, Sam, but he has no part in my death whatsoever, so you probably won't meet him again. A very valuable contact though.) "I can't call him tonight. But I'll give him your number."

"Great! What's his name?"

"Jim Whittaker. And knowing your gift for whips and things—"

"How nicely you put it!"

"—I've mentioned you to him already. He's married—"

"Oh Christ—these married masochists! They're all such frauds! You know the first thing he'll say? 'No marks! No marks!' "

"Believe me, baby, this is one fraud that you will love to put up with!"

"So give him my number." Ordinary? A routine trick, passed on . . . Well, so was the atom bomb.

And that was the whole banal conversation: a piece of tail shared among friends, no more . . . Little did I believe that less than a year later I'd be laughing out of the other side of my ass!

He arrived. Three nights after my call to Sam. ("I'm a friend of our favorite hairdresser. Want to?"—on the telephone.) There occurred that dire moment at the door: what if the trick's not attractive—oy vey! But he was. He was spectacular. In a dapper checkered suit—and wearing that grin he always wears: it suggests some secret he knows, which is his advantage, never yours. I gave him a drink, we played a little verbal footsie, and then—me being the big butch thing I am, and obviously my notices from the hairdresser had been highly favorable: it therefore being my job to start it—I put my hand on his knee. (How's *that* for originality?) And said to him, simply, "Strip."

He began to undress right away. And alacrity, not mere obedience, is the seasoning in a master's feast. "Did Sam tell you I'm married?"

"I know. No marks."

His grin became specific. "You've had married men before."

"My specialty. They're the best."

He was piqued—"Why so?"—and sipped my general compliment, as he took off his pants.

"They usually want from me what they can't get from their wives."

"What's that?" He knew, of course—his smile showed—but he too took pleasure in verbalization.

"A dick up their ass—and maybe a belt across it sometimes." (That damn strength of porn again!)

I was coming on very strong—not knowing the jelly I'd become in a month—and he appreciated it. (What I said, however, was true: Rumpelstiltskin is a present—given by God's Antagonist—to married men who have strange cravings.)

And that first session: My Christ!—I had never made love like that before. It is not true, by the way, that ugly people can make good love. You have to be pretty cats. And I find this man to be beautiful. (I'm not all that bad meself.) So we met, psychically, on a high plateau of confidence. And on that plateau—infallible sex! There was no one else there, but we both were exhibitionists, demonstrating ourselves to one another. I went into my role, and he into his, but both of us remained aware that this polarity—Master-Slave—was an act of creation, an improvised play; that in a while we'd revert to ourselves, but also that, while the play went on, it was far more real than the world that lay in wait for us. The reciprocity grew to perfection. And at the end, we both knew simultaneously we were heading for the cliff. He instantly assumed position, and after a little manipulation, we fell—rather ran—off the edge of the precipice together.

And I'm glad to report—I do so in the low, discreet tones of professional modesty—that when he left, there were no marks. Nor have there been any in the year in between. And there were no marks last night.

(Say, that's a great title for a kiddies' book, isn't it? *No Marks! No Marks!*)

"Hi, lad!" he said, when I opened the door last night: buddy-buddy—big friends for fifteen minutes, before the play begins.

He did look gorgeous too. He's got a taste for flashy, rapid colors—that's Mercury again—fast pinks and blues that race even when the man stands still. And he was in fine ironic fettle, and the reason soon came out. "Guess what happened today?"

"You took out an appendix and then discovered that the man's gall bladder was sick."

"The husband of my wife's best friend has come down with an ulcer. So guess who'll be doing a subtotal gastrectomy about a year from now?"

An opportunist? Oh my! my! my! . . . The fox manipulates the meadow. And Mercury, who smirks as he waits on the gods, always takes home a handsome tip. But he does it with such a gleevil malischievous charm that his worst traits become his best, for me. Especially when they're exercised at my expense.

And a pragmatist? Halfway through our first drink—"My wife's expecting me by seven"—he usually starts to take off his tie. And that coolness too offends and excites me.

Selfish? Here is a rule I was taught on our second session together—which came, by the way, satisfying my ego as well as my prick, the day after the first: "I don't like to neck. At least not with male lovers. That's something I save for the ladies." (An' thweet little Rumpelthtilthkin—who jutht loveth to kith an' kith! With men too. The thrill is quite different than dipping into a woman's lips.) But really—to have announced it like that! So flatly. Of course he added, "When I get very hot, I want you to fuck my mouth with your tongue—but make it rough, not sentimental." That raised my temperature about ten degrees, and constituted another hook in my guts. Yet honestly, I should have known better. I despise a bossy masochist! Why didn't I kick him out right then? Yes—you don't need to tell me—Rumpelstiltskin had already sensed how much damage the motherfucker could do me. Little did ever he know. Or dream.

So last night, when he'd warned me about the time, I obediently—yes, me: the obedient one last night: the tables are turning, turning, turned—I obediently switched on my radio and found *eine kleine sexmusik.* (That's another symptom: that damned old radio. I eat music like ambrosia. Why haven't I bought a new set then? It's just that, till now, my suicide has been too slow.) And we had at it.

And had at it royally. Because despite the fact that I hate the bastard—as you all will have guessed by now—

> *"Odi et amo."*
> Yes, Catullus, I know!
> I hate, and I love.
> You ask—how is that possible?
> I answer—God above!—
> I don't know. But it's hell. It's hell!

Make ready your loudest, most raucous guffaw! My hordes of giggling Valkyries! Love bugs! And various militants!

I am absolutely and hopelessly sunk in love with this man . . .

And *why* am I?

For only this reason: it's absolutely and hopelessly Impossible. There comes that third factor of life again. Outside the palisade, among the rarest nonexistent beasts, the most luminous of the stars that aren't, I found the Impossibility of ever being happy— fuck "happy"!—of even staying alive by falling in love with Jim. So I did.

He genuinely loves his wife. At least he must, the amount of sex they make together. He's told me about that, and doesn't lie. (God, I wish that one time he had!) In fact—all you my witnesses—he's described their married life in intimate detail. Among other pleasures on the mental rack, I've been made a confidant . . . And he simply adores his kids. I'd like him for that. If there were any seashore left in the storm of emotions I feel for him.

I say I'd "like" him—but the truth within the truth is, I *love* him just for that! The fact that he *is* an excellent father, a pretty good husband—despite how much he fucks around—those things are what allure me most—they've magnetized me like iron toward his life: the things that make it Impossible for me to be anything at all except some casual sex for him . . . Terry Andrews—the living dildo, the living whip—that's me! . . . And the sadist has to do all the work!

"I better buzz," he said last night. It had gone too quick.

If only the shit wasn't physically so attractive! And don't think hat I haven't tried that idiocy either. One day last summer I spent .wo whole hours telling myself that, really, he *was* putting on weight. And I can't stand pot bellies. On men—well, maybe. On women—no! (I'm losing it myself, by the way. Twelve pounds in the last two months. The svelte cadaver syndrome, I guess.) It didn't make one damn bit of difference! Those extra pounds are just more of this loved man's body to hold when I get in the saddle and ride his ass. What else did I try? Oh yes—the most ludicrous: he has dentures! That really is pitiful—since a lot of his best service is done when his teeth are out.

But too quick last night. Too quick. I went into the bathroom to take a piss, and when I got back, the couch was out and Jim was lying there prone, legs spread, his arms outstretched above his head: that attitude of pure passive vulnerability—so irresistible in its invitation when one male assumes it in front of another. There's something so damned attractive, something falsely trustworthy, about a hairy, husky, middle-class American ass!

But last night I used Jim's up too fast.

He paused at the door. "And remember, lad, you're coming up to Riverdale a week from Thursday—" Thanksgiving—as if you didn't know. "—if I don't see you before—" Said so I'll dangle the week in between. "—which I probably will."

Hope: the hook I'm lipped into and dangle from . . . Fish—fisherman . . .

On his part I have no idea what it means, his asking me to his home. Perhaps a highly refined Chinese torture. Perhaps he just likes me. (To be just liked, in my condition, is a highly refined Chinese torture.)

For my part, though, I know why I'm going. It's to demonstrate something—my death—to me.

"The kids are all dying to meet you." They've read my book. "And Carol too."

There are still some nifty complications coming. But I'm much too tired to describe them now. It's midnight. And I don't even *know* them yet!

"And Ben especially. He keeps asking, 'When is the *Harold* man coming?' " That child, my intuition says, will provide the final twist of the knife. "So you'll be there—?"

"I'll be there."

"We'll expect you." He again hesitated—a little superciliously. "By the by—there's a funny aroma here."

"Like what?"

"Medicinal."

"It's Ben-Gay. I clobbered myself at the gym last month. My shoulder. I've been slathering it on."

"Such primitive remedies! Ta ta! Be a good lad, now." And he left.

Yes. Primitive remedies. Like killing oneself. They're very effective, however . . .

Oh Christ—I *am* tired. I've been dreading to introduce you all to him. He's been here many times since I started to talk to you in October, but today I knew I had to—gutless wonder that I am. The year works on toward winter, and winter works toward—yes!

"So what!" I hear you muttering. "Another psycho goes over the brink!" Well at least you can relish the irony: I see this man for, maybe, ten or twelve hours a month; for the minutes that we're together, he pretends to be my slave—for the days and weeks that we're apart, I genuinely am his . . . Not funny? I'll make you laugh, though, Rumpel will—our friend. He was so overwhelmed by the sight that greeted him when he came back from the bathroom that he sat right down—he's sitting right down now—to write "Rumpelstiltskin's Hymn to his Sweetie's Behind—"

> You're lovely and you're hairy.
> Oh!—I don't know what to do . . .
> You've got six kids. You're married . . .
> Well—that's just the charm of you!

Absurd? . . . Absurd! . . . But don't doubt this: he will suffice to die on . . . When coupled with another, slower, more quietly deadly failure of mine, Jim Whittaker, I assure you all, will do for this kiddies' author's suicide.

Her kindness—as it did in the beginning—still has about it, for me, surprise, an unexpected suddenness, and at length a rooted sense of despair . . . The third, the most slowly painful third of my life.

And that was what was shouted at me—"Surprise!"—when she opened the door, by Anne herself and two other people marshaled behind her in the hall. A party, it seems, not simply the dinner at home to which she had invited me. The occasion—which I had forgotten myself—the third anniversary of the publication of *The Story of Harold.* Who else but Anne would remember that? And who else but her would have used the opportunity to throw me a party—to celebrate someone she loves.

The other couple don't have any part of—youknowwhat. (Giggleville.) Except as they're friends of Anne. But a bit of description anyway: Kitty and Clive Fairbank. They both are English, but not teddibly and unbeddibly so. He owns an antique shop—yes, my eyebrows are rising too. God knows what their sex life is like, but they genuinely love each other—there's psychic reciprocity. And I make it a point to keep these people just friends of Anne. She's a very chic English secretary, the kind so popular this year. And they both are absolute delights! She especially is just as refreshing as lemonade on a hot summer day. As little as children, they jump up, camp, dance, or sing and show off, at the drop of a hat. And if no one drops a hat—so what? They drop their hats for each other. They never permit a silence to last, they attract attention centripetally, and they're very helpful for someone who needs to retire, at times, to an inner privacy, where he can think about Giggleville . . . How Anne met these people—I don't honestly know. Just the general attraction of particles in the whirling vortex which is New York.

Now Anne . . . Christ—how I've been dreading this! But once you meet, the parts of the splendid apparatus are all assembled. And we have four months to make it work!

But it ought to be summer, early summer: the last week in June would be ideal. There are some souls who are summer souls, some spring, some fall, and some who only feel at home in the dead of winter—my Danny's, my time. She's not yet red July, not tall enough, not sultry enough—she's the last blond week in June. At thirty-seven, with her hair kept short, and the small, soft features of a child—children! damn them for their promising!—there seems more and more of her yet to come. She could easily pass for twenty-four. But she doesn't—she's ruthlessly honest about her age. And everything else as well. (But I'm not honest about my age—and I'll never tell, ya fuck yas—never!) . . . And yes, all of you, come close to her now . . . Good porcelain touched into life—I don't know!—but before I let her description go, I must tell you about one scene last summer. Her apartment, a duplex in a converted brownstone, in Murray Hill—and I like Murray Hill: it's one of the places where real people live—her apartment has three living room windows facing south. In August this must have been. She was looking for something in a brochure and turned, back to me, to get more light. And her hair used the sunshine like something especially prepared for it: the most elegant and expensive rinse that God or our friend had ever invented. It pierced me—and then made me turn away.

Her background is very similar to Edith Willington's. Except in this case, it all works. Whereas Edith is simply a collection of gestures—dresses, furniture, rooms, furs, jewels—the steps of a dance that lack a live dancer, to make them real—in Anne the living girl was there to meld the gestures into a unified upper-class life. She's—grin and bear it—A Woman. And wonderfully enough, a woman with manners but also vivacity, a sense of humor, intelligence, and veins of strength which she very discreetly mines.

Her history—briefly: she was born in New York but sent up to New England, when she was sixteen, to attend a Good Girls' School. (She too makes fun of it.) Then halfway through Smith, she got yanked out by falling prematurely in love with a man twelve years older than she. They had fifteen years—and good ones too. (She did some domestic growing up.) I like to hear her reminisce: it's so without rancor or bitterness. (Damn her too! She remembers decency.) And they also had one daughter, fourteen now. And then one day, while he was shaving—the ridiculous ways that death can happen, unless one makes a plan for it—he died and fell into the bathtub. When she started to trust me and talk about it, she said that that very day the thing that hurt her and angered her most was the fact that he had to look silly, crumpled and cupped in an ugly position, in all that white enamel, with half his face still lathered.

That would have been—1966. The girl—Helen—was twelve. Two years ago, and her husband's death presented the world with the most nervous—perhaps most hopeful—widow that it has seen in years. (And don't dare any one of you make the obvious and vulgar joke about *The Merry Widow!* Yes, merry she may be—but her merriness is the sign of life in an injured spirit, recovering. It's a gift that she gives to very few. And it softly mutilates my guts.)

I met her eleven months after John Black had died. Did I tell you her name was Anne Black? (This is coming tumbling now—but at least the sluice has been lifted.) And we met—you see? from the very beginning, everything was healthy, human—at a fair to raise money for scholarships at the school her daughter was then attending. Anne had charge of the book stall. And *I*—the truth overcomes modesty with great ease—I was to be the celebrity, *Harold* having come out the year before and been a sensation with critics, teachers, librarians, and also the small fry I meant it for. I was there to sign books, which the school had arranged to buy at a discount and sell for the listed price. Noble, ay? I was wearing what I thought was a very plausible and substantial dark gray flannel suit, but discovered to my horror on the subway to the place that it still had a lot of Connie's long blond hairs on it—she and her husband Max and I had been to an orgy the week before—and some of her pubic hairs too. The bitch! . . . It's strange what things stick in your mind. I remember those hairs so well . . .

Anne had giddied up the book stall with crêpe paper and decorations, and arranged a beautiful display of *Harold.* She was sitting on one of the school's little schoolchildren chairs in what, for me, is almost an infallible position. I can't imagine any woman not looking interesting—no, not looking downright lovely in it: bent slightly forward, with one knee crossed above the other, and her wrists crossed over the upper knee—a posture of feminine waiting—irresistibly Impossible.

She recognized me from the picture on the dust jacket. (My editor had advised the company photographer—"Make him look like a young and trustworthy uncle—who just might fuck you some day.") "Mr. Andrews—"

"Yes—"

"I'm Anne Black." She extended her hand. And *that* was good! I like women who like to shake. "It was nice of you to come!"

"I enjoy it myself." (That's true, my teacher volunteer. Nobility apart, while I was alive, I used to like things like book fairs and scholarships.)

Thus we started: selling books. The fact they were mine was an extra pleasure. And we did very well. Sold over a hundred in a couple of hours. And the more we sold, the more light-headed, lighthearted we got, the higher the key that our pleasure went into.

At some point she introduced her daughter: a good-looking girl, but not at all like Anne—dark hair and I'd guess her father's features: reserved and—oh—conservative. (Imagine? In this day and age!) But very contained, with something inside her still staggering—getting its breath back from having her father knocked out of her. I liked her very much. And still do. (About the girl, by the way—last September Anne sent her to prep school. "I could see it coming," she explained last spring. "There was just too much Mom around. Too many old ladies: her and me. God though, I do miss her, Terry!" So instead of keeping her daughter beside her, and using her as a substitute, she chose loneliness.)

Then, when the book fair was finished, in a rush of spontaneity —the first of her sudden, unconsciously cruel, kindnesses—she asked me home "for a pickup supper. Just leftovers." It consisted, as I remember, of half a cold quiche from the icebox, an ordinary omelet, green salad with Russian—because I like Russian—dressing, and lemon sherbet for dessert . . . I do remember. Everything . . . One must. To judge.

The girl opened up. She asked some intelligent questions: where the stories in the book came from, how long they took to write, and like that. I answered what I knew, and admitted the rest of the truth: it's intuition—you hope you'll go on getting presents—and then, when you think you're loaded, you fire. And you either hit or you miss. Eventually she went into her bedroom to do homework. But while she and Anne were there together I had the elusive and disturbing impression that an adult—though, as I say, she looks like a girl herself—was shaping her child in unobtrusive and useful ways. And all done so subtly, understatedly, with slight pressures needed and barely applied: exactly the strength that I like in a woman. There are certain tremendous females whose powers I do love—Kirsten Flagstad's voice, Hannah Arendt's intellect—Hi, Hannah!—but for the most part, I like my ladies modest, and yet potent in the home. (Sorry about that, Women's Lib.)

When Helen had left, we chatted—about an hour, I think. I don't remember a word we said, but if I was behaving like my usual self, I was boasting behind a façade of self-deprecation and secretly begging for compliments. She fed me them, I guess—and did that too with an oblique quality that made them feel more real. The hour still warms in retrospect. On the strength of it—I suppose on the strength of my satisfied egotism—I called her up a week later and took her to see that monstrous production of *Antony and Cleopatra* that the gullible Mr. Bing used to open the new Met.

We began to have things in common. Lincoln Center was one of the first. We had both so much wanted it to work. And when it didn't—to give her a laugh—I wrote this jingle—"Harold's Ode to Lincoln Center"—

> Your buildings all are hideous.
> Architecturally, you're a fad.
> Culture centers all are insidious;
> But really—you are bad!
>
> Your pool still leaks, your art work grates,
> There's nothing true or fine.
> And even your fountain ejaculates
> By computerized design.
>
> But still, but still—the pathos there . . .
> The sense of something spent.
> The money, effort, labor, care—
> The chance that came. And went.

Lincoln Center . . . Who is there who has ever stood on the balcony of the new Met and looked out at those buildings, that fountain, that pool, and who hasn't felt the *frisson* of a nervous civilization taking one long apprehensive look in its mirror—and not finding itself there. The self it wants. Anne and I feel that failure when we go to the Met, but do not speak it out loud to each other. Her silence is *politesse*. And mine is—mine is shame and humiliation. To be there with her . . . The chance that came. And went.

When she read my doggerel, she laughed and kissed me, and folded it up—she was meaning to keep it—and said, "Okay, over to you, Ada Louise!"

She also said, about that dreadful *Antony and Cleopatra*, "The first scene looks like a Bedouin camp. And I use the word 'camp' in all of its meanings!" . . . So you see—ease too: a partner to tease and play with, along with her gentle, persistent, and dreadful love.

We adventured into New York together—everywhere. When she learned about my Fulbright, Rome, and my subjects, Greek and Latin literature—and a comparative study of *both*, if you please! as if one wasn't enough for a life—she did a lovely and daunted thing. "My *lord*, Terry, that's impressive." I assured her I didn't remember a word—that's sadly true, alas—but she wouldn't be unimpressed. "I'm a drop-out myself—" (That's become a running joke with us.) "—will you be the rest of my college education?" And what arrogant susceptible intellect could refuse an invitation like that?

She meant it though. She meant it to be a joke, but she also meant for me to teach her. And if I hadn't been able to write, a teacher is what I would have been—especially if I'd known I'd have classes composed of willing souls like Anne. She's never been to Europe, so—up to the Metropolitan Museum of Art. She'd been there, of course, but never really *been* there. That is, with someone she loved. Her husband had not been much for the arts. I started with Breughel's "Harvesters"—perhaps my favorite in the whole damn place—and worked it into her. That curve that curls into infinity—the warm light: your hands want to reach for the canvas—and the lumpy peasants juxtaposed against radiant Nature: half-baked humanity unaware that the fields it harvests include the Universe. That first time I only allowed her to look at a few pictures: the eyes grow exhausted, bored. The Vermeers. The Caravaggio "Musicians." Some medieval stuff. And—"I *know* that one!" she boasted dryly, after my boasting—the "View of Toledo": a masterpiece of *angst* that doesn't deserve its vulgar fate of postcard popularity.

We go to all the galleries now, as well as back to the Met, for shows. She argues back—and I like that. I try to convince her that Raphael's saints don't really all look like advertisements for facial cream. (She's right though: they do.) And I make supercilious fun of her favorite, Botticelli, referring to him as a hack propagandist, at least in the so-called religious work. And I ridicule that almost—but not quite—unendurable sweetness with which he flavors his paintings: the good sugar of the genuine Christian soul. She knows I love him. But he's her painter, not mine. I understand the affinity. One likes the painters one wishes that one could be painted by. And Anne reminds me—not of the luscious pagan things—but of some of the dry and skeptical, blond madonnas. They do adore that Thing in their laps, but they love It with a kind of bemused irony.

And opera. She wasn't that hot on Wagner yet but pleasurably sweated out *Die Walküre* last year, when it came around. And *Rheingold* last week. "Two hours!" she said. "We'll both get weaver's bottom!"

"Just make sure your bladder's empty," was my experienced advice . . . She liked it too. But added, demonstrating her identity, "I still prefer Bach." . . . Like you, Father, and she's right. But I go in for all the romantic excesses.

So, by innocent affinities, and with the conscious permission of both of us, our lives were woven into each other. And always, like the further clues an excited child finds in a treasure hunt, there were the sudden discoveries. Like my party last night. If she thought I would have preferred a big cocktail party, I know she would have thrown me one. But I loathe those gigantic New York wingdings: rooms full of unreal people chatting, laughing, silently passing gas. No! Four's enough to form one whole.

"How's Iris?" she asked. Everybody I know is aware of Iris. (And also my Greenwich Village foe: that damn collie! My feud with him is another running joke.) It isn't every cleaning woman who's had a kid's book dedicated to her. (My second—*The Whatnot*—one of the best, before *Harold*.)

"She's fine. She sends her love to you."

"Mine back to her."

"The famous Iris," said Kitty. "When are we all going to meet her?"

"I should have asked her to come tonight." (That's not

condescension; it's an apology. If her world was a bit more broad and flexible, she *would* have asked her. She wanted to.)

"Have you met her, Anne?"

"Just over the phone." She called once, on Iris's day at my place, and abruptly I felt myself compelled to make these two lifelike people meet.

"But she's very much aware of Anne. Her first question every week is 'How's Miss Anne?'" And she *really* wants to know! A medical report, and then psychiatric bulletins.

"She's wonderful!" said Anne. "She's what keeps him alive."

(Only I, until I summoned all you, could savor these ironies.)

"She said something great today. I was just about to leave, and the phone rang." And always the ring of the telephone is the possibility of Jim. "I didn't want to answer it—" Since if it *had* been him, the thought that I'd missed the chance to see him would have killed on the spot what little pleasure I could wring from being with Anne last night. "—so I asked Iris to, and tell whoever it was—" "A man," she said afterwards. (It *could* have been him! Shit!) "—that I'd left for the evening. She did. And added, lyrically, 'He's out *so-cial-i-zing* tonight!' And I wish you could have heard the lovely lilt that she put into that one word. There was all the fun of company in it. But the big news this week is—*Death to Cockroaches!* She stormed in this afternoon with a paper bag containing one can of Raid. Which she wouldn't let me pay for. 'It's my fight, Mr. Andrews!' she said. 'It's gotta be me or them!' And she bombed the kitchen prodigiously! Then she said, 'You'll see 'em dyin' for days, Mr. Andrews!'" I stood up, to demonstrate. "And then—if you believe—she did her version of *The Dying Cockroach.* Her head lolled on one side, she reeled around the living room, gagged—and dropped down into a chair. And I'm here to tell you that compared to my Iris's Dying Cockroach, Pavlova's thing with the swan would have looked like an arthritic giraffe!"

They liked my act. I does me best, folks! It's up to me to sparkle a bit, me being a literary type. After dinner Kitty and Clive will take over. Especially if Anne puts a record on. But meanwhile I does me flimsy little best.

"I'll be back in a minute," said Anne. "It's countdown in the kitchen."

"You want another drink?" I asked.

"No, I've still got half my Dubonnet."

Here, if anywhere, she fails. She's sometimes Missy Itsy-Bitsy. It's that girlish thing she's got, of course. But she *is* almost forty, not fourteen. And she only drinks silly little things, like Dubonnet and champagne cocktails and—wild spree!—a daiquiri now and then. It's a very distinct disadvantage, for me. Because I like to booze. Not just drink—*booze* sometimes, with a woman. And then make a lot of unladylike love.

"I'll help," I said, and went into the kitchen after her.

She shut the door behind us, and in a single flowing gesture her right hand hurried to leave the knob and join her left, around my waist. And her head nested into its proper place. She's short, but she likes the height she comes up to—my chest—and has told me so many times, as she played with my pectoral muscles. (Silly vanity, that: but the pleasure I take in it!) For a moment she stayed a part of me, and then lifted her face, expecting a kiss. Which I villainously withheld. She self-consciously pursed her lips. "Come on! I've got to cook!" And while our mouths said, silently, "Yes—?" she played with my new sideburns. (Did I tell you I was growing sideburns? The cutie-in-the-coffin bit.) "They're getting big and bushy."

"I'm going to shave them off." A lie: I'm mad about them— they stand for a decision, made—and I play with them all day long.

"No, don't! I want you to look in style."

"Every time I see myself in the mirror I have the distinct impression that I'm turning into a werewolf." I am. (Just ask Dan Reilly. He likes my sideburns too. And told me that cigarette Sunday he thought they were "virile and mature." What he meant was, a judge might have sideburns who condemned someone to death. Beneath his black mask, a victim tied to a stake might dream that a handsome executioner could be growing sideburns.)

"I love them. And let your hair grow long. Bend down." I did: obedience to her pleases me. Her fingertips lovingly, lightly judged my hair. "It's thick and it's wavy—it's wonderful! Just tell the barber to shape it a little, the next time you have a haircut."

"I'm getting a crewcut—" I stayed bent before her.

Her hands did a little phrenology, and she wryly advised, "I

90

wouldn't, if I were you, my dear. You have a pointy head. Stop that!" I had reached around and slipped a finger, through her skirt, down the crease of her tail. "You won't get any steak."

"That's steak—"

"Get *out* of here! Right now!"

"Okay," I mimicked indifference. "If you don't want to play—" *And the Devil said that! . . . Rumpelstiltskin!*

She pulled me back into her arms, and her eyes hidden in the place she likes, said, "I want to play more than—"

It wasn't a joke, what I had teased. It was a lure that I knew this woman's heart would take. It was tempting her with something she will never get . . . *And the Devil said it! God damn his soul! . . .*

We made love the first time a couple of months after that book fair. We'd been to the Met: *Die Frau Ohne Schatten.* The first time I'd seen it. Strauss is sometimes too thick for Anne but the stunning production carried her. We both flipped our lids when that whole first set started solemnly, silently to drift straight up. A taste for magic she does have. And me—I live off it. Did. My machinery doesn't work as well as the Met's. They've had their breakdowns too, but theirs are reparable.

We came back for the ritual nightcap. I was pleasantly oiled. Been belting Scotch during intermissions at that fentsy soipentine bar. (As if the Strauss wasn't enough!) And our mood was euphoric and fulfilled. Her daughter was asleep. She was—what then?—thirteen, and Anne trusted her to be left alone. The three of us had had an early dinner there. So she got me my Scotch, and fixed herself a glass of half-assed Dubonnet. The air was ripe with happiness. I hadn't met Jim Whittaker yet, and that half of my life was satisfied with trips to the baths every now and then and a little tricking around the town. We had a half-hour of wonderful nonsense talk—about the opera, about Kitty and Clive, about everything, nothing: the real conversation—ourselves, together— took place beneath the words. I got ready to leave. And at the door I kissed her harder than I meant. Or perhaps I meant it just that hard. I always kiss women on the lips. Can't bear the alienating cheek. And my tongue went a fraction in, unconscious. Anne misread me. Or maybe she read me right. But like twin kindlings, her arms went around my back, and her head, like someone rushing home, arrived at its destination, my chest . . . God damn my vanity!

I had known it was coming, but not that night. But why *not* that night, I said to myself. I opened my mouth completely, and Anne opened hers, and after a visceral caress—our tongues two travelers in a wilderness where they thought they were all alone—we weren't youngsters, remember—she took my arm and without a word—but a finger laid across her lips, because of Helen—led me into her bedroom.

In a fit of finally released desire, she stripped all at once, while I, controlling male, took my time. I went slow for two reasons: to prolong that first phase of bodies about to make love but still—an infinity of minutes—untouching, and also to let my eyes, the primary and most sensual sense, eat up her nakedness. Because— blond skin, blond hair, blond heat—hers was clean, like the nudity of the new moon, the total exposure of an ear of corn just husked, untouched.

I think I was the first one since her husband died: a great moment to cash in on. But—and I say this honestly—I didn't cash in. Never once—I think this is true, and let it be!—did I forget that this must be for her. And it was. And therefore, naturally— the sublime equation—it also was for me.

It's an interesting, curious thing that when you make love with a woman who's had a husband—or only one lover—you know right away what he was like. And Mr. Black must have been slow. Because Anne had no idea at all how fast she could be. He must have been one of those mountain climbers, who work their way up from ledge to ledge, until at last they reach the peak. They're good men. Believe me!—I don't put them down. And many good women were made for them. But Anne, although she didn't know it, had altitudes. She was starved, of course, after such a long time. But that excitement—mere eagerness—was only the fuel for the first few minutes. We necked conventionally, upstairs, for a while—then I turned my tongue loose. And he is an adventurer, an indefatigable explorer with a passion for out-of-the-way places, like armpits—if the lady is clean—and the back of one's neck and inside the nostrils of one's nose. And always, after the interesting but dry and familiar Northern lands, he wants to wander toward Southern climes. But that night he didn't wander: he roared, with a quick stop into her belly button—a Bermuda of an island that is!—straight down to the tropics.

There was a slight aroma, but not enough to stop me. (Although I can be stopped by that. In all good sex a cleanliness is necessary. And that's equally true of fist-fucking, or just eating a pretty cat like Anne.) If the jungle reeks a bit too much my tongue departs for the North again. And leaves the whole steaming continent to another, less subtle, adventurer. One who comes there only to exploit, unencumbered with senses like sight, smell, taste—who hacks his way in, if necessary, in stupid pursuit of his own aggressive selfish interest. (The name of my colonist, by the way, is—Roderick Usher?—no—Louie!)

So her slight smell didn't stop me, and I went to work on her with my mouth. And a shudder and a heave of her groin said—something special happening. I looked up and realized—to my everlasting delight—that this lady had never been eaten before. Her hands were uplifted—in disbelief—and every inexperienced finger stretched into a different dimension of pleasure.

It seemed incredible to me then—it still seems incredible—that a woman in this day and age could have reached the age of over-thirty and never have had her cunt sucked. (Mr. Black, if there is an afterlife, you and I will soon meet, and I will tell you how sorry I am for you that you, Anne's first husband—*the Devil said that! made me slip!*—that you never got down on your wife.) Well, if a girl married at twenty, in 1951, a White Anglo-Saxon Protestant who was ten years older than she—and a lawyer at that—I suppose she might have lost out. It certainly couldn't happen now. (Thank God, some progress has been made! But for all I know, even now there may be a few vegetarians left. Oh gentlemen, you're mad! That meat was made to be tasted too!)

And taste her I did. And probed and pried. And my tongue was half pilgrim, half battering ram. Eventually, when Louie took over, I don't think she even knew it. She'd gone to a height—depth—so unfamiliar that she couldn't distinguish between my colonists. However far she went though—or goes—she never made those clumsy noises I hate. This is not a sloppy or grunting fuck . . .

Then afterwards—what she said I will not repeat. Not even in front of unliving witnesses . . . It was most just the gush of her gratitude . . . But more too . . . More. (And *damn* all those I love!)

Do I even remember what it was I felt? That cheap masculine pride, I'm sure, at having satisfied a woman. A genuine tenderness for her, I hope . . . No, I don't remember, really. Nothing . . . Oh yes I do! It was *dread*—at this coming commitment . . .

One thing, though: in the half-hour while we relaxed afterwards, I found out that she liked to play. Apart from the oceanic surf, she also enjoys the little waves. Dirty words, for example. I said something about her "nifty little quiff"—and she started to giggle. (Remember, this was before the Free Speech thing.) There never yet was a well-brought-up young lady who didn't delight in the four-letter words when used right time, right place, right person. I pity you promiscuous people out there who use them indiscriminately: it takes their special charm away—the mischievous joy of things that happen behind the barn. And physically, she liked to play too—in a kind of wicked innocent way. Again, its essence is something left over from childhood. She never said this, but what she seems on the verge of saying, when we get going together sometimes, is, "Isn't it nice to live in bodies! All nice bodies, with all nice holes! And all nice things that fit in holes!" When we're not going after the high, deep moments, we play games, she and I, in that moist, crisp little dell of hers. Because I, with my hoe—my tongue, my prick—I become a moist, crisp little farmer.

That was the mood she was in last night. I could tell from her perkiness in the kitchen. Until Rumpelstiltskin deviled into sentiment.

The dinner was great—she made delicious filet mignon. And there was a birthday cake—a deathday cake—sorry, an unworthy play on worthy words—with HAROLD printed in golden icing, and three red candles. A child's joy, it should have been. But it felt to me like an old man's taut despair. But after coffee, as I had hoped, Clive and Kitty went into one of their very best acts. And Kitty claimed—the new nudity—she could strip to anything. So Anne put on a Mozart quartet—and the elegant little bitch did! She peeled herself very nicely too. Although, between the elaborate drops of her garments, I kept thinking about that telephone call—and *had* it been Jim?

"Kitty, you're not to take that off!" said Clive when she started, operatically, to finger the strap of her bra.

"Well, mayn't I take off half of it?"

"No!"

"Such a prude."

"The record's over anyway."

"But Mozart wrote a *lot* of quartets! I can do it to Beethoven's too, you know. Especially the last. Or the *Missa Solemnis*! Just anything!"

They camped on—both in glorious form. Clive demanded that he be allowed a striptease too. But he wanted some primitive music. *The Rite of Spring*—least primitive of all compositions—was provided, and he met its challenge splendidly, even going so far as to accidentally rip off one sleeve of his shirt in a fit of stylish neopaganism.

I enjoyed them in intervals. These days I'm divided in parts. In particular when I'm with Anne. And last night a separate little splinter—like something under your fingernail—kept wondering if Jim had called. Then, since October—D Day—and that stands for—*guess!* You're wrong! No, you're right: it stands for that too, with a capital. But I was thinking of *decision*. Since October I've had these passionate reveries, that occupy a lot of time. But as usual when I'm with Anne, my driftings are up into Impossibility. I seem to float above the scene—I look down at myself and exclaim, "You fool! It's all so easy. You have to know *some* human beings, don't you? And her friends are certainly more entertaining than any other group you've found. The child is no problem. And apart from what Anne feels for you—she's really pretty rich. If only you were a pragmatist! Or as skillful in duplicity as your shitty friend Jim Whittaker. You could rent a little separate sex pad, and make out with the men—him too—on the sly."

I say that to myself. And this is what I answer back. Or rather our friend—R.—does. "No good to try and be reasonable! We've had this talk before. You know I've got him programmed to love just the Impossible. It's the ease—exactly the ease of Anne—that I'm using to keep him from being complete. Remember the other times—men and women—it was always the same. That Catholic boy who wouldn't make love, although he admitted he wanted to.

95

Of course that didn't last very long, because the bastard does like to fuck. And that married lady—Tina Farr—you know he fell in love with her just *because* she was married. And such a selfish little bitch that she wouldn't leave that nest she was in. And well you know that if she had—and made it possible—he'd have split like a child in a theater that had just caught on fire. That's why Jim Whittaker is absolutely ideal. Jim doesn't love him—oh, did he ever make that plain!—his life is altogether elsewhere—what more could a gleevil malischievous dwarf require? He's just what I've been shopping for these past few years! What allures me in Jim is the totally Impossible—that's always been what Terry looked for in his men. When some of those poor faggots threatened him with love, he'd cut from them too. You know that. And now—right now!—this minute, while he's watching Clive and Kitty striptease —what distances my slave from Anne is the too easily made real!"

"You two should really go on the stage."

"Anne, darling, what do you think our marriage *is?*"

Or perhaps if I just had had Kitty's cool, and sense of humor, I could have made it all the way to my life.

"We're off then. You staying a while?" Matchmaking—the married woman's sport—Kitty gave me an accomplice's grin.

"Drambuie?" Anne asked in the living room, now gently emptied of the public need to have fun.

"No, Scotch. I'll get it. For you—"

"A little crème de menthe?"

"You sure you wouldn't rather have the dew from a rose petal?" If I didn't razz her she'd feel deprived.

"Oh all right! I'll become an alcoholic like you! Make it Scotch."

I got her a crème de menthe and fixed myself a Scotch.

"They were in great form—"

"The geometry works with the four of us."

Devil!—as if this group had years of friendship ahead of it!

"You help a lot."

"I does me little best."

She laid her head on the back of the couch and removed her earrings: next to putting them on, the most elegant gesture— hands, two by two, at each ear—that any woman can ever make. And lay back in a leisure of certainty. Rumpelstiltskin took her hand. This is the moment he waits for, with Anne. To his lasting delight, to prolong my failure, I've taken to staying the night through with her.

"You were nice to arrange this tonight."

She chuckled at a plan that worked. "You really *were* surprised! You should have seen your face—"

"I was stupefied—I've never had a surprise party before."

Her hand, just resting in mine till now, went intimately tight. "Then high time!"

"And the dinner was great. As usual."

"That reminds me—" Into the kitchen—I knew what she was doing: stowing away my Care Package in the refrigerator. The first had been, the first night I met her, a second frozen quiche. "It's another filet," she said, coming back. "Just shove it in your rotisserie. And a big slice of Harold cake."

"I'm dieting!" I insist. "All winter!"

> (The aforementioned syndrome:
>   Most modest, yet mod,
>   Most delectable bod
> In the Campbell Funeral Home!)

"Oh phooey on your diet! Eat."

"How's Helen?"

"Oh *most* grown-up! Her letters are all full of 'consciousness expansion' and sex. I don't know whether to spank her or take lessons from her. But you can't spank them when they're fourteen."

Oh wrong, my dear! You can spank them at fourteen—you can spank them at forty. At seventy-four . . . How old is Jim? Thirty-eight.

"What *do* you do?" she wondered.

"Well, you're much too short to play a *grande dame*. I advise you just to ask her who she's screwing now."

"Don't joke. The sex thing worries me—"

"Whose?"

You bastard, R., darling! You got what you wanted: the stab I felt, when she took and squeezed my hand again.

She giggled at a memory.

"What?"

"Iris and the cockroaches."

"She'll go mad when I tell her about this party."

"You tell her everything, don't you?"

Not quite, dear. Iris has constructed her idea of me from my books—and especially that fact that I dedicated one to her—from the real affection that passes between us. And from my relationship with Anne. Unbeknown to herself she sometimes goes into partnership with Rumpelstiltskin. As on one Wednesday, when her voice took on a teasing lilt, and she sang elusively, "I have an idea about you and Miss Anne." I bite, of course: What, Iris? "I won't tell you yet." Is it something coming soon? "It might. Or it might take years." As she vacuums with a subtle smile and weaves a web of transparent mystery . . . I wish to God I was just my cleaning lady's fantasy!

"She *demands* to know all about you."

And slyly, in her wise black way—don't mean to condescend—Black, if not all beautiful, is not Impossible—she suspects and, I'm certain, makes accurate guesses about the other half of my life. Not all that accurate, though. The pits I keep covered. If she knew about Dan Reilly—at first she'd disbelieve, and then quit me in a minute. Like any symbol of life.

"She's lucky to have you."

"You mean that the other way round. I'm lucky. I'd have drowned in cockroaches long ago."

"It isn't every cleaning woman who gets a book—" She stopped. Because the practice of this love is silence. (The practice of my own insane love is to shout its stupid fucking head off! And you all will be forced to listen to it!) "—a book dedicated to her."

And the mimicry began. This is our friend's finest hour. He savors the lash, but this choice imitation of what might become, in a single second, real—and never will be—is wine for his palate and perfume for his pimpled nose.

"Now I saw *Das Rheingold* last week—which you threatened to beat me if I *didn't* see—!"

Oh never! Never . . . Not women. To their great disappointment sometimes.

"What is it you want?"

"As you know I'm a drop-out—"

"Spit it out!"

"To watch the Johnny Carson show!"

Just loves it, in fact, Rumpel does! It makes the whole imitation more total and unbearable. I switched on the omnivorous machine, and for an hour we watched the Johnny Carson show: some idiot nightclub comedian and that fluffy broad who's always on, and the usual uninteresting dreck. And every mundane detail, as we sat on the couch and listened and laughed, was another quick cut of the knife of my life. The consciousness of hypocrisy—of duplication, forgery—grew tight as a vise around my head. Grew so tight, in fact, that I almost couldn't hear him laugh.

The show ended. Anne said, "I'm tired."

"You want to go to bed?"

"Yes."

You'd think that I'd be impotent. But I only failed her once like that. (You'll hear. Don't rush me!) Since October I have had no problem. The decision, by some supernatural chemistry, is sexually stimulating. Salome was wrong: Strauss, the mystery of love is not greater than the mystery of death. But really, in the past two months, the two have become one—yup!—and they'll both be solved together . . . You see—death is the truly *big* hard-on.

"However—" Her face created great mystery. "—before we do our Tristan und Isolde routine—I have a present for you." She went into the hall and opened the closet.

"When *will* you stop being so damn—!"

"When I damn well feel like it!" She was talking abstractly, impersonally, from the hall, where our eyes couldn't meet. "Harold's a special person for me." The practice of this love is silence. "I never forget what you wrote in my copy."

(What I wrote, two years ago, when I'd seen her for three or four months—and long before Rumpelstiltskin had won—was "Harold's Song for Anne Black":

> Heart athirst never can savor,
> Nor can perplexed mind even guess
> At the wine-dry indefinite flavor
> Of this lady's quick loveliness.)

(Oh why damn all you again?)

She came back with a record, party-wrapped. "I asked the man at Sam Goody's which was the best Wagnerian record ever made. And he said—that thing we saw last year."

The first act of *The Valkyrie*: Lotte Lehmann, Melchior, Emanuel List. "Oh but God, this is *beautiful!* I used to have it in seventy-eights."

"Well now you've got it long-playing. Put it on while I do my tidying up."

I did. And listened. And loved it again.

Anne called from the bathroom—that former aroma is now replaced by a single delectable drop of cologne—"You're going to have to take home your shaving equipment. Or else I'll find a place to hide it. Helen's getting here Wednesday for the Thanksgiving weekend."

I stay all night—of course—and do all kinds of domestic things in the morning. R. revels in all the natural acts, extracting the nectar of irony from them.

Anne came into the bedroom where I lay, naked, except for her bra. It's curious, how a woman in nothing but a bra can excite you much more than she can completely nude: so take-offable it is. But a man in a T-shirt or just the top of his underwear looks silly and vulnerable. By her attitude—easy and almost nonchalant—I saw that it wasn't to be a high, deep night—*not* Tristan und Isolde—he's another cunt—or prank-playing either, behind the barn. She was in a third and more recent condition. His favorite: simple intimacy. I was stripped myself, and in a gesture of wifely possession she reached between my legs and squeezed.

"Get down on me."

She did. Not very well yet. (*Yet*, he writes—as if there were time for her to learn. Or as if I really wanted her to.) But I added that act as well to her sexual repertoire. She stood up.

"Can *anyone* take it all the way down?"

Jim can. In a sudden fleshy thrust that sends me up the wall.

"Oh, plenty can. And plenty do."

"You rat!" She slapped my prick proprietarily. It needed a stronger blow. (I'll damage my shoulder.) (It'll outlast *you!*)

"Lie down. I want to look at you."

She unfolded, without embarrassment. "Oh, and Terry—one last time: we would *love* to have you eat turkey here! It'll just be Helen and me, and a friend of hers who can't get all the way home to Hawaii. And maybe a Hawaiian boyfriend from Hotchkiss, but—"

"I accepted another invitation. And I can't get out of it"—it being even more of a fire than what you offer me, my dear.

"Well, all right. But we'll miss you. Now stop your staring and join this mortal in the sack. That's better—" Her arms around my neck. "—that's much better. Your shoulder's still sore, isn't it?"

"Yes. Can you smell the Ben-Gay? It stinks." (Do you smell it too, gentle deadly complicitor? Oh I hope you do! I need you—)

"I don't mind."

Oh you would, good Anne! If you knew what it stood for, you would.

I pressed my death shoulder against her breast and began to make love to her—*Rumpelstiltskin and the Mask of Marriage*—like an ordinary normal man!

November 28

No, the twenty-ninth now. It's after midnight. I have drunk enough to put it down . . . I'll kill myself—swell! It'll be a breeze. But to go through emotions like those again—never. Before God: not ever again, in the couple of months—

As it happened:

He had said toward two. And hadn't called, by the way, since that time eleven—*eleven*—days ago! (A nice long dangle, that one was.) If I got there at two, we could booze and chat—"You can get to know the family"—then we'd have the monumental feast around four.

Well, gang, I can tell you that by noon today Rumpelstiltskin was in a fit of delicious *angst*! Just sitting there—here!—gritting his teeth inside me—and urging me to make haste slowly, so he could get the most out of it.

I started dressing, and started drinking, around twelve-thirty. And no, I did not get plotzed. But a little cushioning was absolutely necessary. A couple of Scotches as I put on my favorite suit. I have three decent ones—and they'll see me through nicely—but the one I like best is a charcoal gray flannel job. And—what the hell—I decided to do the vest too. After all, I was being introduced as a sort of small celebrity. And when one's going to one's own execution, well, you have to look your best—right? Right!

At one-fifteen, I was ready—the dressing and drinking purposefully slow—but delayed another fifteen minutes, just for delay's sake: the build-up of the Impossible—*I was going to have Thanksgiving dinner with Jim Whittaker and his family!*

So at one-thirty I was launched. He'd given me directions—"the Two-hundred-seventh-Street stop on the A train"—and then very elaborate instructions about how to take a bus, which ended up, "but it doesn't run on holidays so you'll have to take a taxi. I could meet you at the station, if you knew what time you'd get there."

Oh no. No, no. Don't bother. Our old friend R. wouldn't dream of softening the blow: the front door opens—and there he is, and his family behind him—ka-*pow!*

One final slosh. And a toast: your day, R. baby—enjoy yourself! I picked up the present I'd wrapped this morning and left.

At the Eighth Street subway station I had to wait a long time for an A train. But I didn't mind waiting. The graffiti in Greenwich Village are the wittiest in the city, and I love to look for new ones. Nothing much this afternoon. Except one sturdy little poem.

> Peewee was here,
> But now he is gone.
> He left his name
> To carry on.

Isn't that gorgeous, in its own tiny way? And touching. The simple rhymes of sanity. Why are they lacking in my life?

A train came. And I settled into the long ride up to Riverdale. I don't like the idea of Riverdale. It's one of those smug elevated suburbs overlooking Manhattan, from which a successful bourgeoisie rather casually observe the bubbling of this troubled island. Which at least, in its agony, is alive. (My definition of life: agony.)

A very long ride it was, and crowded at first. But halfway there the car started to empty, and I had the chance to pull a favorite stunt of mine. A beefy middle-class lady got off, and after standing and a moment's phony inspection of a subway map, I sat down in the lingering warmth she had left on the seat. You can do it on buses too. Then the rest of the ride I spent staring guardedly at the faces of the other passengers, memorizing them like irregular verbs.

On the way to Riverdale I'll take the time to explain a couple of things to you all.

Carol Whittaker knows about Jim and me—that we're "seeing each other" in that commonest of euphemisms. Jim told me after one of our first sessions, while finishing off his drink, that he'd told her before they were married that he was bisexual. And said that he intimated he wasn't going to give up the other half. And she took it. And *that's* a domestic mystery that I'd like to understand! About me she found out by chance, by Jim's simple unguardedness, and by R.'s artful inventions when his intuition detected the fact that this might be another—perhaps his greatest—Impossibility. Jim happened to see a copy of *Harold* lying around their living room and dropped the remark that he knew the guy who wrote it. Big stir! Their kids' favorite book. And especially Ben's, their son. He reported the scene, as an unimportant but flattering incident. And here, of course, Rumpelstiltskin pricked up his pointy ears and suggested that I send back with Jim a couple of my other ones. Which I did. And they already had them too. They were fans of mine, it seems. When R. heard that, he rubbed his horny palms together, sensing, correctly, that the situation was eminently workable. As far as the Whittakers were concerned, I became a possibility: and for me they became—Jim was already—the largest of all the vehicles that I've ever built to run over myself. It has led—the children begging, his wife saying, "Yes, why not?" with Jim's shrugging indifference—to my being invited to Riverdale and a happy Thanksgiving dinner. And guess who is the happiest? Oh is he ever! Doubled up within me, arms locking his knees against my chest, he was rocking back and forth—just as giddy with anticipation as a seismograph in San Francisco!

("Self-destruction," you murmur, Father, and shake your head. I'll let you in on a little linguistic secret: within every adjective there's a germ of a verb that wants to act. And I'm going to let the verb in "self-destructive" out.)

Riverdale was disconcerting. I'd never been there before. Very much like—like another city of quiet arrogance. In a different state. The houses—twenties and thirties houses—architecturally uninteresting, but majestic with a self-confidence that this country will never feel again. Yet our present designs, in their nervousness, are far more exciting . . . And I *was* making notes on the architecture, as the cab drove along—hoping it would slow my heart.

We stopped in front of a house that I think you'd call Dutch colonial: a bulky kind of neonothing, but it too had the neighborhood's assurance about it.

Paid the fare. Tipped the driver. Said good-bye to him. And wished him a very happy Thanksgiving! All, of course, as slowly as possible.

Straightened my tie. Pulled down my vest. And with at least the grace, I hope, of Marie Antoinette as she mounted the guillotine, walked up to the front door and rang the bell.

It was opened very quickly by someone who had to be Carol, Jim's wife. She's tall, for a woman. I'd guess at least five feet ten. I'm five-eleven myself. And Jim lords it at six feet two. (Have I told you that already? Sorry.) But she did something wonderful, there in the door: relaxed in her height, she made me feel that she'd stopped her growth, just under mine, quite consciously, to be polite.

"You're Terry Andrews—" Behind her eyes a sudden flare-up of interest. Was she as curious about me, I wondered, as I about her? I think she was.

"Yes I am."

She extended her hand. "I'm Carol Whittaker. Please come in."

"Thank you."

"I recognized you from the picture on the dust jacket."

She's blond—yes, that would have to be! As if there weren't blonds enough in my life! But whiter than Anne. Anne's hair is honey, Carol's flax. And cut quite short and frizzily.

"It's taken you much too long to come to Riverdale."

"I came as soon as I was asked."

"Well, that's Jim's fault, not mine."

Her face is—not pretty. But I had the feeling God made a mistake. He should have spent ten more minutes on her. Because you know that the girl he made next is one of the world's true beauties. Her voice, though! God, you spent too much time on her larynx, and not enough at balancing features. I don't know what Kathleen Ferrier sounded like when she talked. But if she was like Carol Whittaker, she was just as much of a turn-on in the living room as the concert hall. A luscious velvety feminine contralto. And low. Low. She speaks *sotto voce* most of the time—which only makes it more thrilling, for me. But the body, alas, like the face. Her limbs are not joined smoothly enough. Yet there again, a woman within whose awkwardness you sense a locked-up grace.

"Anyway, here you are at last, and—"

We'd been talking in the hall—a wall-to-wall rug with square pattern, a telephone table, a grandfather clock, the wallpaper, pseudo-neoclassical: a broken column, vines—when a sudden commotion occurred at the top of the stairs that led from beside the telephone table up to the second floor. A commotion of colors, noise, lives, that resolved itself into the flowing descent of five girls, in spic-and-span holiday dresses.

"Nancy, Barbara, Jane, Liz, Lucinda—this is Mr. Andrews. Don't try to keep them straight. I barely can myself."

And you witnesses, don't you try to keep them straight either. We will *not* be going back there again! They're five little girls, who vary in age from eleven to one and a half, in different stages of unbudding. One thing, though: as Rumpelstiltskin had hoped, apart from their being extremely pretty, their hair ranged in color from Carol's near white to, in his son's case, Jim's own fox's auburn, that makes the skin of my fingers tingle when I weave them into it.

"There's the lad."

At the top of the stairs Jim was coming down slowly behind his son. The boy's hand hovered like a hummingbird just above the familiar railing.

"And this is Ben," said Carol.

"I'm glad to meet you, Mr. Andrews!"—in a high excited voice.

And that sensitive hand, a divining rod, now tipped to shake, sought for and found my right direction.

He's blind.

Microphthalmia. An enigmatic affliction. The eyes in the embryo fail to develop. And apparently the ophthalmologists don't know why. The signs are a narrower iris, a somewhat sunken socket—in Ben's case anyway—and strange sporadic movements of the whole eyeball. As if the right slot still existed somewhere, and the eyeballs, like marbles, were rolling around in search of it. If they found it, and fell in, and fit—why suddenly there'd be sight! Jim told me about the disease after one of our sessions. He saw I was truly interested, and as always with parents of handicapped children, to explain the cause scientifically objectifies their suffering and somehow makes it more bearable. It must have for him, for a while, that night: before leaving he gave me a long and affectionate, unJimlike kiss.

And the boy is beautiful! Already, at twelve, his features are formed—but more like Carol's, if she'd been finished. A thin, straight nose and perfectly balanced chin—and then Jim's hair. And blind. He'll never be able to look in a mirror and see how handsome he is. (There *is* no God! I take it all back.)

"Hello, Benjamin," I shook his hand.

"It isn't Benjamin," Jim corrected. "It's Benedict. Or Ben. *Never* Benny!"

Benedict! A lordly, challenging, noble name—which went through me like fire. Jim must have sifted a lot of names and picked this one out before Ben was born, imperfect. But then, out of loyalty—to the boy, himself, the name perhaps—he had used it anyway. And after Ben's birth he had tried, through a squad of daughters, to have a second, whole son.

"I apologize, Benedict." I made a slight solemn bow, before realizing—what's the use? A blind boy can't see an adult's irony. "But I have something for you to make it up."

"What?" The eyes of a normal child would widen, but in Ben's case his flickering fingers expressed his curiosity. And his louder than natural, blind voice.

"It's a copy of *The Story of Harold.*"

A letdown, on all sides: they *had* that!

"And we can use it!" Carol manufactured enthusiasm. "The first one's been read to death."

"And this is a copy," I said objectively, preparing—I hoped—their ultimate pleasure, "that Ben can read himself."

Carol shot me a glance of warning, incomprehension. "*I'll* read to—"

"No—" I interrupted her coldly, and repeated myself, for the big effect. "—I said Ben could read this himself." And undid my package. *"The Story of Harold*'s been published in braille."

Furor! Mad joy! A *coup de théâtre!* It would have to have been. Or else the greatest *faux pas* in history. But it worked. Ben's thrill was at the center of it, but it radiated out, through five vibrating little girls, and engulfed Jim and Carol too.

And riding the whole delicious scene, just out of his mind with excitement was—yes, our friend, who knew that he finally had brought me to the brink of the pit, the worst day in my life . . .

And *I* need another drink . . .

That's better. Stronger, is what I mean . . .

Now where was I? Oh yes! In bliss/misery. Blissery! . . . Getting drunk, thank God—and none too soon . . .

So—after the dust of excitement had settled, we went through a little ceremony that I hadn't anticipated. I should have, though, having seen all those pictures of Helen Keller. It seems, with the blind, with certain of them, that they want to "read"—"see"—you.

"Mr. Andrews," his little high tenor asked, "may I touch your face?"

"Of course," said I, all nonchalance—and my heart an abrupt racetrack, where quick fear was suddenly chasing affection. I bent down. "Help yourself."

And his fingertips did see me. I don't know if any one of you has ever had your face read by someone who is blind. But those fingers—so articulate and intelligent! They do fly, like sight, from feature to feature. And if any of you Hobbits should have your face tested by a blind soul's fingers, you'll experience how every cell becomes self-conscious.

"You have sideburns!"

"Do you like them?"

"Yes!"

"Because if you don't, I'm shaving them off tomorrow morning."

"No, don't! Let them grow! Daddy has sideburns too."

Ah, Ben—if you knew how often I've kissed and licked and loved your daddy's sideburns!

"Let's go into the living room." He took my hand and tugged me out of the hall.

The blind leading the—a child shall lead them—I don't know

what, but something happened. As his fingers, grown, but not quite grown, gripped mine and he guided me into the living room, I experienced a minute of what I can only call bliss. There *are* those most infrequent moments when Paradise pierces the world.

"Would you like to sit on the couch?"

"I would like to very much."

He knew the geometry of the room—has to know it for the whole house, of course—and led me to a homelike sagging sofa. The decor, by the way, I'm sure was Carol's—good, solid, and conservative: Jim giving her the home. His own taste would have been more exotic and adventurous.

"A drink, lad?"

"Sure!"

"Scotch?"

He shouldn't have said that. He should have asked what I'd like. She'll register the fact that he knows what I drink: we've been drinking together. "Great. Love one."

He made drinks for Carol and me and himself. And then—are you there, my black militant, Snow White?—Mary Wicks came in. She's their colored maid. Black maid! No—dammit!—colored maid! She was formed before the revolution. And she's big and brawny and beautiful. And very much a part of the Whittaker family. I was introduced, by Carol—"Mary, this is Mr. Andrews. He wrote *The Story of Harold.*"

I stood up. And *not,* I promise you, in a gesture of affected respect. She had a presence that said—"Stand up!" Thank God there are still a few colored domestics around! She's not like my Iris at all—not thin, not lithe: she's—pardon—the last of the Mammies—but she added to our happiness. I agree, I agree: she shouldn't have had to add that way. But for blessings—of any kind—one can only give thanks.

"I'm pleased to meet you, Mary," I said.

"You wrote that book." A queenly inquisition took place, eyes fixed on me as only a servant's eyes can judge: deliberate, deep, and accurate. And I think I passed. "It's a pretty good book, I guess." She set down a tray of canapés.

Now somewhere in here—the kids playing, Ben too, with those hands like antennas—two more guests arrived: a resident in surgery at Columbia-Presbyterian Hospital and his recent fiancée.

And I can't tell you very much about them. Not what they looked like, not a word that they said. I was so tight on the Whittakers. Well, a twenty-six-year-old doctor and his recent fiancée—of course they were invisible, consuming themselves in each other's sight.

You all must have been in this situation: the violins of small chitchat playing conversational melodies above the drum beat of actual fact: "Can you honestly believe it? Thanksgiving? And no snow yet?" "It could go until March, as far as I'm concerned." That was me. I hate winter. Until this winter. I let the old self talk. "Jane's old enough for skates—" "Lucinda and Liz'll have nervous breakdowns—" "Do you skate, Mr. Andrews—?" "Oh, come on now! Terry." "Terry—"

"No." My eyes were trying not to study the elegant fit of Jim's pants to his ass. "I'm afraid I'm a hothouse athlete. I belong to a gym, but that's mostly to get me out of the house—"

"You work at home?"

"Yes." When I lived. "It's important to get away. Sometimes. The rut's a threat. When I write my autobiography, I'm going to call it 'The Drain Yawns.' " Not really very good. But I does me little best. "As far as the real sports go, though—like skiing and skating—I guess I'm a bust." Not at fucking, however: just ask your husband's ass.

And in half an hour—a second round of drinks. Thank God for the Scotches I'd had before! Slow drinkers—timing one's glass to theirs—are a problem for us apprentice alcoholics. (A.A.) And another dish of canapés, which I had been hoping for, because it called forth Mary Wicks again, in her sumptuous colored Mary-Wicksedness.

The children, who also had their "drinks"—grape juice or lemonade—had flickered around the room awhile, and then gone into the sun porch adjoining. We heard them laughing: the motiveless laughter—most beautiful because it sometimes does lack a cause—of children at their play. And the boy's voice, already masculine amid the giggling girls.

"I think he's so great, that Ben!" I said.

"So do we," said Jim, with a quiet paternal authority that felt like a hand pressed against my chest.

"He's so—merry."

Carol smiled. "It surprised us too."

"What did?"

"His merriness." Her shaded voice went low, so the children wouldn't hear. And her eyes were aimed, with an intimate specificity, at mine: I knew what was coming was something not shared with everyone. "When Ben was born, it was—"

"Catastrophe," said Jim, remembering.

"It was a catastrophe," said Carol. "But the pediatrician we had—a wonderful man—"

"—and one of our best friends—" Their unity: another of Rumpelstiltskin's fangs.

"—yes, one of our very best friends—he said something neither of us believed at the time. He said, 'You think this is the worst. The worst thing in the world.' And we did."

"I would have thought so too."

"It wasn't. He said, 'You won't believe this for several years, but if you two survive—the boy will too. To be blind'—he said—'it's a strange, strange thing—'" She clicked herself off editorially. "Is this boring you?"

"God no! Please—tell me." Another shiver went through Rumpel's listening.

"Well, he said that blind people reach *out* for life. And someone who's, for instance, deaf, has a tendency to withdraw from it."

"Is that true—?" I disbelieved. "No one would choose—"

"It's true," said Jim. "You can take my word: we've studied this."

"Just look at Ben," said Carol. "He's merry. As you said. And Ben's black—"

"I don't understand that."

"It means he has no vision at all. His disease—microphthalmia —do you know what that is?"

"I've heard of it." In your husband's arms, my sweet.

"There're degrees of blindness. Some blind people can register shades of light. It's brighter, it's darker—without any form. But for Ben, it's all pure—nothingness."

My God! Compared to the dark behind a blind child's eyes the interstellar void must glitter like Times Square.

"And black as Ben is—he's merry." She glanced at her husband. Her husband! " 'Merry'—that's the word we've been looking for." And returned her eyes to me. "You've got to come to see Ben's school. It's right up here in the Bronx."

"Does he go there every day?"

"Every school day, yes. In a big bus. You *must* come! Especially now that you're in braille."

"I don't think I have the guts."

"It *isn't* bad!" A note of true passion swelled her voice. And made it even more musical. "Not after the first fifteen minutes—"

"Will you get me through the first fifteen minutes?"

"The children will!"

"You ought to go, Terry." Jim's voice—a high baritone, by the way—was paternal and reassuring. And I wanted to lay my head in his lap. And I've tried to, in fact. And the bastard won't let me. "We've lived with this for twelve years, and it took us a hell of a lot longer than fifteen minutes, but these kids can be an inspiration—"

This reasoned and reasonable inspiration, the cool maturity in his voice, was interrupted by a cry, a thud, and then a body's thud on the floor—all coming from the sun porch. The silence that froze us so-called grown-ups was a whole ice age contained in five seconds. Then, in the sun porch, Ben started to cry. Jim and Carol rushed in, and the rest of us followed.

When a blind child falls and hurts himself badly, you feel as if the whole wrong world was going to split and fly into fragments. As if it *should* split and fly into fragments! Because the boy *had* hurt himself badly. There's a desk in their sun porch, and he'd tripped and fallen against a sharp corner. His cheek was already beginning to swell, and with more than a bruise. The flesh above his cheek was torn, and blood was streaming down his face.

Jim got to him first and gathered him carefully off the floor. The blood poured all over his crisp, clean shirt, dripped down on his pants—he never even noticed it. "Come on, Ben—it's all right—" In the singsong voice that always brings peace. But his doctor's hands went over Ben's face, to see if there might be a broken bone. And his own face—strange: with a blind child parents can show their true feeling, but only visibly—his own face, handsome as it is, grew even larger in love and pity and in rage. "Who moved that stool?"

"Oh, *I* did, Daddy," a frail girl's voice admitted, in terror. "We were playing house down here this morning—"

"*You must not move the furniture!* I've told you!—over and over again! That's the number-one rule in this house!"

"I know, Daddy, and I—"

"*Never move the furniture!* How else can Ben know where things are?"

It wasn't rage now. It was—Wrath: a gigantic and all-consuming, very beautiful anger at the injury that had been done his son—an injury for which one sobbing, miserable daughter was only the innocent instrument.

"It isn't Jane's fault," Ben croaked through his strangulated throat. "I was running too fast. At school they teach us that we have to be careful."

Jim's face went mad, in an access of futile tenderness, as his son's arms circled his father's chest, for comfort and also to hold Jim's splendid fury in.

And I, in the doorway, in even more useless love, knew that I was right, in wanting to die . . .

Another drink! Another drink!
It helps you not to feel or think! . . .

He lifted Ben up, and kissed him continuously—his own face was covered with blood now too—and kept saying, "Come on! Come *on*, Ben!" And at twelve, almost grown up, to be lifted in your father's arms must be—Christ, yes!—a very special experience.

There was comfort and love from Carol too. And after a while, some very dry talk between her and her husband in which they arrived at the sensible conclusion, very audibly, that Ben wasn't going to die. Jim carried his son upstairs to tend him.

"Well—that happens too, sometimes," said Carol, to break the stiff stillness that had imprisoned our bodies left down below. Our emotions had gone with the two of them, to the bathroom on the second floor, where Jim was patching up Benedict.

The daughters drifted in guiltily from the sun porch . . . Why is it, when horror hits a family, that everyone feels responsible?

"Come on in, Jane," Carol called. "It's not your fault."

The self-judged culprit had been off in a corner chirping despondently. "It *is!*"

"Just leave things alone." Already, woman to woman.

"I will!" And a kiss.

Mary Wicks came in, I know on her own initiative, with a saucer full of tiny hot dogs and toothpicks and a hot mustard sauce. "Lots of shouting out here," she commented reportorially.

"We had a little accident," said Carol.

"Oh—we have lots of accidents!" she boasted airily. "Is he okay, Mrs. Whittaker?"

"Yes, Mary. He's fine."

"Dinner in a half an hour?"

"Yes, please."

The circuit of affection between them—not mistress, servant, not woman to woman, just you, me, *us*—is wonderful!

And Jim came back, with Ben, by the hand. "I'd like you to meet our invalid!" A big gauze bandage covered one cheek. "Now I ask you—apart from an appendectomy—which I may perform later on—"

"No." A fake complaint from the invalid.

"—did you ever see a dressing as beautiful as that?"

The boy, though reassured, was still a little dithery—he had really been hurt—and so was hoisted up into Jim's lap: to occupy the throne. That place where I've often wanted to lay my head. But no. Not unless I'm down there to suck his cock. Which I don't do awfully well, poor lad.

In the next half-hour, while our concern for Ben relaxed, while we chatted and asked the young couple what their plans were, where they wanted to live, how many children they wanted to have—I went through what must have been the worst thirty minutes in my life. (And they were. Until, an hour later, after Thanksgiving dinner, we came back into the living room.)

I tried to keep my eyes off Jim. Off Jim and Ben. He held him in his lap for the whole half-hour, and fathered him. Occasionally he kissed his hair, and combed it once. His arm was light around Ben's waist. His cheek, now and then, slid next to his son's.

And I—on the other side of the room—what did *I* feel? In my vileness?

Envy!

ENVY!—of that permanently hurt and additionally wounded little boy.

I envied Jim's arms around his waist, and Jim's whispered

113

private words in his ear, and his comb and his lips in his little boy's hair.

And at the moment I thought I'd erupt—and throw myself across that suburban living room—and throw my arms around them both—Mary Wicks came in and announced, "It's dinner."

November 28: Half an hour later: And several drinks later. Oh yes—several drinks!

I sat on Carol's right: the place of honor, if you please. And next to me was Ben. And that was the true place of honor: to be trusted to sit beside Ben. The help he needed—the help that Carol trusted I'd give—was the true unspoken domestic honor that made mere etiquette seem as superficial as it is.

"Would you give Ben some cranberry sauce, Terry?"

"Glad to—"

"And if you could cut his turkey up—"

"I can cut my own turkey up!"

"All right, you surgeon's son," she laughed, "go ahead and cut your own turkey up!" And to me: "He gets so far ahead of us sometimes. But Ben, you won't mind if Mr. Andrews puts some gravy on your mashed potatoes—?"

"No," he allowed. And then, for some reason, dispassionately confirmed his decision: "I won't mind."

I tried not to watch him too obviously—but the techniques of sense in someone who doesn't have sight are absolutely incredible. His fork now grew nerves. It tested the toughness of turkey, the squishiness of mashed turnip, the semisoftness of mashed potatoes, the crunchy round hardness of creamed onions with breadcrumbs. And when he was unsure what he had, the pause of his fork before his nose—an instant's pause—his sense of smell must be razor sharp—described precisely what it carried. He seemed to want to know in advance; as in people with vision, to anticipate a taste enhanced its actuality.

There were spills too, of course—"Oops! There's a goop"— which Carol did me the honor not to ask me out loud to wipe up:

a white dab on his miniature man's sport jacket. "We do much better with potato chips."

"I think we're doing very well—with a very delicious Thanksgiving dinner"—me. (Aren't I gracious?)

"Do you need anything more? More turkey? More onions?"

"More stomach!" (No, I'm not. I'm not gracious. I'm a closet full of oily passionate rags.)

"I have more stomach!" said Ben. "And I want turnips and turkey!"

"Well, you *could* say please," his mother suggested.

"Please!" And it always sounds like what every child has to repeat in the police lineup of being polite.

"What are you writing now?" Carol asked, as Ben's plate made its way toward Jim, the *paterfamilias,* at the head of the table.

"Nothing. Right now." That gate shut tight, on a late September day. Except for this journal: my sickbook.

"Oh no—?" Her look was rapid and—it seemed to me—anxious. "I guess an artist has to let the springs fill up."

"That word sort of bothers me—"

" 'Artist'—?"

"It sounds so important. For an author of children's books."

"I don't mean it to. I mean, bother you. But *The Wind in the Willows* is going to last longer than *A Farewell to Arms.*"

"You think so—?"

"I know so. Don't you—?"

"Yes, I know so too. But I wonder how many of us there are."

"There are enough." A guarded intuition momentarily escaped from her eyes and shared a mind she had with me. "I think *Harold* will last too—"

"Now stop that. I'm already stuffed with this turkey." Ben's plate came back, loaded, and I set it down in front of him. "You'll never be able to eat all that."

From the heat they felt his fingers judged how much there was. "Oh yes I will."

"How did you get started? In writing children's books?"

"Do you want the truth?"

Her smile mocked me an instant. As if I should have known better. I should. "Either that, or something more interesting."

"I spent a year in Europe, then came back to New York and wrote a couple of plays. Which didn't get produced. So in a year or two I realized I sort of was starving to death. Meanwhile I had made a friend who worked as an editor in the children's department of my first publisher. He suggested I try a kiddies' book."

"I wish you wouldn't say 'kiddies' book'—"

"I just did it to tease you. So I did try to write a significant work of children's literature—"

"All right!"

"And it was absolutely rotten! It's out of print already—thank God!—but the idiot company published it. And that led to the next—"

"And that one was good. We have it."

"—and the next, and the next—and there you are."

"And to *Harold* eventually. That's wonderful!"

"I don't see why. If I'd managed to get a play produced, I wouldn't be in this field at all."

"But—" Her puzzlement, that I shouldn't be perfectly happy, was naive and lovely to see. "—it's your vocation."

"What about you? Did you ever want to be—excuse it, please—an artist?"

"Oh I had no vocation for the arts. I've never been creative—" She dismissed herself offhandedly. "—to write or paint or anything. But when I was little, I dreamed about being a ballet dancer."

That sounded, somehow, right: within her bulk, an imprisoned ballet dancer. "Did you take any lessons?"

"Yes, and I whirled and twirled around. But then I began to grow this—" big thing, she meant, that she's living in.

"What's wrong with your body?"

"Nothing. It's great. For having babies. But it's *not* a ballet dancer's body. So when dancing left me behind, I decided, rather grandly, that I would learn to sing."

"That's more like it. You've got a luscious voice."

"It's all right when I talk—it's not luscious—"

"It's pretty luscious. Go on."

Her smile recorded the compliment. "—but when I sing, I squeak."

116

"I don't believe it!"

"It's true. Whether it's fright, or just not strong enough vocal cords—I really do squeak. And terribly. So that's my story, as regards the arts: I had no vocation for any of them. And anyhow, shortly after the singing thing collapsed I met Jim."

"Do you know what 'vocation' really means? What it comes from?"

"It comes from *vocare:* to call."

"Well bless us and scratch us! A Riverdale matron—and she remembers her Latin!"

"We had to take two years of it, the school I went to." She shrugged and grinned—at what she once had wished was her life. "The arts just never beckoned me. But as I said, then I met Jim—" She looked toward the opposite end of the table, where her husband was persistently reminding a middle daughter that it was time to use a napkin.

"—and found your true calling after all."

Her head snapped toward me. "And found my true calling after all." For an instant she stared at me hard: at my face, then through my eyes, where she searched for me. But all she found, behind what I hoped was a friendly and impassive smile, was a consciousness of herself. A blush began to harry her cheeks—she dropped her eyes and busied herself with turkey and cranberry sauce.

And cued by her, I had my turn to look at the opposite end of the table. I expected the usual double shock that I get when I look up and see Jim there: a jolt first of love, and then despair. But Carol's sanity had been contagious. I may have seen him the way she did—with peace and confidence—after fifteen years of a happy if somewhat unorthodox marriage. Or perhaps I was interested enough in her to see him simply as he was. But I had an interval of fleeting normality. And these lapses from madness are Rumpelstiltskin's most brilliant coups. I do get them sometimes—infrequently, and they never last very long. But I see—as tonight, through the fire, I caught a glimpse of—an ordinary man. Poor Jim, poor Jim! I suppose any other handsome prick would do. A man who was wiping a middle daughter's chin. A monstrously handsome man, to be sure, and an excellent doctor, I'm certain of that. But basically unworthy: incommensurate with the furnace into which he has turned my existence. Suppose he is an artificial masochist? Suppose he fucks around? So what? *This* is his reality: six children, one of them blind, poor bastard—his wife—the rugs on the floor, the columns on the wallpaper: his whole life. I almost forgive him for being himself. But then *him,* it quickly comes over me, this not extraordinary man, who's exactly the key that fits in the lock of my weakness: that complex, broken machine of a heart. And then the Impossible blazes up around me, like kindling, like tissue paper, on fire: something horribly painful—bubbling, flaking, peeling skin . . .

Oh, Danny Reilly—what I felt then—and what you crave—which is the metaphor? Which stands for which? What is the reality? . . .

We all had—naturally—mince pie for dessert.

November 28: The wee hours now. And how wee—I don't give a living shit!

It took longer than I thought: the drinks, Ben's brutal accident, and the huge Thanksgiving dinner. It was almost seven o'clock when we went back into the living room . . .

Game time—play time—for the children now.

His youngest, just staggering out of a toddler, was charging around with a plastic-nippled bottle of milk. She would take it to Jim, he'd lift it up, pretend to drink—"Gug-gug-gug!"—and then hand it back with an elaborate "Thank you very much!" And she'd gleefully "gug-gug-gug!" away.

But for the older children, the game, at the Whittakers, is called "Hidden Billy." It seems there's this grasshopper—invisible—and his first name is Bill. Billy Grasshopper. And he has this habit of jumping in everybody's clothes. And the person he jumps in gets to shout, "He's in *me!*" Which provides the chance for everyone else to search—with their hands, of course—and do a lot of tickling.

It takes place on the floor. The children and Jim participate without any reservations at all. Carol tried—but sat there, propped on one hand with legs awkwardly folded, unaccomplished ballet wings, beneath her, in a proper pose—and couldn't be part of it. But being Mother, she had to do one "He's in *me!*" before she was allowed to excerpt herself from the game and come back on the couch. That body of hers again. I guess the only moment she trusts it must come when Jim is fucking her.

"Come join us on the floor, lad," Jim offered. "You've got a lot of jumpable pockets in that suit of yours."

A simple offhanded invitation to play with him and his kids—and if I'd been strapped in an electric chair I couldn't have felt more paralyzed panic: electrodes were fixed to my head, to my chest. I looked at Jim and shook my head.

"Come on, Mr. Andrews!" Ben chorused.

"Some other time, Ben," I governed my voice into steadiness. "This is an uptight Philadelphia gray flannel suit, and it doesn't know how to play 'Hidden Billy.'"

Jim glanced at me, puzzled, an instant—then shrugged. "He's in *me.*" And was inundated with his children.

They played "Hidden Billy" for half an hour. Carol half watched her family, and half sneaked sidelong glances at me. There was nothing suggestive in the looks she stole—mere tentative curiosity. And I watched the game with a growing fascination. A gesture of Jim's, instinctive and quick—he may not have been aware of it himself—had established itself as a recognizable pattern. I'd seen it before, in the living room, when Ben was on his lap. But I thought that then it just might be the comfort that the moment demanded. It isn't. He does it continuously. He'll suddenly cover Ben's sightless eyes with his hands, as if embarrassed by the blindness there, not wanting the world to see, but beyond that—and this I felt very strongly—exactly the opposite: as if to shield some secret vision lingering in the useless sockets from sights that shouldn't be witnessed. It's the fastest and most complicated human contact that I have ever seen.

Carol worried about my isolation, and drew me into an artificial conversation about the young guest surgeon's career. His specialty turned out to be something glamorous—neurosurgery, it was. I asked him the most elaborate questions I could—the ones it would take him longest to answer. "What *does* it feel like to spend eight hours in the human brain?"—et cetera—so that while he discoursed, and I ignored, politely, all he said, I could live, through the corner of my eyes, in that game of "Hidden Billy" being played on the floor.

The game broke up—the children went into the sun porch to play—"And no more running! And *no* more moving the furniture!" "No, Daddy." "No, Daddy." "No, Daddy."—and we so-called grown-ups were left alone. When children leave a room full of adults, my first impression—and lasting one—is how dull and immature we are. The things we speak are just as much nonsense as any infant's conversation, but lack their uninstructed passion.

There was medical talk—between Jim and the nondescript resident. Trouble in Surgery. Trouble in Neurology. Apparently Columbia-Presbyterian Hospital is nothing but a kind of Aesculapian United Nations, with all the departments bitching each other . . . Carol and the fiancée twittered on about weddings . . . I hung between the two discussions—one interested smile—and bored as hell with both.

There were liqueurs. For them, that is. For me there was Scotch. I hate those icky things. And something told me I was going to need Scotch. But I didn't remotely guess how much.

At nine o'clock the *éminence grise*—no, the *éminence noir*—of the Whittaker household appeared—one substantial fact at last—and announced, *ex cathedra,* it was time for the girls to get ready for bed. Ben, being the oldest, being a boy, and especially—unspoken—blind, was allowed to stay up for a little while longer. "But your time will come," Mary Wicks advised him magisterially, as she herded the giggling platoon upstairs.

The young couple left now. And I tried to too. But—

"Oh do stay a while longer," said Carol.

"Stay and chat with us, lad."

"Jim'll drive you to the station—"

"Sure."

—and Rumpelstiltskin, whose intuition was humming like a tuning fork, aware that something—not yet how much—was waiting for him, minutes away, said nonchalantly, "Well, all right."

The girls streamed in to say good night: a flight of five spirits, in nighty-like pajamas. Though one, that youngest, the stumble-bum cherub, sailed into the living room rug three times—to her own, and everyone's, loud delight. Those girls—I still can't keep them apart—but they gave the whole house such an air of joyous turbulence. Their medium seems to be the air. They exist, at all times, one foot off the floor—just *one* foot, but it's quite enough. There were kisses for everyone, little wing beats of arms and legs, the demanding flutters of soft white wool—and the troop was stampeded back upstairs.

And we four remained alone. Ben sat on the couch, beside his mother. Jim occupied a corner easy chair. And I another.

For the three of them the lull that the girls had left behind was the full round period that punctuated a happy day. For me—and R.—it was the terrific deadly stillness that precedes an earthquake, a revelation—the one I had come for: fulfilled necessity.

"Where's my book?" Ben began it, poor kid, unwittingly.

"Here." Carol handed it to him.

"Maybe Mr. Andrews would read you a chapter." Jim—did he know? No. Just as innocent as his wife and child. I had a last quick glimpse of him: a perfectly decent, well-wishing man.

It was, of course, I—or rather R.—his voice sounds amazingly like mine, when he talks through my vocal cords—who suggested, "I'd rather hear Ben read a chapter to *me*."

Jim and Carol stirred with pleasure: at the chance to show off their damaged but viable son.

"Yes, do, Ben!"

"Read the first chapter, Ben."

"Okay."

The first chapter in *The Story of Harold* is one of the gentlest in the book. I wanted to start it in a minor key—and also introduce Sylvester, the rubber plant, the second lead—a sage—to the story.

Ben's gifted fingers opened the book, and read everything. The title page—the dedication: "To my living friends—who will know who you are"—and "Chapter One: Sylvester and the Drop of Pure Water."

"Harold woke up one morning, and as usual his first thought was that something was wrong.

Is it a storm? Maybe a sou'wester?
No.
A sick angry worm then? . . . Oh—it's Sylvester!

(Sylvester lives in the lobby of a very fashionable hotel. After having been schlepped from one Upper East Side bar to another, he ends up at the Plaza, naturally. But he's very badly mistreated there. Men empty their pipes in him—ladies butt their cigarettes—and he never gets enough to drink. So he sent out an SOS to Harold. And one night, in the dead of night—Harold put the cleaning ladies to sleep—they worked on the problem of Sylvester's thirst.)

> Niagara Falls! That's just the ticket!
> By magic I can surely trick it
> To watering you both day and night.
> We'll try it now. All right? All right.

"But there was too much of Niagara Falls. 'I'm washing away, Harold! And the Plaza's lobby's getting all dirty.'

" 'Oh rats!' And then a snap of his fingers—so the Plaza wouldn't have rats. 'I've got it!—

> The Pacific Ocean's big and wet.
> It holds both calms and wild typhoons.
> That's what you need! And I'll just bet
> You'll like it more than chic saloons.

" '*Glug!* I'm drowning, Harold! *Glug!* There's too much of the Pacific Ocean. And also, it's so *salty!*'

" 'Phooey!' Harold snapped his fingers, and the Pacific Ocean left Sylvester's tub and went back off to California.

"And then Harold gets a *little* idea: a little drop of glistening water.

> Oh little drop! Oh little drop!—
> If you'd go on and never stop—
> If you'd be crystalline and pure,
> And keep Sylvester watery—
> You'd get to love him just like me.
> You would! I'm absolutely sure!

"And Sylvester, in the deep bass voice that a rubber plant would have to have, heaved a huge sigh and said, '*Ah!*' "

There was more to the story, of course—and the boy was reading it very well.

What it meant to him, I assume, was simple happiness: he could read his favorite book now, alone.

What it meant to Carol was—a mother's satisfaction, I guess. She was feeling rich in Thanksgiving, and rich in her children, and rich in her love for Jim. And happy too, I think, that I was there, and listening.

What it meant to Jim—God alone knows. And He, Who does not exist, may care. Probably something like Carol's still joy.

What it meant to me—about halfway through the story—was the deepest, most choking desperation that I've ever felt in my life. I looked at the three of them. The room was quite dark—one big floor lamp above the red couch, that's all. So I could see them without seeming to spy, with my eyes reserved in semidarkness, where they couldn't be seen.

And the passions that fought each other: real pleasure, that I'd made that little boy happy—respect for Carol, and affection—and Jim I—"love" I was going to say. Can you call a heart's cancer "love"? Yes! Jim, I do love—malignantly! Within my head the question tolled: what can I be for the three of these people? For that heroic little boy, who doesn't even know he's a hero? For that woman, who wears her heroism as casually as old-fashioned clothes? And above all, what can I be for Jim? And the answer knelled back, in three dead strokes: *Nothing! nothing! nothing!* By the end of the story I had sunk through so many different depths I believe I had reached a perfect emptiness: the absolute tranquillity that comes—but does not last—from absolute despair.

It doesn't last. Ben finished the chapter. I stood up. "Thank you, Ben. Now I *have* got to go."

Good nights . . .

At the door—"Thank you." "Thank *you!*" And a kiss from Carol and from Ben.

Jim's driving me to the station, his hand—a casual occasional question—testing my knee. "I wish I could come back. I'm hot."

"You couldn't—could you?" Idiot infantile hope!

"No, not on Thanksgiving night. I'll call you next week though." We stopped. A final touch. His fingers authoritatively entered my crotch—"Thanks for coming, lad"—but just to locate his mastery.

"Thank you!" And Jim—Rumpelstiltskin meant it: *thanks!* He'll have this to work with for days and days.

"Ta ta!" He drove off. And called through the window, "Be a good lad now!"

And drugged with hopelessness—which can sometimes become as strong as hashish—I rode back to Manhattan . . .

So—as I said—to kill myself—swell! With pills or guns or ropes or even Danny Reilly's way . . . But to go through emotions like those again—?

My handwriting's gotten illegible. And I think—thank God!—that with one more drink I can fall asleep.

November 29

Hung over. And dreadfully sick: headache, stomach, everything. I went through half a quart of Scotch last night. Apart from what I had at Jim's . . . And my feelings are still in tatters today. Being about as substantial as a Muslim's lady's veil to begin with.

All you fags out there, who fall in love with married men—listen! There is a special Hell reserved for you that even Dante never dreamed of. Your passion—which you think is the very best in you—will hold little handy pocket mirrors up to your every imperfection. Good luck!

And to give the coup de grace to whatever little muscle of life was still twitching, around noon Carol Whittaker called me up. I was going to call *her*—R. was—and thank her for a charming Thanksgiving Day that, in all kinds of specialized torments and twinges, exceeded his expectations by far!

"I just want to thank you for coming to Riverdale yesterday."

"You want to thank me—? It's up to *me* to thank you! And write you a note. If I wasn't such a lazy slob."

"No note."

"A nice well-brought-up thank-you note."

"Absolutely no note! But I wanted to tell you how much everybody enjoyed you. And Ben especially—"

"How's his head?"

"It's fine. He's wearing that bandage like some kind of helmet. And he does so love your book! He's been reading it all morning. You really were very thoughtful."

"You were. To ask me to come at all."

A double pause: of how to hang up, and something else that she wanted to ask me.

"Will you come and see us again?"

Remember my vow last night? Before that God Who does not exist? *Never!* Not ever go back there again. Automatically I answered, "Whenever you ask me." The emotional robot I am! You would have thought I'd have been permitted at least five seconds to *think*—wouldn't you?—I'd have had the quick intelligent instant to ask myself—is this wise? is this right? Not a bit of it! The programmed answer was blurted out: "Whenever you ask me." (*Her* fish, as well as her husband's.)

"Then that'll be very soon." This pause was simplified. "And thank you again. Good-bye."

"Good-bye."

It brought the whole evening back again. The worst parts of it, at least.

Had I really been jealous when Jim kissed his children good-night?—with a lingering hug and specific look—*you*—for each one?

Yes! . . .

Had I envied a crying blind child's comfort?

Yes! . . .

> Ah, something's wrong! There's something wrong!
> Because something's been bugging me all day long.
> Is it a buzzing? Like a big beehive?
> Yes!
> Is it the feeling you still are alive?
> *Yes!*
> So something is wrong! Yes, there's very much wrong!
> But believe me, my friends, it will not be for long!

December 3

"Well, the week after Rumpelstiltskin and the Three-Legged Nothing began collecting kindling wood—"

"Nooooo—!" A whine of frightened impatience: he is bored with that joke, though he hasn't been told it yet. And so are all of you, I've no doubt . . . But it's no joke, and it's real, and it frightens me too . . .

Edith called me this morning and said, in an affectation of reproof, "*Ber*-nard is very angry with you."

"I'll bet he is. I promised him a Thanksgiving story." And I've got a great one to tell, all right! I'm still drinking on the strength of it.

"Terry—" Her voice, but always within its cultured limits, went worried and urgent. "—I wish you *would* come up. If you can."

"What's happened?"

"That weekend with Frank. Disaster area! And Frank tried to be so nice! He brought him a lot of toys. And *Ber*-nard hated every one. So Frank swallowed that. And said that he'd take him to F. A. O. Schwartz—" Of course! Nothing but the useless best—for a kid who's lost. "—and buy him anything he wanted. And you *know* what he wanted? A stuffed animal! And *Ber*-nard's too old for stuffed animals." Oh I am too! (Gleep!) "And apart from that—can you guess what *kind* of a stuffed animal?"

"What?"

"A rat! Now *really!*"

Was that a tug of tenderness toward the little bugger? No! "Edith—if he wants a rat—for God's sake get him a *rat!* He's in a dismal period."

"That's what Frank said. But they don't sell rats at F. A. O. Schwartz. We settled on a very large, quite delightful mouse."

"Any rodent, in a pinch."

"But since Thursday he's been whining and sulking—"

"Okay, okay."

So here I am—in Bernard's bedroom. Drinking cocoa and munching cookies. It's foul weather outside today. And the room is awash with unplayed-with playthings: abandoned toys that never had even the slightest magic.

Edith has left the apartment completely—a wise and motherly move that was made on her own initiative: some pretext—a shop—in the neighborhood. She leaves it to me to fill the rooms with something living, if I can. She's obviously upset, and in the minutes we had alone I detected driblets of humanity seeping in through the cracks in her composure.

"Are you absolutely *positive* that you don't want to know what happened the week after Rumpelstiltskin adopted the Three-Legged Nothing?"

"Yes!"

"All right then—" I untease my voice.

"Harold—and the Rat's Thanksgiving."

Seems Harold woke up Thanksgiving morning, and he knew right away what was wrong. Taking the Rat to the Whittakers—and the name did leap out: that's what you get, when you try to live your life like fiction—was going to be an awful risk. To keep his courage up, Harold sang a silly little song—

> Oh the Rat's going to have a delicious dinner!
> Courage, Rat!
> You're where it's at!
> (In family life Rat's just a beginner.)

(One does parenthesis in confidential whispers.)

Harold wrapped up his present for the Whittaker boy, and then down to the Village, to pick up the Rat—and there he is in a dirty shirt and khaki pants . . . Much consternation on Harold's part—and he finally induces the Rat to wear his good gray flannel suit . . . I was trying to work in as much of the real experience as I could. Without driving the boy insane. And myself as well . . . The Rat had been drinking too. "Okay," allowed Harold, "but just don't get so damn"—yes! a swear word—"fortified that you fall on your whiskery kisser" . . . They almost have a fight in the taxi, because Harold, to relieve that Rat's obvious anxiety, sings—

> Oh the Rat's going to have some delicious turkey!
> Courage, Rat!
> You're where it's at!
> Perk up now, Rat! Be a *little* perky . . .

The Rat threatened to bust Harold in the nose if he didn't stop singing those silly songs—the silly songs that keep me going, while I'm telling a story—but the driver of the taxi in Riverdale—yes, *Riverdale!* we are that far now—the driver of the taxi, who was a young sea lion, with a beard, said, "Not in this taxi you don't."

I get us there, relaxing the Rat, by describing the Whittaker family . . . "A family!" groans the Rat . . . Five little girls and a blind boy—oh boy! that's all the Rat needs! . . .

And at this point, to my amazement—delight—Barney asks, again, the metaphysical question. He interrupts me, in fact.

"Are these people real?"

"The Whittakers—?"

"Are they really real? And the Rat—?"

"I told you that he was real. And the Whittakers are far more real than the Rat! Now shall I go on? Or shall I stop?" His dropped head, eyes embarrassed, down, is the plea I need.

Then on with the story . . . Mrs. Whittaker opened the door, and shook Rat's claw, and made him at ease . . . Then the flight down the stairs of five little girls. And behind them Jim and Ben . . . and Jim said heartily, "Hi, Rat, Lad!" I had to make him lovable, because—Christ alive!—he is . . . Then the blind boy, to Rat's great jitteriness, felt his whiskers and his buttony nose and his funny little pointed ears—they made Ben laugh—I said "Ben"—and the Rat felt as if his face had never been known so well before . . .

Well—well, well—the cocktails and the canapés. (I left out Mary Wicks—although she surely could have been one of the ones to pull old Barney through.) And Rat got nervouser and nervouser. "It's this house," he said, "it's just like my parents' house on Ninth Avenue—the rugs, the furniture—"

> Courage, Rat—Harold softly, almost magically buzzed—
> This is where it's at. (He wondered if, perhaps, it was.)
> Just trust the love in this family.
> There's enough for you. There's enough for me.

Then on to dinner—after another Scotch for the Rat—and I did include the booze. And Barney's face told me, after I'd asked him, that yes, he did know what Scotch and vodka and gin really were . . . At gin, in fact, he said, "Martinis." . . . His mother's tipple, I would guess.

Hyddy-ho! . . . Somewhere here I went into Edith's kitchen, to make myself a drink . . . Reliving it—even on Harold's terms— was brutal, though it did kind violence to the facts. And I hadn't decided on an ending yet . . .

So on to dinner. I make the Rat even more of a celebrity than I had been. After he'd tucked his napkin under his chin—because that's the way well-brought-up rats *do* eat Thanksgiving dinner—

it's "More turkey for the Rat!" and "The Rat doesn't have enough stufffing!" and "Quick! The Rat needs more cranberry sauce!" . . . Rat accepts the kindness grumpily. Because, when people seem to like him, a happiness sort of flares in his heart. But doubt puts it quickly out.

Now here I said, Terry—remember: this is a little boy. "Do you know what I mean?" I said out loud. "About the doubt."

"Yes."

Well—with the intuition of children—God knows, perhaps he does!

After dinner—I explain "Hidden Billy"—the feast of fun on the living room floor. And to Harold, who was sneaking looks at the Rat from the crannies of his eyes as he chatted with Mrs. Whittaker, the poor furry thing looked even more dejected than ever, as he watched the playing in front of him . . . And then—then—

"Yes—?"

Then Jim Whittaker asked the Rat to join them all on the floor, because that gray flannel suit looked as if it had a lot of nice pockets in it, where Billy could hide. But the Rat, in a voice that was tight in his throat, said no, he couldn't. Because this was an uptight Ninth Avenue suit.

"The Rat wouldn't play 'Hidden Billy'—?" Barney's face is a map of the land of sadness and failure.

"Now wait! Jim Whittaker looked puzzled. He glanced at Harold. And Harold, who had been listening, made an urgent plea with his eyes. It said, 'Take him! Please, Jim. Take the Rat—' And Jim heard what Harold's face was saying. Before the Rat knew what was happening, Jim had picked him up, laid him down on the floor, and shouted, 'Hidden Billy's in the Rat!' And before you could say 'Rumpelstiltskin' there began such an orgy—that means everybody gets mixed up together—there began such an orgy of tickling and giggling and rolling-around as the world has never seen before! And the Rat was laughing and rolling around just like the human beings." And that, I think, thank God, is that. "Then all the children went to bed, and—"

"What was Harold's present?"

"What present?"

"To the Whittaker boy. You said he brought one."

"His name is Ben." I'd forgotten, but he had not . . . My God, this kid is in league with my demons. "It was a copy of *The Story of Harold*. In braille." And *I* am in league with my demons! "That's writing blind people can read."

"Did Ben like it?"

"Yes. He read the first chapter out loud to the author."

" 'Sylvester and the Drop of Pure Water.' " He too knows how to do capitals. Devil! "Did Harold like it?—listening to his own story?" Yet amazing!—for the first time the child seems almost optimistic. "How did Harold feel?"

As if Hell was closing over him . . . "As if—" But then Harold says to me—"No! No!" And flings his arms up and down . . . And I say to him—

Oh Harold, Harold—the next few minutes, please—
Be real! If I can't, let this kid have peace . . .

"Harold was happier than he'd ever been in his life before. He loved these people, the Whittakers—the girls, Mrs. Whittaker, and blind Ben—and Jim—" Every inch of whose skin he has kissed and caressed and adoringly flogged. "—and he knew that Mom and Pop had been touched to their hearts by hearing their blind son read, through his fingers . . . And Harold too, because of them, the both of them, felt as if two hands were holding his heart. But he couldn't meet the Whittakers' eyes. Eyes sometimes are very hard to meet. So he just stared into a middle distance, in bliss."

In the living room Edith is discreetly rustling, letting me know she's back . . . And only in the nick of time. My fictions are failing.

"Then it really was time for good-nights. And everybody hugged everybody. And much to the Rat's embarrassment and secret joy, Jim kissed him on his woolly cheek, just above where the Rat's long whiskers begin." I stand up. "And all the way back to New York the Rat kept saying—as if he couldn't believe it himself—'I really enjoyed that! I really did.' And every now and then, just to keep the Rat's happy memory going, Harold would say, 'Yes, Rat, so did I.' "

I put my hand on Barney's head and scratch the soft, short downy hair . . . His face, now that I'm leaving, now that the story is finished, has such a woebegone look of loss in it.

December 7

I discovered how hopelessly I'm in love with Jim because on September 21, 1968, not out of malice, just negligence, he failed to make a telephone call . . . And I can confess this, *now this minute,* because I've been watching—and laughing hysterically—a Road-Runner cartoon! (God bless *The New York Times* for religiously listing the cartoon shows—along with its more pompous opinions. Indeed I think God and *The New York Times* must have the same personality: something vast, abstract, and faintly, vaguely, benignly ironic.) Presented in our most lifelike masks, Jim and I are the Road-Runner and the Coyote. Masochist though he is, he shouts, "Beep! beep!" and absolutely flattens me. (Among the deeper philosophical questions—"Does God exist?" "Is love possible?"—there exists this one: "Whom do you identify with?—the Road-Runner or the Coyote?")

For almost a year I had thought I was managing things very well. A married man—so, sure, nothing serious: a damned good piece of ass, that was all. And I *believed* what I told myself! It's one of the glories of self-deception that you can make it last so long. So on the twenty-first of September Jim went to a friend of his, for drinks. No sex—they'd had a go-round years ago—but now they were simply—Impossibly, to my thinking, as far as Jim is concerned—just friends. And my motherfucking friend drank enough to get hot. And he wanted—I blushfully admit this—me.

He called and said, "I'm at a friend's. I've got to go back to Riverdale and have dinner with Carol and the kids. But I need you tonight. Are you free?"

And his need—oh my listening voyeurs!—expressed so audibly, urgently, is an expert's groping hand in my crotch. Through short breaths I offhandedly answer him—"Sure."

"I'll call you just before I leave."

"About when?"

"Ten, I guess. Thereabouts. See you, lad."

And he never called back. Simply that. The explanation, two days later, was—"Oh. When I got home, I found a houseful of people there."

"And you couldn't go upstairs and make a call, to tell me that you couldn't come?" asked a voice which two days before had belonged to an altogether different person.

"It didn't seem that important."

Oh Jim—you shit! you prick! you cunt!—my honeyed unforgivable—it *was* that important!

For here is where the Coyote comes in. Like him, I'd been walking along for a year—yes, a year I'd known him!—but then, in the hours I waited for Jim to call back, I happened to look at the ground—and discovered that the solid earth had been left far behind. I was out there above an abyss. *Uh*-oh! And in that instant, like the dumb cartoon brute, I literally *fell* in love. The phrase is well chosen. Or perhaps I only realized that I had already fallen in love. It amounts to the same: the drop was catastrophic.

Or rather, it wasn't at first: to fall is not a painful sensation. It's landing that breaks your bones. And I landed two days later. I was pissed off at Jim that night, as the hours became millennia, for not bothering to call, but at the same time so narcissistically engulfed in this new understanding—"I am in *wuv!*"—that the fall was thrilling: a sky dive into romantic passion. I had hope for Jim, you see: that he sort of, a little, returned my affection. That was to be my parachute.

"Of *course* you're married, baby! And you've got a family." The vulgar mawkish dialogue—alas, all accurate—was printed in words of gold in my mind. "I wouldn't love you as much as I do, if you weren't the man you are." How can truth be made so ordinary? "But—?"

But—? Yes: but. For two days I lived in that "but": that despite his situation, which I didn't want to change, despite his love for his children, his wife, there might be a dab of the cosmic cream left for me. The sex was not diminishing: the opposite, in fact. We'd begun to talk—about his son, about his work. And the fluttering little thing inside me—and it's inside you too, my dears: *tua res agitur*—just didn't believe there was such a word as "no."

In two days he called up and nonchalantly apologized about "the other night. But I'm sure as hell hot right now!"

And I, in a fit of immature rapture—believe me, Juliet herself was Godzilla by comparison—I said in a voice made of butterflies, "Well why don't you come on down?"

The thing is—I hadn't *meant* to tell him I love him—

(*Liar! Liar! Tell the truth! . . . You can, you know . . . Your witnesses do not exist! . . . Nor do you!*)

All right then. I knew that I'd have to tell him sometime, but I hadn't meant it to happen so fast. The session was spectacular. In fifteen minutes I had him shivering—not only his buttocks, revolving up into the stick I use—but his whole body trembling uncontrollably. And, what turns me on most, his hands pressed tightly against his head—I think to prevent the sensations he felt from becoming hallucinatory. And this on two Scotches and only two blasts from our trusty popper!

I didn't want him to come with the stick—but I do permit him that sometimes—so as his moans grew desperate—the difficult pleasure of coming, postponed—I flipped him over and entered him. And then it was I who hallucinated. And my hallucination? . . . Love.

In the lull that followed I stroked his stomach, a sticky forest of auburn fur, till I got him a towel. While he wiped himself, he began to make his usual mundane remarks.

"Wow! Where were you?"

"I was here. With you. Where were you?"

"I was here. But someplace else too."

"Where?"

"Someplace with a lot of lights. I began to hear those lights. I began to feel those lights—on my ass, when you were strapping me. By the way—am I—?"

"*When* have I ever left any marks on you?"

"Okay. Don't get mad. You're the only one I trust enough not to worry about it, when I fly."

That must have been what triggered me. With my hand still in his now dry glade—and red is the color of magical trees—I offered, as an interesting but not very critical comment, "By the way, Jim, there's something I have to tell you."

"What?"

Still petting that fox's fur of his—"It doesn't happen to me so often that I can afford to let it go by in silence." I was looking at his crotch: the triumphantly shriveled ruin of what had been a whole city of pleasure. I thought my ease of not looking in his eyes, my casual and unbothered indirection, would make it easier for him to reply. "I love you. Very much. That's all. No sweat. But I *do* love you."

A silence, behind my head, where his head was pressing the pillow down . . . A silence I misinterpreted.

"I wouldn't want anything to change. It's just—it's time for you to hear. I know that your life is located somewhere else. And that's the way I like you to be." Oh, Father, was I mature! Was I adult! Was I a *fool!* With my shoulder on his chest, propping up a head full of unreal dreams. "The thing I love most about you—apart from that red-headed ass of yours—" That was thrown in to prove that I was grown-up. "—is the fact that you're a family man. But I think—" Here the guillotine's knife went up. Here the torch was placed. "—you feel something for me—"

"I don't." His voice had become some other man's, a bureaucrat, who worked in an office and answered questions he really wasn't interested in.

"You don't feel anything—?" The devil in me pursued to question.

"No." His body slipped out from under mine, and left me propped on my failing hallucination. "If you mean love—no. I don't. But welcome to the club anyway."

There are times when a body is hit so hard that it takes several minutes before it can register pain.

Before I could register mine, Jim had showered and dressed, said, "Ta ta!" and left. I will not put down that night. Can't. Sorry. Or the day that came afterwards. (Lucky for you.)

When Joan of Arc was burned at the stake—like my Danny— she really was very lucky. It must have taken twenty minutes at most. And being a very fashionable martyr, she probably had flames designed by Dior.

It was Rumpelstiltskin who supplied my fire. And he kept it going as long as he could. . . . Would he call me again? Or was that it? . . . But the passions are matter too—like wood or like water. You can boil or burn them for only so long before they consume themselves.

I was burned out, burnt up—for the first time: unfortunately wood and water replenish themselves—by the next afternoon. I'd had twenty-four hours of what Dan Reilly's flesh dreams of. And my ashes, exhausted, felt nothing but shame. As usual—as has happened all too often in my life—after being obliterated completely, I felt compelled to write a letter: to uselessly try to undo the absolutely done, the past. And this is what I wrote—addressed to his office, marked *private*.

Dear Dr. Whittaker,

Well, now you know the worst. Our friend is too embarrassed to write to you himself, so he asked me to apologize for him, for that Forty-second Street scene he pulled. He has played it over many times since you left, and each new showing makes it seem worse. And he much regrets the egocentric question—request, rather—that he made of you. It will not happen again—he promises you that. If you'd like to continue to come around . . .

What else was I supposed to say? Well, a lot of nonsense about the hairy glories of that behind of yours. And the tricks he's got up his sleeve—in his pants is actually what he said—that he hasn't tried out on you yet. (That is meant to be provocative—keep you coming around.)

One thing, though. He asked me, very urgently, to remind you that, better or worse, you're now part of his life. That—

If you want a son, if you want a father,
If you want a friend, if you want a brother—
Whatever you want—he does love you—
You'll get. And I'll keep him cool, but true.

Yours, in embarrassment,
Harold

So that was the first of three days. And that night, September 24, according to destiny's flawless mathematics, I had a date with Anne . . . But I'll tell you about that tomorrow . . . Right now I'm hot. I'm going to go out and get loaded and lauded and laid. Every nerve in my body is overtuned, and a bow is playing across each one: high, deep, and demanding notes of lust. And their silence maddens me. I've got to hear my flesh sing—out loud.

But a man or a woman—I can't decide. It'll either be the Turkish baths, where I'll fuck as many as I can, or one of the whore bars on Third Avenue, the lower part of Third Avenue, where one of those five-and-dime floozies will zero in on me—naive, in my gray flannel suit—and then will find, when I get her home, that this smiling, ordinary man has some rather extravagant needs to be filled . . . A filthy little bird just told me that I'm going to get rimmed tonight. And maybe go into the bathroom too . . . We'll see . . .

December 8

It turned out to be a woman. Picked her up in that bar between Twenty-first and -second. Very much in Connie's type. I miss those people. Their charm is a gemlike commonness. She wanted me to go back to her place, but no thank you!—I've had the badger game played before. And almost had my brains beaten out by one bitch's pretended fiancé. But that's another story—one that comes from the years when I still was alive.

Her name, deliciously, was Maxine. And *a* Maxine was what she was; bleached hair, fingers glittering with worthless rings, and reeking of a vile perfume that smelled incredibly like pure sex: an ideal representative of that ordinary species: Maxine.

I about had to break her back—no, her nose, the way I wriggled around—before she'd lick my tail. But when she did, and realized I was completely clean, her mood—and mouth—delightfully altered. You'd have thought that my rear end was caramel candy. Hers, when I'd showered her, certainly was . . . Enough of that.

The sex was violent—not sadistic, but full of suddenness—and dirty and good—no bathroom, though—and on the strength of the memory of it I will tell you the second day of the trilogy that ended in Giggleville: an iron town.

I burned all day, September 23. And the weather was very pleasant for a private holocaust: that surfeit of summer, a swollen sun, that aches into autumn. And within this city of New York, that glowed and rejoiced in a beautiful day, I walked around with every single cell on fire. Till six, when I had my date with Anne.

We were having dinner at her apartment, as per our routine, and then going to see *The Thief of Bagdad*. It's a relic of my childhood—the Sabu version, *not* the one with Douglas Fairbanks, Sr.!—that old I'm not quite, yet—and I see it whenever it comes around, and sit in a trance of pastness, watching: a trance of all things that are lost for good. (Pop took me to see it one

Christmas afternoon.) Last fall it was playing in one of those dippy, invaluable little theaters that specialize in old movies.

I got through dinner pretty well, my Dior flames all being invisible—the hottest kind there are, did you know?—but Anne knew that I was being consumed. Her eyes were nervous and extremely careful not to look too deeply into me. And our conversation—voices and subjects too—was a few notes higher than usual.

Then off to the Upper West Side. Where through the smoke and through the heat I caught a few glimpses of Sabu and June Duprez. That big genie. That huge ruby of the All-Seeing Eye. I remember at a certain point I half-laughingly asked myself which one was more painful: the past or the present? And the answer, when one's at the stake, is now! *now!* NOW!

We went back to Anne's apartment.

I thought I could make it—fake it: spend the night with her—make love.

I could not.

Anne was puzzled and nervous and, I guess, afraid. But she went through the preparatory motions—our having a nightcap, a bit of talk about the film—automatically. Her training—etiquette, in the best sense—showed itself here: she knew that since something extraordinary, and probably bad, was happening to me, it was up to her to provide a surface, for my sake, beneath which I could hide. She even went so far as to invent an out for me, for that night. "I think I'm coming down with a cold—"

And God—I should have taken it! But I had this idea: that if I could be with her, stay with her, make love to her and make her come—I still might be alive. So I laughed, with the phoniest masculine assurance that ever has been heard, "I'll marshal my antibodies."

We went into the bedroom. She wasn't expecting a high, deep time, she wasn't expecting fun and games—she wasn't expecting anything; she was taking all her cues from me, and prepared to do anything to make it as easy for me as she could. I stripped, and she undressed. (There *is* that difference: men strip, and women, garment by complicated garment, undress.) We lay down, side by side.

I was telling myself that the way to start was just naturally to kiss her. I rolled over—and her eyes were embarrassed by tears. And a psychic bone—what's the most important bone there is? The backbone. My spirit's backbone broke. It snapped inside me audibly. I flopped back on my back and lifted my hands halfway to my face. Before they reached it, I felt Anne's hand in my groin. It was sheltering, with that abstract sensation of blessing that only a woman's hand can give, the utterly futile and useless append-ages that were shriveling there.

She said softly, yet austerely, "You know how much I love you, Terry. I'll be here."

The only time that Anne's love ever talked.

There's a state beyond the destruction of flesh by fire. It's possible for a soul to burn—burn literally—in a substance that makes ordinary flame feel like a cooling glass of spring water. And, Father, this is the true meaning of Hell.

"I don't think—" I began, in as much voice as I could muster up, as a lead to a—yuk! yuk! and hardy-har-har!—guess-who-can't-get-a-what-on gag.

But Anne, in that same authoritative yet feminine tone, took the words from me and used them with intelligence, "I don't think you ought to stay here tonight. No good to force."

"You kicking me out?" This offer I took.

"I'm kicking you out"—pragmatically.

So under the guise of being kicked out, a mask of friendly expediency that worked for the minutes it took me to dress, I left . . .

And the evening and the morning were the Second Day.

December 8: An hour later

I've just been out and gotten a not very satisfactory blow job in a subway john. And from a kid who looked young enough to spell Rapeville if the fuzz busted in.

This business of sex—that floozy the other night and junior just now—is all part of the thing that happened when the mental Red Sea had parted and I saw my way to the Promised Land. Death *is* the really big erection! If I don't fuck every day—and I haven't bothered to put down them all—I usually jack off once or twice . . .

September 24 was Anne.

September 25—and what is the opposite of your birthday? The day you die? The day you believe you'll die? No, the day you decide to die . . . Dan Reilly's day.

He called in the morning. I had burned up everything combustible—for about the thousandth time—and was in a state of apathy that I prayed would last for the rest of my life. "Sir?—can I see you this afternoon?"

"You not working? Servicing humanity?"

"No—" Then that drop in his voice, "—sir"—into pure servility: the essence of audible masochism.

"Okay." An automaton in me answered. Or did something already suspect? "Come around at two."

"Yes—sir."

And at two—*precisely* at two: the difference between a real slave and a fake shows itself in details like punctuality—the buzzer went, and I let him in . . . I had a joint ready, but didn't need to light it.

We did our usual tricks. He insisted—oh, very obediently!—on our cigarette routine, although, at that time, I hadn't ever really hurt him. I fisted him—and my God, I don't see how that cat does it! He must have guts like the BMT subway!

Don't *any* of you even smile, however. Because after his climax—I didn't want to come, and I brought him off with my fist, on his back—I found myself in the midst of the farthest, most airy conversation I've ever had in my life. One only has one conversation like that.

I was still living in blessed apathy, and as we lay there, side by side, out of nothing but curiosity, I happened to ask him, "How did you learn to like that thing with the cigarettes?"

"Cowboys and Indians."

"What?"

"When I was twelve, I was playing with some older kids—"

"How old?"

"Sixteen or seventeen. And I was the white prisoner."

"They put butts out on you?"

"Yes. We went out into the woods, and they tied me to a tree. I was the white prisoner."

Life—as in our first encounter—had entered poor dead Danny's voice as he began to narrate the central experience of his existence. "Go on."

"It was fall—there were plenty of leaves and dry branches around—and they piled them up to my knees."

"Go on."

"Then one guy, the oldest—he was eighteen—the handsomest— he looked like you—"

"Skip the compliments!" Something much deeper than vanity had been hooked in me now.

"No, sir—he really did. He had those green-blue eyes you've got. And he took out his cock and began to jerk off. And then all the others did too—"

"Go on." (*Fool,* me! The lure of porn is reality. Fool, you too.)

"And one of them took down my pants. I was twelve—I had this dopey little thing—they all laughed at me. But the older guy—you—said, 'Play with it. Before we burn him up, we'll torture him and make him come.' And they did. They opened up my shirt—and they all had cigarettes and matches—and they started to butt me."

"And did you get a hard-on?"

"I don't know. Can you?—at twelve?"

"You sure as hell can!"

"Well I was slow, developing. But I think I came. They sure all did!—all over me."

"Then they cut you down?"

"The hell they did! They went off and left me!" Of course, of course. And you're still there, tied at the stake. "It took me an hour to get those damned ropes off. And their come was all dried, all over me." Here, with a curious reserve, almost flirtatiously, he laughed. "So that's how I got to be a fire-freak."

"A what—?"

"That's what guys like me are called." (The lure of the real is pornography. He was living this.)

"Oh. I see." (So was I.)

A silence. And though I didn't know it then, it was the dead stillness of the two of us being becalmed in the center of a madness of oceanic proportions.

In that same coy, enticing tone—not feminine, but alluringly, like a prisoner demurely asking a guard if he couldn't open his cell, a little: "Course the cigarettes are just because no one's got any guts any more."

The boat that we both were becalmed in—a sailboat—was lifted slightly by a swell.

"Some people have guts."

"I've never met one."

And a breeze sprang up, behind us, and pushed.

"The cigarettes are pretty dull, aren't they?"

"Yes—sir!"

"You want a tree trunk—" I left it for him to create.

"No, sir, a tree trunk isn't necessary."

"Not outdoors—?"

"No, sir. No. I'd rather be indoors. In a home."

Does this exchange read ridiculously? Does it read like violence? It wasn't. The boat was coasting now. Have any of you sailed before the wind? There's truly no experience like it, when a light boat sails before the wind! And the sentences we exchanged were like a duet sung by only one person: we had turned into the same idea. The tune beneath the song was supplied by the lilt of the waves we went over.

"Whose home?"

"My own, sir." The wind increased. "Why do you think I live in the suburbs?"

I was going to say something like, maybe, economy—up till now I had thought that *was* the reason—but it would have broken the boat's momentum, and I caught myself in time. "I know," I lied—in the moment that I didn't lie, and the truth took hold. "But you tell me."

"So I'd have a place, where—"

"Where—?"

"—where, if somebody had enough guts—he could really play with me."

The wind died, a little.

"You don't mean 'play,' do you, Danny?"

"No—sir!"

A gust rushed us forward.

"Then tell me what you mean."

"Where someone could really—"

"Out loud." Softly.

"—kill me."

Not enough. The boat, the momentum, had taken possession. I had to hear it all said. I reminded him gently, "That isn't what you mean. How?"

"By burning me to death."

In the silence of its at last being infinite—we sailed and sailed and sailed. The sky above us was bright and sunny, and the sea was green and blue beneath.

I didn't say, "All right, I will." I didn't say, "Yes," or anything. The pure motion we both felt together, lying unmoving, side by side, was his question and my answer both.

When we started to talk again, it all had been taken for granted. His pitiful savings—my practical suggestions: "Don't draw it out all at once." It seemed weird to me to hear me talk. I thought that the change that had occurred would make me sound different, look different, the way I was different. For the past two days I'd been in the hell I built for myself. But all that I'd felt about Jim—the rage, frustration—and everything that I'd felt about Anne—shame, failure—they had all been lusciously painful emotions, but at least they'd been human. Even when they are at the stake—no, most when they are at the stake—the victims, martyrs, are human beings. But what I felt now had gone beyond. The peace, tranquillity, happy speed—the motion of that boat we were in—was utterly inhuman. And it was wonderful! I felt the end of the voyage at once: by killing him I could kill myself. I would have to—I couldn't do anything else.

It was at that moment, when I saw it all—already existing, a few months off—that after two days of impotence my sex came back in a tidal wave. I made Danny do eight different kinds of stunts, and came so many times—*enough!* . . . And of course he knew very well what my orgasms were all about . . . No, not completely. He thought it was *his* death that I was fucking.

When he'd dressed, at the door, on his knees, the slave risked impertinence. "Sir?—will you swear?"

"Swear what?"

"That you'll do what you said you'd do."

"Don't dare ask me to swear!"

He persisted, however, in arms that tightened around my waist. In the dialectic of master and slave he is far my superior. "Please—sir. Please swear."

"But what could I swear by? I don't believe in God."

"You could swear by Yourself." One does capitals with a tone of voice. And Danny knows the trick . . . We all do!—damn us all!

"Then I swear, by Myself—that I'll kill you."

"How—?"

"By burning you to death."

His face in my belly: *"Thank you!*—sir."

December 8: A couple of hours later

No sex in this intermission . . . I took the same walk that I took that day, when Danny had left that afternoon: to the ruins of the Washington Market: an atmosphere commensurate.

You remember the note that Harold wrote Jim? This is the letter that should have been written. And wasn't, of course.

Dearest Darling Doctor Whittaker—may I call you Jim?—

At last, my love, we are one! You sort of suspect me, don't you, dear? There never yet was a masochist who didn't seek revenge somehow—except those like Dan Reilly, who already are truly dead. But the *poseurs* of obedience, who only like to feel their skin tingle, they always find ways to strike back. So you must be aware of who I am and that you and I are partners, Jim. I've suspected all along that my final accomplice would be a man. (Although I still remember with relish the six months that that married bitch Tina Farr put him through.) But that day, when the fool risked everything, your dry-ice "No!" was the richest moment in my life. The single syllable pierced his heart with an icicle, but it went through mine like a ray of white fire—for I knew I had found you at last! . . . love bug! As for how to proceed—just be yourself. Your family, your beauty, your promiscuity—it's wonderful that you're a

143

whore! That adds insult to the injury we intend him. And above all your divine indifference! It's precisely the combination that I've been waiting for. A word more about your whorishness though. I can work that wonderfully! You see, friendship may be democratic, but love is totalitarian. So don't neglect to tell him a single detail. Like that time last summer when you described how you got completely plastered and went to the baths and left the door open and lay down flat on your stomach and spread your husky legs apart and greased your tail—and then didn't even bother to look around to see what pot-bellied middle-aged queen was spilling his scum up your ass. A story like that is invaluable! I'm taking down everything you say—and I'll play it back to him, over and over! And I'm filming all your deeds—not just the ones that you do with him, but all that you tell him about. With that vivid imagination of his, believe me, he *saw* that scene! And now that he's declared his love, he'll see it even more painfully . . . The ladies too are an added thrust. That student nurse you told him you groped in Harkness Pavilion a week ago. (He can cope with them though. Emphasize the men.)

Oh and yes!—do remember this: he's told you he loves you, so *now* is the time, when you meet some chick or a groovy young intern, for you to say, "Now *there's* someone with whom I could have a love affair!" He'll get the point, all right, all right!

What else?

Just this: if love can be said to be one of those hectic and futile passions of his, he does love you. As that idiot Harold wrote to you. (I know him remotely, by the way—and he's no obstacle.) But it's more than that. He's addicted to you, Jim. So give him a fix every once or twice a week—and we'll keep him alive for as long as we can. That won't be for very long, I suspect. But we'll make this winter something special. For both of us.

We'll be in touch, lad!

Yours, in partnership,
Rumpelstiltskin

That accurate letter was never sent.

Nor was a pair of earrings—a superfluous, but preciously painful gift—delivered to Anne Black, with the following note: "With thanks for being a decent lady. Just keep it up, lass!" Signed: "An Unknown Admirer."

Nor was a postcard sent to Hempstead: "*Build* your pyre, you

maniac! Not yet—but soon, soon, soon!"
September 23, September 24, September 25.

> Three days to build a suicide:
> The first was Jim, the second Anne,
> The third was Danny, a real madman.
> A lock snapped shut. A process began.
> And look—how great!—I've hardly tried,
> And already the best in me has died.

December 17

Unbelievable! . . . My God, my God—the absurdity of human
existence! Its worst attribute.

Yesterday I was playing, on my lousy little machine, that can't
do it justice, the first act of *The Valkyrie*. Anne's present at
Harold's birthday party. (Another lovely thrust coming there!)
And who should give me a call, around five, as he's leaving his
office? Why yes!—Dr. James No-I-*don't*-love-you Whittaker. And
down to my Nibelungen apartment he came, me finding that I
could spare him, just barely, a couple of hours—or the rest of my
life.

I had his double Scotch ready as soon as he—"A new record, I
hear."

"And a great one. It's—"

"The first act of *Die Walküre*."

"Since when were *you* a Wagnerian?" Our encounters are all so
fast and sexual—except for Thanksgiving, and except for my gush
last September, and Harold's subsequent letter, which worked: he
returned—that I really don't know what his tastes include.

"Lad, I *come* from Manhattan! I heard Melchior and Lehmann
sing those roles in person."

"You prick! And I never did."

"Start the record over again." He began to take off his clothes.

Now here, just here, a scrap of something—bemusement, I
guess you could call it—was thrown in the cauldron of despair
and desire that I always feel when I'm with Jim. My intuition
lifted an eyebrow and whispered, "Jim likes Wagner. In fact,

Wagner turns him on. In *fact*—Wagner turns him on sexually! At least this piece does. Use it, lad!" But reason, wearing glasses and sitting behind her editor's desk, replied immediately, "That's ridiculous! Don't be absurd! Just wishful thinking." "We'll see," said intuition dryly, as I too took off my pants. And then removed the belt from them.

And reason, as always, like every other intellectual, was absolutely wrong!

He responded quickly, instinctively, to the music, as if he felt it in his skin. I, behind him, with my equipment, kept pace with his speed, accelerating him when I judged that a workable space lay ahead.

And—for the first time since I've made love with Jim—behind his back I was smiling. The nonsense of it! The idiocy! That one could use Siegmund and Sieglinde's duet to activate a masochist struck me—and struck again, like a bell in my head—as the richest joke I had ever been told. But don't think that the silliness of the scene interfered with me physically. Jim's excitement has always been my disease, and I catch it from him instantly. Yet in my stiff there was now a laugh . . .

That was yesterday.

And today—it's now about eight in the evening—the laugh, understanding (a margin around insanity) became power. Because the exact same thing has happened again. From the office his call at five o'clock, and down he comes. Of course there were drinks, and of course there were poppers—thank God that I've got an unlimited supply!—but the big thing was Wagner. And the tingle he kept from yesterday . . . It was even better this afternoon . . . "Let's hear that record again," he suggested.

"Okay," said I, in precise imitation of his affected ease.

But a whole ritual can become established in just two incidents. And I'll do it—God damn it! I'll do to that bastard what Pavlov did to his dogs! I'll program the motherfucker so that every time he hears *"Winterstürme wichen dem Wonnemond"*—he rears up on his knees and begs for the belt. And will I give it to him?—oh, I will! And when he begins to worry about marks—I'd say that comes around the time when Sieglinde says, *"War Wälse dein Vater!"*—I'll train him to spread the cheeks of his ass, already prepared with spit, KY, and—

Ah, one thing I do know: it's a use for Siegmund's "Spring

146

Song" of which Richard Wagner—who was another first-class Rumpelstiltskin—would have thoroughly approved! He would!

> Dear Richard—thank you! Thank you, sir!
> I call you "sir"—as he calls me.
> The three of us make love together.
> While listening to *The Valkyrie*.

And you out there, whom I'm talking to, when your roars of disbelief have subsided, I hope you all understand one thing: I am only telling you this—*since it's absolutely true!* . . . Oh my God, the absurdity of human existence! It's another good—no the very best—reason for—Hi there, *Götterdämmerung!*

December 17: An hour later

I am still so spaced out by this new thing with Jim! I wonder if anything else would work? . . . I'll buy the whole damn *Ring!* . . . Birgit Baby, they can hear you in Newark, and you've racked up another sale! . . . But no. Better stick with the dependable . . . It's enough. It'll add a lot of zest. I want these months violent, hectic, fun . . . And with music! I'll sing along too!

> You doctors out there—are you listening?
> Beware when—*Ho yo to ho,* Mr. Bing!

December 21

Boy, when the Management knows that you're packing your bags, they do try to supply you with some novel experiences!
    As it happened:
    Yesterday afternoon—and I have a visitor. *Ber*-nard Willington, no less. Earlier in the day the usual pained, strained call from Edith—"You're the *only* one—" Blah, blah—et cetera. So about four o'clock the gork and I—that's a great title for a kiddies' book!—are taking a walk. The afternoon is still pleasant then.
    I've prepared a story—stupidly—but I want to see—more as a

challenge to my talent than anything—if I can't get his unleavened little soul to open up to me again. The danger is going too close. So before the main event, I've ficted up a comedy.

We walk beside the park . . . "You want to hear a silly story?"

"I want to hear more about the Rat."

"There's no more about the Rat. For today. Nothing's happened to him since Thanksgiving." Except that he's beating his beloved's behind to the tune of the Wälsungs' leitmotifs. "But I'll tell you a silly story called—*Harold and the Clothes.*"

"Can I see where you live?"

What—? That stops this author dead in his tracks. "Barney, why do you want to see where I live?" His head swings silently away to that lonely private place of his. "I live way downtown."

"I don't mind," he apologizes for pressing his request.

So—"Taxi! Taxi!"—and the strange ride down Fifth Avenue, while I wonder what in hell I am doing.

"Now this isn't as nice an apartment as the one *you* live in—" His utterly defeating silence, as we trudge up the stairs. "Here it is—" He scans the dreary living room—"Needs paint, doesn't it?"—but finds, above the couch, one thing that's familiar.

"That's the Rat's picture of Harold!"

"So it is. It's on permanent loan to me."

He stares at the simple but beautiful sketch, hypnotized by reality: it's a vindication, irrefutable proof that everything I've told him is absolutely true.

"Now sit down. You want some—" What do you give a kid? "—milk?" I've got half a carton of skimmed milk—diet! diet!—in my wretchedly small refrigerator.

"No, thank you." He sits on the couch, right under the Rat's drawing of Harold—my God, I'll begin to believe it myself!—and as always his feet don't reach the floor: that most touching of danglings.

"Now do you want to hear a silly story?—or don't you?"

Without too much enthusiasm—"Yes."

"Harold—and the Clothes!"

"Harold woke up one morning, and as usual—*uh*-oh!

> Is there a puppy with a snuffly nose?
> No.
> Oh,—said Harold gloomily—Then it's the Clothes.

"Now the Clothes were quite a large and rather well-to-do family who lived in an apartment on the Upper East Side." Edith's living room is—? "The living room of their apartment was white, with lovely molding around the ceiling. And the furniture was the most beautiful and expensive that anyone could buy anywhere. The head of the family was Bluesuit, and he was a very handsome blue gabardine suit. And the lady of the house was Minkcoat, a lovely elegant—" Edith's is—? "—chocolate-colored mink coat. But there were a lot of other members of the family too. Such as Stole—do you know what a stole is?"

"Yes. Mother has one."

Progress!—progress! "And Tophat, and Suedejacket, and a couple called Blackshoes, and—oh, lots more! And off in their own case lived the Jewels: a very special part of the family. And did they ever know it! They were the most valuable part of the group, and they never let anyone forget it.

"And I'm sorry to say that all was not well with the Clothes family. They were constantly feuding and fighting and bickering with one another. Even—" The first risk. "—Bluesuit and Minkcoat, the heads of the family, who should have known better—even they had their quarrels sometimes.

"Harold drearily walked up to the Upper East Side. He liked the Clothes, but he did get a little sick of having to go visit them so often, and listen to their squabbling and then solve their problems—at least for the time being.

"He rang the bell, and Minkcoat let him in. 'Well, here you are at last,' she said. 'It's taking longer and longer.'

" 'I came as soon as I could,' said Harold, trying not to sound too much as if he'd have rather been somewhere else. 'Now what?'

"Minkcoat sighed wearily. 'Oh, it's Hanky and Necktie—as usual.'

"Hanky and Necktie were two young cousins, twice removed, who were in love with each other but always were having spats. 'Did you drag me all the way up here just because those two are at it again?' said Harold dismally.

" 'Well, it oughtn't to take long,' Minkcoat began her usual fret.

" 'Bring 'em in!' Harold interrupted her. 'I've got a feeling that somewhere in New York City there's something a lot more wrong

149

than *this,* for me!'

"Hanky and Necktie were summoned. And Bluesuit came in too. 'Morning, Harold,' he said with the reserve that one would expect from a blue gabardine suit.

"Hanky—who was yellow, with two lavender polka dot eyes in one corner—was sort of tearful—she usually was—and Necktie, red, with bright blue stripes, was his usual cocky self.

" 'Okay,' said Harold, 'let's have it.' He wanted to get this over with as quickly as possible.

"Hanky whimpered a bit, and then wiped her eyes with herself and said, 'Necktie called me—*flimsy!*'

" 'Oh my God,' Harold groaned. 'And I came all the way from Greenwich Village!'

" 'Well, she called me *rude!*' said Necktie defiantly.

" 'It's a major disaster, as you can see,' said Minkcoat superciliously. Do you know what that means?" . . . Respond!—respond!

"No."

"As if you were looking down on someone. 'Yeah!' growled Harold. 'So you ruin half my day!' He took a deep breath and collected a little angry magic. 'All right, here it is—and it better work!' He sang, in an irritable tone of voice—

> Hanky's not flimsy—
> She's just full of whimsy.
> Why shouldn't she be? It's her right.
> And Necktie's not rude—
> Just a little bit crude.

" 'Hmm!' muttered Necktie.

"Harold finished his song:

> Why don't you two kiss and make up? And *not fight!*

"The song had worked. It always worked—with Hanky and Necktie.

" 'Sweetie!' said Necktie.

" 'Darling!' said Hanky.

"They rushed into each other's material. And then went out on the balcony to look at the new moon.

" 'Now what brought all that on?' said Harold when they'd gone.

" 'The Jewels,' said Bluesuit.

" 'Who else?' groaned Minkcoat wearily.

" 'Those damn Jewels!' exclaimed Harold. He flung his arms up and down. 'It's time I had it out with them! Go get 'em!'

"Bluesuit went off to call the Jewels out of their case."

I'm about to launch my second risk here, when I happen to glance at my clock: an electric clock on the top of my bookcase. It's six.

"Good Lord, Barney!—we're way overtime! Your mother must be frantic!"

"Please tell what—" He begs to interrupt my progress to the telephone in the bedroom. And there I discover, through my unwashed windows, that it's snowing—howling!—a blizzard, outside.

"Edith?—Terry. I'm terribly sorry! I had no idea what time it was. That cab ride downtown, to my apartment, at rush hour—and I'm telling him a story—"

"Terry—it's all right." Her voice is not panicked, like mine. Why not? *Her* son. "As long as he's safe. You're nice, to let him see where you live."

"And it's *snowing* outside—!"

"Something off Cape Hatteras came in when it should have gone out."

A pause, full of unconcern on her part—full of God knows what on mine.

"Look, this may be just a squall," I find myself saying. "Suppose I give Barn—*Ber*—nard—his supper here?"

"Oh Terry—I can't ask you to do that!"

"It would actually be easier—" Plausibility objectifies my voice. "—than trying to find a cab right now. I suppose you'd scream—" And weary worldly wisdom makes a joke of the whole thing. "—if I gave him a TV dinner."

"I think that would be just lovely!"

"You've never had one, I see." Oh—I am *so* mature!

"I have. But *Ber*-nard hasn't."

"Then let me give him his first TV dinner. And I'll hustle him back by nine o'clock."

"You're an angel!"

No. I'm a sadomasochist. And if you knew that, Edith Willington, you'd fly down here on your broomstick—or send the police down on theirs.

"I'll call you before we leave—"

"Angel, Terry! How *can* I thank you?"

By not calling the fuzz, not telling the nation's librarians what their favorite author is really like . . . And not taking Barney away too soon.

"Bye, Edith."

The commitment—three hours: he is my responsibility—oppresses with an abrupt sensation of lifetime fatherhood.

"Hey, Barney—" However, I'm casual. No. But I hope I sound as if I was. "—you're having supper with me. Okay?"

"Here—?" Is it hope, indifference, despair in his voice?

"Right here. If it's okay with you." Or are those emotions only what I hear in myself? "It's snowing outside. I'll get you back in time for bed. Okay—?"

"Okay."

"Good! We're going to have something awful to eat—okay?"

"Okay."

"Great! TV dinners. You put them in the oven and—"

"The Rat eats them!"

"That's *right!* And you heat them up for half an hour, and presto—chango!—monosodium glutamate!"

"What?"

"Nothing. Which do you want? I've got—" Into my minikitchen. "—fried chicken—or turkey."

"Turkey."

"Why turkey?" I know, but tell me . . . Silence . . . "Why turkey, Barney?"

"Because it's Thanksgiving food."

Quite right!

For the next three-quarters of an hour I heat up two dismal TV dinners. And go on with my story:

"What happened then?" His question is for a narrative: life. *What happened then?*

While the TV dinners heat—"Then the Jewels glittered in: Pin,

Ring, Bracelet, Necklace, and Tiara. A tiara's like a crown. Now you know how they moved, don't you?"

"No." Is he vivid in his interest?

"Well, the way that Jewelry always moves. Minkcoat and Bluesuit sauntered along the way grown-up ladies and gentlemen do. And Hanky more or less drifted—and Necktie strutted on the ends of himself. But the Jewels—Ring rolls, of course, and Pin does a one-legged limp, and Bracelet and Necklace sort of slither. And Tiara—she rolls too—but much more grandly than little Ring.

"Now Harold understood the Jewels. He had just enough magic to do that. The thing was, they weren't like the rest of the Clothes. The rest of the Clothes had been alive—Minkcoat had, and Bluesuit too, at one time—but the Jewels were stones. Inanimate. Do you know what that means?"

"No."

Neither do I. Except I am it. "A something that's never been alive. And Harold understood their problem. They jabbed at each other and at everyone else, but they couldn't really be hurt because they were minerals, precious stones. They just were pretty. And sat around."

"Like Mother."

Oh wow!—the wrong identification! She was meant to be Minkcoat . . . Well—too late.

"So the Jewels wriggled in—and Harold gave them all a strong talking-to: on how they ought to behave, and they shouldn't cause quarrels, and things like that. And the Jewels just smirked and simpered and sparkled—'Of course!' 'Well of course, Harold!' '*Really*—you don't need to say that again!' "

Which one does he locate his mother in? She has no tiara, as far as I know. "And which one was it, do you think, who asserted that *she* at least had never said *anything* to upset *any*-one?"

"Pin."

That sumptuous diamond clip of hers—"Right!" Now how does one take the curse off a diamond pin, who happens also to be your mother? "And in this case Pin was telling the truth: she *hadn't* said anything nasty. It was Bracelet and Necklace who hatched the plot. One whispered to Necktie that Hanky was flimsy, and the other simply stated to Hanky that Necktie was downright rude. But Pin was perfectly innocent. So, as I said, Harold gave the Jewels his usual lecture, and they writhed and rolled back into their case again. Harold shook his head. 'It won't do a damn bit of good,' he said. 'They'll be up to some mischief in a week—you'll see.'

" 'Well *anyway*,' said Minkcoat, 'Hanky and Necktie are settled—temporarily.' She fluffed herself a little. 'Bluesuit, dear, would you mind?—I'd like to speak to Harold for a moment. Alone.'

"Bluesuit was a little put-out. 'I don't see why I—'

" 'Be a dear,' said Minkcoat, rather icily, as if she didn't mean 'dear' at all. 'It won't take a minute.'

"Bluesuit shrugged his shoulders—that's something that suits learn to do when they're young—and sauntered off.

" 'Now what?' wondered Harold gloomily. He'd suspected all along that something worse than Hanky and Necktie's quibbling was wrong in the Clothes family. 'Well, Minkcoat,' he said, 'what is it?' "

It's the third risk, old unevolved self. You're mistaken to take it.

"Minkcoat smoothed her collar—something she did very beautifully. 'It's Bluesuit and I,' she softly said. 'We're thinking—' "

What in God's name *was* I thinking of? (Another good reason to commit suicide: to keep oneself from meddling.) It was *Pin,* for him, not Minkcoat!

" '—we're thinking of getting a divorce.' Do you know what a divorce is?"

"Yes." And no sign at all that anything is amiss.

"Minkcoat went on, in a very mature tone of voice, 'I heard he was seeing Dressinggown.'

" 'Oy!' exclaimed Harold. You know what 'oy' means?"

"No."

"It's what Jewish people say when they mean 'oy.'" Harold hadn't expected that the trouble with the Clothes would be as bad as that. And now—I think that our TV dinners are done! The story's to be continued later."

Just as pleased as Punch with my smug and utterly unreal maturity, I pull the card table out from behind the bookcase—no room for a table in my midget kitchen—set it up, and—presto chango!—two steaming aluminum trays of monosodium gluta-mate. A Scotch and water for me, and milk for Barney.

I'm resolved, in my newfound authority, to make him talk. "What subject do you like best at school, Barney?"

"Reading."

"That used to be my favorite too. How are you at arithmetic?"

"Not very good"—in his eternally toneless voice. Which I now interpret as being a superficial distraction, while the wonders of my understanding are working deep within him.

I pry mechanical monosyllabic answers to mundane questions out of him. Has he seen Walt Disney's *Pinocchio*? (Yes.) Did he like it? (Yes.) Me too! Better than *Snow White*? (Yes.) I agree! And I pride myself, over tasteless fried chicken, that at last, apart from abstract words, I have reached a living child.

We finish. He can't finish all of his. But I, setting a good grown-up example, polish my artificial platter clean.

"Do you want to hear the rest of the story?" As I hear myself over now, I must have sounded like some fortyish spinster storyteller brought in to embarrass the third and second grade.

"Yes"—in his helplessness.

"Well—Harold demanded to know where Minkcoat had heard that Bluesuit was seeing Dressinggown.

"Minkcoat replied, sort of haughtily, 'I think that a person's confidence should be respected, Harold.'

" 'It's one of those Jewels!' said Harold angrily.

" 'As a matter of fact,' Minkcoat admitted, 'it is, but—'

"Was it Pin?"

His anxiety ought to have warned me, but "I don't know who—"

"It was Pin!"

Oh, I hope you Freuds know much more than I do, about a child's life. "Well yes, it *was* Pin. But it took a long time before Harold could make Minkcoat admit it. 'But *why* do you believe Pin?' Harold demanded to know. 'You've just seen how they act.'

" 'Oh of course.' Minkcoat ruffled herself again. 'But it's something that I've suspected myself—for quite a while.'

" 'Oy!' said Harold again, to himself. It really means—'This is bad and useless too—and why do people behave like this?'

" 'So I'd start working on a charm, if I were you,' Minkcoat advised. 'That is, if you think Bluesuit and I ought to stay together. And Harold—' Minkcoat smiled and her voice went as smooth as her fur. '—do try to make it something more interesting than that "Hanky's-not-flimsy-she's-just-full-of-whimsy" thing you recited before.'

" 'Don't knock that charm!' said Harold angrily. 'It worked, didn't it?'

" 'Well, but Bluesuit and I are *hardly* Hanky and Necktie,' Minkcoat sleekly advised him.

"Harold muttered something impolite, which Minkcoat, with her good manners, did not understand, but the gist of which was that Harold wished to hell that Bluesuit and she were as easy to handle as Hanky and Necktie. But he promised to think about the problem, at least. Then he left."

Now—are you all ready? Are you truly all ready for my phony grown-upness?—for an altogether unreal understanding that presumed it could comprehend that boy, while in fact it can't even begin to penetrate the child who lives in my own chest? Here it is: "Harold thought about the Clothes all the way home. He happened to be living at the time in a hardware store in the Bowery. You know where the Bowery is?"

"No."

"Not a very nice section. And way downtown. But Harold liked to live everywhere. So he had a long time to walk, and think. An especially long time, because the birds had eaten the bread-crumbs. And what he thought was this: if he used up some magic—and remember, he didn't have all that much left—and thought up a really powerful charm that was sure to keep Bluesuit and Minkcoat together—well, that was one thing. But what if they didn't *belong* together?" Get it? I had it all planned, in the course of a few more stories, to justify, hypocritically, his mother's divorce. "If Harold kept them together by a spell, why then he would be responsible. It was one thing to send Miss Amanda back to Iowa to open the bake shop, or to make Jake Moth crash-proof —that was what they both wanted. But to keep two people locked to each other, when they really didn't want to be—the thought of that sort of worried Harold. And you know how easily Harold got worried! His arms began lifting a little, up and down, as he walked along the Bowery. After all, he thought, Minkcoat might be much happier with big Camel's Hair Overcoat. He was someone who lived in another part of the Clothes apartment." Is Edith's fiancé—what's his name?—Frank Henderson!—is he big, I wonder? He must be, with a big pubic name like that. Isn't everybody from Denver big? I make a little smug mental note to check her out, without her knowing, so the next installment will be more close, more accurate. " 'And Bluesuit,' thought Harold, 'why he might be much happier with Eveninggown!' " This merely is fiction: rounding it off. " 'But I don't think he ought to go flirting around with Dressinggown though!' " And that's just the cancer of the imagination. God, when an author gets going there's no telling what he won't throw in! " 'Or Bluesuit and Reddress might do well together.' Harold started to chew his fingernails. 'Like Minkcoat and Overcoat.' Do you see why Harold was worried, Barney?"

"Yes." Does he? . . . *Does* he?

"I mean—Clothes have to sort themselves out. And find their right partners. Do you see?"

"Yes."

Does he? . . . Do *I*?

"So Harold was really worried by the time he reached the hardware store in the Bowery. He went in and sat down amid the nails and decided he'd have to think a lot more before deciding what to do."

The pregnant end of Chapter One. And this time I interpret his silence as being the dawning of Wisdom, Tolerance—all the TV Madison Avenue things that the human state's supposed to revere. I look at him in an overripeness—which now stinks in my nose—of self-satisfied kindness: a benign paternity.

And Rumpelstiltskin—never asleep, and he may have known what was really happening inside that kid—now prompts me with a holy thought. I look at the clock: it's half past eight. I look out the window: it's snowing still. There are flakes as big as elfin boats drifting in the street light's weird green glow.

I go to the telephone. "Edith?—it's getting on toward nine."

"Don't worry if you're a little late. This is a very special night."

"No, the thing is—it's still snowing pretty hard, and taxis'll be Impossible—I was wondering—wouldn't it make more sense if I kept Bar—*Ber*-nard—here overnight?"

(Is *that* what you're thinking? Men, yes. Women, yes. Dogs, cats, and kangaroos, yes! Oh, and especially the latter. But who knows? If I'd lived for another ten years—who knows? There's nothing like aging to rot, with a rampant imagination acting on boredom, a person's sexuality.)

"Oh Terry—I can't ask you to do that!"

No, dear Edith, I'm asking you. "Why not?"

"It's such an imposition—!"

"No it's not. I've been brainwashing kids all my life—" Why not admit it: it's so Poplike and nice. "However, I am *not* serving breakfast!" A taste of the acrid old Terry that they all know and trust, just to make her believe that I haven't turned into some old fart of a saint.

"You can have breakfast *here!*"

"Seven? Seven-thirty?"

"About in between."

"His face'll be washed."

"You *are* so good!"

"I've been dreaming about Albert Schweitzer lately. That may mean something. Night, Edith. I'll see you tomorrow."

Done. Almost before I knew it was going to take place. He is mine for the night. And if I knew what the night contained, I'd have hired a Kerry limousine, if necessary, to get him back.

"Hey, Barney—" I stroll back into the living room. "—you're going to stay here all night. Okay?"

The same look, the same intimidated question—"Here?"—as when I told him he was eating with me. Intimidation?—or is it his warped code for joy?

But my feelings are hurt. (Absurdly enough!) I'd expected recognizable pleasure, and his venturing disbelief—whatever it stands for—is alum on my enthusiasm.

Superciliously—you parents, do you too forget with your children?—I comment, as if he could grasp my tone, "You don't have to, you know. If you'd *rather* go home—" I am smirking haughtily: George Sanders putting down a disturbed little boy.

"No."

"You sure?"

"Yes."

"You *sure—?*"

His eyes fail, before mine. His head drops into subservience. "Yes."

God—I made him repeat it! I actually made that seven-year-old devastated child psychologically grovel in front of me.

> Destroying children, you all know—
> One does it with success
> If, when their minds, their hearts, say "no,"
> You make them just say "yes."

His abject defeat replaced my hurt feelings with guilt. "You'll sleep in my bed, inside—I'll make it all up fresh for you—and I'll sleep out here on the couch. It opens out."

And God forbid you should sleep out here, Barney boy—in patches of dried up female secretions and the crusted come of Jim and my other male mares.

To make up for having humiliated him, I do a big production of changing the bed: I yank off the old sheets—top and bottom both, both pillow cases—and throw them, unworthy, into a corner. And then the new linen: the smell of it—something that all of us love. The air of my bedroom, which isn't big, is filled with flying sheets—white sails—as I try to find precisely the right location: the middle crease exactly down the center of bed . . . Nope—no good! Another try—and the linen wings go up again and land—what a curious accident!—all over Barney. He stands there like a kidnapped child. I listen for giggling inside the white shape. And think that I hear it. But probably not—his hard breathing only: his being trapped, in fresh, flexible linen: his being Barney. I unveil him—"Whoopee!"—and he stands motionless—his face works in embarrassed joy—he is turned to stone in a sense of fun that he can't quite trust.

"Now get on the other side of the bed and help me make it—okay?"

He stations himself, and those little blubbery arms of his do yeoman work in straightening, folding, tucking.

"Did you ever make a bed before?"

"No."

"Very valuable experience." I learned at prep school where my parents shipped me off—at fourteen—as soon as ever they were able. "And *this*—is how you fold a hospital corner!" I do the elaborate ritual: the tight white angularity. "Nice, ay? Now you do it—" And he muffs it, of course. "—oh well, just cram the sheet in any which way." At least once, in this shrunken, deadened bedroom, a sheet is tucked in spontaneously. "Very good! A little haphazard around the edges—that's the boy! Push that in!—but really, Barney, very good!"

It's quarter to nine—and nine is the hour when everybody who's underprivileged goes to bed. I give him a half a glass of skimmed milk, which he doesn't really want. But I'm doing a nourishing thing in my heart. "I'll drink the other half. I know it tastes thin, but it's very good for you. Harold drinks it all the time."

"All right." He swigs down skimmed milk—my dopey diet: I don't like it very much myself—and Barney doesn't dig it—a grimace of drinking—but he finishes it, skimmed milk being Harold's drink.

"Very good!"

Ten of nine: ten minutes while this noble altruistic soul continues his developing, watering, nurturing, of this undernourished child. (I'd had about three Scotches—five—by now, and was feeling triumphantly paternal.)

More artificial talk: "Barney, who's your favorite teacher?"

He never boasts. At best he admits. Most often, as now, he apologizes: "Mrs. Dickinson."

"What's her subject?" Oh—I am so objective, so bright! I'm a laser beam, powered by five Scotches and water, of sheer intelligence.

"Reading."

It's nine o'clock. I've begun to supply his absent personality. He can sit there like a collapsed soufflé, and he only has to answer questions. My pride in making him talk at all pearls success around his every word.

More school talk. Then—"It's nine-fifteen. Time to turn in, Barney, I think—don't you?"

"Yes."

I don't know what he wants. Does he want to talk to me? He *can't* talk! Does he want just to stay awake? Too late: past nine—children turn into haggard wraiths after nine o'clock, don't they? That's what I was taught to feel. Does he want to hug me—and trust someone? I am far too obtuse in my half-squashed children's author authority to recognize that, if it *is* what he wants.

"Hop out of your clothes then! First time you've slept in your underwear, I'll bet."

His undressing—pitiful. Below shame at the flesh that he's living in, there is an uncertainty that ought to be called "existential," if such a pontificating word could be used to describe a seven-year-old: he doesn't believe he'll be there. But he is, despite himself—in white childish shorts.

And I have a new image for innocence. Up to now I've had three categories: people eating ice cream cones, people sitting in bathtubs, taking baths, and people wearing white socks, nothing else. To these are now added little seven-year-olds, in pristine underwear . . . Poor lad.

"Now into the bathroom. I've got an extra new toothbrush" (Alas for the need for clean toothbrushes!) "And it's just for you! Do you mind using Colgate toothpaste?"

"No."

"Is it what you use at home?"

"No. Gleem."

The details of his little domestic existence seem suddenly precious gems to me. "Well, Colgate's good too. Brush hard now." *Now*—what do I say? "Then wee-wee?" "Then here's the potty?" "Then have your good-night tinkle?" How *does* someone utterly ignorant of children advise a little boy to pee? I lift the seat of the john, and say, like a middle-aged trained nurse, "Then finish up—and we'll say good-night." And I leave the bathroom and close the door.

And in a raw fit of human curiosity I remain motionless, with my ear pressed against that bathroom door, listening to his small rain.

"Okay?" He comes out.

"Okay."

I had heard a little dribbling, but not much. Shall I ask him if he's really finished? No. Bladders are nervous things at best. When they're questioned they can actually become paranoid.

"Okay then—hop in!"

And here a lovely, funny, unexpected thing happens. Before mounting the bed too big for him, he hesitates, looks at me sheepishly—then ducks down quickly to look under the bed.

"Why Barney Willington! What *are* you looking for under my bed?"

"I thought—I was afraid—the Three-Legged Nothing—"

Before I know it, I've burst out in a gust of laughter, and snatched him up, hugged him, and set him down again. "Barney, the Three-Legged Nothing is *not* under my bed! I told you—Rumpelstiltskin adopted it. It's off somewhere, in the streets of New York, in a wattle hut. Now—quick!—under those covers—"

He creeps, crawls in—a wide-eyed little animal, in a prairie of linen.

"One pillow? Or two?"

"One."

"None?"

"No. One's what I have at Mother's." Not "What I have at home."

"One then." Do I kiss him good night? Does he expect me to? I'm sure Edith does: a meticulous cheek-peck or on his rigid lips. Suppose I bear-hug him again? Would it scare him? Would it save his life? Would it save *mine*? . . . I don't know what I want to do.

"Night, Barney." A compromise: I reach out my hand and ruffle the downy fur on his head.

And shut the bedroom door. "I'll leave it open a crack—all right? You won't mind if a little light comes through—?" Or is he old enough to have come to terms with the dark? (Dark stars are the most passionate.)

By now I am feeling like—*wow!*—St. Francis in no-trump! A little boy peacefully asleep in my bedroom—I think. A half-told, but fully prepared little story, which will justify his mother's divorce—I think. Am I ever a latter-day saint! . . .

I do believe it deserves a drink . . .

In an hour, I'm very pleasantly plotzed. If I'm going to go to bed this early, I've got to be. Or pop a couple of sleeping pills. So one more Scotch—I get a blanket out of my misplaced dopey closet, opening into the living room—unfold my unlovely couch, its discrepant colors and stiffnesses—and prepare to fantasize, over one last highball, on dreams of human decency . . .

It is almost eleven.

From the bedroom, through an unreal alcoholic veil of contentment, I begin to hear noises. They are not human noises: the groans, moans, whimperings of a young—unhuman—beast. They increase in intensity.

I am instantly sober. That's a funny thing, about my drunkenness: when something unexpected happens, or danger, or when I'm with someone tighter than I, I sober up at once. As if ice water had been thrown on my mind.

And those sounds now, from my bedroom, are infinitely more sobering than a drunken homicidal stud, or one of my editors who drinks, or the edge of the subway platform, along which at two or three in the morning I am doing a pas-de-one. They are sounds of fear, and also the realization that all that is feared has come to pass. A horrible moment. Like the assassination of a president: when the whole fabric of reality is shaken, and one wonders—will it hold? . . . That child goes on crying.

I sit up, sweating already. I'm prepared to cope with hustlers who want five dollars more—with floozies who claim that they'd like to see me again, no charge—with dim-witted librarians who want to know "*How* did you get the idea—?" But I'm *not* prepared to cope with a ruined child in the throes of a nightmare.

I widen the crack to the bedroom. His crying—screaming: the awful roar of pure panic—is not as old as he is. It's more like three or four than seven. He writhes beneath the blankets. I go in and turn on the light. Our physical contact has been minimal—but I've got to do *something*—and put my hand on the back of his neck, to brace him up. "Barney—Barney—" He's sitting now, but still—it sounds to me—hysterical. "Wake up, Barney. Do wake up!"

Then I realize—and my fear quadruples—his eyes are open: he *is* awake. This is a waking horror, for him. And he won't stop sobbing. His cries work deeper and deeper in me. Do you slap someone? (No, that's only in Susan Hayward movies.) Do you take them in your arms? Yes—but only if you've got the guts. His eyes blaze with infantile terror: the most appalling kind, because the titanic fear comes out of the utterly unknown, the world. And I too am descending, drawn by him, to his depths of dread.

I suddenly shout at him—*"Harold!"*

His screaming stops. He stares at me, uncomprehending but quiet now.

"Harold," my disciplined voice repeats, "says to stop it. Right now! Stop crying, Barney. It's all right."

He doesn't stop crying. Indeed, he *is* crying now—but humanly now: he's a little boy. The hysteria has vanished like a rampant ghost at the lifting of a wizard's wand. And my fright too begins to diminish. A devastating sympathy, pity, takes its place—for that lonely, isolated soul, sitting straight up, fists into his eyes, in that desert of bed: a terrible icon of all childish misery.

"Come on now, Barney—" I sit beside him. "—it's all right. What happened?"

"I—" gulping, "—dreamed—"

"Dreamed what?"

Gulp! Swallow! The sounds of a young distraught child whose feelings are verging on consciousness.

"Everyone has bad dreams sometimes."

"I dreamed—" Gurgle.

"What?"

"I dreamed Pin stuck me and I died."

I blurted out—"What was it like?"—at the same time that into the margin of sanity, that goes by the name of intelligence, there was scribbled a terse note: another failure, you inexperienced fool! My story, my allegory, a bust: it will have to be written off. But this, a day later, I find to be incredible: when that little wreck said he dreamed he died, I couldn't stop myself from asking him what it was like. And I honestly *did* want to know!

"I can't tell—"

Was it dark? Was it light? Was it fire? Was it ice? I came inhumanly close to pressing him for information. But the margin widens, as I watch his baffled floundering, and I say, "Never mind. It's just a dream." An imitation of comfort and wisdom that he—as well as I— can't believe.

For I notice a new anxiety, humiliatingly specific. His eyes dart sideways, frantically; beneath the sheet his knees tighten. I don't need to see the yellow stain—which I do see, in a couple of seconds—to know he's pissing. I pull back the sheet and the single blanket, and most journalistically I suggest, "Let's go into the bathroom, Barney."

He doesn't answer. Can't. His face is an ugly, fast, but unerasable sketch of despair. His shorts are running—he's unable to stop it. How much self-consciousness can the degradation of a seven-year-old have? (I remember once Pop found me looking at mother's sewing kit and sweetly asked, "You planning to do a little sewing, dear?")

I pick Barney up, leaky faucet and all, and carry him into the bathroom. And stand him up in front of the john. And lower his shorts. Still dribbling, he is. And I hold his tiny tap while he finishes his last few sporadic spurts.

"Now *this* underwear will have to be replaced," I say, and make a pragmatic fact of it—with a joke in the back of my voice, I hope.

"I'm sorry—" He weeps and wee-wees at the toilet bowl. Poor little bugger!

"It happens to the best of us." I coolly—except that this is the Impossible: I have never had to take care of a child before—slip him out of his shorts. "Do you think that you'd fit in a pair of mine?"

He looks up at me with decaying embarrassment, with a question—Am I putting him on? "I don't know."

"Well, you surely won't fit in my pajamas! And I don't have pajamas anyway. So how about a pair of my underwear?"

"All right."

I get him a pair of shorts and a T-shirt—he's pissed his own underwear top—and make my second production of the evening in getting him into them. They don't fit beautifully! He really does look comical. "You want to see something funny?" I stand him in front of the full-length mirror on the bathroom door.

He looks at himself—and doesn't laugh. But I think something in him *may* be laughing, would like to laugh, at least like to smile—his quizzical look is clearly asking, "Is that white goony thing in the mirror there *me*?"—but being Barney, the laughter can't escape.

I take him back into the bedroom, where we're greeted with yellow wet reminders. He turns away from the scene of shame. The mattress must be soaking too. Again, the pragmatic, the eminently realistic Terry Andrews: "How about if you bunk in with me for the rest of the night?" And that look in his eyes: the unknown, the disbelieved. "An' I'll whop you if you gouge me with your elbow or take more than your half of the couch!" Does this rough-and-tumble talk—slang—put him at ease? I don't know. (It appeals.)

But he says, "All right."

He lies down, I get the pillow from the bedroom, fortunately untouched by his flood, and pull the red blanket over him: wooly, wine-colored, and comforting. I tuck in the edges. "That's really Woolyville, ay man?" For good measure—*liar!*—because I want to—I jounce him around beneath the blanket. *"Woolywoolywooly-wooly—!"*

I turn off the light. That organic glare from the street light comes in through the blinds. I walk around the bed and slip in beside Barney.

And there we lie, side by side.

The room is full of our wakefulness: there's no one dozing, no one falling asleep.

"Barney," I say, "there's something that I forgot to tell you. Before Harold left the Clothes' apartment, he had another talk with the Jewels."

Is he interested? Yes. In a minute his voice beside my head: "Did he?"

"He went over to their case, and there they all were—sort of slithering and rolling and curling around. 'Well, *look* who's here!' said Ring. 'It's our little Mender-of-broken-romances!'

" 'Mr. Advice-to-the-lovelorn!' Tiara chuckled huskily.

"But they couldn't get Harold angry or upset. It just made him sad to think that people like the Jewels had to go around jabbing—" No, he said, "*stuck* me." "—had to go around sticking other people. He really didn't know what to say, so instead of saying anything he sang softly to them all—

> Oh rubies, diamonds, emeralds—
> You beautiful rare Jewels—
> I know you're only minerals—
> That needn't make you cruel.

"The Jewels stopped twisting and snaking around. And Harold

decided that as long as he had them listening, he'd give them a little warning.

> Be happy in your beauty, and
> Try not to be perverse.

"That means nasty.

> I *could* turn you to simple sand—
> Or something even worse!

" 'Well really!' exclaimed Tiara loftily. Being something of a crown, and also the largest of the Jewels, she enjoyed becoming indignant. And she did it awfully well. 'I've *never* been so insulted!'

" 'What does he mean by—"worse"?' asked Ring a little worriedly.

" 'I think he means something—organic!' murmured Bracelet nervously."

What I mean is shit. But I can't say that to Barney. So I say—

" 'I mean vegetables!' said Harold. 'All those emeralds in you, Tiara—I'll turn them into little green peas!'

" 'Oh Harold!—you wouldn't!' Tiara got flustered—very rare for her—and rolled back into a corner and flopped back upside down.

" 'And your rubies, Necklace,' said Harold sternly, 'I think they'd make lovely red kidney beans!'

"Necklace didn't say a word. She collected her links and tried to hide in a fold of the velvet case where they lived.

"Now I hate to admit it, but Harold was getting a kind of a kick out of scaring the Jewels like this. It was Bracelet's turn next. 'And about you, Bracelet—' Harold folded his arms majestically. '—such lovely sapphires!' " But, dammit, there aren't blue vegetables! "He clicked his fingers. 'I'll turn you into a string of blue jelly beans!'

"Bracelet moaned. And collapsed as only a bracelet can."

"But *Pin*—!" Barney interrupts.

And thank God—he is following!

"Oh, for Pin Harold had a very special warning. 'And I'll turn Pin into a piece of crystal candy!' He tightened his eyes at her and sang—

And I'm telling you right now, you Pin—
Behave! And don't you be malicious!

"That means naughty.

I'll give my Barney my permission
To eat you. And you'll be delicious!

" 'I have this friend, Barney,' Harold explained, 'and I'll send him over to gobble you up.' "

Another *coup d'inexpérience*, meddling, madness: I've told him he could gobble Big Mama up. Better that, though, than pricked to death by her.

(*Pricked to Death*—another great title for a children's book! Those who live by the sword shall die by it too!)

There's no motion, no sound, on my couch. Have I taken the killing point off Pin? Or is this tale a failure too? Is he bored? Have I put him—"Barney," I whisper, "are you asleep?"

"No." And he too is very whispery, in the darkness, imitating my tone.

"Well anyway—that's what I forgot to tell you. Harold had this talk with the Jewels a little while before he left."

"Did they—?"

"Did they what?"

"Behave?"

"Oh yes! He scared them good. They all behaved. Especially Pin. She decided that to be made of precious stones—to be beautiful, the way she was—wasn't such a bad life after all. Her diamonds brightened. And in the new light that she shed, she was happy and content."

Is that the end? . . . No—it has to include him too.

"And it was a good thing for them that all the Jewels reformed. Because otherwise Harold *would* have sent you around to gobble them up! You'd have gone too—wouldn't you?"

"Yes!" His excitement invisibly lights the dark stars . . . At last!

"Let's get some sleep now."

My right arm cups his pillow. I believe he feels its pressure. And the scent of a child's hair!—the burgeoning young animal. Even my Barney's hair smells like that. And all his burgeoning has been stolen already.

In half an hour his breathing tells me that he's asleep. And I need to see what he looks like. The light would be too bright. I get up as stealthily as I can, and go to the window, and raise the shade. That aqueous luminescence floods the room. He *is* asleep, but his face hasn't changed. As awake, he still looks worried, puzzled—as if something he'd been expecting was not going to happen after all. The resentment that he ought to feel is transformed into something worse—acceptance and despair. I think he must be the *oldest* child—in his eighties at least—that I've ever known. I pull the shade and creep back into bed, next to him.

I sleep a few hours, eventually. And I know I dream. But I don't remember what.

Toward six I wake up. He is still asleep. I lie beside him, waiting: an hour . . . Then wake him up . . . I feel nothing. I'm numb . . . I make him get up, brush his teeth, get dressed.

And I want to feel nothing! . . . Barney's numbness too is, reassuringly, back.

A taxi to Edith's apartment house. I say good-bye in the lobby. "Tell Mother I've got some important appointments—I didn't have time to come up. Bye, Barney."

He doesn't say anything. He turns, with that doomward trudge of his, and enters the elevator . . .

I don't want ever to see him again!

I come home—to you, my fictitious companions—and tell you what has happened . . .

> Oh Barney, you disturb me so,
> You hopeless, wiped-out antichild.
> There's nothing in your face but sorrow.
> Asleep too, have you never smiled?
> In sleep at least one should find peace.
> You don't. You scream and cry.
> You dread the night—it's no release—
> Ah well, but so—

December 21: Fifteen minutes later

I've changed the bed. His yellow stain, dried now, was all over both sheets. I felt a sudden urge to kiss it—but being the sophisticated gnome I am, I manfully restrained myself.

December 22

I should have known she was plotting generosity. She always is—and especially now: the holidays.

Helen was going out later on with some friends, but the two of them had half decorated the big Christmas tree in the living room when I arrived. The three of us had dinner together, Helen very articulate and urgent on the subject of Civil Rights, and Anne very impressed and I very earnest and a little bored as we listened to her arguments—with now and then a glance at each other to share the strangeness at this transformation, more violent and beautiful than the larva into the butterfly. She apologized, as she raced through dessert, for having to dash off and meet two classmates. We had coffee in the living room. Sanka for me, of course. (Anything real would keep me awake.) And there stood the unfinished Christmas tree.

"A year ago she'd have rather died than not put the last ornament on herself."

"The star on the top?"

"John used to make a ritual of having that be the last. And when Helen was old enough—" Her face, approaching middle age, was steeped in melancholy, and seemed forlornly pretty. "Well—that's what it's all about, I guess. Growing out of Christmas trees."

"She'll grow into them again," I philosophized. (Maturity?) "In a different way."

"I hope so." She stared at the whole unknown future. "But not with me. And in the meantime, buster—" Jauntiness. "—that leaves you an' me to finish with the tree! How are you at hanging icicles?"

"I majored in it at Harvard." (My ancestors welled in New England, but then they all dribbled all over the place. *Mayflower* bilge we were. I'll try not to boast about that. But you must have guessed it already. What sensibility but a decayed Puritan's would enjoy the things I do?)

"Oh, and speaking of Christmas trees—" She went into the bedroom and came back with a little midget pine on a stand. "—you've got to do this one too."

"Who's it for?"

"A nobody-else friend. You know—one of those once-a-year people. That string of little green and blue lights will do the whole thing. And this box has some green and blue ornaments."

"This person likes green and blue, I take it."

"It's a nice combination."

We decorated a while, carping good-naturedly at each other's choices, sometimes praising—"That bird on that branch is *brilliant*, Anne!" "I rather thought so too"—and the job got done.

"Do you have a star for this little tree?"

"No. But there's one white bulb. If you lift the string up, so the white bulb's on top—"

"Like this?"

"Very nice. It'll do for a star, won't it?"

"In a pinch." She rummaged in a cardboard box. And brought out a five-pronged star, with different-colored bulbs at each point. "Can you reach it without a chair? For the big tree?"

"I think so—"

"A little way this way. Perfect! Stop! Plug them both in!"

The big tree: multicolored lights, a treasure trove of ornaments —and the little one: a conscious restriction to blue and green, but elegant. "They're great."

"They *are* sort of great, aren't they? And now—" She was brisk in her festivity. "—since the Yuletide spirit's upon me—we're going to have some mulled wine!"

" 'Mulled' wine—?"

"Have you ever had mulled wine?"

"No. I thought it went out with Nicholas Nickleby."

"Well neither have I. But I've got the ingredients and a recipe, and I'm going into the kitchen and mull us some wine!"

"Can I watch?"

"Don't be dirty!"

She looked at the Christmas trees for a second: a dissolving expression, without any anger. "It takes you back—"

"It doesn't me."

"You and your family didn't decorate your Christmas tree?"

"Mom and I did, sometimes. Pop, never. He'd come back from the office, see it there, say 'beautiful,' and start reading *The New York Times*. Most of the presents were gifts from his patients anyway."

"But you and your mother did decorate it—?"

"It wasn't a ceremony—" Oh wasn't it! "The only thing—"

"What?"

"Well, the thing of Christmas, for me, was stockings."

"Hung up in front of the fireplace?"

"Yes."

"Tell me."

"It's nothing. It's just that the stocking bit felt more like Christmas to me than the tree."

My crisp response cued her into the kitchen. "Be right back, Terry."

"Mull well, my dear." . . . That game I played—"Peekin' Aroun' the Corner"—to see my stocking hung up.

Anne left, and for some reason that I don't understand, I felt a kind of blissful apathy. I began to groove on the Christmas trees: the lights on the big one were constant, steady—the lights on the little one flashed on and off. And in that difference—enduring multicolored lights, blue-green lights winking off and on—between them the stars were released. It was like being high on pot. The grand abstraction—reality—was possible, *there!* . . . The thing of Christmas, which at one time meant much, had been processed into philosophy.

"Mulled wine!" Anne warned, as she came back in with a tray, two glasses, a pitcher. "It isn't hard at all. You just heat it, add spices—those two big things are cinnamon sticks—and serve."

"So serve. I'm thirsty."

"Lush!"

"Good!"

"Good?"

"Really good!"

We settled into a lulled two hours. It was one of those intervals of sanity that I sometimes have with Jim. With Anne the sensation is dulled mellowness—assisted last night by the wine, I'm sure—not the cold clarity of understanding, as when I see Jim as simply a man. In those moments I live in her past, her present, young Helen, what she expects her future to be. She tries to share, to talk about me, get me to talk—but it has to be all her, and I'm only there as a torpid witness—to my own absence . . . As are all of you.

It lasted until eleven: her Christmases on Fifth Avenue, then on Central Park South, with John, then without him, in Murray Hill. Her mourning by now had been compressed, like coal into diamond, its wet sentiment squeezed out leaving only the valuable.

"I better get going."

We came to our exchange of presents: the last phase of our pre-Christmas evening together. Mine to her: the complete recording of *Die Frau Ohne Schatten*—since we'd liked it so much two years ago. (And after all, she'd given me Jim's sexmusik. A luscious irony, that.)

And hers to me: a turtleneck sweater, from Sak's. "I've never owned one before!"

"I know."

It was white—splendiferous! "How did you know?"

"When we went to the Met—to *Rheingold*—you saw a man wearing one instead of a formal shirt. And you said that you thought it looked tacky."

"So that's why you got me this—?"

"The way you said 'Tacky' I knew you were eating your heart out for one."

"The clever little cunt you are!"

We exchanged the holiday kiss that one only gives before Christmas.

"And that's not all." With the glee of a twelve-year-old—benign deception a success!—she sprang her surprise. "Here's your Christmas tree—"

"My Christmas tree—?"

"When you asked me who it was for, I was going to say 'a shut-in,' 'a recluse'—I don't know *who* you are—" She was laughing triumphantly. "—so you wouldn't recognize yourself!"

But that gift, the blue-green little Christmas tree, sprang a trap beneath me. My contentment had been abstract—the mere idea of

Anne's immediate happiness—but the solid gift, which smelled like pine, was pine, was decorated with *Christmas tree lights*, winking, visual phenomena, let in the world with a rush.

"And don't worry how you'll get it home! I've thought about that too." So preoccupied with her *coup* that she didn't notice my own collapse, she stormed into the bedroom and returned with a sheet. "Now put the tree in the middle. Right! And we lift up the ends of the sheet like this—and we tie them together—and we've got—" A shrouded white shape. "—what looks like a kidnapped child!"

"My God, it does!" I tried to meet her euphoria.

"You'll *never* get back to Greenwich Village! The cops'll arrest you."

" 'It's just a little boy I'm abducting, offither.' "

She went into another riffle of laughter, propping her mirth with one hand on my arm. And as she rose, in exactly the same proportion, the scales of my own emotions sank. I wish I *had* been smoking pot—no, you can go on some bad trips too. Because the Christmas trees, both of them, the covered and the glimmering, stopped being abstractly beautiful and were turned by memory—and by present fact—into weapons. The bulbs of the open tree—red, yellow, blue, green—began to burn inside my brain, as if I was back in the sun porch at home, where the Christmas tree always stood, and the ornaments were organic growths—malignant, every one.

Worse: Anne's hand wouldn't leave my arm. She was getting high on *her* pot—joy—and I felt it evolving into desire. Thank God her daughter was home! It would have been another disastrous episode like that one in September. Not even the fantasies of nonbeing could have gotten me through love-making last night.

"Too bad Helen's here—"

I kissed her hair, since I knew I was safe. "She does turn up at the most inopportune moments—"

"Of course we could both take this Christmas tree home—"

Her perpetual dream, since I've known her, is to make love in my apartment. She's been down here a couple of times—demanded that. We've had dinner in the Village, but always gone back to Murray Hill. But her hinting, pretty obvious, that she'd like to have sex in the bed where I slept— "It's so tiny, this bedroom! Instant claustrophobia! How'd you ever get this big bed in here?"—her hinting has gone blithely ignored. And as for the place as a whole—"Oh Lord, Terry, this needs paint!"—it's exactly the same whoever you are: a psychotic welfare worker, or an eager widow from Murray Hill, or a black cleaning lady.

"—if I'd be allowed in the sacred precincts."

"The sacred dilapidated precincts."

"Oh Terry, that apartment could be so nice! If you'd just *use* the fireplace—!"

"All right—I'm a slob. But it doesn't make very good sense for you to come back there tonight. And then come reeling around back here at three or four in the morning. When Helen's a senior, or junior maybe, we can pull those tricks on her—" Too late then—blessed time! Will she remember these words? I hope not. Don't, Anne! "—but not on a freshman."

"Okay, Dr. Spock!" Short-circuited, she lifted her head from my chest, with a grimace at the practical world of a parent. "But anyway, merry Christmas, Scrooge!"

"Merry Christmas, Anne." The relief of being free, being on the way out, made my kiss sincere. "And say all the good words to Helen. Like merry Christmas, and happy Chanukah, and congratulations on being a woman."

"I will." Her arm within mine as we walk to the door. Me holding my kidnapped child by his sheeted top knot. "You ought to walk home with that. Just to see what adventures you'll have! Apart from the cops. But it's snowing again."

"Is it?" The New York City snow, this year—clean—means strangely much to me.

"Started while we were eating."

"I'll take a taxi and skip the Dickensian scene."

"Oh—your Care Package." She went into the kitchen. "Two lamb chops and a bottle of our mulled wine."

"You've *got* to stop—!"

"Have a good Christmas in Philadelphia."

Oh, I will! If I'm lucky—twenty-four hours of deadness. "It's just a duty thing. I have to check in once a year."

"I wish you were free for New Year's Eve—"

"So do I. But when your publishers invite—"

"I know."

"Good night then. Thanks."

Her fingertips flickered up—good night—but before she shut the door, she said, "At least once in a lifetime everybody should be given a completely decorated, completely illuminated Christmas tree!"

I found a taxi, and with that dead white shape in my lap—the driver did not inquire about it—drifting into the emptiness I sought, I came home.

December 23

Carol Whittaker called this morning.

"It's insulting to be this late—but if you were free for Christmas dinner—"

"Stop being so polite." The whole thing of Jim—his family, like another limb: articulated, fingers, wrists—was suddenly sensitized. "But I have to go down to Pennsylvania. To see my family."

"I know that it's awfully late—"

"It's not that. But I *have* to go."

"Then here's something else. We're giving a party, on New Year's Eve—"

"Ah! That's more possible." And the hell with my publishers! It's a mistake to know them personally anyway. I can always call them up two days later and say I had *A Stumik Ake*! (The name of my third book—and one you teachers liked very much. Despite the spelling so criticized in all the school journals.)

"It's not going to be very interesting—"

"Then *why* are you inviting me?"

"Because we want you to *come*!" She met my aggression evenly. "I mean—there'll be people from the hospital—some friends of Jim's—"

"Not doctors—!" Horrified.

"Yes, *doctors!* And their wives. Who can be even worse."

"You know, I'm a fugitive from a medical family."

"Then all the more reason—"

"Too late! I'm coming. You asked me—"

"Any time after seven." A pause occurred, while Madame Hostess shifted gears into someone whose first name was Carol. "Is there anything new?"

"Not really—" Except I'm now flogging your husband to some of the most sumptuous love music ever composed by mortal man. "—nothing much. And with you?"

"Oh, you know the life a housewife lives—"

"As a matter of fact, I don't, no."

"You writers!" she laughed, in that dusky contralto. "I expect you all know everything!" I know why he loves her.

"Don't believe what it says on our dust jackets."

"You haven't started on anything new—?"

"No." Her silence came close, pressed me. "Don't take it as a personal insult."

"I don't."

"I'll see you then—" I created an artificial space—no Whittakers—between today and the end of the year. But chances are I'll screw Jim at least once. "Say hello to Ben."

"I will. He'll be glad you're coming." She hung up.

So will *he!* With any luck our old friend—whom we haven't seen for quite a while, have we?—can do an even better job on me than he did on Thanksgiving.

December 25: Merry Christmas, folks!

Back at last. And better than I expected. My induced deadness—a lot of Scotch and valium—got me through the day pretty well. (Good ol' Val! Prince Valiumt.)

It's ten o'clock now. That goddam Penn Central Railroad! We were stalled for half an hour, outside of Newark . . .

To the baths? To the brothels? Just to bed? . . . Oh no!

> To the baths? To the brothels? Can't sleep. Don't know where.
> To black holes?—S-M star-bars? I really don't care.
> But out! Can't sleep. So I can't go to bed.
> Drink? Yes. Pills? Yes . . . Rhyme now. "—ahead"? "—said"?
> Come on, my witnesses! What rhymes with "bed"?

January 1

As it happened:

It wasn't the first trip to Riverdale, so R.'s anticipation wasn't quite as vivid as it had been a month ago. Still, that house and its occupants is the seat of maximum discomfort, so he was pretty thrilled anyway. And besides it was New Year's Eve. Rumpelstiltskin far more than Harold or I delights in wearing funny hats and blowing noisemakers. Of course there'd be none of that at this party. But Rumpelstiltskin's noisemakers are totally soundless. Like his knives and his torches, and pins and needles, they all are internal.

On the ride up I was loose and cool and bemused: a transitory mortal state which I thought might last for as long as six hours—with the usual liquid fortification.

I arrived at eight. And a flock of children opened the door: three girls in the vanguard, Ben behind them, hovering in his uncertain space, and in his arms—"What's his name?" I enthused. (I do like dogs, you kennel club members. Except that damn collie!)

A silence—full of private mirth. Much giggling.

"Benedict!" I suspected that I was the butt, so I made myself stern, adult, vulnerable. "What *is* that puppy's name?"

His dead eyes search, and find my voice. "It's Harold!"

More uproar: affectionate, and at my expense. Ben lifted the puppy—a corgi, I think—at an angle to my arms. "Well, at least it isn't Terry," I said to Carol, the spectator in the hall who dramatized the scene by seeing and enjoying it.

" 'Harold' was Ben's command."

"I accept the name with gratitude." With a formal bow that Ben couldn't see, I replaced the puppy in his arms.

Then into a crowded living room, devoid of the children's life in the hall. Jim stood up as I came in, with that private look—"Hi, lad! We're sex!"—that he always gives me in public, and that knocks me out, and we shook hands.

Introductions—which I will not bore you with, except one. The interesting guest—"This is John Ciodotti"—was a man somewhere between forty-five and fifty, and still tautly good-looking. When Carol and I had gone the rounds, and I was trying to put

178

husbands and wives together, I asked which one he was married to.

"Oh John's single. He runs an art gallery on Sixtieth Street." She said it quite innocently, unaware of the devastating deduction: the logic of certain professions and sex.

I read the history instantly: he was one of Jim's old tricks, now turned into a family friend. He'd appraised me closely, perhaps guessing—or knowing, if Jim and he were still confidants—that I was the current contender. I wondered for a moment—will I become one of those lonely old fags who fall back on the sentimental generosity of familied friends when the desolate holidays roll around? (But then the use of the verb—"will?"—tickled my funny bone.)

"We've known John for fifteen years," said Carol.

(Time! Time! Until I realized that I love Jim, time had been for me what he is for all you: an expert anonymous waiter, who takes the courses of life away so unobtrusively that you're hardly aware he exists at all. Until he presents the bill. But loving someone changes one's chronology. It dismembers your history as well as your heart, and you measure your epochs against his or hers. Fifteen years ago Jim was shacked up with that man. Fifteen years ago I—ah, Time! The sweetest sensation you have to give, like coming to the end of a very good book, is to know you are strictly limited.)

The redoubtable Mary Wicks came in with shrimps and cocktail sauce. "Hello, Mista Andrews." (And she did say "Mista." Sorry. We both are old school.)

"Hello, Mary. How do you like the new addition to the household?"

She gave me the wry look of one who has cleaned up puddles. "I'll like him better in a couple of weeks."

The children had been fed already, but were being allowed to stay up late—"but *not* till twelve!" Carol's contract read—and romp around the living room, while we so-called grown-ups boozed ourselves.

Jim ignored us all and sat on the floor and played with them. As before, I couldn't keep my eyes off this father and his kids. His degree of participation—a double role: both as an equal and their Pop: *The* Adult—was perfection, and beautiful to watch. And that gesture of his, hands suddenly covering Benedict's eyes, was as weird and emblematic and indecipherable, as it had been on Thanksgiving.

Carol moved in on me with a familiar questioning expression.

"Now don't you start!" I warned.

"I'm not going to say a word."

"I'll begin another book when you take up singing and dancing again."

A flush began. "That'll never be."

I was feeling good: the Scotch, Jim, there, this woman. Her blush was a cue to tickle a little. "I'll bet you do right now. Behind closed doors. I'll bet when the kids are off at school, and Mary Wicks is down in the laundry, you lock yourself in your bedroom and dance around like crazy. Naked!"

Her contralto rumbled sumptuously. "No I don't—"

"Yes you do! I know what you suburban housewives are like. Beneath those domestic exteriors, inside those Bonwit suits, you're drunken maenads, all of you!"

"Lord, I wish we were!"

More flirting, more laughing—and I with my eye on her husband and children, deluding myself that she didn't notice.

In a pause in my ribbing, out of nowhere except her watching, she said observingly, "You have the strangest smile when you're looking at Jim play with the kids."

It took me aback, and jolted me into a moment of honesty. "It's the smile I smile whenever I'm looking at human beings."

"I'd love to know what's in it."

"I can tell you exactly: respect, contempt, envy—and puzzlement. And love."

Her eyes quizzed me for a minute, and made me feel like an artifact dug up in Mesopotamia, or a dinosaur egg embedded in glacial ice. She shook her head, now pretending to smile at her own ignorance. "You live on a whole different planet, don't you?"

"I only wish it was inhabited."

She was going to object, at what must have seemed like a vulgar plea for a compliment instead of the simple truth it was, when the children flocked around us. They had finally agreed to go to bed, Jim having delivered a *paterfamilias*. Kisses. Wishes of "Happy New Year!" And then Jim pulled his surprise. He'd gone into the hall, and came back with a box that he held above the children's heads: a place of living mystery. A couple of minutes of relished suspense—he opened it, turned it upside down—and out cascaded the noisemakers and funny hats that I thought I was not going to see: a gift for people the proper age to enjoy them.

Still acting daddylike, but benignly now, Jim gave permission: "There may be one extra half-hour tonight. For rumpus and other necessities. Upstairs! And there *also*—" Lordly *largesse d'esprit*. "—may be one minute of rumpus down here!"

A *coup de confusion!* The girls scrambled to snatch up the gaudy equipment. But Jim picked out the wildest hat and put it on his son, and put a noisemaker in his hand. A glorious and legitimate din began—because it arose from a crowd of children. I couldn't hear all he was saying, but Jim bent next to Ben's ear and talked softly. I heard the word "red": he was describing his paper hat to his son. Ben nodded enthusiastically. Jim whispered something more, and the boy blew a blast on his noisemaker. His dead eyes jiggled, with their crazy questing little flickers.

I must have been staring at them too intently; someone's eyes, I felt, were fixed on me. Carol Whittaker's stare was dawning somewhere between ignorance and quizzical understanding.

I felt my cheeks get hot and gloppy. "Now you're looking at me the way you said I was watching your kids."

"I can tell you there's no contempt in it."

"Look, Carol—don't misunderstand—"

"I don't."

"—what I said. The contempt I feel is for—"

"I *don't* misunderstand!" Her expression went general, and surveyed a hostess's living room. "Jim—I think that may be enough, don't you?"

It was not enough for Jim. He looked up from his children's madcap delirium with a boy's expression of—"Aw, Carol, come on! Not yet!" (They have that between them too, this husband and wife. She sometimes summons him—his face changed now—into proper maturity.) "Okay, you bandits!" he ordered. "Upstairs!"

And away they herded. I was near the hall and saw the girls fly. Ben went last, his hand drifting like a radar antenna above the banister.

181

The lull in the living room—abrupt absence of children—made me feel as if the party was over. It wasn't. How much it wasn't I had no idea. If I'd guessed, I'd have had no appetite. Excitement, desire, kills hunger.

Carol trooped us into the dining room. I was seated on her right, and on mine—it was fortunate, in a way: a woman you only needed to look at probingly every now and then to keep her talking, and no question of needing to listen, much less of answering.

Dinner parties—indeed all parties—have had a dispiriting effect on me for about the past ten years. I remember how, as a child, I wondered what it would be like to be grown-up. And this was it: the emptiness of this conversation, this postponement of life—when life was still possible—the margin around reality: adult existence. That's what it's turned out to be.

My dismal reverie, at having arrived at all that I'd looked forward to as a child—this table of large human beings who utterly bored me, except for the one I adored and his wife—led to even more macabre thoughts. It occurred to me that there was one way that this dinner party could be brought to life: the Impossible—the truth. If any one of us simply stood up and tapped a glass, and then spoke the whole truth—if I said quietly, like a metaphysical master of ceremonies, "My fellow guests, Jim and I are this, and we do this"—if one single word of truth were spoken, anywhere, by anyone, I feel certain this world, not just this house in Riverdale, would instantly vanish. Because a fact of total truth, encountering the lies we all live, like matter meeting antimatter, would combine with it violently—and end in nothingness.

The temptation to test the theory grew. Grew dangerously. I'd had quite a lot to drink. With a bow I could say, "Carol, and ladies and gentlemen, I happen to be in love with that handsome man at the end of the table. And I'm whipping and fucking him."

"Carol—" I aborted the urge with a little small talk: the ideal's best antidote. "—do you ever get into the city?"

"Sometimes. For shows and things."

"I mean in the day. If you'd like, we could have lunch."

"Are you making a date with Jim's wife?" Our Lady of Loquacity, on my right, glittered with illicit malice.

"I'm trying to," I said. "If you'd like to relay the information, her husband's sitting at the other end of the table."

"Oh, I'll certainly relay it!"

We finished dinner—thank God!—and went back into the living room. Then liqueurs. Then the emptiness again. It was ten forty-five: a long time to wait before we could all pretend to be festive. One of Jim's doctor colleagues was getting plotzed, ranting about the hospital, to Jim's embarrassed annoyance, but not to the doctor's wife's. She had obviously given up on him years ago. I decided that as long as I wasn't going to blow up the world, it was time I did me little best.

The chance came when some wife or other said she was thinking of buying a relaxicizor. That triggered a memory. "Oh, they're very dangerous!" I made my voice dire: a storyteller's warning. "I knew a girl who tried one once—and I could a tale of woe unfold—"

"What happened?" Carol prompted.

"Well, once upon a time—"

I launched into the story of—*Yvonne and the Relaxicizor*! A true story too, in part. Edith Willington's best friend at Smith was a witless, skinny nitwit named Yvonne Maccabe. And being as thin as a bean pole already, she decided to lose some weight. And called up some relaxicizor company, and whom did they send around? A diesel dyke named Bertha! At the use of the words "diesel dyke"—which I did use, aloud—Jim winked me a smile that said, "Go man! But don't go too far now." I explained to the elderly doctors' wives who were there that a dyke was a lesbian, and a diesel dyke was a lesbian who grew a beard, drank whiskey straight, smoked large black cigars, and drove an oil truck between Tulsa and Oklahoma City. Thus far the story was true. Yvonne opened the door and there did appear a bull dyke who should have been a tank in the First World War. The poor frail bitch, with all the electrodes attached, was almost electrocuted once—I made it twice in retelling it—and fainted at the first shock. (But that's what storytelling is all about—isn't it, Daddy Dickens? You take the fabric of Reality, and then, as if it was not enough, you do your own embroideries on it.) I made a great character out of Big Bertha—as her tomcat friends must have called her—"Okay, Yvonne, strip! Now up onna massage table! Atsa girl!"—and led—not to the true end—"Please leave," said Yvonne—but to the best I could, "Sorry, kid, but yer my first case." Then, confidentially, "Ya wouldn' like to try it on *me* sometime—would ya?"

Oh well—me little best . . . And one of the older women got the giggles . . . A very good sign, at an Upper Middle Class party.

"So beware!" I warned the doctors' wives. "When you order a relaxicizor, you may get a bull dyke too. Hey, that's a great phrase—*The Bull Dyke and the Relaxicizor*. I'm going to use that for the title of my next kiddies' book!"

And midnight came, finally—long overdue. There were ritual kisses and words—"Happy New Year!"—that had sounded real when the children had shouted them.

I wondered how long I'd have to stay, to be polite: at least half an hour. No, till one. Champagne had appeared, but after one glass I went home to Scotch again. One has one's loyalties up to the end.

John Ciodotti maneuvered through the living room—we hadn't talked privately yet—and arrived, after several talk stops, beside me, and said, "I'd like you to see my gallery."

"I'd love to."

"Do you like paintings?"

"Very much!"

"Come in any time. I live right above it. We'll have a drink."

Was it an offer of genuine friendship? Has Jim told him I'm okay in bed? And described what we do? Was he trying to pass me on? . . . The cocksucker! *Damn all those I love!* Him in particular!

The phone rang around twelve-thirty. "The doctor's lot—" Jim came back from the hall. "—I've got to drop down to the hospital. A gallbladder I did yesterday has decided to celebrate New Year's Eve by spiking a most exciting fever."

A chorus of social "No's!" and "There you are's!"

"It's early, Terry, but if you like I can give you a ride to the One-Sixty-eighth-Street subway station"—Jim, in his businesslike baritone.

Hallelujah! I was free. And apart from being bored most of the night, R. hadn't scored a single point. Except, perhaps, for my joyous pain when I watched Jim play with his kids. "That *would* be a help—"

"John, you'll have to be host till I get back. And I don't know when that'll be. The guy's in real trouble. Why don't you stay over tonight anyway?"

"Yes, do, John!" said Carol.

Good-byes—lies of false familiarity—to everyone.

In the car—his driving too excites me: easy, confident, masculine—Jim said, "Thanks, lad."

"For what?"

"For keeping the party alive after dinner."

"It's a true story!" Almost.

"True or not, it's the only good time I had all night."

"You mean, after your kids went to bed."

"Yes."

"That was quite an event, all that equipment."

"Weren't they great!" He grinned into the windshield, living his children's celebration again.

Here, for the first and—I thought—only time last night, Rumpelstiltskin was able to shout "touché!"

"Tell me, Jim—" I had a human being there; I might as well interrogate it. "—as far as Carol and the kids are concerned, which do you love most—her or them?"

Now he laughed out loud—at the windshield flashing with surface lights. "You don't differentiate. Only a single man could ask a question like that. She's them, they're her—I'm all of them."

Ancient artifact time again. The jillion-year-old egg in the ice.

"Hey, stop." We had come down the West Side Highway. "That's the turn-off to the hosptial."

"I know where we are."

I'd be damned if I'd ask him what he was doing. I instantly knew—and desire, like dozens of elegant female fingers, with nails very long, began softly to scratch every inch of my skin—but I'd be damned if I'd ask! No need: my silence was vividly questioning him.

"That telephone call was just a wrong number. Some drunk shouted 'Happy New Year, Shlunk!' and hung up."

The audacity of this bastard! To assume he can have me any time—

"I thought you wouldn't mind if I drove you home—"

—and he can!

"—and maybe came up for a little while."

"I don't mind."

"It's New Year's Eve, everybody's out celebrating—we can play our record."

"But look, Jim, if Carol should call the hospital—"

"She won't. She never does. Besides, I think she knows where I'm going."

"I don't under*stand* human beings—!"

"She loves me," he patly explained. "She knows I love her."

"I don't understand—" Defeated by all that was real, I slumped back in the front seat of Jim's Jaguar. "I honestly don't understand human beings."

He laughed again, and gripped my knee. Then tested my crotch with his fingers, where—like a black star—I was ready for him. I sat in a gathering fit of love, lust, whatever the passion is that locks me onto that man. His bravado in whisking me off, in front of his wife—in front of *myself*—worked on me like hashish.

But did I say that Rumpelstiltskin had gotten to me only once last night? He got to me again, on our way to the Village. Jim, making conversation, said, "You know that half-assed psychiatrist—we *had* to ask him: forgive us—he's got the wildest new secretary. She's someone I'd like to have a quick love affair with."

(Rumpelstiltskin honey, in your own fiendish way you *are* a genius! To have anticipated that—congratulations, champ!)

It didn't matter too much though: I was keyed up sexually. I'd had just the right amount to drink, and Jim had had just the right amount to drink, and God knows, Richard Wagner, when we got back to my apartment, had had just the right amount of drink when he composed the first act of *The Valkyrie*!

He fell asleep. I had a half-hour of the kind of simple happiness that I haven't known since last fall. It was not that I believed he loved me, but it was all right the way it was. Like that time at Thanksgiving, when just for an instant he became what he was: a young father approaching middle age who was sitting at the head of his family's table. Last summer I had an hour like that too. He'd come down one Saturday afternoon, and after the scene he said, "Come on out—I'll buy you a beer." We just had two beers and two hamburgers at an outdoor Greenwich Village cafe. Two guys we were—it was one of the few times in my life that I've felt like a "guy," not a male or a female or a freak or a genius: my usual categories—two guys, drinking beer. Jim looked around and breathed and said, "I love Saturday! I love the feeling of Saturday!" There's something so ordinarily sweet about Jim. If I could just disinvent him as someone I love. But I can't. I've always invented the people I love, as I'm inventing Jim Whittaker now: a monster of beauty, family—Impossibility—but based on a very plausible, if somewhat oversexed, man. It's just this—my imagination: the great space of the unreal—that's the reason that I often enjoy more thinking about him, masturbating about him, than actually making love with him. Last night he lay beside me, an exhausted human animal—man—potbellied, graying, snoring— yes, *snoring*, really snoring: *zzzz*, like a Ritz Brothers' movie—and my hand moved over his puffy stomach and turned it into Mercury's.

I let him sleep the half-hour out, then woke him up, and—"Ta ta!"—he went home. And Father, I ask you—how many sadists do you know who wake their victims—victim! that's a laugh— wake their victim and/or master up to make sure he gets back to his wife in good time?

I had thought that my commonplace bliss would last at least till I got to sleep. It didn't. Jim had been gone only fifteen minutes when I fell in love with him again. And all my other emotions began to report drearily in to my love, as if it was really the dentist, not pleasure—my desire: I was hot for him again—curiosity: had he and John Ciodotti been lovers?—envy: if so, had he *loved* John Ciodotti, as he didn't love me?

I hopelessly, endlessly fight against these insidious guerrillas of love, the thoughts and passions that attack you from ambush. But why perpetuate this interior Vietnam? Why not cut my losses completely? . . . Why *not*?

I shall . . . And Mr. Nixon, you most unlikely, yet most depressingly inevitable of presidents, I advise you to do so too.

Later: January 1

Called Carol, to thank her. The usual social two-step: "So glad you could come!"—"So glad you asked me."

But before she hung up she couldn't keep herself from demanding, "Now *write* something!"

"You sound like a grammar school teacher I had."

"I don't care. I only know that if I had a gift—"

"All right, I'll write something! Good-bye!"

And this is what I wrote—

> When one has given up on life,
> One shops around and one finds Art.
> And after years with genius rife,
> One finds one hasn't been so smart.

Enough of this merciless self-pity! . . . The suicide's dreary narcissism.

Poor Carol! Still nibbling at her heart because she isn't "*Kdeeaytive*"! (To be pronounced in the most cultured tones!)

"Harold's Song for Carol Whittaker": That she should never, ever, be unhappy again! (This I *liked* to write!)

> My dear, don't regret for a single second
> The fact that you cannot create.
> If the arts, in their privacy, never beckoned,
> That does not mean you've been left behind.
> For when human abilities finally are reckoned,
> I know no one who's famous or gifted or great
> Who could cope with a child, her own child, who was blind.

January 3

"What did the Rat do for Christmas?"

"He went home to Ninth Avenue to see his parents."

"Did he have a good time?"

"No. He only stayed a few hours. It was just a duty call." Be honest with him. "He didn't have a bad time though. He felt nothing."

"Was Harold there?"

"No."

"He should have taken Harold. Why didn't he?"

"Harold was not available."

"Where *was* he?"

"He was hiding from the Three-Legged Nothing! Who had just come down with the mumps! How the hell do I know where Harold was? I don't keep track of him *all* the time!" I am shouting at him, angrily, truly shouting at him. That little four-foot collection of dulled emotions, with no defenses at all. When I ought to rejoice that he talks back, answers me now a little bit.

We're in the Museum of Natural History, walking amid the skeletons of dinosaurs, star sapphires, the stuffed cadaver of a giant blue whale, immortal insects embedded in amber: the necessary proofs that the world and time are real.

We blissfully ignore them all. He wants only to hear me tell a tale. I want—I don't know what. Having sworn that I'd never see him again, as soon as his mother called this morning, I instantly promised to take him out.

"*However*—" I retract my anger in a big, bold, grown-up conditional. "—if it means so much for you to hear about the Rat—" A moment of melodramatic suspense—which I'm sure I enjoy much more than he does. "—it just so happens that Harold *did* see the Rat a couple of days before Christmas. He took him to meet one of the nicest people he knows." I will *not* go on until he makes himself part of it!

And he does. With intimidated curiosity—"Who?"

"A lady named Anne Black."

The question of questions: only children know what to ask. "Is she real?"

"She is very real. And Harold likes her very much. And knowing what Gloomsville Christmas usually was for the Rat, Harold thought that the best thing he could do for his worried furry friend was to take him up to Anne Black's—for mulled wine. Anne had asked him to come up for dinner on the night of the twenty-first. And that afternoon Harold began thinking about the Rat. He called Anne up on the telephone and told her he had this dismal rodent friend—would she mind if he came to supper too? She naturally, being a giving kind of person, said she'd love to have the Rat come too."

I launch into the story of *Harold—And The Rat's Christmas Tree*
. . . It's much the same as Thanksgiving: what should have
happened, but didn't. Couldn't. And never will.

"Harold knew he was taking a chance, because nothing made
the Rat more nervous than pretty, lovable women. Who loved
him. He didn't mind—" Now steady on, I tell myself. I was going
to say "tramps from the street" or "the female half of some balling
couples," but I get control in time. "—he didn't mind the sort of
ordinary little ladies you meet everywhere, but a woman as real
and nice as Anne, Harold knew, could give Rat a conniption fit.
Do you know what conniption means?"

"No."

"Neither do I. But it must be something awful! Anyway, as
Harold waited, down in the Village, to be buzzed in, he sang,
rather nervously to himself—

> Oh the Rat's going to have some Christmas cheer!
> So courage, Rat!
> You're where it's at!
> And don't be afraid—Anne's really a dear.

On into the story. Of course Rat objects—"I'm not going
anywhere!"—and Harold threatens to have to use magic. Although his magic is low these days . . . The gray flannel suit . . .
But Harold thought that beneath his sulk he could hear the Rat
being glad that he was forced to go.

> Oh the Rat's going to have some lovely mulled wine—
> So courage, Rat!
> You're where it's at!
> Just trust me, Rat. It'll all be fine.

And the cabbie—a walrus this time—definitely states that the
Rat is not going to bust Harold in the snoot in *his* taxi . . . "Oh
wow! A *really* Merry Christmas," moans Harold. But then
apologizes—because he knows how Rat feels about the holidays.

On—on—Anne's making the Rat feel at home; her gesture,
when shaking paws or claws or hands, of covering the back of
one's right hand with the palm of her left . . . I demonstrate to
Barney . . . And then into the two Christmas trees. With a wink,
while the three of them decorate, Anne lets Harold know who the

little tree is for. He turns away, to cough a hidden laugh into his hand . . . Then dinner . . . Then—*mulled wine,* which the Rat likes so much, along with the Scotches he's had before, that he gets absolutely euphoric. No gloompot for the Rat tonight! . . . After letting him ask who the little tree is for—"A recluse," Anne says quietly. "A shut-in, I mean"—I allow the truth to appear. Because I don't think it can hurt Barney much.

" 'Who decorated your Christmas tree, Rat, when you were little?'

"Harold flashed her a warning look, which said: that's a touchy subject for the Rat. But much to his surprise, the Rat was willing to talk about it. 'I did sometimes,' he said. 'I'd come back from school, and my mom would have it almost done, but she left out a bunch of ornaments for me to hang up myself.'

" 'Did your pop help too?' Anne hung a toy robin on the big Christmas tree.

"Harold trimmed his ears to listen to how the Rat would answer, 'No, never.' But there was only sadness, not anger, in his voice.

" 'He must have been busy.' Anne hung up a toy bluebird.

" 'Oh he was busy, all right!' laughed the Rat. But still, not angrily. 'He was busy reading *The New York Times.*' The Rat hung up a blue ornament. 'One thing though—'

" 'Yes?' Anne softly coaxed.

" 'He used to pin my stocking up, on Christmas Eve.'

" 'On the mantelpiece?'

" 'Yes. And that second, when he pinned my stocking to the wood, it felt more like Christmas right then than at any other time.' Rat hung up a little green ornament. 'Christmas morning, when we opened our presents, it didn't really feel like Christmas. Most of the stuff that was under the tree were gifts from Pop's patients anyway.' " Steady. " 'I mean, they were gifts from his grateful customers: the people he collected garbage from.' " Such garbage as tumors, cysts, diseased intestines. "Rat strung the green bulbs around the tree.

" 'The white bulb goes at the top,' said Anne. 'We'll pretend it's a star.' " (Black star! God curse it!)

" 'But my stocking,' said Rat, 'that really was Christmas. Coming down on Christmas morning to see what Mom had put in it—' A memory stuck Rat. Like a pin. 'Why, I even made up a game,' Rat remembered. 'A sort of rehearsal it was. I'd creep downstairs and peek around the corner from the hall into the living room, as if it was Christmas morning already. "Peekin' Aroun' the Corner"—that's what I called this game I invented. I'd play it for days before Christmas when I thought no one was watching me.' Harold and Anne had stopped decorating the big Christmas tree and were listening to the Rat. But in a pause the Rat suddenly heard them listening and got embarrassed. Beneath the fur on his face he blushed. 'May I have some more mulled wine, please?' "

On! on! . . . The Rat, of course, gets smashed—"Hey Harold, I'm mulled to the gills!"—and when he does finally understand that the little tree is for him—and Barney's joy surpasseth the Rat's: *his* tree too, I see by his eyes—why he resolves, at Anne's advice, to walk all the way home, just holding it. "You'll have strange adventures," Anne prophesies.

At my mention of "strange adventures" Barney's face grows huge with expectation.

"By the way, Barney," I casually ask, "are you in any special hurry to get home early this afternoon?"

"No."

"Oh." I'm journalistically informed, no more. "In that case—"

And do I ever invent some adventures!—while Harold and Anne have a quiet drink alone . . . After Anne's blessing—"At least once in a lifetime everybody should be given a completely decorated, completely illuminated Christmas tree!"—what can happen except adventures! (Only the bliss of nonbeing, I guess.)

Adventures!—here they come! . . . Rat happens to run into Kitty and Clive. I describe their apartment—red, red, everywhere! And Kitty calls up Anne—"This Rat happened to say that he knew you!" I narrate what Rat did. "Well, first he undid his Christmas tree, and lit it up—and *then* he went into the bathroom and wee-weed without closing the door!"

Barney's giggling! He's got the giggles! (A very good sign in a well-brought-up child!) Oh—does he dig that wee-wee bit! The child's gesture I've always most prized: knees knocking together in ecstasy.

" 'Then,' Kitty said, 'he reeled out the door, singing something like this—

> Oh the Rat, he's had some delicious wine, mulled!
> You're grooving, Rat.
> You could beat up a cat!
> Do you feel like having your whiskers pulled?

(Of course what I mean is, does the Rat feel like getting laid? But as frequently happens, some sleazy adult symbolism is cleansed by the literalness of a child: the Rat is in a grooving mood, and he may want to have his *whiskers pulled!*)

Another adventure—another telephone call to Harold and Anne. Seems the Rat got stopped by a cop—a grizzly bear in a blue uniform. "Is dat a kidnapped little boy you've got in dat wrapped-up package?" "No, officer, it's my Christmas tree!"

"Hahahahahaha—!" No language can capture laughter. Especially a child's.

Does the star sapphire fascinate my Barney? Does the blue whale hold him? Does the dinosaur? Does anything in the whole real world? . . . No—I do!

"It's late, Barney—"

"No! Please—?" He can't bear an ending. "Weren't there any more adventures? Or telephone calls to Harold and Anne?"

"There were lots. And I'll tell them to you as we cross the park."

He takes my hand as we cross the street, and won't let go when we enter the city's countryside: gray, desolate, wintered Central Park.

Well—there was the episode of the weasel, wearing dark glasses, who tried to steal the Christmas tree—but the Rat rassled the gun from his hand. And there was—I can't even remember—a half-dozen stories. I give Rat the giggles too, as long as Barney has them . . . And all of them involving telephone calls uptown. Where Harold, with his penchant for anxiety, was doing his worrying thing. "He's really swacked, Anne, by now." But Anne just keeps on pouring mulled wine, and says, "Don't upset yourself, Harold. Nothing bad can happen to someone who's carrying home his Christmas tree."

And finally Rat lands in a bar in the Village. Where who should he meet? Jake Moth. And a floozy named Josie. (I explain that a floozy's a barfly. Right. Barney doesn't doubt that. Who else would a kooky moth drink with, if not a barfly?) Jake, Josie, and Rat make a call all together, and shout, "*Merry Chrishmash,* Anne an' Harolharol—"

I fall silent. The filthy, pitiful New York City snow . . . And this child—who will not leave my hand.

He ventures the question. "Weren't there *any* more telephone calls?"

It isn't teasing now, my silence: I'm trying to decide. "There was one." From a Greenwich Village police station? No. From Bellevue? The morgue? My mood, in the winter twilight, sinks. "When Rat got back to his apartment. 'Anne—Harold—I'm home. I decided I could go one night without having my whiskers pulled. So I came straight back from the bar.'

" 'That's good.' Harold heaved a sigh of relief.

" 'And Anne, I set up the tree on a table beside my couch. I'm looking at it right now. The bulbs are flashing on and off. And I'm never going to take it down, Anne. I'm going to leave it in my living room always.'

" 'That's very nice, Rat,' said Anne. 'But the needles'll begin to fall.'

" 'Let the needles fall where they may!' said the Rat. 'I'm never going to take down this tree!' " I want nothing. I don't want to get my whiskers pulled. I don't want to hear music. I want—nothing: not to feel. But I've got to end this story for Barney. "And here is a funny thing," I say. "All this took place last December twenty-first. But as Anne and Harold and the Rat all knew, it secretly was Christmas Eve."

January 4

The Three-Legged Nothing is after me. It grew huge last night while I slept . . . I got the fears. It ain't fair either. Most people have to take LSD, or at least smoke pot, to go on a bad trip—but my God, Father, I can come down with a case of the willies on a single Carnation Instant Breakfast. And I have one every morning! . . . And what *is* this horseshit about sleep being a healing agent? Cancers ripen in the night. (A lot of you, my innocent witnesses, are contracting cancer right now.) You wake up with a cold—so sleep can be just as destructive and deadly as consciousness usually is.

That poor kid! But I've been with him before. So why now? And the holidays are over—thank God!

I've got to get out of here for a while—

January 4: A couple of hours later

The hypocrite I am! Or rather the creature of habit and vanity. In my panic to flee my apartment I still took several minutes to comb my hair in front of the full-length bathroom mirror. The things it says to me range all the way from "Hi, cutie!" to "Fuck you, old timer!" Today the glass winced and muttered, "Oh Jesus—avoid all things that give back your reflection."

Outside it was as I thought: the Three-Legged Nothing was at large. It was running up and down Greenwich Avenue, waving its four arms and shouting with its two heads, "Oh I'm angry! I'm angry! Find me someone to kill!" All the people were jumping out of its way. A couple of panicky ladies even tried to get into the women's prison. And Sutter's Bakery was a packed mess of terrified faces. But I needn't be frightened of it now. It only eats living human beings.

Then went down to that open pier at the end of Morton Street. And whom should I meet there but Rumpelstiltskin, in a very pensive mood—not his usual fiery self at all—staring into the gray and clouded Hudson River. But even he wouldn't talk to me. Or stick his little pins in me. He just looked me in the eye for a deadly minute or two. Then softly said, "Not yet. But soon, soon, soon." And with his arms folded behind his back, he strolled off toward the Washington Market ruins. Temporarily—for the rest of the winter I guess—he has pitched his wattled hut there.

Came home. Called Iris—a human voice—on the pretext of wishing her Happy New Year. I try to apologize, in advance, with phone calls and sometimes little presents, for the great favor I will ask of her: that she discover me. Cleaning women often do. If their employers have any decency, they make restitution in their wills.

Our litany: Anne—how's my shoulder?—still sore.

"Lord, Mr. Andrews, I don't know whether that gym does you more good or harm!"

"You want me to keep nice and trim, don't you?" The secret of keeping a cleaning woman, at least for unmarried men, is a little outrageous flirtation.

"I sure do! But I can't stand the smell of that stuff."

(Ben-Gay: the acrid aroma. The distant screaming of the Three-Legged Nothing. A sky that has never known a sun. This Saturday: January fourth.)

We chatted on—about her best friend, Holly, whom she can't *stand!* They see each other once a year, and fight like alley cats, but are soul mates over the telephone. And about our New Year's resolutions. She won't tell me her most important. No—she *won't!* It had something to do with me. The secret, for a cleaning woman, of keeping a generous unmarried man is a little outrageous flirtation.

But she did give me one good idea. "We gotta clean out those closets!"

Yes! It is time to start throwing things away. I looked around the living room—the closets aren't possible: no visible difference for me there; she'll have to do them herself, poor soul—and saw my runners. I've got a not barely wall-to-wall rug. The strips that were left, when I had it circumcised, I use as runways. When I used to work, I would tramp and tramp—a sentence: tramp!—a paragraph: tramp!—and in order not to blaze a trail in the carpeting—a single word: tramp!—I used these skinny leftover shreds as paths on top of the under-rug. And just now, when I hung up, I knew that they had to be thrown away.

So I lugged them down to the street, to the trash can . . . And I wish I hadn't.

Because that God damned collie next door heard me rattling around, and stuck his snout out the window, and began to bark at me! That bastard! And the worst of it is, he's so beautiful: a shade darker than most collies, and with beautiful auburn—yes, auburn!—markings to his mask . . .

Oh Jim—Jimmy—I am really in bad shape when a few hairs on the face of a dog that hates me can send me into a tailspin that has only to do with you.

Why couldn't you have returned my love? At least for a little while?

Oh well—as Salome sang to John the Baptist, whose hearing had been impaired, *"Warum hast du mich nicht angesehen, Jochanaan?"* And then playfully added, as she chucked him under the chin of his severed head, *"Du schlepper, du!"*

Because your heart is in your family . . . Where it belongs.

January 5

Whoopee! (Thank God I'm normal! As Connie said one night, "I just like good old-fashioned sex."—as I replied, "Oh so do *I!*")

Now we have some fun at last! . . . " 'Bout time!" I hear you muttering . . . A call from my friend, Sam, the hairdresser. The one who introduced me to Jim. "Hello, Terry? Sam. Some couples are coming around tonight."

"Great! And boy, do I need an orgy! Max and Connie?"

"And those new ones you met last fall. Who you never introduced me to. You shit!" Sam is moderately effeminate—there *is* a tradition to uphold after all—and rather waspish. But one feels he's a wasp whose sting has been plucked and replaced with vermouth. But he still delivers his gifts of charity as if they were little injections of venom.

"I apologize, Sam. I meant to. He's great. And goes both ways. In front of her too. I meant to pass them on, but I've been preoccupied"—with Giddyville.

"That's what you say, sweetie! You're just a selfish prick."

"You're right!"

"The star's going to be a football player from California. Who's supposed to go both routes himself."

"Most football players do—the darlings!"

"A friend of Hal and Dorcas's. They'll be here too."

"The clan's really gathering!"

"One thing, Terry: will you behave? No trying any mean things now—"

"I'll behave." No I won't! "And I've got something for you too."

"For me? What?"

"I picked it up at Mark Cross last week. It's a bona fide, certified, calf's hide—tittywhipper!"

"Terry—will you behave?" His patience is monolithic, like a schoolmarm's before a disruptive child.

"I'll behave." No I won't! "But what if some husky young husband comes up and says, 'Thpank me, thir—*pleeeeeeeth!*'"

"Terry—God damn it—!"

"I'll behave." Yes I will. "Cross my heart!"—and hope to turn into a hairdresser.

"Eight o'clock. Tomorrow's a working girl's day."

The Balling Couples! What a big drink of Grape Ade it'll be to see them all again! I feel just like them tonight. Like them, or a beastly widow, or a slightly alcoholic middle-aged head nurse.

I met them about two years ago, through Sam, whom I'd met at the Turkish baths. He's seventy percent gay, but when drunk enough, or turned on enough by some guy in the room, that thirty percent has been known to do yeoman service for the ladies. And women do like him: he's charming and funny and flattering. The girls are much more realistic than male homosexuals. They don't demand a phony, often impotent, Hollywood mask of masculinity. What they like is a stiff not too ugly prick, with a dash of personality.

Sam and I weren't really each other's dishes of tea. He was too femme for me, and I, with my need to fuck and, if possible, beat a behind, was too violent for him. But despite the sexual misfit, before we knew it, behind our backs, we'd become good friends. (He *is* funny too! Can't stand a trace of faggotry. Conversations with strangers often run thus: "I *adore* your loft!" "Do you?" "Yes. You've done it beautifully!" "Get out!") When he found that I had a taste for the ladies—and with them, didn't try to beat their asses red, white, and blue—he invited me to an orgy. And even—a sweet guy, really—provided me with a date: a squat dyke named Marcia, to whom I didn't need to do anything except appear with her at the door. The couples are touchy: as a rule, they don't like stags. But of the stags who *are* allowed, there's one poignant couple—Andy and Hank—who, permitted because they're so beautiful, will only make love to a woman together . . . Oh, many and many are the rugged buddies who ball gals together—"Hey Hank, man, go!"—and whose eyes, at the moment when one of them comes, meet incompletely above the abyss of the woman's body between them. For the rest of us single fucks, you can bang a wife, in front of a husband's glittering eyes, but you have to have brought a girl along. It's more a question of balance, of geometry—but ethics is what it really is: a primitive morality—than anything else: there has to be equalization, even if the guy doesn't like the broad. So Marcia and I met down at the door, went up to Sam's loft, and I didn't see her again that night. Sam told me later that she'd had a splendid time: gotten down on about five wives.

That first orgy was really delightful! At least fifteen couples, all sprawled on the floor, walls, ceiling of Sam's Ninth Avenue loft. And at one point, after I'd creamed a few times, I just walked around and tried to memorize what I saw. It was like a scene from a D. W. Griffith movie—but the scene that got left on the cutting room floor. In retrospect I seem quite naive to myself. Things like that go on every day in the grand old Puritan-founded righteously imperialistic United States of A. The lasting thought that I took home and chewed over reflectively for days, had to do with the pregnancies in these sessions. Despite the pill, rubbers, oral contraception, they do happen, you know. But perhaps, gentle reader—ya fuck ya!—it may be that our happy-go-fucky promiscuous age will necessitate a return to tribal society: an Eden condition in which mere kinship—"Me human being! You human being too?"—will replace the bonds of known parenthood.

But I had a real wingding of a time, that first time. The tone of the whole thing—social, psychological—was set, for me, in the bathroom—appropriately enough. I had screwed some nameless chick, who had a wedding ring on, and being the well-brought-up youngster I was, with a medical background at that, I went in the john to piss and wash my prick. So there stood I at the sink, scrubbing up as if I was just about to operate, in a bemused daze of finally realized total promiscuity, when this stark naked broad came rushing in, without knocking of course, and sat on the toilet and started to urinate. I continued washing, with as much nonchalance as I could muster, and above her hissing I heard her sigh deliciously, "Oh Jesus, nothin' feels as good as sitt'n' on the crapper when ya really hafta!" I heartily agreed. "Say, you're groovy!" she looked up from her seat to observe. "I'm here with my drinkin' partner. Name's Sally—you met her—?" No. "An' a couple of studs. We just had a groovy scene. Come on out an' chew the shit a while. Then we'll *bang! bang! bang!* again!" Swell, I'd meet them outside.

She left. And I disintegrated into hilarious hysteria. For I had this vision: Terry Andrews, that prominent author of children's stories, has finally achieved his life's ambition: sittin' on the crapper—chewin' the shit—with his drinkin' partners! (Hi, Mom!)

Does this sound condescending? I don't mean it to. The Balling Couples are refreshing. And real! Like powdered lemonade. Like TV dinners, off which I live. Like plastic. Like all the artificial indispensable things on which you too, my unliving witnesses, have come to depend. The advertised world! A little girl, munching her corn flakes, and you know that she's saying, "I eat shit too—an' Mummy, it's yummy!" The world the object of advertising! I dig it! For I too have been convinced that if I use the right hair spray and mouthwash it'll prevent me from getting underarm syphilis. There's some subtle connection between the vulgar gullibility of our lives and an orgy like tonight. Oh, the American middle, lower middle class: an artifact that fascinates me. I used to sip it, suck it, fuck it, love it at every chance I got. And those of you who are jet-setters—you're fools! The excitement is not in Rome, St. Tropez, Palm Beach. It's in a loft on Ninth Avenue, and it consists in unleashing mediocrity, the madness of the ordinary.

I didn't meet my drinkin' partner again that night. Instead I met the most charming of dim-witted little females, Connie, and her dum-dum husband Max. He works for the city: a tiny cog in some utterly unimportant urban machine. But possesses one amazing gift, according to several women that he's been down on—on whom he has been down: one tries to keep this elegant—he's got a tongue that nature intended to pillage ant hills in central Africa. Short and potbellied, he is only for the ladies. But believe me, girls, it is no loss for us.

The great acquisition that night was Connie. Her hair a badly bleached blond, her body, at thirty-two, on the brink of sagging middle age—but not over the slow precipice yet—she beguiled and totally charmed me with her dazzling banality. She is like a find—some glorious gadget—you might make at the bargain counter of your local five-and-ten-cent store. We instantly clicked, our eyes asking each other impatiently how long it would be before we got into bed together. A modicum of *politesse* demanded that the three of us drink and talk for a while, and then I could take this man's wife away and fuck her in another room. In the course of our manufactured conversation she learned that I wrote children's books, and I learned that she had a delicious little speech impediment: she couldn't pronounce her "r's!" I was "Tehwy"—she was going to go to the "libwawy" and get all my books out for her three kids.

Our dutiful ten minutes' dialogue done, I screwed Connie. Max stripped and watched the preliminaries, but then went off in search of a strange lady's orifice. And Connie and I had at it on a mattress in a corner of Sam's tactfully darkened bedroom. As a lay she was great—abandoned, out of control—but the wonderful moment was something she said. As we reached the peak—she was squeaking deliriously—she took time out of her mouse's rapture to give me one of the great lines in my life: "Oh Tehwy—oh Tehwy—I swea' ta God!—ya' my vehwy favowite childwen's autha!"

That whole first orgy was full of superb lines, as well as ordinary bodies. When Randy and Pauline came in—but it wasn't Randy. Randy's her husband—and a nice piece of ass, and loves to get fucked—but he was sick that night. So instead she brought her brother, Al! I was talking with Sam when they both came in. "Sam, this is my brother Al—Randy's sick."

Sam shot me a glance that said, "This must certainly interest an author!" And when Al had gone off to get two drinks, he said, "Pauline, do you, like, make it with your brother?"

"My own brotha—? Nevah! We nevah have sex! I mean, I blow him every now an' then—but we nevah have sex!"

And in the bedroom, later on, from a crowded dark quarter where some guy had tried the wrong nether gate, I heard a plaintive female explain, "Oh honey—I don't like to be Greeked."

A great verb—what? I Greek, you Greek, he she or it Greeks. (Well, maybe *it* doesn't.)

It's eight o'clock. I've had a light supper of monosodium glutamate and various cyclamates, and Scotch, and I'm off to the orgy!

One couple—Hal and Dorcas, I think—have a genuine claim to fame: they're two of the people who heard Kitty Genovese's screams and did nothing. They've been interviewed on television and written about—"We've heard screams out there before"—and generally established themselves as celebrities of apathy.

Here I go!

The name of tonight is—"Rumpelstiltskin—and the Balling Couples!"

> Tonight my Randy's ass I fuck!
> Tonight my Connie's cunt I suck!
> And lucky I am they both don't know
> That their lover is a corpse. Ho! ho!

January 6

The beginning, at least, was splendid, and commensurate with my mood: physical fireworks and lots of fun for all the grown-up little kiddies!

In the taxi I began going over their names. Because names are fascinating—the attraction that certain names have for names. (Secretly I have always wished that Hortense Calisher and Clementine Paddleford would run away together.) And I realized that of all the couples I've met at orgies—there must be thirty or forty at least—I know the last names of very few. The anonymity, of course, is part of the promiscuous charm—still, I felt a slight pang at the thought of strangeness, unfamiliarity, enjoyed for its own sake, and R. said to himself—

> You Balling Couples, don't forget
> You have a hidden last name too.
> You're Hal and Dorcas, John, Yvette—
> But I am I, and you are you.
>
> You're Dorcas Kurtz and John Coudert,
> Max Moscavitz and Marcia Pitkin,
> Pauline and Randy Odalaire—
> And I, of course, am Rumpel Stiltskin!

Should I have had another Scotch? I decided to pick up a bottle. Besides, it's *nice* to bring a little gift to an orgy! (Apart from a stiff dick, I mean.)

Sam's voice through the door, backed up by hard rock and, I suspected, hard cock. "Who is it?"

"Mr. R. Stiltskin to see Mr. S. Tyson."

"You nut!" The door opened—in that special clandestine way that a door to an orgy opens—and like the pure penis that I'd been invited to be, I slipped in. The living room, lights lowered, was shivering with half-clothed bodies, still separate.

"Stark nekkid!" I observed. "Has it started already?"

"Just beginning. You've lost weight—"

"You better believe it! Sixteen pounds."

"—and grown sideburns! I hate to say it, but you look halfway human."

It occurred to me, with a flash of joy, that this might be my last orgy. I gave Sam's peter a friendly pull! "You look pretty great yourself."

"Off mit de clothes." I stripped to my shorts. "Them too!"

"Not yet. I want to cool it a little while."

"That's the football player over there."

"Splendiferous!"

On a couch was sitting an heroic figure—I'll risk that adjective, yes—with his feet crossed neatly in front of him and his hands folded in his lap: some mother's well-behaved little boy, patiently waiting for the orgy to start.

"Pretty stupid too. But what do you expect from Long Beach?"

"Any action with him yet?"

"No. He's playing it cagey and straight. Carl—come over and meet a friend of mine. This is Terry."

"Hi, Terry."

"Hi, Carl."

A handshake, a grin: and buddies already. And he really was scrumptious! Deltoids like grapefruit, a mat of black hair, a nose that had been broken at least once—damage is an enhancement sometimes—and flat blue eyes no deeper than the tint on a china plate.

And a great behind! TU ES PETRUS, ET SUPER HANC PETRAM AEDIFICABO ECCLESIAM MEAM! Or at least I've tried to. It doesn't work. But the most stupendous pun in history! If we're to believe it, Christ, in the moment he was founding his church, took time off to crack a joke. Oh, I hope he did! And I hope he and Peter had a good laugh together.

"You are *really* in great shape!" He too still had his briefs on, but beneath the cotton the bulge down there looked pretty impressive. "Do you work out in a gym, as well as play football?" I was counting on the usual California narcissism.

And wasn't disappointed. "Uh-huh."

"It shows."

"Do you?"

"A couple of times a week. When I see a physique like yours, it makes me want to quit."

"Don't quit." He believed me. Beautiful! The jerk. "But you gotta eat the right foods."

"Like what?"

"Like protein powder. Tastes lousy, but it's not so bad if you mix it up in orange juice. But you gotta be careful. It corga-lates."

It does *what*—? "It does what?"

"It corgalates. Gets sticky and thick."

Coagulates! He was a natural! A Mrs. Malaprop—with a chest like the front of a Cadillac and thighs you could prop up a skyscraper with! I began to like him.

"Hello, Terry." Marcia, already in action: nekkid as a jaybird, and unembarrassed by being bare-assed—a faculty I have yet to acquire.

"Hi, Marcia. Marcia—Carl."

"Hi, Carl."

"Hi, Marcius."

Marcius! And he called her that for the rest of the night. The victim of numberless Roman Hollywood epics, I suppose he was confusing my rugged little Volkswagen dyke with a bit-part centurion. He *was* beautiful. I take back the "jerk."

Then Connie—"Tehwy!"—came rushing up, in panties and bra, and her fingertips, nails, did their crazy little dance in the hair on my chest. "Long time no see."

"Too long!" I really am mad about her! My hands, inside her panties, made friends again with the cheeks of her ass—so lacking in malice she is—so ready to have her ass caressed. "You know Carl—?"

"Mmmm!" She imitated Marilyn Monroe's moan of affirmation—ridiculously, and all the more appealing because it was absurd. "But not intimately yet."

She squirmed in my arms, and I got turned on. "Him later. Me now!" The football player, for all his flesh, sank into insignificance.

"Mmm—yes!"

Before the bewitched and bewilling audience of Carl and Marcius—and you—I hugged, tugged, amorously lugged her into the bedroom at the back of Sam's loft.

And there, in the demilit darkness—a magic scent!—

> Fe! fi! fo! fum!
> I smell a popper—an' I want some!

Amyl nitrite has hit the heterosexual, bisexual, unisexual couples at last! . . . Golden treasure trove! Amyl nitrite—commonly known as "poppers," because they pop when you break one of them—they are little glass vials of joy encased in knitted yellow jackets. (At least the good ones are.) They're an aid for angina pectoris, cardiac asthma, and debilitated desire. They give you a couple of minutes of thick, tangible intensity as all the blood vessels in your brain dilate, and an inner uncontrolled explosion takes place. I use them often. And enjoy them very much! And, in fact, here's—

> A whoop for all my groovy poppers!
> We've had great times! We've had some whoppers!
> But let's not discuss physiology.
> I'd rather not know if you're killing me.
> Groovier to do it all by yourself
> And not be done in by some little yellow elf.

A box, on the night table beside the bed. Along with an even more discreet tube of KY. Unnecessary—but fun—those poppers were for Connie and me. We have our pattern without them. (With Jim I sniff them constantly. And that prick! A doctor he is, and he won't write me a prescription for any! It shouldn't surprise me: he's been guzzling Scotch in my apartment for over a year, and in that time he's given me exactly one bottle.)

"Haul it up here," I ordered, after I'd come, "and crouch over my mouth. Make it hover now. Spread your knees a little farther apart." I dove—dove upwards—for what surely is the world's most precious sunken treasure. In what surely—a woman's nether flesh—is the world's most primitive ocean. Cave. You might call this spelunking, orally.

When I swam up for air, having nipped her clitoris enough to get a lunging thrust on her part, along with a couple of squeals, I found we had an audience: Sam was standing above us, watching. "I suppose *that's* what they mean by rapport," he observed.

"You want a taste?" I offered to share my cellular candy bar.

He grimaced. "No thank you." A woman's inferior mouth has no savor for Sam at all, poor boy. Nor does much else that has to do with girls. These parties are thrown to net him men. "I asked your friend, but he couldn't come."

"What friend?"

"Jim Whittaker. He said Sunday was his 'family day.' Rather dear of him, I thought."

As the hive of jealousy swarmed toward my head—"I didn't know you still saw Jim."

"Sweetie, in the past month alone I've passed him on to at least five guys."

The hive landed. And each separate suspicion, envy, quick visualized fantasy of Jim and at least five other guys, put their needles in. I was glad that the room had been darkened. Neither Sam nor Connie could see my face clearly. "You were always wonderfully generous."

"And *he* is wonderfully popular. He says that you're seeing quite a lot of each other."

"Oh we are," I airily allowed, as the stinging went on incessantly. "We've become good friends." And God *damn* that word "friend"!—to be forced to apply it to what I feel!

Sam arched an eyebrow—"Don't let me interrupt your compatibility, you two!"—and left. And left Connie wanting to mount my mouth again. And left me wanting to—ah, I do try your patience, don't I? But "wanting to kill Jim Whittaker" was what I was going to say.

"Ya wanna come again, Tehwy?"

"Sure."

A casual and altogether unfounded masculine boast: because my masculinity—Roderick Usher—was in a state of complete collapse.

She stroked my chest, as if it was the hairy back of a dog she liked, and inquired easily, "Not weady yet?"

My God—women are good to me! . . . Why *do* men have to be beautiful?

"I guess not." I wanted to reach her in some way though. She's so like that little fourth-grade girl that I met at a book fair once. She looked at me with enormous round eyes and informed and warned, "Oh I wike *Heidi*—" And with a sigh: "—but I wuv to waff." Her problem was with her "l's," not "r's." And so does Connie love to laugh. I looked down in affectionate disappointment at my limpotent little friend, and waggled him back and forth, and said, "Aw Louie, yer a grave disappointment ta ya motha'!"

She hugged me and tongued my lips, then crept her tongue—lovely lizard—little by little, inside. And slithered it out and said, "Maybe *I* can do something—"

"That's a great idea. Try."

Around she swiveled, and down. And for a girl, she's a very excellent cocksucker. (Look to it, ladies—all you traipsers up and down on Third Avenue—the real girls are getting formidable.) I tried like hell to get an erection. I fantasized—a nymphomaniac—that football player in the other room—a wild scene I had once: a mother and daughter, both named Marie—an even wilder one: a father and son I picked up at the baths—that *really* was a fantastic two hours. I had to wheedle the truth, dredge it out of their quiet complicity, from this forty-five-year-old man and his twenty-three-year-old boy. The memory of it almost always works. But it didn't last night.

I was lying in the classical masculine posture: on my back, legs spread apart, her in between on her knees, with my arms crossed—rather theatrically: too nonchalant—behind my neck. We began to collect onlookers. The football player and Marcia came in. Several other sets of eyes were watching from the door. I heaved my most masculine sigh and said, in an operatically baritone voice, "Boy, that girl puts the right kind of lip on a dick!"

And I have a nice little lip curl I do, to present an image of perfec[t] male complacency; it's based on the basic snarl, and like a[ll] successful gestures it started as instinct and ended as art. But a[t] least something started to happen to me.

"Hi, Carl. Any action yet?"

"Marcius give me a headfuck."

"A what?"

"A headfuck. A blow job."

I feel very old sometimes. The next generation has a who[le] different vocabulary. But whatever was happening got harder an[d] harder. "You want to fuck?"

He grinned. "Sure!" And reached between Connie's legs for he[r] vegetal canal.

"Not her, man. Me!"

A ripple—excitement, and also the shiver of some leftove[r] moral indignation—ran through our assembled witnesses. (You[!) Football was taken aback for a second; then his grin flickere[d] brighter: he too was turned on, as I had been, by the chance to b[e] exhibitionists. "Sure!"

"Hey, Connie, try Carl a while."

"Mmm!"

It was he and I now. And ladies—why should I call on yo[u] ladies only?—I don't like to get fucked. It's happened about half [a] dozen times—and no, just no: it is not my stage, my act. But Ca[rl] and I had undertaken, apart from giving each other pleasure— only hoped!—to provide entertainment for our on-wishing, wel[l] looking spectators. The psychological glow of exhibitionism la[y] over both of us. It's an inner light that I enjoy—and apparently h[e] did too. I felt that our smiles mirrored each other—although I ha[d] never been about to perform in the under position before.

I took a fistful of KY and tried to relax as much as I could. Bu[t] naturally, being the uptight tight-assed semivirgin I am, I re[-] mained about as free and easy as the door to a safe in [a] Chase Manhattan Bank.

There were other aids available. I tugged him toward m[e] steadied him, and reached for a popper—without the inhaler: th[e] total momentary jolt was what I knew I was going to need. Befor[e] pure sensation took over, I had a last critical look around: Marci[a] Connie, and two or three couples pressing in through th[e] door—(And oh ladies, ladies—that strange pleasure you take when you watch two men make love with each other: your faces turn into a thrilled amalgam of envy, joy, rage, and a crazy belief.)—then snapped the popper and said to Carl, "Now take it slow and even, lad. And don't pull back till you're all the way in."

He did as he was told—the darling! (Football players usually do.)

My fantasies? A kaleidoscope at first. There was so much physical pain involved that I closed my eyes and went on some kind of a retinal trip. Then—Carl was good: he *was* a sweetheart, and waited for me to engulf him completely—then out of the abstract flashing lights, *made* out of the lights, a figure materialized. It was Jim. In the many times that we've had sex he hasn't fucked me once. But this was what Jim loved and did: this violent passivity. I began to rise toward Carl. Good lad, he was careful and timed himself to meet me pulse for pulse with the wing beat of his thighs.

I fantasized that I was Jim Whittaker, dying . . .

I fantasized—completion—he was dead . . .

The jock—God knows what *his* images were!—was extremely considerate in saying bye-bye as smoothly as possible.

And the show being over, the audience, with murmurs of approbation, dispersed.

What did not disperse was the lingering dream I had of Jim Whittaker killed. It buoyed me like a tidal wave, or as a bird must be buoyed when it sails before the wind. It was easy, this feeling—pacific. And it floated me into my clothes—

"So *early?*" said Sam.

An apology: two times with Connie. He hadn't seen the episode with the muscular honeybunch.

—and floated me inches above the seat in the taxi coming home.

After all, an anaesthetized voice was saying, any death will do. Won't it? . . . After all, Dan Reilly would just have to take up a second quest—

It's two o'clock in the morning—yes: sung to drugged three-quarter time. And I haven't been smoking pot or hash. And I'm not even drunk. On booze . . . I am drunk on the close Impossible.

January 6: Three—in the afternoon!

No! No! No! *No!* . . . *Killing!* Am I really that far along?

January 6: Six o'clock

It has to have been that getting fucked. I got jarred into an area where rampant imagination took over. . . . And I wish to hell that I hadn't been jarred! ("Jarred"—that's a spelunking euphemism!) My asshole is as sore as hell!

January 9

"Uh-oh!" said the watchman.

> By the pricking in my thumbs
> Something evil this way comes.
> By the pricking up my ass
> Something evil that way passed.

A warning I've never had before. And if I'm right—it will serve me right! . . . Anyway, I've called my trusty gay doctor—who will, no doubt, enjoy a few discreet physicianly chuckles to learn that my nether portals have been forced at last . . . VD, I've had enough for a regiment of Cossacks. But out front . . . Another good reason—

That motherfucking football player! . . . No, no—I'm sure he didn't even suspect. Let us preserve our images of childhood innocence . . . Except God help all the wives at that orgy!

January 9: Two hours later

Yup . . . I got da "gongareeah"—as my first contact pronounced it, lo, these many years ago.

What a nuisance! And what a bore! No booze for all these days and the shots in my ass. Let us hope, my fastidious audience, that I've got a strain that responds to those needles.

You, Mr. Auden, may live in The Age of Anxiety, and you, Dr. Oppenheimer, may have lived in The Age of the Atom Bomb— but I live in The Age of the Antibiotics. And thank heaven I do! By now, if it weren't for the wonder drugs, my genitalia would look like the picture of Dorian Gray!

> Oh penicillin—many thanks!
> And thanks to Terramycin too.
> I'd be one living chancre now,
> One painful drip—if not for you.
>
> Too bad you don't work in the soul,
> And cleanse infections there as well.
> There's just one cure for lives diseased:
> The drugs of Heaven. Or the drugs of Hell.

January 10

Two telephone calls: from Jim, and Dan. (My deadies. Steadies. Yes, I am that far along.)

I've been dreading a call from Jim, because being asexual and analcoholic while the cure lasts, I can't have a session. When I heard his voice—"There you are, you rascal!"—my guts began writhing like snakes in a fire. But I was saved. "I can't come around tonight, but you feel like an outing this Sunday?"

"Yes!" An outing with you, my adored disease, for which Terramycin *doesn't* work—anywhere! A Hackensack dump, East Harlem, that fabulous cemetery in Queens. "Where?"

"South Hampton. This old-fart millionaire patient of mine, who's actually an old-fart dear, has come down with a bellyache. He had cancer fifteen years ago and naturally suspects the worst. I know it's nothing, but I've got to go out and hold his hand for a while. You want to keep me company?" In Hell, if that's the only place possible. "Thought we might come back to your house and hear a little music."

"I'd like an outing," I offered, throbbing offhandedly.

"I'll call you Sunday sometime around noon, when I get away from the family manse."

"I'll be here." With my hand poised above the telephone from eleven-thirty on.

"Ta ta!"

Then a moment of panic: was Sunday long enough? Yes. Four days from the first angelic injection.

For an hour I drifted in giddy expectation.

Then Danny called. And—how to tell it?—for the first few moments his voice sounds normal, masculine, even pleasing in its mildness, but then you get those reverberations that do come from a Queens cemetery: "Good morning—sir."

His tone always chills my blood with excitement. "Fine, Danny."

"I haven't seen you lately."

"Well—the holidays. I had to go home."

"I was wondering if you'd like to come out for dinner some weekend"—luring me with food.

"I *would* like that, Danny."

"Any time you say, sir."

"I'll call you—"

"Will you?"

"I really will."

"Sir!—don't hang up for a little minute. Please. I'm smoking a cigarette, talking to you—"

Oh, God! Why couldn't I have been bored? Or annoyed? "Dan, you know that I don't dig these telephone scenes—"

"One thing, sir—tell me to do one thing—"

Yet his plea—fish, fisherman, as always.

"Press the coal of the cigarette—"

"Sir—?"

"—in the palm of your left hand."

His ambiguous cry of pleasure-pain—"Ah!"—is always followed by a huge in-drawn breath. "Thank you—sir."

I hung up.

Just to talk to that man leaves me groggy—drugged.

January 11

"Harold—and the Scream."

"Now you won't like this story—" Nor will I. So why am I telling it to Barney? I'm not even tanked. Yes, the kid's got me so bugged up that the past few times I've had to have drinks before I could face him. But no Rat story is available—nothing's happened to him since Christmas. Except that he's got a dose of clap up his ass. *Harold—and the Rat's Clap!* How would that be for a title? Surely Harold has enough magic to cure a case of gonorrhea. (I only wish the little bugger did!) But don't worry—I am not about to tell Barney that tale. "You sure you want to hear it?"

"Yes."

We are walking along the promenade that runs beside the Hudson River, past the boat basin at Seventy-ninth Street. The sky is a breathing, breathtaking blue: the great flowing water, polluted and unimaginably defiled, retains its majesty, and the air is astonishingly warm: we are having a January thaw—the rarest, briefest, most delusive of springs.

"You sure?"

"Yes."

"Well—Harold woke up one morning, and—oh boy!—something was *really* wrong!

> Did a bat have a perfectly terrible dream?
> No.
> Oh—Harold's face sank. —somewhere there's a scream.

"Now there were certain things that Harold didn't like. He did not like bloody noses, he did not like black and blue marks, and most particularly he did not like screams. And he realized that on this special day there was a scream inside someone somewhere in New York. And he also realized that he had to find the person and let the scream out. Because a scream does damage if it doesn't get out.

"Harold wandered around the city all day, searching for the scream. And the day was gloomy and overcast—not at all like today. A chill wind was blowing, gray clouds were lowering in the west, it got dark very early, as if the night—with its black stars—against the rules, was nibbling at the afternoon—and all the people were hurrying, the way people hurry when they're being chased by something but they don't know what it is they're chased by, with looks back over their shoulders and a worried tightness around their mouths.

"Of course, a lot of the people knew what they were being chased by. It was the Three-Legged Nothing—"

"No!"

"I am *sorry*, Barney—but the Three-Legged Nothing was out that day! It was running through the streets waving its four arms and shouting with its two heads, 'Oh I'm angry! And I'm hungry! Find me someone who I can kill and eat!' Whom. It knew its grammar, the Three-Legged Nothing did.

"And I'll tell you who also was abroad that day. Rumpel-stiltskin was roaming around New York tearing down buildings that should have been left in peace, being old and worthy of respect. It was *that* kind of day, I'm afraid . . .

"Harold slogged on through the fearful city. A few days before, there had been a snowstorm, but the snow that lay in the gutters now was all black and dirty and awful-looking. Harold felt very sorry for the snow of New York. To keep himself company he sang it a little song—

> Now don't feel sad, you New York City snow.
> I'll write you one good poem before I go.

"But today was just not a day for poetry."

"Go where?" Barney's face is screwed up in *angst*.

"Just go, Barney." Caught off guard by the little avaricious listener. "Harold was going to have to leave. Go away. But don't worry about that now. That comes later.

"So—Harold slogged on, in search of the scream. Was it somewhere on the Upper East Side? No. There were a lot of concealed squeaks up there—but no terrible scream. Was it in Murray Hill then? There were sighs, and a few moans, in Murray Hill, but no scream. Well, how about Greenwich Village? Only yowls, and howls, some sobbing too, but no scream.

"Harold began to walk uptown again. He was walking up Eighth Avenue. It was late in the afternoon, and he felt despondent. That means that he felt the way the sky looked.

"'Where are you, Scream? I'm looking for you,' Harold mumbled to himself.

> Don't be afraid. It's only me.
> It won't hurt much—but I've something to do.
> Just trust me, Scream. I'll set you free.

"At the corner of Eighth Avenue and Fourteenth Street Harold

214

slipped on a piece of ice and fell on the sidewalk and hurt his left shoulder badly. 'Dammit!' he swore. 'I wish I was home instead of here.' At the time Harold was living in a very comfortable closet in a penthouse on Central Park West." (Ah, Johnny and Fran! The summer you asked me to live up there, while you were in California. What a wonderful summer it was!—amid the emblems of your humanity. Living friends, Father, who have no part of this.) "But despite his shoulder, which he thought might be broken, but he didn't want to waste any magic on it, since he knew his magic was going fast, and despite the night that was coming on, Harold slogged his way uptown.

"At about Twenty-seventh Street something happened: Harold thought he heard a silent shriek.

Is that you, Scream? I think you're near.
Scream silently again. I'll hear.

"And there again came a silent cry of desperation. Harold hurried on. And at the corner of Twenty-eighth Street and Broadway—there stood the scream. Or rather there stood the man that the scream was inside. He wasn't a very prepossessing man—that means you don't look twice at a person—just big, and sad, and ordinary. And his eyes were dull and dead, as if he'd seen things, or felt things, that had just put out the lights in them. Harold didn't much like the looks of him. You know, Barney, there are some people you just don't want to say hello to. And this man was one. He was standing under a street light. Smoking a cigarette.

"Harold steeled himself and went up to the man and said, 'Excuse me, sir—'

" 'Huh?' said the man in a flattened-out voice.

" 'I don't quite know how to say this,' said Harold apologetically, 'but there happens to be a scream in you.'

" 'Hey, what do you want?' said the man. But a spark flared up in his eyes.

" 'No really, there *is* a scream in you—and I'm here to let it out. That's all.' Harold smiled as pleasantly as he could. A *real* scream is a very rare thing, and Harold sensed that the scream in this man was as loud and horrible as anything he had ever heard. 'If we could just go somewhere—by ourselves—I'll be able to let the thing go.'

"The man just looked at Harold. And for a minute Harold thought he was going to lift up his big human hand and hit him so hard that Harold would die. But he didn't. He only blinked, and murmured, 'All right. Do anything you want with me.'

" 'Well—let's go down to that open pier at the end of Morton Street,' said Harold. 'That ought to be deserted now.'

" 'All right,' said the man automatically.

"As they walked to the pier, Harold introduced himself, and asked what the man's name was. 'Dan Reilly.' "

"Is this man real?"

"Now Barney, you've got to stop asking that. You know Harold well enough to judge for yourself." He does judge: his face sets. But whether he really believes, I don't know . . . *I* believe.

"Danny and Harold solemnly walked through Greenwich Village, down Hudson Street, then right to the docks—" Where there's always a little action, even on the chilliest winter nights. "—and out onto the deserted pier. In the west, across the Hudson River, some gray light was trying to die and be gone, and behind them the lights of New York looked muffled and dull and unwilling. They walked all the way out to the end of the pier. The water flowed by in absolute silence, like liquid night.

" 'Here we are!' Harold tried to say hopefully, but it came out pure despair instead. More than anything else Harold hated to liberate screams. That means let them out. But it had to be done. Again and again. Sometimes he would hit someone with his fist, and that would do, even though Harold wasn't very big. But sometimes he had to use—" Steady now, lad—steady on! "—he had to use something besides his fist. And he knew that with Danny Reilly he would have to use something horrible. Because this scream had been down there in the dark in Dan Reilly collecting so long. 'Do you—um—do you have any ideas how we can let the scream out?' said Harold.

" 'No—sir,' said Dan Reilly dully. His eyes were as gray and fading as the light in the west, above New Jersey. 'But I think—'

" 'No, wait!' Harold interrupted him. 'We may find something not quite so—so drastic.' He fidgeted there at the end of the pier for a minute. 'Um—Danny—I guess you'll have to bend over and I'm going to sock you on the jaw.'

"Obediently, like a child, Dan Reilly bent over and said, 'I told you before, sir: do anything that you want with me.'

" 'Well, it's not that I *want* to!' Harold shouted. 'But I've got to! We've got to let that scream out.'

" 'Yes, sir,' said Danny drearily. He bent over, Harold made a fist and took a breath and shut his eyes, remembering where Dan's chin was hanging, and then hit him with all his might.

"And nothing. Dan didn't even say 'Ah.' But Harold did. He said *'Ouch!'*—three times in fact and hopped around the pier, shaking his hand up and down. Because he had actually broken a knuckle.

"Danny stood up silently. And just *stood* there, waiting. 'All right now, Dan,' said Harold almost angrily, as he breathed on his actually broken knuckle, 'we don't need to try that yet.'

" 'No, sir,' said Dan.

"Meanwhile, Harold had to repair his hand. He sang to it softly—

> Come on now, Knuckle!
> Don't you buckle!
> Dammit! That hurts! Moans and Groans!
> Knuckle, please repair your bones.

"And his knuckle healed itself whole again.

"And Danny stood there, like a lifeless living statue, waiting to have his scream let out.

" 'We'll try a spanking!' said Harold briskly. 'Give me your belt.'

" 'Yes—sir.' Dan took off his belt. And held onto his pants to keep them from falling down. At the summit of Heaven one dismal black star had been forced to shine. I assume you know what a spanking is—"

Barney's eyes glitter with the terror and excitement of a child about to be spanked. "I know."

(The one time he did it to me—he boasted about it for years afterwards . . . At least *that* I remember from my first twelve years.)

"So Harold took the belt and said, 'Bend over, Danny,' and Danny did, and Harold gave him a very good spanking.

"And nothing. Danny didn't make a peep. He knew what was coming. What had to come.

" 'Oh all *right!*' shouted Harold. He flung his arms up and down. 'If that's all that'll work! Go on!—light up a cigarette!'

"Dan did as he was told. He always did as he was told. When the cigarette was lit and bright, and burning like a hot small hole in the winter night, Harold told Danny to give it to him. Or rather he begged for the cigarette. He had been defeated by the scream and he felt very weak and impotent. That means you have no power at all.

"He took the thing in his hand and said, like someone who was giving up, 'Hold out the palm of your left hand, Danny.'

" 'Yes!—sir.' A light came into Danny's eyes as he did as he was told; it was like the dead light that was lingering in the west.

"Harold closed his eyes and sang softly, so Danny couldn't hear,

Oh Fire, why must it be you
That liberates his shriek?
It's such an awful thing to do
To someone big and weak.

It *is* you, though: he's chosen fire—
So do it! Set it free!
Oh God—this world: all black desire . . .
But why must it be me?

(Curious, my own fear of fire. The worst fear in the world, for me. When I was maybe four or five, I saw my mother, wearing only a slip, try to fix the furnace. And a tongue of flame leaped out at her.)

"And with that, with his eyes still closed, and holding Dan's left hand in his own, Harold pressed down the cigarette into it.

" 'OW!' screamed Dan Reilly. And his eyes suddenly seemed to come to life: they looked startled, puzzled. 'Hey, that hurts—'

" 'Of course it hurts, you idiot!' Harold shouted. 'How did you *think* it would feel when someone butts a cigarette in the palm of your hand—!'

"He would have gone on and ranted and raved—because he felt like ranting and raving awhile—but he had other things to think about: namely, the scream. It was circling above their heads on the pier, in the growing darkness, going *'owowowowow!'*—like

218

those horrible new police ambulance sirens. And also—it was getting bigger. That's the thing about a scream: once you've let it out, you've got to take care of it—or it grows and grows until it deafens the world. Already this scream could be heard all over Greenwich Village. But there were so many sirens and screams in New York that nobody was taking any notice yet.

"Harold got a little panicky. He had known that Dan Reilly's scream was big, but this was the worst scream he ever had heard. He could feel the gusts of wind beat down as its huge invisible wings went flapping—and they were getting larger too—and always that dreadful rising shriek: 'ow*ow*OW!'

"Harold jittered a minute, then said to himself—

Shall I try for soft clouds? Shall I try for soft rain?
Send it south? Let it fertilize meadows and grain?

"But then he decided—

No. Let it be snow. Yes, that is the best!
White particles drifting—

"He flung his hands up as high as he could.

—Oh Scream—*be at rest!*

"And in an instant several wonderful things occurred. The dead light in the west disappeared completely, but the night that fell was somehow brilliant: even though it was black, it was clear and bright, and it seemed to shine. Away to the north the Empire State Building rose up like a tower of trembling lights. And there was abruptly this sound in the air: the scream stopped, and it was as if the whole island of Manhattan had turned into some huge kind of harp. And all the avenues were the strings running up and down. And the sound that Harold heard was as if a great hand had swept over all these living strings. The air shuddered with the splendor of it. And finally, as Harold looked upward, the radiant black was filled with falling snow. It settled lightly on Harold's face, it settled lightly on his hands, it settled on Danny Reilly's face—everyone in New York looked upward and felt the snow, which had been a scream, settle softly on his face.

" 'Whee-*oo!*' Harold sank down onto the pier. He was so exhausted that he had to sit down for a minute. Dan Reilly was standing motionless. 'You sure take it out of a person, lad. Where do you come from anyway?'

" 'Hempstead, sir,' said Dan.

" 'And don't call me sir! My name is Harold. *Harold!*'

" 'Yes, sir—yes, Harold,' said Dan apologetically.

"They walked back from the end of the pier, through the snow that had been Dan Reilly's scream. On the corner of Hudson Street they stopped. 'Go home now, Danny,' said Harold. He put his hand on Danny's back. 'Go back to Hempstead. Or wherever the hell it is! East o' the sun and west o' the moon. Have supper. If necessary, look at television. But try not to grow another scream.'

" 'I'll try,' said Dan, 'Harold.' He shuffled around on the sidewalk a little and locked his arms behind his back. Then he asked, embarrassedly, 'Can I see you again?'

" 'Yes,' said Harold. 'I live all around. Just want me enough and I'll find you.' He held out his hand. 'Good night.'

"Dan gave Harold a quick, kind of nervous smile and said 'Good night,' and walked off in the darkness. Harold watched him walk away under a street light—he was pretty round-shouldered for such a big man—and shook his head. He knew he'd be seeing him again.

"Then Harold walked home too. He walked all the way up to the Upper West Side, to Central Park West and that lovely penthouse. Danny's scream kept on snowing for about an hour. By tomorrow morning it would begin to be trampled and nasty and filthy, but at least for tonight—Harold breathed in and swallowed some crystalline flakes—for this one clean night the New York snow was beautiful. And Harold looked at it and loved it. Because he knew he was going away."

January 13

Yes! *Let* this be a genuine curse!
God damn his children! And God damn his wife!
God damn every atom of that bastard's whole life!
God damn his blind son—
                         Yes! And worse—
God damn myself!

                Yes! Yes!—God damn

The man I would be, could be—am!
God damn the best there is in me!
God damn my soul eternally!

January 14

All right: as it happened—

The thaw continued on Sunday unbelievably. I have never felt or seen such glorious false mildness, such lying in the lustrous sky.

Jim called at eleven, from the hospital—he checks on his patients Sunday morning too—I like that—to say that he'd pick me up around noon. So out we drove—I haven't taken you out of the city all winter, have I?—through all the mechanical desolation Long Island has become. Jim railed at the ugliness of it, but I believe—Barney's question, "Are they real?"—that real heedless people do live on Long Island.

I stayed in the car while he tapped his patient's tummy: an excuse for him to get out fast.

"I want to show you a place," he said. "I was out here last year, baby-sitting Claude, and just for the hell of it I got lost on some dirt roads in Montauk. And I found this great spot. But I'll probably never be able to find it again."

The two of us in his car; his driving confident, almost unconscious; in a quest for a lost place: now sum those up, my witnesses. Then add that thaw: the air of May exhaled over sea-gray oceanscapes. Now put in my love. And my credulity. And my trust in the Impossible. And stir well!

He found the spot. At the end of an almost impassable road, in a hollow that opened, one end, on the boundless silvered Atlantic Ocean, there was—a dreary little house, unoccupied. "That five-and-dime shack isn't much." I studied it, in determined objectivity.

But Jim swept it up in a glance and dismissed it accurately. "A decent architect could make something wonderful of it. The site's the thing. Come here—"

We walked to the end of the dell. About a mile out, on the water like watered silk, in illustration of one of the world's great poems—I saw three ships go sailing by, sailing by, sailing by. Jim was looking along the shore, east and west. He hadn't noticed the fishing boats. And I said to myself—him—Please look at them. Just let them exist in your sight for a second. Then they can be real for me. "Jim—are those fishing boats?"

"Yes."

He studied them a second. Their black shapes leaped into my mind ineradicably. "Oh." Reality is something that one intuits, precipitates, in bits. And the catalyst has to be love. "I didn't know they fished all winter."

"Great spot, what, lad?"

"Yes. Wonderful." I turned away from the fishing boats: their outlines, substance, was burning up my brain. But the land too had entered my life, in its essence: every dry, pearly January shrub was a Burning Bush in my veins.

"You want to go back?"

"When you do, Jim."

"I can't stay out too late tonight. We better start. If we want to hear some music."

My ears blinded, my eyes deafened by music I'd never hoped to hear before, I said, "Okay then, let's go."

His life, the familiar, intruded upon him, and made him grin. "Lucinda's learning checkers. We've got a date at eight o'clock."

This city, seen from across the East River, does suggest in its elevations an ideal that waits to mate with reality. And we saw the view—broke over a rise in the highway, and there it dawned in the sunset: complete—at exactly the right time.

Dante, you must have dreamed of New York!

> *Era già l'ora che volge il disio*
> *Ai naviganti—*

> It was the hour when voyagers want to cry
> For home, the hour that turns their hearts to clay
> The day they've said to their sweet friends good-bye;
> The hour that strikes the pilgrim just away
> With love, if he hears soft bells ring far off
> That seem to mourn the dying of the day—

Dante is where the action is. And the Hell with you, Saul Bellow! . . . Idiot! Two days ago I believed that after Purgatory came Paradise. (How optimistic you were, Dante lad!)

In my apartment, I locked the door and went into the kitchen to fix us drinks. And unexpectedly, as I faced the sink, felt Jim's arms snake around my waist and his head lie flat along my right shoulder, with his ruddy hair—and it *feels* ruddy to me now as well—pressed against my neck. "You're unnaturally affectionate today."

"That was fun, that driving out there. I like to drive. It makes me hot."

I swiveled around, and into his arms. "Let's have another outing soon."

"You know what I feel like—?"

"What?"

"Turning on. Have you got any pot?"

"No." We had never smoked grass together—but the thought of it, the fantasy, was almost as effective as the stuff itself. "I know where I can get some though."

"Now?"

"A cop I know, who lives in the Village, does a little pushing on the side."

I knew that he'd love the irony. "Great!" You see, if one is going to break the law, one should always try to make a policeman an accomplice: it adds a valuable vibration.

And my friend, Officer Kevin Molloy, came through. I called, he was in, he lives only a couple of blocks away, and said to come over and pick up as much as I wanted.

"But look," to Jim, as I hung up, "if you've got to be home by eight—" Idiot!—that I cared if he jilted his daughter Lucinda.

"If I'm not home by eight—" Pragmatically: does anything come between him and his fun? No. "—my wife knows how to play checkers too."

"Be back in fifteen minutes. Relax—drink your drink—"

He started to take off his clothes. "I'll relax."

Kevin, who comes from a long line of cops, delights in all that's illegal. He giggles deliriously while he's selling you dope. I suspect he enjoys it even more than molesting children. No, he does not molest children—quite. But he loves screwing youngsters, male, and makes out like a bandit in the subway johns, being handsome, being young, and being—risky—in uniform. (Dear Kevin, I have complete confidence in you! And I know that sooner or later you'll make it to jail.)

I bought not only our tea-for-two but a little toke of hashish as well.

In ten minutes: "I got some hash too. Have you ever had hash?"

"Lad, I've had everything. You should mix the two." He was naked, and had moved the furniture and opened out the couch. "There's a synergistic effect—"

"Don't use your medical terms at me! Get over on your belly and let me see what I'm going to work while I fix up my trusty pipe." The air of the room was smoldering and smelled of the lust of men for men: an animal odor—burning hair—that lacks the musk of a female's enticement.

"Have you got a pipe? Why, Terry Andrews, I'm going to report you to—"

"Look at this pipe!"

My pipe, all glistening bronze, unscrews into eight or nine separate pieces. It was once described by a writer friend as looking like "a hobbit factory." So naturally I call it Bilbo. I packed it, lit it, whistled the first draft in—"Now don't choke. This is strong"—and passed it on to Jim.

"Lad—don't tell your uncle how to smoke."

"On your belly again. Quick!" Alacrity, since it leaves no marks, since it costs the masochist nothing at all, is something that Jim does very well.

How many of you have smoked hash? To those of you who have had the experience, I say simply that it happened to us . . . To those of you who haven't, I say that nothing that I say now will be even barely commensurate. It's untranslatable.

The first effect for me, the first elevation up out of all that's ordinary, is a neural crescendo: a ruffle of blood in the drums of my chest that deepens, heightens, intensifies—till it reaches a pitch of pulse where, as if by the blood's own choice, it stops. And stays. And maintains a corpuscular drumroll that holds off and also makes imminent some climax of the flesh. But not necessarily orgasm. The body has many crests in it that have nothing to do with sex.

The time thing, by now, will have started to work: a second—is still a second, but savored as if there were minutes in which to enjoy it; and minutes are arbitrary huge slices out of the inexhaustible pie of time; and hours are inconceivable! An hour would be the time it takes for a species to evolve. (A species that might be yourself.)

I have never been in a hydrofoil. But there must be a moment when the boat goes faster and faster—a single moment when it lifts itself into the air. (The image that everyone uses is "flying"— "I'm flying on pot"—et cetera. For me it's sailing, only not in a hydrofoil. In a boat that has no machine in it. Does a catamaran get out of the water? The sailing I do is all internal. But it has to do with a surface beneath you, a wind behind you, a sun above you—and suddenly you are *up*, and traveling faster, motionless, than you have ever traveled before.)

What Jim felt, I don't know; we all have our own solar systems, and I suspect that his planets wheel slower than mine.

This I do know, however: at a certain moment I was kneeling, Jim lying supine in front of me, with his legs locked around my thighs; I was stroking his guts methodically—stroking them with my stiff, adoring self—propped up on my right arm, with my left arm supporting the back of his neck, and lifting him rhythmically into me.

I must now, despite you neoclassical critics out there, do a short, taut ode to this man's face. And especially to those lips of his that knock me out: so particularly formed, with a high pink in them—his facial color's unusually high—and barely, just barely, protuberant. They are lips on the way to becoming Romantic. Baroque, in the best sense—overripe, with a hint of the rottenness yet to come . . . (Can't stop this, folks.) With his head tipped back, in the cradle of my left elbow, his mouth slightly open, an elliptical gate, ruddy membranes inside, and above it his eyes half open too—it's permission: an urgent, passive invitation. I began to spit spears of saliva, which his throat, like an athlete, reached to catch.

Then I had to withdraw—talk—stroke his hair—to keep him from coming. "Where are you?"

His eyes swung from side to side. "I don't know."

"I know where I am."

"Where?"

"In a place where two men—" As I said it, the hash cloud

condensed and rained visions within me. "A place no one ever has been before."

"Tell me, Terry. Talk to me!"

I started to talk.

Anesthetically, I don't remember all that I said. He and I were high: remember that. It would read ridiculously. But while I spoke, we both believed. I invented a place—say, California: Yosemite, before the first Indians had crossed over the Bering Strait. And I peopled it—I animaled it—with Eohippus, my favorite creature, whom Jim hadn't met before: "The tiny dawn horse, the ancestor of all living horses; and he galloped with joy in a level meadow, to think of what sons and what sons of sons, he would have!" There were other delightful souls in that valley: friendly reptiles—and fish that stood upright in the water and chatted with one another, with their fins on their hips: all clear and bright and colorful, like the illustrations from a children's book. There was also—and what is funny when you're sober is sublimely hilarious under hash—the Three-Legged Something. Jim started to giggle when I told him how the benign thing slid in from its cave in the West, doing its usual three-legged waltz, and singing a wordless song in its two mouths, and keeping time clapping with its four hands. It seems that the Three-Legged Something—but no one knew what: an Impossible animal—was the clown of the meadow, the most popular creature there. It visited from species to species, and always was a welcome guest. And Jim loved it! His giggles flourished, rooted, roared—he began saying over and over again, "The Three-Legged Something! The Three-Legged Something!"—and pulled me down onto his laughing chest.

The proximity, friction of flesh on flesh, lit desire in both of us at once. "Now we have to go down to the coast," I said.

This meadow had been a high plateau—there were black stars up there—ringed round by the summits of sheltering mountains. But a pass at one end, where a stream descended—"We only have to follow the stream"—would lead us to a shore, upon which there pounded the surf of an ocean that no ship had ever crossed. The beach where we settled, the linen beach, had only the footprints of animals on it. An immense sun that burned in our blood also towered above us, at noon. The beat of our bodies against each other was given us by the waves. The breath, which I drew through his nose, through his mouth, through my mouth, to my lungs, had begun, somewhere, as a wind off the sea.

I took care—took care! caretaker! you Harold! you fool!—to let Jim flower first. And he did: that flushed color of his, like a masculine self-satisfied rose, expanding beneath and in front of me.

The blossom of love that gnaws on the heart . . .

Alerted by—what? by everything: by the pitch I had tuned him to, by his total submission, his willingness, by the nerve of pure pleasure that he had become, by a look in his eyes that I mistook—it was only pure pleasure—as I got there myself, more totally there than I had ever been before, Mr. Stiltskin—who was *not* having an orgasm—who was waiting for his opportunity, said, "God, Jim, I wish you'd admit that you loved me. Just once." And Harold and I dissolved. I kept my eyes closed, while the cells of my body, mind, soul—what the hell!—reassembled themselves.

When I opened them, Jim was sitting up. His face was strange: editorial and preoccupied: a scientific expression. It must be the look he has when he's performing a fairly interesting operation. If he hadn't yet come—what would he have said? But, orgasm past, the effect of hashish is sometimes to transmute, instantaneously, pure passion into exactly its opposite: a glacial objectivity.

In a gesture of casual negligence, he swung his legs over the side of the couch, preparatory to getting dressed, and wondered aloud, "I don't see why every dopey, lonely faggot I let get up my ass has to fall in love with me."

The open sore, bandaged, which my life is, had its gauze torn suddenly off of it. There were bits of scab, stuck; there was blood; there was—oh, just all *sorts* of interesting infected things!

I remained where I was, lying back on the couch, as Jim put on his shorts and pants. And Rumpel, who has an exquisite sense of decorum, said, rather blandly, to smooth things over, "Can you drive?"

"I can drive."

"You're not too high—"

Preoccupied, in his hash trance, with the mystery of his wrist watch, he didn't answer. Put on the rest of his clothes. And left.

It took a whole day, in the emptiness that I had become, for me to be angry. I had to work to summon up rage, against the truth of what Jim had said. But I worked! I did work—

> So let this be a genuine curse!
> God Damn his family! And God Damn his wife!
> God Damn every atom of that bastard's whole life!
> God Damn his blind son—
>
> > Yes! And worse—
>
> God Damn myself—

Ah well, no need to repeat it. The second half is already in effect.

January 16

A third of my life has been taken away. (Advice to the lovelorn: cast off your ballast! Get rid of him, her, it—that high-heeled shoe that you're mad about. If you live through the first two days, you'll find that you're flying. Despair is weightless: the inner equivalent of outer space.)

I'm sailing! It has been a great day! I've taken a concrete step. (No, I'm *not* drunk, Father. Nor am I swacked on pot or hash. You funny, lovable old Pope—surely you know what the big High is.)

It came to me like in a dream: pills! One has to decide scientifically—say I, as I pound my voodoo drums!—on the way one is going to do it. Pills! I'm afraid of heights, and I don't like the idea of leaving a mess for wonderful Iris to have to clean up: no gun then. So pills.

I already have some Seconal: a doctor's prescription, two years old, and drearily practical: just sought and purchased to let me sleep. But the pills I prize, the precious and special pills—the precial pills—these had to be bought particularly. And they were. Today.

I felt like a Bach fugue—or like a computer: programmed for a specific action.

Out with my suit! And out with my suitcase! The given plan was to walk up Eighth Avenue. And the mask was to be a salesman, an out-of-towner who needed to buy some sleeping pills. The mask was to be a guy just—Hi! hi fella!—just in need of a little Seconal.

I have ascertained that thirty-five of the grain and a half, plus a lot of Scotch—a whole bottle if necessary—will do the trick.

And this thaw—incredible. Will it never end? May in midwinter . . . And my birthday comes in May.

> Good-bye, my birthday. I am proud
> That you occurred in lovely May.
> A joyous month! Spring shouts out loud—
> But doesn't quite know what to say.

With the certainty of the damned and/or blessed I began my pilgrimage uptown.

It was given that I should buy five Seconal in seven drugstores. Illegal, without a prescription. Precisely! If I fight—and defeat—the boundaries, then I'll be allowed to die.

My quest, if it did nothing else besides get me my pills, proved the value of small enterprise. The chains were disagreeable, but the neighborhood pharmacies—a stranger, who just wanted to get some shut-eye—even some with candies in big round glass jars—the neighborhood pharmacies, with their funny names, their bribability, their sweet and healthy unconcern, were not. The fireplugs outside their doors—

> Beyond the seven waterfalls,
> Across the seven asphalt hills,
> Young Rumpel Stiltskin gaily strolls
> To buy the necessary pills.
>
> He first tries Whelan, then Rexall,
> And then the locals must he try.
> They all are kind, and patient all,
> And don't believe he wants to die.
>
> But oh you druggists, do beware
> The soul who comes in cool, with needs.
> He may be suave and debonair,
> But he will not grow old. He pleads.
>
> You say that it's against the law.
> He winks and says he knows that, yes.
> Just five he wants. Just five? No more?
> He's new in town. You will? God bless!

Don't worry, Sam, it's not your fault.
Go sell your laxatives and lives.
A drugstore lures all kinds of guilt.
Not yours the choice of who survives.

Fate kissed, caressed Eighth Avenue!
Light flowed in gold through mundane streets!
Outside your shop—the "Sam 'n' You"—
I stood where death rejects, flirts, greets.

January 18: Eleven at night

He still is alive. I can hear him breathe, feel his breath on my
cheek, as I bend above him.

How *can* this have happened? I'm not a murderer—yet. And
when I become one, it must be by my choice.

Damn Edith! And damn the wretched believing child! And oh,
most damn my own obscene stupidity!

She called this morning—"with a very special request. And it's
all your own fault too!" Seems the fetus has been pleading to
come down to my apartment again. When what he ought to have
been asking for is to be aborted! "—and if you are kind enough to
take him out to dinner—on *me!*—since you are the only human
being alive who can get a proper meal into him—"

"How about tonight?"

"Oh Terry—!" A mother's, a very well-dressed mother's, gasp
of gratitude.

"Would he like to stay overnight again?" As long as it's saint
time, why not shoot the works?—the halo, the lily pinned to my
nightie, the shit-eating smile: the works. St. Francis, you're a piker
compared to St. Sadist of Greenwich Village.

Well, *Ber*-nard would simply be thrilled!

And why not, on my part? A third of my life is completely gone.
A third is spending a weekend at Miss Porter's: some Freshman's
Parents' Day Do. Why not tell the third third lies?—sweet stories
of a world where the Rats are happy.

So down Barney comes—in his very own taxi: looking lovely
and forlorn in the back seat—I was watching from my window,
and went down to the street to haul him in—like a tadpole in an

oversized goldfish bowl. And up to my apartment, with his usual eager reticence. The idea of eating out is absurd: a TV dinner is all he wants. A Scotch, several Scotches, is all I do. I decree—franks and beans—with a muffin in the right-hand corner compartment, stewed apples in the left. He winces with pleasure at my lordly gesture, right hand upraised, as I make my announcement: "We're going to have—franks and beans! So there."

I have a story prepared too, based on fact. When I first moved into my tomb, ten years ago, I tried to paint the place myself.

> Is it a tornado? No, that's what it ain't.
> Oh my God—
> Harold jumped up.
> —the Rat's trying to paint!

" 'Well where have you been?' screams the Rat.

" 'Now now, take it easy, Rat,' says Harold. 'I got here as fast as I could.'

" 'All you people who keep telling me my apartment needs paint!' the Rat sulked. 'Just look what I've done to me!' He unstuck a claw from one side.

"Harold had to do something fast. Because he was about to burst out laughing.

> Poor Rat! You're covered with paint. You're a sight!
> Don't worry, Rat—it'll be all right.
> Your whiskers are sticky. I touched one. *Ik!*
> I'm afraid this'll take quite a bit of magic.

" 'Just sit down now, Rat,' said Harold.

> White paint in splashes large and small,
> Up now on friend Rat's living room wall.
> White paint in splotches fat and thin,
> A nice smooth coat. Okay—begin!

"Immediately the air in the Rat's apartment was full of flying globs of paint. Harold and the Rat have to twist and duck out of the way.

" 'But what about *me?*'

" 'Oh. Sorry, Rat.

> P.S. You, paint that's on the Rat—
> Up on the walls! You too. That's that.

And the paint job is finished. Imitating the "Sorcerer's Apprentice" section of *Fantasia*, I have a demonic paintbrush do a fabulous performance on the molding, with Harold and the Rat shouting "bravo!" after each virtuoso flourish. They get a little squiffed—as I do too, while I tell the tale—and it ends with Harold staying the whole day—he makes the plaster plaster too—and that evening he has supper with the Rat. It is one of the few times that the Rat has a guest. (Their meal, coincidentally, is a TV dinner: franks and beans.) (And God damn my urge to invent!)

Our meal, story ended, for the first few minutes is eaten in silence. But Barney's puzzlement has to break out. He looks around, at my disappointing walls, and quizzes me seriously: "But why isn't everything *white* now?"

Good question. "Good question." I scratch my chin elaborately. And pretend to twirl some whiskers. "No answer."

The believing little fiend! He's so difficult to talk to! You parents out there—don't your kids talk? Don't they rattle on, ask questions—"How? Why? *Why?*" This uncooked hamburger hardly says a word. Just scoops up his beans, his apples, and munches on his bun. And waits to hear me say something.

It drives me mad! I begin to get bored and angry. (Why didn't I know enough to send him *away* then?) Jim's gone, for good. Anne's gone, temporarily. But I could have gone out and gotten laid—at the baths—or picked up a hooker on Third Avenue. God knows, I could have done *something* besides sit across a cardboard table, eating a TV dinner, with this vacuum of childhood.

"Hey, Barney, how's school?"

"All right."

I feel an impulse to crush his skull. I would love to hurt him physically. Yes! "Just all right?"

"Miss James was sick. We had Miss Malinski."

Yes! To hurt him physically. "In which subject?"

"Reading."

"Your favorite—you said."

"Yes."

The room shivers—or do I?—in the dawn light of the Impossible. "Is Miss Malinski as good as Miss James?"

"She's—"

"What?"

"She's different. She reads to us better. But she interrupts when we try to read."

His head, his arms, his whole body—ungrown—seem to pulse with vulnerability. "How—how—" I swallow—no food. "—do *you* read? Well? Are you a good reader?"

"I don't know." His answer, in its uncertainty, is sacrificial: seems to plead with me.

For a moment the madness is giddy, delicious. Dan Reilly, Jim Whittaker—or *Ber*-nard Willington: any death will do. Won't it? "Do you want some more milk?"

"No thank you."

I stand up: my dizziness needs to be vertical. And go into the kitchen. And make a Scotch. In the tiny room a breeze that began a thousand miles away breathes softly over me. And the floor seems to rise and settle in swells.

Long silence, while I wonder—truly wonder—if I could kill him. While he wonders, finishing dinner, if I could tell him another story. So then what will it be?—a story, or death?

He reads my mind! The underdone devil! "Where's Harold going?"

"Away."

"Where?"

"*Away!* And how did you know that anyway?"

"*Harold—and the Scream.* But why is he going?"

"His left shoulder hurts him, that's why! And what are you?—some kind of midget detective?"

He giggles: a midget detective he'd like to be. Questing after the soul's destination.

"Is it in New York? Where he's going?"

"No." Or is it? It may just be some dingy eternal suburb. Or perhaps Hell's that interchange on Bruckner Boulevard. "But maybe it is. It may just be the Bronx."

"How is he going to get there?"

Like that old radio program: "Let's Pretend." How do you get to the adventure? A fire engine?—a friendly dragon, with seats on his back like a 707? "He sleeps his way there. He takes a handful of magic pills—and he wakes up in Oz, or Middle Earth. Or the Bronx."

"May I see them?"

I am still in the kitchen, coasting in front of this nonexistent wind. The inevitable, the necessary, is not an iron chair; it is merely a breath against the back of your neck. "Would you like to—?"

"Yes—"

Like a kite at the end of his timid request I am tugged—I slip sideways—the wind carries me into the living room—

"—please."

—and into the bathroom, where the pills are in their plastic jar.

I must say now that in the daze of that soaring, I foresaw what would happen.

I empty the jar in my hand—"There"—and the innocent, lethal, small bullet-shaped pink things swarm in my palm. "There." I memorize their attributes, as Barney also studies them.

And as he has to, he suddenly stretches out his half-formed paw, snatches up as many as he can, and jams them in his mouth: perhaps his first act of initiative.

I must say now—I watch it happen. It is not till I see him start to chew that the panic explodes inside my skull. His face is determined—and old, very old, an old man's face, as he concentrates upon the hard task, as if he were gumless, of chewing up my Seconal.

"Spit them *out!*" I shout. And cup my hand in front of his mouth.

He grins at me, and keeps on munching . . . R.S.—I finally see your smile.

"Barney—spit them out," I reasonably request. "They aren't what I told you they were." My reason abruptly is oxidized, and I think of grabbing him by the throat. Except that way I'd just choke him to death. His jaws keep on grinding methodically. He is trying to swallow. "Barney—if you will spit that silly stuff out—I will tell you a story that Harold has never told anyone. His most secret story. The one that puzzled and troubled him most." His jaws relax. His eyes, skeptical, are quizzing me. "I mean it, Barney—" I am aloof, aloft: a balloon above a volcano. "—but you'll have to spit that nasty-tasting stuff out."

It slithers into my palm: the empty shells of the Seconal, the white scum—how much of it has he eaten? Shall I call a hospital? Shall I jam my fingers into his throat and make him vomit?

Shall I kill him—the thought lingers—and then kill myself?

"I'm going to make you some coffee. Yes, coffee! You'll need it. This is a very hard story to hear."

It takes a few minutes to steady my hands, to put the kettle on, as I ransack rejected Harold stories and try to find one to make grand and difficult. "All right now, the name of this story is—*Harold—and the Teddy Bear who went Berserk.*

"That means cuckoo: lost his marbles completely." I stay in the kitchen and start to talk, as the water heats, in order not to see the child. If he's going to die, he'll make a little squeak, won't he, first? "Harold did *not* wake up one morning—this happened late at night. He was still living in that comfortable closet on Central Park West. Well, about midnight Harold was fast asleep, and dreaming of yogurt with brown sugar on top. Because plain yogurt and brown sugar go very well together. When all of a sudden a pair of little wings started to pound him and he heard a voice—a very garbled voice—that means, 'blublub'—saying, 'Harol'! Hey, Harolharol! You gotta wake up.' It was Jake Moth. You remember who Jake Moth was—?" He couldn't have died, without a sound. Could he?

"Yes," he calls from the living room.

In the drop of relief, a physical space that I feel around me, I make him a cup of pretty strong coffee—lots of milk, lots of sugar too. "Now sip on this. 'Cause it's going to get grisly." He holds the big cup in both hands and sips.

But *should* I take him to the hospital? Don't you turn a certain color if you're going to die? And isn't there time, once you turn that color, to get you to the hospital? St. Vincent's is only four blocks away . . . I could carry him, if he lost consciousness.

"Harold jumped up, terrified. You know, most of the time he was terrified anyway, but Jake Moth had really frightened him. He flung his arms up and down and shouted, 'What's wrong, Jake! For God's sake, what's wrong?'

" 'Ish Ted Bear,' said Jake, who had been smoking one of his kooky little cigarettes. 'He—like, wow, man!—flipped out! Ish a real bad shene, Harol'!, not groovy at all! You gotta come quick!

Jush lucky for all the animalsh tha' Mrsh. Bottomthrottle'sh apartmen' ish in the shame buildin' ash theirsh!'

"Harold whipped on his vest, and whipped on his coat, and he and Jake dashed across Central Park to the Upper East Side. Of course Jake Moth went dashing, zigzag, through the air."

He is held: his eyes follow, in a middle distance, Jake's zigzag dash through the air. You don't die if you're interested in listening to something, do you?

"Now Harold had had some experience in dealing with teddy bears. And he had found that many of them were very excitable. Just a year or so ago a bunch of teddy bears at Columbia University had raised the black flag of anarchy. That means they misbehaved—but meant well—and had an awful lot of fun. It *is* fun, when teddy bears raise the black flag of anarchy. Barney—? Harold had been called in by Mayor Lindsay, and his suggestion was buckets of ice-cold water. But the mayor, acting very mayor-like, suggested negotiations instead, and Harold gave in. But the point is, Harold knew teddy bears. 'Is Ted raising a revolt?' he asked.

" 'No, no, ish worsh,' said Jake. 'Ish pershonal. None of that New-Left-teddy-bear jive.' The New Left is something that teddy bears just found out about. It's everybody being good and nice. But the idea has been around as long as there have been left hands." My voice is possessed of a life of its own: it says—it blabs—anything I can find, just to keep him listening. " 'Ish Jimmy,' said Jake.

" 'Ted's Jimmy?'

" 'Yesh. He shaid it wash okay for hish mom to put Ted up in the attic. Ish a good thing Jimmy an' hish parensh are away for the weeken'.'

" 'Oh Lord!' Harold started to run. It was worse than he had expected.

"Ted Bear and the other stuffed animals lived in the apartment below Mrs. Throttlebottom's. Along with Ted, there was Art Panda, Anita Peacock, Dick Pig, and a senile owl named Isaac with a music box inside him. That means he was old and forgetful and funny and sad. His music box kept going off at all the wrong times. It played patriotic songs. Barney—!"

"Yes?"

"When Harold and Jake Moth got to the apartment of Jimmy's parents and went into Jimmy's room, they saw a very awful sight. There were smashed toys everywhere: a broken top, a ripped-apart Monopoly board, a toy train crushed and its tracks ripped up—everything sadistically destroyed. But even worse than the ruination was the sight of all the animals. They were standing awkwardly around the room with tightened-up faces and eyes that were trying not to see anything. And what they were all trying not to see was Ted Bear. He was sitting on the floor, with his arms tied behind him with Christmas-tree ribbon around one of the legs of Jimmy's bed. And he was staring down into the rug, pretending not to be ashamed.

"Harold walked right up to him and said in an ordinary voice—an especially ordinary voice—'Hi, Ted!'

" 'Hello, Harold,' said Ted, without looking up.

" 'He hit me!' Dick Pig burst out. Dick was made of white velvet, and he had been given to Jimmy by a very rich aunt. Named Gladys. 'He hit me right here!' Dick poked his tummy.

" 'Well, with all that fat,' said Harold matter-of-factly, 'there must have been plenty to cushion the blow.'

"Art Panda, who was quiet and nice and Ted's best friend—except for Jimmy, his boy—said, 'Did Jake tell you what happened, Harold?'

" 'Yes,' Harold began, 'and—'

"But Ted Bear started to shout and tug at the ribbon. 'How do you like that, Harold? How *do* you? Eight years we've been together! His very first toy I was! All those years in the crib! And now he tells his mother—it's okay, up to the attic with old Ted Bear!' His eyes snapped as he stared around at all the other animals. 'And don't you look so dumb, all you! If *I* go up to the attic, sure as hell you all are coming up there too!' Drink up that coffee, Barney. It's going to get worse. Is this too hard a story?"

"No."

He slurps up what's left in the cup. He does not change color. His eyes are not dull. " 'Do you *know* what it's like in the attic?' Ted Bear demanded. 'I'll tell you! There's this storeroom on the top floor of this building. With all ugly old furniture crammed into it. And that's where we'll be—for the next forty years! Then they'll burn us all up. I don't mind the fire though. It'll be horrible, but it'll be quick. It'll be a relief! I'll go fast, I'm so dry. God, Harold, you can't imagine how dry my stuffing is! I'll go fast. It's those forty years that worry me. With Anita Peacock crying—I mean, not really crying out loud—I could stand that—but just sort of whimpering. For forty years. And Art Panda sighing. And Dick getting sootier and sootier. And Isaac Owl trying to play all the wrong songs. But his music box will have rusted years and years ago. But we'll all hear him trying—grating and trying. And we'll hear birds too, in the spring. And see snow through cracks in the winter. And all the different slants of light, as the sun goes all around the year.' Ted tugged at his ribbons and bashed his head against the bed leg. 'I can't stand the thought of it, Harold! It gives me the fears!'

" 'Now take it easy, Ted.' Harold laid his hand on Ted Bear's shoulder.

"It didn't help though. Ted jerked his head sideways and started to cry. 'But the worst—the worst—'

" '—is Jimmy,' said Harold. There are times when you do have to say the worst.

" '—is Jimmy,' sobbed Ted Bear. 'Eight years. I mean, I love him, Harold—I really do love him. And now he wants to stuff me into a cardboard box and put me up in the attic.' Ted swung his head away, so the animals and Harold wouldn't see him cry. But they saw him anyway.

" 'Ted,' said Harold quietly, 'if I undo the ribbons, will you behave? And not break anything?'

" 'Yes, Harold,' said Ted Bear softly. He couldn't have broken anything, even if he'd wanted to. For he was exhausted. He felt the absolute tranquillity that comes—but does not last—from absolute despair. That means you have no strength left to be unhappy. How was the coffee?"

"All right."

"You want some more?"

"I shouldn't have coffee."

True—"Okay, Mr. Know-it-all!"—unless it keeps you from being killed.

"Harold untied the Christmas ribbons. Ted Bear stretched his arms to get the circulation back into them, but he stayed where he was, sitting on the floor, staring downwards, at nothing. 'Now Ted,' said Harold, 'I'm going to do exactly what you want.' Ted looked up, puzzled. 'I mean that, Ted. You're in bad trouble, and I can see that. So whatever it is you want, I'll do.' Harold cleared his throat and sounded as much like a newspaper as he could. 'As I see it, there's three things that I can do. The first is—kill Jimmy.'

"Ted's head jerked up, and all the other animals winced into themselves. 'Yes!' said Harold, almost angrily. 'All you silly little toy animals! You think just because I rush around New York, making moths crash-proof and sending old ladies back home to Iowa—you think that I can't kill. But I can! I've got plenty enough magic left to do *that!*' He stared at Ted Bear sternly. 'And I will! I'll kill Jimmy. Tomorrow, when he and his parents get home. Burn him—or hit him so hard with my fist—'

" 'Now wait a minute,' said Ted nervously. 'I didn't say that's what I wanted.'

" 'All right.' Harold's voice was as blank as linoleum. 'Then here's another idea. When they get home tomorrow, I'll put some slipperiness on the doorstep. And Jimmy will fall and hit his head. And he'll never grow up. I'll make sure his brain gets broken. He'll stay a child for the rest of his life. Even when he gets big physically, he'll still stay a child inside himself.'

" 'Will he get big?' Ted Bear asked.

" 'Yes,' said Harold. 'I happen to know what Jimmy will be like, if he should survive.'

" 'Tell me,' said Ted Bear.

" 'Well,' Harold dreamed, as the future came into the present, 'he's going to be big: six foot two. And his hair, which is blondish now, is going to turn reddish. Auburn, you'd say it would be. And he would have been a doctor—'

" 'A doctor?' said Ted. He looked over in a corner where a smashed medical set was lying. 'His father gave him that last Christmas.'

" 'Well, that may have been what would have started it. But he wanted to be a surgeon.'

" 'What's the third choice, Harold? For you to do?'

" 'The third choice,' said Harold, in his voice like a page with no writing on it, 'is to let him grow up.'

"No one—not any toy animal, nor any human being either, had seen Harold look as cruel and impersonal as he looked right now, staring at Ted Bear.

" 'I don't know what to do,' said Ted. 'You choose, Harold.'

" 'No,' said Harold icily. 'It's up to you. But think, Ted—' His voice turned silky and sweet. '—if you want the second, even when Jim gets big, when the red hairs grow out of his chest, he'll always want his teddy bear. When he goes to the home too.'

" 'What home?'

" 'He'll have to be put away,' Harold prophesied calmly. 'But in the home, with the other gorks, he'll have his toy animals with him.'

" 'Stop it!' Ted Bear jumped up. 'You stop it, Harold! That can't happen! I choose the third!'

" '*Do* you?' said Harold, with a face like transparent glass.

" 'Yes!' said Ted Bear. 'Yes, I do!'

" 'Then you have to say some words,' said Harold. 'You have to repeat after me—

> Let him grow—let him grow—let him outgrow me.
> Let him even forget me, if need be.
> It's not his fault he's a little boy.
> It's not my fault I'm a nursery toy.

Now say that, Ted. If you mean it.'

"Ted said the words.

" 'Thank God!' sighed Harold. His face came back to what it ought to be. 'We survived.'

" 'Well, it's up to the attic tomorrow!' Ted Bear said hectically to all his friends.

" 'And don't be so sure about that either,' said Harold. 'As a matter of fact—Jimmy's going to change his mind. You all stay here for another year. And as for the attic, it's not going to be what you think at all. I happen to know something about attics. And closets. And places where people get put away.' "

He's yawning! Oh Jesus! Do you yawn when— Do you get to yawn first? Or do you just lose consciousness, like a thimble of water evaporating? Or go into convulsions, like a mechanical toy that's having fits?

"Barney!—are you sleepy?"

"No."

"There's more to this story. Do you want to hear it?"

"Yes."

"Well, before Harold told the animals what the attic would be like, there were all those broken toys to be repaired. Harold rolled up his sleeves and addressed himself to the split Monopoly board and the ruptured railroad train.

> Come on, you toys—back! Be unbroken.
> Ted's sorry and apologizes.
> Good words and prayers have now been spoken.
> You meant them, didn't you, Ted Bear?
>
> Yes.

"So the toys were fixed, and to make the occasion more festive—that means *whoopee!*—because Harold knew that Ted Bear was still quite upset, to make the atmosphere party-like, Harold conjured up a chocolate cake with white icing and a pitcher of lemonade. And a lot of paper cups.

> Okay, you chocolate cake, be cut in pieces!
> Now help yourself, folks—and I hope it pleases.

"Barney—do you like chocolate cake with white icing?"

"Yes." But his eyelids grow heavy and heavier.

"Well—when everyone had had enough—which means Dick Pig had eaten half the cake, because he was the kind of person who could forgive a punch in the stomach if he had some cake to eat—and when Isaac Owl had tried to play 'Oh beautiful for spacious skies' but it came out 'God bless America'—and he reached down and pounded himself on the stomach where the music box was, and said, 'Damn that Kate Smith!'—because Isaac was a very old owl, made in the time of Kate Smith, and given to Jimmy by his uncle George, Gladys's husband—and Kate Smith was a fat and jolly lady who sang on the radio, but never mind—*Barney!*"

"Yes."

"Are you falling asleep on me?"

"No."

"*Anyway*—when the cake had been eaten, and the lemonade drunk, and when the animals were all in a party mood, Harold explained about the attic. 'It's really just like this,' he said. 'It's parties.'

" '*Whoopee!*' Dick Pig shouted. 'More parties!'

" 'There's toy animals in almost every attic in New York,' said Harold, 'But instead of being downhearted and gloomy, and lying around in cardboard boxes for forty years, they have parties. They find each other by going out the skylights and walking across the roofs.'

" 'Um—Harold,' Art Panda interrupted, 'I hate to bring this up, but there isn't a skylight in the storeroom upstairs.'

" 'Minor point.' Harold flicked off the minor point like a fly from his cuff. 'I will make you a skylight! If I say so myself, there's one thing I'm very good at—and that's making skylights. And ladders that go up to them. Why, every single warm night of the year, the roofs of New York are creeping with toy animals who are going to parties! There are very few black stars and they *don't* hear the Three-Legged Nothing screaming!' Forget that, Barney! They don't worry about the winter either. 'I'm also quite good at making secret passageways.' Barney—"

"Yes."

"You're falling asleep."

"No, I'm not."

"Yes you are." But it's late: it's ten-thirty—he ought to be sleepy. If only I could trust this sleep of his tonight. "Just a little bit more, then we'll both go to bed." Oh no I won't!

" 'The thing is,' Harold said, 'you animals have to remember this: there's always ways for people to meet. If the people are little toy animals, they meet one way, for parties and boasting about their children. If they're human beings, they meet in a very different way. Takes more time.' Barney—come on now. It's time for bed."

Limp doll, he allows himself to be undressed. I strip him to his underwear, take him into the bathroom, into the bedroom, tuck him in. And wonder if I have murdered him.

"You won't mind if I leave the light on in the living room, will you?"

"No."

"I want to read a while." An unplanned event: I bend over and kiss the short fuzz on his head.

"Woolywoolywoolywooly!" It ought to be a jouncing code for love and bliss, not a last attempt to forestall—

And my vigil begins.

January 19: One o'clock

He still is alive. I can hear him breathe, feel his breath on my cheek, as I bend above him.

January 19: Three o'clock

He still is alive. I can hear him breathe, feel his breath on my cheek, as I bend above him.

January 19: Five o'clock

He still is alive. I can hear him breathe, feel his breath on my cheek, as I bend above him.

January 19: Seven o'clock

I can wake him up. I have shaved and showered, put on clean clothes, and am ready to take him home . . .

I can wake him up!

January 19: Twelve o'clock

I cannot swim in this surf . . .

Being raised, during summers, on lakes, I am used to manageable waves. But last summer I went out to South Hampton to stay with a friend for a weekend. And the surf was high and beautiful. I thought you could get through those great oceanic breakers like the ripples of childhood, that I was used to. My friend—a living—said that for about five minutes all he saw was a cartwheel of my hands and ankles.

This morning—the surf is high inside me.

He wakes up as if sleep was literally two eyelids shut and nothing more: they snap up like shades—he grins at me sheepishly, as if being seen, by me, asleep, is somehow a cause for embarrassment. Poor little bugger! Just like myself as a child: the world, in its essence, is only a place that affords opportunities to be ashamed.

"Did you sleep well?"

"Yes."

"Are you hungry for breakfast?"

"Yes."

"Well I don't have any TV breakfasts—if there are such things. And I *don't* think you'd like a Carnation Instant."

"Yes I would!"

"All *right* then! We'll have two Carnation Instant Breakfasts!"

He trots into the bathroom, thrilled at the prospect. He weighs too much: his trot's a waddle. From the kitchen—"You know, Barney, you ought to lose some weight."

"All right."

Just like that: "All right." And he will, if I tell him to.

As he dresses, I begin to become aware that the flat relief, the dead peace, of his not having died in the night is starting to grow into turbulence. There are waves being generated, far off.

"Vanilla for both of us—all right?"

My compliment—that we have the same flavor—makes him squeagle. But he doesn't answer. Just takes his glass and stares into it as he drinks.

"That's not much to eat. Your mother'll make you some real breakfast when you get home. And—" Lordly, I condescend, from an artificial eminence that I know he'll enjoy—I dramatize with a princely phony gesture, fingers flicked up, of my right hand. "—if your mother should ask me to stay—I'll eat three hundred pancakes."

He sequesters delight behind a face turned away.

The schemer in me senses here, pragmatic even in an approaching storm, that this is the time to say, "And if you don't tell your mother that you gobbled up my happy candy last night—I won't."

His silence is complicity.

In the taxi—a raw winter morning, with gusts of sunlight that strike me like breakers—his puppy crew cut works on me. "Hey, why do you keep your hair so short?"

"I don't know."

"Long hair is all the rage these days. Does your mother like it like that?"

"I guess the barber does," he fatalistically explains.

A devastating witticism!—I roar with laughter—on the strength of which I reach over and shake him by the shoulder. "More hair and less weight is what we want."

Edith is unmade-up and wearing a housecoat when she opens the door. One sees something ragged, almost frumpish, beneath that Bergdorf artifact. For the first time I like her. "*You're* early—"

"Up and doing! Up and doing!" the early bird—Christ, I'm crazy!—

"If you'll wait a minute—till I get something on—"

"Take your time." A Patton tank could not dislodge me from this apartment.

Barney flops frenziedly after her, into her bedroom.

And when she comes back—I fight to keep on liking her, though she's smart now, chic—"I see! I don't know whether I can make three hundred—"

"Just try."

"All right." It's Barney's "all right," the first word a few notes above the second. That's where he got it. But in his voice the clay is still wet and fresh. "And meanwhile why don't you make us both bloody marys or screwdrivers or something else you're allowed to have in the morning. The bar's over there."

Barney has paddled in beside me. "Come on—" I propel him toward the bar. "—I'll teach you how to make a drink."

Regretfully I confess it: I do not eat three hundred pancakes. I can only eat ten—ten middle-sized ones. But that's something of a triumph in Barney's eyes. I become euphoric, as he watches me down them, one after another. Or it may be only the bloody marys. But beneath the surges of good humor—"Edith, do you remember Yvonne's relaxicizor? We will *not* talk about that before you, my lad!"—the rushes down into laughter, the crests of

245

wordless happiness, I feel these swells rising, and they frighten me. At ten-pancake time I am not only stuffed, I am terrified. I have to find some shore. (And your listening—yes, *yours!* my witnesses—please exist!—is the only beach in which I believe.)

I make a flourish of good-byes: "See you soon!—Thanks, Edith!—Bye, Barney!—I do better with waffles."

I exit as a madcap character, having made Edith laugh, having found an excuse to touch Barney's head—a clown who cracks jokes and does tricks while he's drowning . . .

It is cold out today . . .

I haven't worn an overcoat, and my topcoat is only a flimsy reminder that this is January. But I need to walk all the way home.

My shivering I can excuse as a chill. Even in my living room, where the radiator is going full blast.

I must try to identify this sensation.

It isn't desire: the loss of Jim.

It isn't regret: the loss of Anne.

> Between desire and regret
> The world entirely vanishes.
> Matter and antimatter, met,
> Create an ideal emptiness.

He had my death in his mouth . . .

Oh my God—I do love that little boy! . . .

January 20

You poor people who haunt schoolyards!—you're not all rapists, you're not all exhibitionists, or child molesters—there are some of you who simply love.

If I'd had the guts, I'd have gotten up early today—a Monday: dreadful school—I'd have hidden outside his apartment house and watched Edith walk him to school. (At one time or another she'd told me his latest torture chamber was in the neighborhood. "Conveniently! I can walk him to school. And he walks home *all by himself!*")

But no—I've no courage, no courage to hide in doorways, casual smile, nonchalant slouch, all those masks of deceitful normality that one puts on a life that's become so alive that all the ordinary gestures grate on one's skin like steel wool. I can't craftily spy on someone I love. Instead I go up to the Frick—my favorite place in the world—and sit in the courtyard beside the superbly audible pool, ignoring the treasures on every side, and fantasize thus:

I could go to every private school on the Upper East Side and ask if they had a student named Bernard Willington. And when I found him!—

"I just happen to be this well-known children's author, and I happened to be walking down the street, so I thought I'd come in, and—*where is he?*" Or—

"I'm the handyman at *Ber*-nard's apartment house. Mrs. Willington has a message for him. Now—*where is he?*" Or maybe—

"I feel faint. May I have a drink from a water fountain, please? Preferably the one outside Barney's homeroom?"

The smells of school: antiseptic in the lavatory—floor wax in the hall—the myriad odor of humanity in the classroom. How I hated those smells once! How Barney must hate them now, poor lad: so un-at-home in his life.

Do kids still have recess, I wonder? Do they come piling out at ten-thirty? I dread what I dream, having lived it myself at his age: an outsider. I was skinny and Barney is fat, but the grim experience of not being part transcends physiognomy.

Is he coaxed by a teacher—"Join in! Join in!" They are playing some improvised game with a ball. And you see the types already set: the jock-strap athletes, before they even have pubic hair—the determined, disciplined little boys who'll be in Congress in thirty years, or running IBM—and the Barneys. Some of whom do survive and live happily ever after. They do not live happily now, however. For now they exist in corners. They shine, sometimes, in geography, or reading, but out of the structured field of a classroom they are whirled apart, spun off like desolate satellites, and they orbit the unknown all alone.

Has she got him to try, that kindly teacher? Someone throws him the ball. He misses it . . . The Frick fountain splashes . . . I missed it too.

Could I find his school? And then go in, an honored guest,

when the teachers learn who I am, and make Barney a star?

No, no—it's absurd . . . Just brood on that sorrowful water before you.

And after recess—arithmetic. The new math, I suppose. He's as bad at it as I would have been.

Then lunch . . .

Then naps. Do they still have naps—little kids his age? I am so far away from everything real and young and necessary . . . But the naps of children!—I'm drowned in the peace and terror of small complicated sleeps . . . Do they sleep on cots? Or do they fold their arms on their desks . . . "Fold your arms," Mrs. Jackson crooned. "Fold your arms on the top of your desks. Now head down. Yes—that's right. That's right"—in the singsong voice that always brings peace.

And after naps, reading . . . Miss Malinski, who interrupts . . . Mrs. Jackson, who never interrupted me . . . Is that why I write?

But now it's gym time. Oh shit! . . . It's gym for little kids . . . Poor Barney! With your blub-blub stomach! Your Mesozoic coordination! Before God, I don't know what his regimen is—but I know he's undergoing the daily hell of gym! I did mental flyaways, looptheloops, but nothing made up for the physical hell of basketball. I remember once—

They are playing basketball right now! Some seven-to-ten-year-old-version of the adult game. And Barney is hiding around the court in a desperate attempt not to be thrown the ball.

—when I couldn't avoid it, I caught the damn thing, and dribbled like a terminal neurological case—toward the wrong basket! And almost scored a goal! If "goals" are what you do score in that lousy rotten game!

Then, of course, in late adolescence my vanity, which had planted itself in mental accomplishments, sank roots into my flesh. I began to work out at a gym. And thank God I did! Apart from keeping me healthy thus far, you make out much better with a sizable chest and presentable arms.

Will Barney become a fag, I wonder? I only hope he acquires enough self-confidence to think of himself as attractive to anyone.

> You parents out there—don't get desperate
> If Junior turns into a full-fledged queer.

Don't trust those words "fag" and "degenerate"—
It's better there than neither there nor here . . .

It is three o'clock. I have dwindled, through reverie and regret, beside a fountain, within a museum, into the middle-aged child I am . . . And I could not stop myself!

I begin to prowl the Upper East Side. Especially Lexington Avenue, since that's where Edith's apartment is . . . Am I cruising? . . . No, no . . . Like Saint Christopher, who has been lately devaluated, I want only to carry a child on my back . . .

And I find him—miracle!—plodding the blocks back home, as if home was only another school. I shadow him, hoping—but he isn't *alive!* . . . I'm shouting, without a sound—"At least, for my sake—please be alive! At least, for God's sake, be curious! Your classmates may hate you—certainly your teammates do—and why not? You're the clumsiest on the floor—but the world is an interesting place. Just look in the window of that glass shop! Those paperweights! They're not like that thing you've got in your bedroom—with the *real* snow, when you shake it up! They're glass flowers planted two centuries ago. Will you look at them, please! They will never die."

Oh—for heaven's sake—the Ordinary! The Impossible! Has that no fascination? A stationery store you walk by: those drab holiday cards—aren't they thrilling? A delicatessen: the simple foods—don't you have a sense of the mystery of the familiar? No? *no*–?

No. He doesn't.

Well—jail or not, I must risk an encounter. "Hey, Barney! Hey! *Hey!*" He turns around. I'm a revelation! It shows in his face. "I was up here on the Upper East Side, visiting the Frick Museum, and I saw this little boy walking along, and I thought—that's Barney! You *are* Barney, aren't you?"

"Yes." He's amazed and thrilled. As am I.

"What a coaccident! You know what a coaccident is?"

"No."

"It's a combination of a coincident and an accident." We swing into a brisk stride which I set. "Oh but, lad, you don't know how to walk down a street! Harold is going to have to give you lessons in seeing beneath the skin of things. As a matter of fact, just the other day I was talking to Harold about what a coaccident the whole world is: half chance and half kind of crazy secret plan. He was feeling very philosophical, Harold was, and—you know what philosophy is: it's when you think about things and enjoy the thinking—and he said to me, 'Terry, the coaccidents of life are truly amazing. Now stop!'" I halt militarily, as if having reached some preordained destination, in front of another dreadful delicatessen. "Now look in that window! What do you see?"

"Food."

"Right! We're making progress. Now what kind of food?"

"Cans of soup."

"Right! What else?"

"Cheese. And meat. Ham."

"Absolutely correct! And this is what you call philosophy. Because instead of turkeys and hams we could have been looking at rubies and emeralds. But in *my* opinion, the turkeys and hams are just as valuable since they're *here!* Out of nothingness just these real things came to *be!* Do you see?"

He doesn't understand, doesn't say a word. Nor do I "understand" myself. But I hope that all I say is true. (No, he'll never be alive.)

"Anyway—now you're a philosopher. Come on, I'll walk you home."

I glance down, but I can't see his face; the visor of his cap hides his eyes. I reach out and tug the visor farther down: he can't see anything now except the sidewalk in front of him. And he leaves it in the exact position to which I have tugged it. My love fills out his willingness, and I wonder why, so swollen with all the surprise with which I should have inflated him, he doesn't float up to the level of my chest.

In front of his apartment house, Edith is disembarking—knees bent and packages held becomingly—from a taxi. "Now *here* is another coaccident!"

"Terry! Hi! A what?"

"Barney will explain upstairs."

"Oh you're the one! I might have known."

"The one what?"

"The giver of strange nicknames." Oh Christ, is she going to fuck that up too? Till now I'd been extremely careful not to call him that in front of her. "He told me that that was his secret name."

"If you let him keep it, I'll make up one for you too."

"That's tempting. But 'Barney' sounds like the bartender of an Irish bar." She ignited her smile, so pleased at her dreary alliteration. "But what are you doing here anyway?"

I love your young son, lady. And I've been bleeding for him all day. "That's just the coaccident. I was up at the Frick, and on the way to the subway station, guess who I see walking home from school."

"Ah ha! Come up for a drink—"

"No I can't—" I am so choked that another fifteen minutes would probably make me gag. "—I've got a date."

She lifts her eyelids —"I see!"—and does some coquettish jealousy. "Some other time." (They never forget.)

"Definitely. In the meantime, however—with your permission— I'll bounce a few stories off your son. I need a listener for the next few weeks."

"You hear that, *Ber*-nard? Mr. Andrews is going to tell stories to you that he may *write* some day!" But thank God for his sternly maintained tugged-down visor! She cannot defile his innocence. Not even when she airily states, "I think we'll enjoy that very much!"

"Good night—" I want to say "Barney," but can't—and Christ knows, won't say, "*Ber*-nard." "—lad." I snap up that visor. "We'll go for a walk in a couple of days."

He looks at me with his eyes like marbles. Does he understand anything? Certainly not my coaccidents: my grab bag of causality: my kindergarten metaphysics . . . Perhaps, though, he does understand that I love him. Halfway through the lobby he stops and turns to look back at me—at me, who can't move till he's entered the omnivorous elevator: at me, with a funny, perplexed expression. We mirror each other.

So perhaps he knows . . .

Sometimes we do know whom we love, we secret people, we hiders in plain sight . . .

> You want a fist, fire—a coaccident?
> Just listen! (*Shhh!*) Be very patient . . .

Sorry to seem so giddy, Father, but this much excitement leaves me kittenish.

Oh well—as it happened:—incredibly!—

Jim called this evening—"There you are, you rascal!"—at six o'clock, as if the last thing he'd said was "Ta ta!" and nothing at all had happened. And when one gets struck by a third of one's life, falling back like a ton of iron, one doesn't have anything to say. "Can I come around?"

"You want to?"

He seizes, as always, a cool initiative. "I wouldn't be calling if I didn't." Why can I not play those vocal games of his: the scrabble of easily found indifferences, the slapjack of casual contempt?

"Sure."

"See you shortly, lad." He hung up.

When one's—you've—*I've*—been delivered a blow, a blow of great force, we don't know what we feel for a while. We walk around waiting for sensation to strike: pain, anger, relief—anything which is something. I ended up in puzzlement, a condition I often fall back on, when "life," "all," seems Impossible.

The easiest explanation—he's simply forgotten. No, there was an even easier: he remembered what he'd said and it didn't matter a goddam bit. He was hot, that's all, and had called me up. But disliking all simple explanations, I manufactured complexities: an abyss of recrimination—he was sorry for what he'd said—fat chance!—or else, to the melody of *"D'amour l'ardente flamme,"* he'd discovered how much I meant to him. Anyway, there are states of shock which truly are pleasant: I wandered around my apartment, dazed, and the drab rooms felt like a banal mask that had been placed on the face of mystery.

He materialized in half an hour, and was veering toward being drunk: sporadic, short sentences and gestures of his head and hands like some kind of unfinished code. "Good lad—" At the door. "—to see me at such short notice."

"Your notices have always been short." I defended myself with an unreal objectivity. "And I'm glad that you're not operating on *me* tomorrow morning."

"No surgery tomorrow. Don't worry—" He flung off his coat and suit jacket with a manifest abandon that started to act on me. "—when I operate, I don't booze the night before."

"Aesculapius would be proud of you." I was falling back on an utterly unavailing and pretentious classical education—the remark delivered, of course, in a mannered academic tone. But the child's life—curiosity—demanded to know: why?—and asked, beneath a comment, "I didn't think that I'd see you again."

"You *were* pretty silly, weren't you?"

I remembered that one of the first times we'd been together he spilled a drink and said casually, "Now why did you do that?"—"*I* did that—?" "I never apologize"—with cool editorial confirmation. And the motherfucker had the gall to add, "You *were* pretty silly, weren't you?"

Then rage did strike. And I reveled in it internally, dreaming, instant by instant, of how I could hurt him—how many ways there were to hurt him. And the most choice cruelty was whispered thus in my ear: "Say this! Yes, darling, say this to him! 'You deserve Benedict. He doesn't deserve to have been born blind, but you, you motherfucker—with all your egocentricity, and that vein of raw and insensitive, selfish iron in your soul—you deserve just what you've got: a hopelessly damaged son.'" The dwarf leaned near and crooned, "Do say it, my dear! He's got it coming."

Yes! True! true! true! And somewhere in my brain there's a single living cell of certainty: he has earned—does earn—that little boy. And before God—*I rejoice in his curse!*

But then, "Now wait," said Harold, with some passion concealed in his realism. "Just wait a minute. He's drunk now. And he was stoned on hash last time. And even if he had been cold sober—the boy is an endless crucifixion. *Nothing* he says—and nothing he does—could justify your wielding the child to hurt him. And you're wrong, lad, and you know you're wrong: no one ever earns a curse like that." The moralistic little bastard even ventured to add, "Whatever happens—there's Benedict! That hatred you're feeling right now—and you know this very well—is just love turned inside out." But then, recognizing me for myself, he hastily went on, in a voice that shook—he knew I was that close to wounding Jim viciously—"And besides—just look how pretty he looks tonight. In that mod blue suit. With that graying red hair. Let your flesh decide."

I did. "Take your clothes off."

"Yes, sir."

"You want the record?"

"Yes, sir. And everything." Jim's is softer, conscious of its theatricality, than Dan Reilly's "Yes—sir."

The skin is an instrument—so are vision, hearing, taste, and smell—and the music that one plays is sensation, orchestrated by desire.

Ah, Rumpelstiltskin, you outdid yourself! But no, it wasn't you. And it wasn't Harold. It was some weird archangel of sensuality. Who must have a biblical name. (Mavis? Or Priscilla? Jim? Barney? Anne?)

After endless love-making—drinking, whipping, popping poppers, fucking, *not* coming—I had been turned into a kind of phallic Frankenstein. (The monster, I mean, of course, not the doctor.) Pure cock from head to toe, with somewhere inside my head a tiny little inventive mind that was thinking and thinking up things.

Now for instance—rimming! I does it, says I, very modestly— but not very often—the last was that hooker last fall—and not with much pleasure. But last night what Jim was sitting on seemed like the sweetmeat of the world. I had flogged it enough to satisfy pride, so I decided—oh neophyte, why not worship a while? The altar: flat on his belly—the priest: on my knees—the host: somewhere between his cheeks. I hadn't done it before, like that, and Jim, with his voice, disbelieved. But with his ass, that levitated into my tongue, in a while he had no doubts at all.

Perhaps we had a recall of the hash. Without his viciousness. But we got to that planet—Jupiter—if sopranos sing on Jupiter, they sound like Flagstad—where every gesture is ten times larger.

"Don't come!"—me.

Jim—"I won't."

And that curious angel prompted me. I was slavering like some rabid dog, licking my spit and the sweat of his ass off my lips. I smacked his tail, hard.

"Hey!" (He has a threatening baritone that he uses when one

goes a little too far: the kind of sound—"Hey!"—that I'm sure he believes that a sergeant might growl to pull up a recruit.)

"You think you're an adventurer!" But I too—Mr. R.S., at least—had my own challenges. "You're a tame cocksucker—a Riverdale fuck—that's what you are."

"You want to strap my ass again?" His curiosity—un-Jimlike—would have made me laugh, if I hadn't known what I meant to propose.

"No." And my nonchalance was about as ordinary as Elizabeth Taylor's latest diamond. "You're pretty proud of that ass of yours, aren't you?"

"It's made a lot of people happy."

"How about we please your tail, for a while?" (The lure of words is pornography.)

"You want to fuck?"

"Not with my prick."

"Got a dildo?"

"Yes. And it's growing at the end of my arm."

"Come on!" In disbelief. But the whole lower half of his body strengthened. In fear? In excitement? (In words—?)

I challenged, "Big swinger! Big quester after sexual adventures! You're a Riverdale fuck."

"It can't be done—"

"Doctor—I'm certain you know that it can."

"When I was an intern, a guy came into the hospital with a flashlight stuck up his ass. He almost bled to death."

"One does well to stay away from amateurs and fetishists." True, true. My increasingly nervous voyeurs—or is that jitteriness something else?—when you read in the paper that a handsome young bachelor has died of "internal hemorrhages," it may only mean that he had the wrong fist, flashlight—or crowbar for that matter—shoved up his ass.

"And you're *not* an amateur, I suppose?"

"No complaints yet. *Or* deaths," I met him reportorially. "It depends on the person. If he's got the guts for it. And I'm speaking literally." Was he near the idea emotionally?—intellectually?—an insane speculation? Quietness was requisite. "Surely, doctor, you've performed more than one sigmoidoscopy yourself."

"In my office. With the right equipment."

"This bed is an office," I truthfully said. "And the equipment's in the bathroom. And right here." I spread out five fingers on the top of his back, and began to caress his spine, up and down his vertebrae, like silent notes.

He lifted his hands, palms flat on the mattress, aligned beside his head. He was shivering—the nerves' giddiness before the unknown—like a colt. "Will you hurt me?" The instant of commitment.

"No." But I wondered whether love or hatred would manipulate my puppet's hand. One thing I knew: *I* would have no part of it. "I won't hurt you," I quietly promised, and lied again.

"Okay." His head swung from side to side: abandoned—an animal in heat. "I've got to take an enema."

"I dislike that word. Say 'douche.' There's a bag in the medicine chest in the bathroom. Go do your duty."

He was far out now in willingness. "You wouldn't like to do that too—"

I sensed a huge advantage in this area of untapped sensuality. "We'll save some experiments for another time—shall we?"

"Yes, sir."

He was in the john for quite a long time. I got the couch ready: a pillow for him to lie prone on—four towels—a jar of cold cream, by far the best lubricant—

> My witnesses, cool off now—do!
> This is going to happen to Jim, not you.

—and three inhalers loaded with fresh amyl nitrite.

He came back sheepish, with reservations. "This isn't going to work."

"Lie down."

"Will you stop if it hurts?"

"No. I'll press right on till you feel my fist in your throat."

"Look, Terry—"

"Don't worry. I won't get pleasure unless you do."

And Please, God, I added—"Lie down"—let that be true.

"On your knees now, Doctor. Right shoulder down."

"I can't—*hey!*"

"Shut up"—affectionately. "Put your right shoulder down on the mattress. That's right. You'll see stars, love bug!"

"No, Terry—" He tried to harden his voice into fact. "—I can't—"

"You already have. The last problem we had were my knuckles. Relax."

"Are you there—?"

"No. But there's no more problems. This is where you begin to enjoy it." My hand, with the hot wet pressure of flesh around it, seemed to seed itself with brain cells. "Now say it, Jimmy—" I called him "Jimmy"—an affectionate verbal gesture—

> A lovely touch, *gentle* feelers, that.
> When I had my fist—
> Yes, up to the wrist—
> Into, Dr. Andrews, you know what!

"—you like it. Out loud, Jimmy. Say it!"

"I like it. Yes, sir."

"My boy—you are a natural!"

I will not try to write his groans. "Oh!"—"Ah!"—seem very inadequate, when describing pain or ecstasy. He did make sounds, though, that are far beyond words.

"Kneel up. Kneel up!"

"I can't—"

"Yes you can." I gently propelled him toward the wall. And finger by finger, he inched his way up. And achieved another world: unbelievable verticality.

"Oh Christ—I'm going to pass out—"

"No you're not. You feel that corner there—?"

"Terry, don't—"

"I'm around."

"I *will* pass out—"

"No you won't. You'll come. Throw your shoulders back."

He *is* six feet two, remember—"I can't!"—and has a back that proves that the primates were right.

"I said!—throw your shoulders back! Be a king on your knees!" And then—

> "You could kill him," someone whispered to me.
> (Unwritten moans.)
> "Do you feel that pulse, that artery—?"
> (Unwritten groans.)

257

"Just pluck it. Pluck it hard. And wait.
He'll bleed to death around your hand:
Warm love, wet love, red love, yes, and
Commensurate with all your hate."

His pulse went quick; his delirium fluttered at the tips of my
fingers and affirmed itself, tightened around my wrist. I gauged
the time—a disbelieved infinity for him—by the length and depth
of his breathing. Then said, in a different voice, "Now easily,
easily down now again."

"You're still inside me—"

"That's all right. You have to help me. Help me *now*—"

"You'll kill me—!"

Ah! . . . But: "No. It's okay. I'm out."

"Is there blood?"

"No." There wasn't. If there had been, a couple of drops or two,
I'd have lied. (Of course if his life *had* gushed out, these pages
could have ended right here—you'd all be free—and Iris would
have found us both.)

"Did that happen? My God—" He sprawled before me, prone,
still floating in an unreal space. Like someone safe, already on the
ground, I had to guide this blind pilot down. "—I'm a doctor."

I gathered him in, a male harvest in my arms. And I felt him
drifting, sinking back, out of madness and into the practical
world. It was time to make him laugh. "As far as that goes, I think
that for an unregistered nurse my technique has been proved to be
quite adequate too."

An arm circled my waist, he chuckled, and landed, upright, in
reality. Alive, alas. "My guts are readjusting themselves."

"Nature's way, baby." Any banality—words—to make it all
seem possible.

A silent few moments: he is reveling in the accomplished
unknown—I am half high on his excitement, and half embarrassed by the mundane accessibility of his flesh. His ecstasy, in
retrospect, seems vulgar beyond belief. My gratification seems
equally coarse and commonplace. Even death—which *was* an
alternative—feels like a crude organic failure.

"Ben wants to know when you're coming to see us again."

Now there, Father, we have either reached a new fever of

sickness or else a new plateau of health, on which I have never existed before. I have just whipped, fucked, and fisted this glorious Rubens creep—and he wants to discuss his blind son! The tentative and apologetic tone of his voice says he does. I lay back in the decadence of my *Mayflower* ancestry—I mean that!—and listened.

"He's kind of got a crush on you."

"Oh, the glamorous author! I know, I know." A world-weary sigh—as authentic as a plastic orchid. "How's Mary Wicks?" Curious: I needed to name someone real.

"She asks about you too."

"She's splendid!"

"But Ben—" He must revert to his son. "—every night at the dinner table—" When you're not out getting screwed at a gangbang. "—it's 'When is Terry coming back?'"

"Not 'the Harold man' any more?"

"No. You've got a first name now."

You must picture this: he was on his belly, and I beside him, stroking his back, that I'm sure you've heard me praise too much, while we talked about his little boy.

> That damn phrase: "little boy"—"little boy"—
> You're sightless! Your toys are just felt joy.

"The report from school says he's very bright—"

"You just need to talk to him to know—" His wanting to boast about his son made me love Jim very much, at that second.

"I keep wondering what that kid might have been if he only had eyes." He unguarded himself, as he had a few times before: his head fell forward, into the pillow, in an icon of hopelessness.

"Come on, Jimmy. It could be worse. He might have been a gork."

"He could have been a healthy kid—"

"He could have been a mindless freak—" Like me. Who repeats words over and over, without understanding a single one. (This is not, by the way, a gratuitous piece of self-derogation. Surely by now you are all well aware that a certain part of my psyche is leading the life of a severely retarded child.) "As it is, he's a smart—little boy, who's going to cope with everything he has to cope with. And he'll be able to."

"I hate him!"

"Jim—"

"I do! And I dream about killing him—"

"No you don't."

"—and I love him much more than my life! More than Carol and all the girls."

My fingers searched his skin for the truth. "This is only a fit—"

"It's the fit that is my life."

And they found honesty: a rigidity in his flesh. "I'd like to kill him."

"No—you wouldn't—" I worked for bored, easy disbelief.

"You know how I'd like to kill him? I look at those goddam jiggling eyes of his—those *futile* useless goddam eyes!—and I'd like to put a knife right through them! Into the center of his goddam brain! Why *can't* he see, Terry? He's such a horribly beautiful kid—!"

"He *is!* And with or without his eyes." I leaned across him and tightened my arms around that back that you're all in love with too. And interestingly I found, you can keep dynamite from exploding, if you hug it with enough love.

"Boy!" He relaxed in my grip. "I haven't let myself say that out loud for a long time."

My reaction? Just guess! What would be most contemptible? . . . Jealousy! (When *did* you say it the last time? With whom?)

But the physician in my tradition was able to note, with maturity, "It's a healthy thing. Better out than in." And I added, majestically self-deprecating, "I only wish I could too. Let out my woes, instead of chewing on them in private."

But I don't, do I, my witnesses?—chew them over in utter privacy? *You* at least I can force to hear . . . You too—my black potent lightless stars!

"I gotta get going." He revolved upright and began to put on his clothes. "But you really have to come up pretty soon. Ben's beginning to think that you've given us up." He slipped on his shorts, and appeared proud and impregnable, now that all I'd ransacked had been hidden. "I'm getting jealous."

"Of what?"

"You. I think Ben loves you more than he does his daddy." You see, *this* was the burning—or the real fist! It wasn't the pleasure I got from violating Jim, in the most extravagant of ways. Jim's grinning, childlike jealousy was a blade that went between my ribs. "But I figure—oh well, if it has to be someone else—" And his willingness was—as willingness always is, for me—the final delicious twist. "—why not you?"

He was dressed: resplendent in a checkered tailored suit. I opened the door. "And Jesus, Terry—thanks!"

I pretended to click my heels and said, "At your service, sir!"—and believed that for a little while longer I owned him.

But no—his panache reasserted itself: "Ta ta! Be a good lad now!"—he owned me.

January 25

Ownership—is a complex thing.

Jim owns me, but a bit more than twenty-four hours after I revealed to him the thrills and sensations of—intestinal spelunking, shall we call it?—he called me up. This morning, at seven o'clock.

"You awake yet?"

"No." In a sound sleep all voices sound vicious, no more. "Who *is* this?"

"Jim. You want to watch me operate?" . . . What I've wanted for the past two years!

"Today—?" Swarms of questions hived in my mind.

"At eleven o'clock. It's only a gallbladder, but ever since we met you've been yowling—"

"Where shall I meet you?"

"In front of the hospital. One sixty-eighth Street and—"

"I know."

"—at nine thirty. We have to scrub."

"Me too—?"

"Sure. You're a doctor friend of mine visiting from—"

"Philadelphia. 'Doctor Andrews.'" Pop's name—a killing name . . .

They're exciting, though, hospitals are: the nurses' soft, quick steps in the hall, the lowered tones, the sense of crises barely contained. The smells of antiseptics. The doctors in liturgical white uniforms.

"Here, lad—try this one on for size."

"Do I get to wear a mask too?"

"Sure. Have you ever seen an operation before?"

"Yes. Several. The only time I was ever taken seriously was while I was being brainwashed. Or trying to be. To be a doctor. I'm a fugitive from a medical career."

"This'll be old hat then. It's a drag of an operation."

"It won't be if I see you do it."

He winked his thanks for my compliment. And he was splendid! Elegant: an economy of cutting—and almost aesthetic in the finesse with which he altered a human anatomy. (Surely an operating room must be the most intense of temples.) I'd suspected that he'd be beautiful, in an operating room, but the dancer's grace of his hands—every gesture filled out to completion, then ended unequivocally—was art in action, pure joy to watch . . . And the slap of the instruments in a surgeon's hands, delivered by an experienced nurse, has simply *got* to be the most exciting sound in the world!

In short: a turn-on. Strange place to get an erection—but I'm afraid I did.

"Well?—how was it?"—in the doctors' locker room.

"You were gorgeous!"

"The operation, I mean!"

"You, it, the gallbladder—you all were great!"

He had stripped to his shorts and was sweating. And I hasten to admit that each wet token of his ordeal—the life that he'd taken upon himself—made me want to lick him clean. He asked, "Got plans for this afternoon?"

"No."

"Want a visitor?"

I tried to imitate the whole impersonal hospital. "You have office hours—"

"Usually. But one day a month I leave for letters and paper work."

"So? Your papers?—your letter work?"

He grinned at my uncontrol. "I'll take a shower—"

"Don't! Just put on your clothes."

"I can stay all afternoon."

"Then we'll have to space ourselves. Time ourselves."

And we did. . . .

And I'd thought that an operating room was the most intense of temples . . . But no—a bedroom is . . .

And today, instead of doing it himself, he wanted me to—

Ah well, Father, Father, I'm sure you've heard things more absurd, and pardoned them, as you shook your head in bemused sympathy.

> I sing the body undiscovered.
> I sing the blood's concealed estates.
> I sing the inch—miles there I've covered.
> I sing the many fleshy gates.
>
> I sing my skill at this new madness.
> I sing my fingers and my hand.
> I sing the danger, risk—the sadness—
> Of such a—starry?—wonderland.

January 27

I take my lumpy little beloved nothing to the Frick—yesterday. I've got to get him out of himself, attach him to the world. And I don't know how to teach him to play with children or get along with grown-ups, since I can't do either one myself, but maybe—and maybe it's a mistake—I can teach him to take some nourishment from things like great paintings. Or will this just be instructing him in my own escapes? However—it's all I can do.

Very curious, how fate contrives these total reversals: all last fall and this winter Edith has been nibbling apologetically at my time, and now it is I who am scheming excuses to see her son. I allow that I'm going to visit the Frick, and I wonder if Barney would like to come. And silently hope to God that she won't ask to come along herself.

"That's lovely, Terry! That's very kind!" Oh, I am so kind I may kidnap the boy and you'll never see either one of us again. "I've tried *Ber*-nard in some museums, and it just didn't work."

We will live on a Greek island, he and I. "But you—you may be able to." And he'll learn to love the classical orders.

" 'Bout three then. My brunch should be finished by then."

As I wandered around and around the block, and waited for the time to come, I brooded on what one *would* make for brunch for Barney. Something special, delicious! Maybe eggs Benedict . . .

Poor Benedict! In your darkness you're so much brighter and livelier than my unrisen son . . .

Three o'clock—and I wring five more minutes out of myself, as spastic proof of my random ease.

Edith produces her bundled-up boy. It is cold yesterday.

"You're going to be very bored," I announced. "You're much too young to enjoy the Frick."

He says nothing. And the nothing he says—averted eyes, head bent—is permission to bore him, to do anything with him I want.

"He *is* too young for the Frick, you know." I create a moment of shared maturity for Edith's benefit.

She improves on it with an understanding, yet delicately contradictory smile. I am warned to brace myself. "You're never too young to see good art, if the right person takes you to see it." Poor lady! Why is it that even the purest innocent truth seems banal in the mouth of some people?

We are off!—to the corner of Fifth Avenue and East Seventieth Street. Yesterday the Frick feels not only beautiful, but human too, since this little intimidated troll is by my side, staring up uncomprehendingly at the cool everlasting works. (It's strange, but even the most passionate paintings seem almost self-conscious in their immortality.)

"Now the thing about museums—" I don't know how to take a child to a museum or an opera house or anywhere; so in desperation I fall back on intuition. "—is this: most of them are too damn big! You can't see everything at once. And when your eyes have had enough—they say 'Enough!' If they're in Italy, your eyes say 'Basta!' If they're at the Louvre, a museum in France, they say, 'Assez!' " Am I talking Italian and French to him? Am I showing off linguistically? You bet your ass I am! "The thing is, as soon as your eyes say 'Enough!' you head right away for the nearest exit. If the weather is nice you go straight to the park and you sit on a bench. Because a bench is a very nice place to be when you've been to a good museum. And you let your eyes digest what they've seen. But after they've said 'Enough!' you *don't* stuff any more paintings in your eyes! Right?"

"Right," he fearfully mimics me. And I playfully twist his ear, to let him know that my shouting is only love, too loud.

I take him to my favorite first: the St. Francis. "Now what do you see in that picture?"

Nothing. And his silence is fear that he's failing me.

I am *ruining* him already! As if I expected a Panofsky appraisal from a seven-year-old unhappy kid!

"What's your favorite color, Barney?"

"Blue."

"Well then, you must like this painting! Because what color do you see in it?"

"Blue."

"Right!" Hallelujah!—he can recognize blue! I'm as proud of him as if he had painted the damned ravishing thing himself! "And what's happening is, this man, St. Francis—" How the hell do you transpose 'stigmata' down? "—is getting hurt the way Christ was hurt on the Cross." And I'm trusting the probability that his genteel Episcopalian mother has sent him to Sunday school. "That's happening because he loves God very much. Because he believes in Him."

He tries to read all I've said, all I feel, up into the glorious canvas. And fails . . . But I think that he does appreciate those incredible transformations of blues.

"Come on—I'll show you a lady I like."

The Ingres portrait of—God damn it! I always forget her name. But that smirking beautiful Ingres young bitch!—the neoclassical answer to the Mona Lisa. And another intuition of the possible permutations of purples and blues . . . It's odd that I like these two paintings so much. My favorite color is red.

"Do you like her?"

His "Yes" is the expected answer.

"Do you see her back in the mirror there?"

"Oh—"

It's got him!—thank God that something has!—just the way it got me the first time I saw it. It's the visual trick that captivates him.

"Of course sometimes when a painter paints a reflection, he makes it different, so the person seems like two people, or two different sides of the one person—" Oh stop *forcing* his first little bud of interest! "Do you like that lady?"

His grin is a question: Do you get to like or dislike all the people in paintings? In my universe, yes you do. "I don't know."

"I like her a lot. But I don't think I trust her. I like her with a space in between."

I try a few more pictures on him—the Corot countryside, the de La Tour—but out of nowhere, except his need, when we're walking from one room into another, he asks, "Has Harold seen the Rat?" Poor bugger. Just starved for a story . . .

Well, as it happens, ol' Uncle Grimm-Wiggily-Tolkien here has prepared for just such a dire eventuality. I steer him into the peristyle—the presence of wetness, vegetation, amid the elegance of marble—and sit him down beside the fountain. "As a matter of fact, he has. And the name of what happened is *Harold—and the Frick!*"

Seems that Harold at one time lived in the Frick. As well as in hardware stores in the Bowery and closets in penthouses on Central Park West. The Rat told him about the place and said there were a lot of things up there much better than that silly little sketch of Harold that he had done himself. And Harold absolutely loved the Frick! (Despite the formidable presence of Miss Frick herself in an apartment upstairs.) He moved all his possessions in: a rabbit's foot named George and a wishbone that hadn't been wished on yet . . . But, but—and that "but" is the crux of all stories—after a while Harold decided to rearrange the paintings. He could do a much better job himself, he thought. So he sent Jake Moth down to Greenwich Village with an urgent message— "Get the Rat up here quick! I can't do all this work myself." So up comes Rat, grumpily, and for a whole night—after the guards had been put to sleep, which doesn't take much magic, because they're already sleepy—Harold and the Rat rearrange the paintings . . . And of course, after all the work is done, Harold decides that the original positions of all the pictures are very much better than his.

" *'Goddammit—!'* shouts youknowwho.

" 'Just cool it now, Rat,' said Harold. 'I'll take care of this myself.' He lifted both his hands and snapped his fingers.

You pictures—right back where you were!
I'm no museum curator.

" 'Good *night!*' The Rat sulked through the lobby—over there—and out into the street.

"But Harold didn't go to bed right away. In fact, that night he didn't go to bed at all. He just wandered around, with a snap of his fingers making the lights above his favorite paintings go on, so he could enjoy them all over again. For many nights Harold did that, after he'd put the guards to sleep—but he burglar-proofed the whole place, of course. He just strolled through the rooms and let his eyes feast on all that they saw.

"And you know something—?"

"What?"

"Harold's favorite place in the whole building is where we're sitting now. After he's looked his fill of pictures, he comes and sits here. Of course the guards turn off the fountain when everybody leaves, but Harold turns it right back on again. And that skylight up there—you can't see through it now, but Harold has just enough magic to turn it into transparent glass. Then, late at night, the star-shine through the skylight and the soft and orderly rain of the fountain change into the same thing. And for hour after hour Harold listens to the stars.

"There was one night he was so in love with this place, and everything in it, that he had to write (composed yesterday morning) 'Harold's Ode to the Frick.'

> You beautiful paintings, I own you all!
> And I live with you here at the Frick Collection.
> I own this house too—I own every wall.
> But don't tell Miss Frick!
> She'd sue me quick
> For damages and then eviction.
>
> There never was a place so right:
> So orderly and so elegant.
> The ferns and the furniture all are polite,
> The fountain speaks low,
> The lights never say "No!"—
> And even the mice are intelligent.

I'm back to myself when I'm home to you,
And every night I drink my fill.
But you lovely things make me sort of sad too.
The Frick lets me see
What this city could be
If the people too were beautiful.

The fountain silence—in which the two of us sit and listen.

Well, I may not have been able to teach my Barney to like great paintings, but the Frick mansion is now an enchanted place for him. He sits on the pristine marble ledge, watches the water's pellucid ripples, listens to the endless plash, and dreams of Paradise.

I allow us several minutes . . .

Then, "Time to go home, Barney." And he stands up, bemused by perfection, as I am myself: a deep and rare experience that—please, Someone—he will never forget.

Coats, street: the winter chills us back into the mundane world. Which still includes fiction. He possessively holds my hand, as we walk down the street, and asks, "Does the Rat see the Whittakers ever?"

He does, yes. And just lately, when Dr. Jim Whittaker comes around, the Rat—"Yes." The truth is a kind of suicidal weapon that one holds above the head of the young.

"Do they play 'Hidden Billy'?"

"They haven't lately." Five paces, while I reevaluate memory. "You remember all that? From Thanksgiving?"

"Yes." Five more, while he relives my lies. "Mrs. Black too—does the Rat still see her too?"

"Say, what are you?—some kind of midget memory bank?"

"She gave him a Christmas tree."

"Now answer me, Barney! *Are* you a nice little boy? Or are you an evil little dwarf, who never forgets anything?"

He smiles, and allows me to play a grown-up teasing a child: becoming the child he pretends to tease. "I'm an evil dwarf!"

"If you *must* know!—the Rat does see Mrs. Black now and then." As a matter of fact, he's taking her to the new production of *Der Rosenkavalier* tonight. "She continues to feed him up with delicious meals." His not speaking now is a very serious questioning. "Well?—what are you thinking?" I demand.

"The Whittakers and Mrs. Black—"

I impersonate an indignant adult. "*Yes*—?"

"They *are* real—?"

"Oh 'real,' Barney—! Does it matter?" Yes. "Must it all be real?" *Yes!* "You keep asking that!"

"I just wanted to know."

"Do you like them? Dr. Whittaker and Mrs. Black?"

"Yes."

"Why?"

I hadn't expected an answer. But the little bastard gives me one. "They made the Rat happy."

We reach his apartment house. With a minimum of leave-taking—his cap tugged down over his eyes: our parting sign—I say good-bye. And walk home.

The afternoon is rich and full—and abruptly incomplete.

January 28

I'll never be able to bring it off. But the idea has been started now—it jumped out like a fox—and I've got to track it down.

"Anne, how do you make a child happy?"

"You ask *me* that?" She was sitting in that chair beside the window, sipping her damned Dubonnet, preparatory to making an early dinner. "You've made so many—"

"Stop that crap!" I was harsher than I'd meant to be—her face flickered into puzzlement—and I went on quickly, "No compliments. I'll wink when I want one, okay? But to write a story that a child can like, and to make one happy—they're two different things. You—diminutive little earth mother that you are—have a daughter. And you brought her through intact. How?"

She searched me in a questing expression. "You mean—?" And she didn't know what I meant.

"I mean—day by day."

"What's happening, Terry?"

"I've met this hopeless little boy—"

"Oh Terry!" The perennial optimism of a human being—a woman!—who's been happier than she's been miserable asserted itself in her indignation; it was mixed too with the generalized optimism of a mother who has done her job. "No little boy's hopeless! You love them, that's all. And keep them in line."

"This one's hopeless. I used to know his mother. Divorced, and a tasteful dope, I'm afraid. But he likes my book—she wanted me to meet him—I've been telling him stories all winter long."

"That's wonderful."

"No it *isn't!* I'm just wiping him out even worse! However—" To the bar, to the bottle, and back to the couch. "—there's nothing else that I know how to do." Sip, and a first hint that I have a specific request. "He asked about you."

"Me—?"

"You remember my Christmas tree?"

"Yes."

"I fitted that into a story."

"How great!" Her body reacted—then relaxed. "A *Harold* story?"

"Yes. And you too. That's how he knows about you."

"I'd like to meet him."

Snap! Trapped! "Interesting you should bring that up. If I should arrange, say, a little dinner—"

"I'd love to!"

"No, wait. And if I should pay for all the food—"

"*I'll* take care of the food. Bring him here."

"No, *wait!* I want it to be in my apartment. But could you, maybe, make a casserole, or something else, we could heat up down there?"

"Your apartment! Good Lord! A party in your apartment. He must be something very special."

"He's a wiped-out little kid. But could you—"

"I could make an eight-course feast! And I will!"

She was wearing a light dress of watered silk. The texture of it made me suddenly feel, beneath my fingers, her skin within. I stood up and sauntered across to her and stroked, exploratorily, her right side. "Well that would be very nice—"

"Now stop that—"

"Any old kind of a casserole." I felt like a tuning fork, struck precisely on the note of desire.

"We are not going to get to *Der Rosenkavalier!*"

"We don't *need* to get to *Der Rosenkavalier*."

"Oh yes we do! It's one of my favorites."

"Strauss, my dear: bad taste. You like Bach!"

"Nonetheless! It's my favorite of his. And there's all the ingredients of spaghetti carbonara in the kitchen."

She stood up, and her appropriatorial smile took my heat—postponed—with her into her kitchen.

I heard about a third of the opera, I'd guess. And, my God, it was glorious! *Rosenkavalier* is *not* one of my favorites. The Viennese whipped cream gets a little too thick. But last night—Richard, baby, the opera that you composed last night was at least ten times better than the last time I'd heard it. I was so turned on at the thought of bringing the three of them together—if the motherfucker only would! (And he will, I know he will, if I ask him as a straight off-the-shoulder favor. It's only my love that he can't endure, not my impulse to make a little boy happy: he'll like that.) I was so spaced out that most of the time even that Strauss huge orchestra didn't make a sound. But Anne's enthusiasm at all the best moments kept tugging me back, like a kite on a string. At one point I felt her hand on my sleeve and realized that we were about to have the presentation of the Silver Rose. "Rofrano!" the chorus off-stage was singing, and the music began its acceleration. And the set was truly commensurate: Von Faninal's salon was backed by huge transparent doors that gave onto a foyer, staircases up, down. At the right modulation—somewhere in the strings, I think—a battery of manservants appeared and threw open those doors—so your spirit swooped down through the huge auditorium and out through those now inviting doors. And—dum da da *dum!*—another upbeat—the nurse and Sophie fell on their knees—and there the young aristocrat stood, in his hand the glittering and imperishable imitation of a flower that could die. Anne tugged my arm again, wanting to have me look at her, with our eyes too to share those sounds. Her face was a hungry metaphor for all that we heard. And—sentimental fool!—there were tears in her eyes. Then she tipped her head sideways and laughed at herself for having cried.

I guess it was the opera—you, Richard Strauss, you bourgeois miracle!—but by the end Anne too was turned on physically.

Perhaps also my admonitory fondling before we left the apartment had something to do with her readiness. We got, I would say, two sips from our drinks.

It is one of my necessities, when I'm really hot—and this with a male slave, a prostitute, or a willing woman like Anne—to take the clothes off the body myself. The unwrapping, unveiling—exposure, at my hands—is indispensable. And—sorry about this, folks, head nurses, you!—but them's the facts—at a certain stage my hands won't suffice: my teeth become prehensible too and drive my fingers off the field. I'm afraid I've chewed runs into quite a few nylon stockings in my effort to mouth them down a thigh. It becomes a game to get one off the foot intact. And being beside a foot like Anne's—placed there by a Providence that knows there is no square inch of articulate body that isn't desirable—what one does is to get as much of the foot as one can in one's mouth. With men too. Rarely, but on occasion, yes! Last week, in the classical masculine position, backed into my crotch, Jim had his legs up over my shoulders, feet close to my head, and it seemed downright unreasonable for me not to clean out his toes with my tongue. (Note, to gourmets: beyond a certain speed of excitement, smells work in ways that you wouldn't expect.)

The thing of teeth, though, is this: they should only come into operation when one layer remains to be peeled. It would be absolutely ridiculous to try to remove a mink coat with your molars. But a bra, now—without so much as a single mark on a shoulder—until you mean to put a mark there—that's a challenge for teeth that may still be evolving. I think they are. Meantime, the tongue helps. Lips help. Nose helps. It nudges a strap to a shoulder—good dog!—where teeth can tug it down.

In making love one does, sometimes, feel the process of evolution in action . . .

Anne vanished for a while, while I was inside her, she inside my arms. They all vanish, the people I love—Jim does, when I'm fucking or fisting him—and leave me alone, like some crazy caretaker of ecstasy. They go into the past, or into the future, or out of time altogether. They go where real creation is, true evolution, if it exists—and *not* my theatrical teeth—and they leave me in an endless conscious present. Like Harold!—the manic little bastard: a born caretaker: worrying that I'll tear Jim Whittaker's guts apart—and I hope to God I will!—concerned to make sure that Anne's orgasm—and Jim's—goes off in their groin like the major chord that it ought to be. (Caretaker . . .)

"Well, come on now, Harold—let's be factual, honest: you cream too—"

"Yes, I do. But the hands of a present consciousness are always pressed around my skull."

However, at times, like last night, the hands are Anne's—and I opened my eyes to find her beneath me, her own eyes closed, and her fingers colonizing my hair.

There was no going home. I fell asleep and stayed the whole night . . .

Mornings—unless I'm hung over, and thus artificially, chemically hot again—are usually another self-conscious embarrassment.

I dressed quickly.

She made us breakfast—"Toast? Or an English muffin?"

"A muffin, please"—and matched my reserve with her puzzled reticence. "I'm still singing *Der Rosenkavalier*. Did you like it?"

"I loved it!" She turned from the pan where she was scrambling eggs and remembered: not *Der Rosenkavalier*.

(Oh Harold—why must you always feel guilty at the love you love?)

"Listen, Anne, about that little boy—"

"Can it wait a couple of weeks?"

"It can wait forever. I think it was just a silly idea."

"No it wasn't. I want to." Her truthfulness, stillness, stared me down. "I'd love to, Terry."

"There may be someone else there—"

"Good!"

"A friend of mine. Who's also a story."

"Just the four of us?"

"Yes."

"Us stories, and you." She slithered the eggs out onto two plates. "But can it wait a couple of weeks? I'm going out to see my sister. February's a good time for San Diego."

"Whenever you're ready."

"I'm ready now." Her eyes clicked away from mine. "But I promised Louise. It's been three years."

And we ate our breakfast in a silence articulated oppressively
by the small talk that we made.

Poor Anne—

> Last night I took you to *Der Rosenkavalier*.
> You cried. You really cried. The Presentation Scene,
> The final trio—and you wept. Beside you I
> Was more stirred by your tears than all the Strauss I heard.
> The corniness—"to cry at Strauss: really, my dear!"—
> Was absent utterly. I think I've never been
> So puzzled. So in love. So wanting—*now*—to die.
> So close to all the human things I've always feared.

February 2

God, the next thing you know I'll be taking him to baseball
games!

I've been thinking all week that he's much too fat—damn a
mother who feels obliged to stuff her son!—it's a vicious
substitute—and by yesterday morning his weight has become an
obsession. The answer—of course—the gym! It's obvious now
that he's come to mean so much to me, that I want him all over
my life. And I spend so much time in that place, that I needed to
feel his presence there too.

Edith is overjoyed! "He *is* rather—sluggish." I dress up my
bodily narcissism as a simple aversion to sports in groups . . . In
short—here we are!—the gym.

I would say it's divided about equally between gay and straight.
With a few limbo people, like myself. We all keep our distance
respectfully, although one does sometimes catch fragments of
rather unguarded talk. As when Big Nick Jacobson, weight lifter
extraordinaire und Prinzessin von Judea, came back from Aca-
pulco—"Bubbles! You're back!" a workout partner greeted
him—and announced that he'd found a sensational exercise for
the calves. And said partner demanded, "What would a tit queen
like you know about good calves?" (It's true too: his pectoral
muscles are breathtaking!) And one picks up snatches of talk
about snatches from the locker-room jocks, but for the most part

the fags, the married men, the confused—we all occupy, territorially, the psychological niches apportioned to us, without much mutual interference.

My own group consists of little animals—I've named them, and they put up with it. The Turtle, sturdy and likable; the Beaver, rich, and busily unbusy; Dead-dead, who curses dead actors on his television screen; and best of all the Chipmunk. He's got the best body in the whole damn gym, and a wee bit too conscious of it he is. But I call him the Chipmunk because inside that splendid physique of his, and despite the harmless suburban narcissism, I sometimes catch glimpses of simple human decency sitting up on its hind legs with two tiny paws dangling in front of a woolly and dependable chest.

I'm afraid that the locker room is an ordeal for Barney. He's got this thing I anticipated: a distrust of his flesh. You sense it right away in a kid. When the other guys have brought in their sons—a couple have—they've been reedy, riotous little boys who delighted in seeing where Daddy worked out. But Barney twists out of his clothes, shamefaced, as if he's being tried in court. The male presences intimidate him: all that hair all over, where he has no hair—and those monstrous fleshy extensions that ridicule his little dribbler. I try to shield him, standing beside him, from anyone that he might think was staring, as he slips—shimmies rather—into the trunks that I've brought from Edith's.

The weight room is an otherworldly mystery. I think he likes the vast red carpet, and is awed by the wall mirrors, doubling, quadrupling space, but the dully shining steel equipment—dumbbells, barbells, the racks where we can press or squat—it's all a mechanical enigma to him.

My crowd is there, and I introduce him: of course not to men—to the Chipmunk, the Owl, and on through my zoo. Mice. Leopards. One elephant. They laugh, and being the good lads they are, indulge me in my game. And Barney, with that cryptic smile of his—the one subtle and instinctively sophisticated gesture he has—is quite willing to believe that this rugged torso is really a Chipmunk, that slippery man a Lynx. He senses a story coming. And he's right.

"Come on now, Barn'—we gotta work out!" I drop into the camaraderie and bad diction of men together, nonchalantly dramatizing, for their own benefit, the roles of their lives. "Did you ever work out before?"

"No." If he had, I'd have swallowed the nearest dumbbell.

"Well, the Chipmunk here is an expert weight lifter. Aren't you, Chipmunk?"

"Do my best, Terry." The Chipmunk grins in self-conscious pleasure. I control an impulse to pat his head.

"And since he's also got a little boy your own age, I think maybe the Chipmunk might be the one to give us some exercises. Okay, Chipmunk?"

"Be glad to!"

To my inner and everlasting delight, the Chipmunk now proceeds to instruct, with the utmost seriousness, my befuddled Barney in the intricacies of correct weight lifting.

"Now first we limber up—" Chipmunk swings a dumbbell between his knees, then up over his head. "I'll get a little one for you." Barney eyes me apprehensively, but I nod encouragement: yes—do as the lovable rodent says.

And a precious half-hour begins: the Chipmunk takes Barney through a whole routine. Chipmunk and I, unacknowledged accomplices in an innocent and ironic pleasure, do not watch too closely. But the vigor with which he instructs my puffy little boy, the absolute belief, is beautiful to watch.

Chipmunk—you're a hero of credulity!

My witnesses—you are knights of smiling understanding!

Chipmunk does curls: arm-ups with dumbbells held in the hands, to build the biceps—he does prone presses: flat on your back, and push a weight above your chest, for the pectoral muscles—he does triceps exercises—he does toe-raises for the calves—he does squats, deep-knee bends with a weight on his back, for the legs—an exercise I hate!—he does *everything*, and he does it with the gilded finesse of one who knows he's observed. Chipmunk—no one else will ever train my little boy!

The rigorous rodent is about to initiate a whole new set of exercises when I break in. "Are you tired, Barney?"

"Yes!"

"Aw, Barn'," Chipmunk bucks him up, "that's just when you've gotta keep pushin'! When every muscle in your body is screamin'."

276

"Now hold on," I admonish him. "Don't lose your furry head completely. My boy needs a rest. Sit down here on this bench, Barn', and catch your breath."

A silence, which Barney recognizes. And the Chipmunk can interpret it too, in a minute.

"So, Barn'—" I need to be coaxed, pleaded with—no—loved, in front of these friends of mine. "—how did you like your first workout?"

"I liked it."

"Did you?"

"Yes." He smiles sheepishly at the Chipmunk. A breakthrough!—the first time that I've ever seen him need to please someone else. My buried genius! My considerate son! For that, I promise, I'll make you happy—I'll make you laugh, if that's all I can do.

"Did you know, Barney, that Harold comes to this gym sometimes too?"

"He does—?"

"Indeed! And the first time here he almost killed himself."

"Oh-oh! John'll have to hear all about that." John is Chipmunk's son. The good lad is cuing me.

"Anyway—the name of what happened is—*Harold and the Latent Weight Lifter.*

"So, anyway, once upon a time—like a couple of weeks ago—Harold, who was still living at the Frick at the time, woke up one morning, and—you guessed it!

> Is it flab? Is my rear end as big as a bustle?
> Yes.
> Oh my God, I'm a mess! I don't have any muscle!

"With a shock Harold realized that he was almost middle-aged and that he was just in *rotten* condition. He'd been leading the cultured life for so long, over at the Frick, that he'd completely forgotten that he was living in a body after all, and that he ought to take care of it. He went to a mirror and took off his clothes down to his underwear shorts, and what he saw did not make him happy one bit. 'I *am* a mess!' he groaned. 'This is dreadful!'

"He whipped on his clothes and tore across Central Park to this gym, which he had heard advertised on the radio. And everyone was here, working out: the Lynx and the Chipmunk, and Owl, the Beaver, Dead-dead—the whole crew." The whole crew is standing around, listening, and grinning and giggling at being fictionalized. I don't ordinarily like to talk to a group, but these guys—guys!—are so innocent, in their childlike attention, that yesterday I don't mind. "And everybody was working out so well, so expertly, that Harold felt kind of intimidated. That means, like when you have to hug your arms around yourself, to keep everybody from seeing what you feel. Harold decided to do a little invisibility on himself and wait till the gym had closed for the night.

"Then later on when the gym was deserted, Harold flicked on the lights with a snap of his fingers, and stripped down to his underwear, and started his first workout.

"He had seen the Chipmunk doing prone presses, so he decided to start with that. Although he knew he could never hope to build up pecs—chest muscles—as big as the Chipmunk's." Oh Chip, can I ever forget your baritone squeak of pride. "But Harold didn't really know much about weight lifting. He piled up the thirty-pound weights at the end of the bar—see? those big round things over there—until he had about three hundred and fifty pounds on the rack there. Then he lay down, and with a mighty effort, he lifted the bar down onto his chest. And there it stayed!

"'Oh my Lord!' Harold groaned. He struggled and pushed—but that bar wouldn't get off his chest. 'Well, I hate to do it,' he said to himself, since you're not supposed to cheat when you're working out, 'but I'll have to resort to magic:

> Get off now, weight! I'm being crushed.
> It's just too silly a fate, to be squarshed.

"But the weight didn't budge an inch.

> I mean it, weight! I just can't breathe.
> Lift off now, weight. Oh won't you? *Pleethe!*

"And the weight didn't budge an inch. You see, Harold did *not* have enough magic to lift three hundred and fifty pounds off his chest. 'Oh, this is *ridiculous!*' he mumbled to himself. And Barney, you know Harold: of all things in the world he dreaded most to appear ridiculous. 'To be crushed to death in a gymnasium. In my

278

underwear, at that!'

"Now just now, as Harold was getting ready to say good-bye to everyone he loved—he was going to begin with his rabbit's foot, George—he heard somebody come into the gym. And 'Help!' he called weakly.

" 'Who's that?' said a voice.

" 'Me, Harold,' said Harold, from under the weight. 'I'm over here—' He heard what sounded like big wings beating, and looking up from his back, he saw a bat hovering in the air above him.

" 'Hi, man!' said the Bat.

" 'Oh, I'm so glad you came in!' said Harold, 'You see, I'm getting—'

" 'Name's Bob,' said the Bat. '*Big* Bob, my friends call me.'

" 'Well, Bob,' Harold began, 'if you'd just help me—'

" '*Big* Bob,' said Big Bob Bat peevishly.

" '*Big* Bob,' agreed Harold, as he choked to death. 'If you'd just help me lift—'

" 'I've got fourteen-inch arms,' said Big Bob Bat.

" 'Big Bob, that is really wonderful.' Harold had about half a minute left of his life. 'But I wonder if you wouldn't—'

" 'Shall I do some squats first? Or claw raises?' asked Big Bob Bat. 'The ol' legs feel really great today! *Eeee-ah!*' he screamed a karate scream and flung out one foot toward the mirror on the wall.

" 'I'm very glad your legs feel great,' Harold wheezed, 'but in all honesty, Big Bob, I have to admit that I'm sort of getting squarshed to death a little bit, I guess, and if you would only help me lift this weight off my chest—*uhhhh!*—' He sucked in what he knew was his very last breath. '—I would really be most grateful. *Urk!*'

" 'Oh. Sure, man,' said Big Bob casually. He flew down and grappled his claws around the bar, and with no effort at all he lifted it back on the rack.

" 'Oh God—what a relief!' Harold sighed. He was still too limp to lift himself up off the bench, and just lay there being glad not to die.

" 'Say, man, you're really in rotten shape,' Big Bob Bat commented after a while.

" 'I guess I am, Big Bob,' said Harold apologetically. 'That's why I came—'

" 'You want me to train you? I'll give you a workout program.'

" 'Big Bob, that would be wonderful!' exclaimed Harold. 'I really don't know very—'

" 'But look, man—' Big Bob Bat flapped his wings once or twice. '—I mean, you'll never look like me.'

" 'Oh, I couldn't aspire—' Harold began.

" 'I've been working out now for five years.' Big Bob hovered in front of the mirror and turned around slowly, up in the air, to see himself better. 'Some pecs, huh? Some shoulders!'

" 'Big Bob, you're really in wonderful condition,' said Harold with admiration. 'I've never seen—'

" 'You got no pecs at all,' said Big Bob. 'And your deltoids—' These shoulder muscles are deltoids. '—the deltoids oughta bulge out like grapefruit. And yours look like lemons. That belly too—wow!—that's really a little pot you got goin' there.'

" 'Oh my goodness!' groaned Harold. 'When I woke up this morning, I knew *something* was wrong, but I didn't think this much was!' He tried to squinch up inside his underwear so Big Bob couldn't see anything more that was wrong with his body.

" 'I have to tell you,' said Big Bob frankly, 'even if you work out for years and years, and do everything like I tell you to, you'll never be anything but mediocre.'

" 'Oh well,' sighed Harold stoically—that means you can take what comes—'I'd rather be mediocre than downright ridiculous. Lead on, Big Bob! I'm yours to command!'

"And command is what Big Bob did: 'Lift, man! Lift that weight! Oh push, man—*push!* Oh man, are you weak!' Poor Harold, he strained and struggled, and moaned and groaned. And the worse it got—for Harold, that is—the more Big Bob seemed to enjoy himself. 'Keep goin', man! Ten more reps! You gotta psych yourself!' That means you make yourself believe that you're something you're not. And you act like an idiot.

" 'I'm psyched! I'm psyched already!' shouted Harold almost angrily, even though he knew Big Bob Bat meant well. He did five more curls and then dropped the dumbbells on the floor. 'Oh my God—!'

" 'Come on, man! We can't quit yet!' said Big Bob Bat

enthusiastically. 'You can't stop until every muscle in your body is screamin'.'

"Harold slumped on a bench. *That* bench, it was. 'Big Bob,' he sighed, 'if we can stop when every muscle in my body is screamin', then we can stop right now. Because every muscle in my body is—!'

" 'Let's do some dips!' roared Big Bob Bat.

"And on they went. Until even Big Bob, who'd been doing all the exercises too, but with three times more weight than Harold— even Big Bob had had enough. 'Wow, man!' he exclaimed. 'What a workout!'

" 'Oh my Lord! Oh my heavens!' whimpered Harold. He was lying flat on his back on the floor—over there—and wondering if he'd survive. Sort of hoping he wouldn't, as a matter of fact.

" *'Eeee-ah!'* Just for the fun of it, Big Bob gave another karate scream and kicked a leg out toward the mirror.

" 'I wish you wouldn't do that,' groaned Harold. 'I can't tell you how nervous it makes me.'

" 'Okay, man,' Big Bob laughed good-naturedly. 'But say, man, if you really want to see what a weight lifter looks like, I could do some poses for you.' And Harold could hear a little plea in his voice.

" 'That would be lovely,' he moaned from the floor.

" 'I'll just fly up here in front of the mirror and beat my wings,' said Big Bob. 'You want to watch me beat my wings?'

" 'Fine. Beautiful.' Harold wearily hoisted himself up on one shoulder. 'Go ahead, Big Bob. Beat away.'

"So Big Bob flapped up in front of the mirror and flexed his muscles and began to beat his wings. And after a rather long while Harold thought that his duty of looking had been done enough and mumbled, 'Big Bob, that really is wonderful,' and flopped back down on his back.

" 'I really should have a spotlight on me,' said Big Bob Bat, as he pivoted in the air, to show himself another side of himself. Harold snapped his fingers drearily and one of the lights—it was that light there—that was wasting its light all over the place, focused in on Big Bob. 'Hey, great!' exclaimed the Bat. 'Wow! Look at those lats!' That's that muscle right here." An opportunity to tickle. " 'Hey, man, you got some magic, don't you?'

"'Oh, I've got a little leftover magic,' said Harold, who was grateful for the chance to talk about himself for a while. 'But it's going fast, and—'

"'I got a favor to ask of you,' Big Bob interrupted him. 'I'll tell you something in confidence—'

"'I'm sure you will,' said Harold.

"'I've been working out now in private for almost five years. And now I feel that I'm really ready.' He paused portentously. That means that you want to get asked what it is that you're ready for. 'I mean, I'm no ordinary bat! None of that crap of haunting a belfry in New England somewhere!'

"'Yes?' said Harold automatically. There were times when he got a little mad at himself for always doing what everyone wanted.

"'I'm entering the Bat's Body Building Beauty Contest!' announced Big Bob proudly. 'It's held every year over in the Brooklyn Academy of Music. And man, I was wondering—' He didn't sound so proud now. '—I mean, I'd really appreciate it, man.' He whispered, 'If you did a little magic.'

"'I see,' said Harold. He didn't go in for rigging races or fixing fights, but he could see how much this contest meant to Big Bob, so he stretched a principle—that means you decide to do something anyway—and said, 'Here you go, Big Bob. In return for the workout:

You judges in the Brooklyn Academy,
Let Big Bob come in first.
That is, if you think he ought to be.
At least don't let him be worst.

"'Well, thanks, man!' allowed Big Bob. For a big husky bat he could be pretty peevish too. 'That's some swell spell you just cast!'

"'You wouldn't want me to make it dishonest, would you, Big Bob?' asked Harold, with a little more wonderment in his face than he really was feeling.

"'Oh no, man!' the Bat answered fastidiously. That means it wasn't the truth. 'Nothing like that, man.'

"And—" Another *fabula interrupta*: I love Barney's puzzlement. "—that's the end of the story."

"Well *what happened!*" He demands to know. "Did he win?"

"No. He came in second," I sadly announce. "And it almost broke his heart. But Harold read about it in the newspapers and got in touch with him, and together—with Harold doing a little bit of magic—they doped out a whole new workout routine for the Bat. And he's already entered for the Bat's Body Building Beauty Contest next year. He's put himself completely in Harold's hands. In fact, Harold's his trainer now."

Chipmunk claps his thighs, and Barney sequesters his pleasure in that private place of his.

"They work out here every night, when everyone's gone away, and after the workout they take five minutes in the steam room and have a shower. Which is what we're going to do right now. Bye, Chipmunk. Bye, Lynx! Bye, everybody." I stand up.

And Chipmunk, with his instinct for humanity, does something unforgettable. At least in the weeks left I'll never forget it. A simple thing, but it elevates Barney, and mans him, matures him, for the instant it happens. Chipmunk shakes hands with my little boy—"Bye, Barney. Come back to the gym and see us again." I feel as if the good lad has put his hand on my chest, and pressed me there, as well as into Barney's timid little fist.

And a great sequence happens! All my friends follow Chip! They all shake hands with the kid. It's a chain reaction of kindness and solemn formality. Mouse, Beaver, Owl, Ocelot, the Tiger, Dead-dead—every one of them has to shake hands—

Well, I can't stop myself—"Harold's Song to His Gym Companions":

> My animals, grow huge and strong!
> Work out like tigers, turtles—mice!
> Be narcissists, if that's your joy.
> Forget that flesh must fade and die.
> Remember though, with this one boy,
> Who is not mine to harm for long,
> When you have drunk your mirrors dry,
> Since you are human too—stay nice!

And they will be. They were. I'll take Barney back to the gym again . . . Perhaps this week. And I'll tell him about the party I've planned.

February 6

God is playing games with me. Or else I'm paranoid. (I *am* paranoid.) But there's only so much coincidence endurable before you begin to believe that you're God's bad practical joke for this week. (Please God—Ya Fuck Ya!—stop it.)

Two telephone calls:

I made the first: to Edith, to see whether *Ber*-nard could come to the gym again. Oh yes, he could, except—she was all adither—they were both going out to Denver this week. And stay for several days. Instead of Frank's coming to New York this time—he *is* going to live in Denver eventually—she was taking *Ber*-nard out *there* for a visit! And a pride-filled pause invited my admiration for her insight and understanding.

The bitch!—to take him away. What I'd like is to keep him here when she goes, and then dynamite her plane!

I raise, in my mask of maturity, the issue of school—

Oh yes, she knows. But this wouldn't be that long. A few days. And Frank *will* be his father, in a little while—

I wonder—does the Mafia still rent killers out? Could I kill them both?—and then pose as a friend of the family, and gravely say, "I'll take the child"? But his moldy real father would show up . . . The receiver in my ear, I fantasize while she talks . . .

But of course, when we get back, he'd love to come to the gym again. Who's Big Bob, by the way?

No one. No one. Put him on the phone. I'll wish him *bon voyage.* Here he is! "Mr. Andrews, *Ber*-nard!"

"Hello." And his pulpy, untoughened voice—he doesn't want to go to Denver—works like Greek fire in my guts.

"Hey, Barney! I hear that you're going to take a trip."

"Yes."

"You'll like Denver. It's a beautiful city." Does my lying enthusiasm convince him, I wonder? I try to be a baritone—Jim's —a father's—but come out sounding like Beverly Sills. "I was there once. Before you were born." It *is* a pretty city too. (And I hate it as much as the City of Dis!) "When you get back we'll go to the gym again. Shall we—?"

"All right."

"And meanwhile—now I wouldn't want this to prey on your

mind—" Oh wouldn't I just! Think of nothing else, my little love. "—I'm planning a surprise for you."

"What?"

"Well, you'll have to come back to New York and see." If he cries, has tantrums, she may get him back faster. "I think you'll like it, though."

We dribble into inconclusive good-byes . . . He hangs up . . . And he's gone.

And fifteen fucking minutes later the phone rings, and it's Jim. "Hi, lad."

"Hi! You free tonight—?"

"No. I'm calling up to say good-bye." It was here that God goosed me. "I'm taking Carol to the Caribbean for a short winter vacation. And knowing your general proclivities for temper tantrums, hysteria, and other unlikable attributes, I thought I'd better tell you. Since I don't want you storming my office."

"I may anyway. For the fun of it."

"That's my lad. So ta ta now—be good—"

"Hey wait!" Blurt: capture him—try, pin him down. "Will you come to a party in my apartment?"

His eagerness is vividly perceptible, even in the dead mechanism at my ear. "A gangbang?"

"No *not* a gangbang! You motherfucker!"

Cooled instantly, he warns, "I'm talking from the office, Bubi."

"I don't give a living shit *where* you're talking from!" The Aztecs were right: the gods live only on human hearts. The god of anger does, at least. I swear by his unpronounceable name, if I'd had the bastard on my bed just then I'd have cut—dragged—his heart from his chest and eaten it lovingly.

Iced over, perhaps for some eavesdropping secretary's benefit, he announced, "I'll call you when I get back."

"*Why!*" And lacking a knife, I had to use one word as I could. His silence was undecipherable. "You don't want me to call you—?"

"Do you think there's any point in it?" Words out, I felt—which one of you has acrophobia? (*You* do!) I felt now the way you would if you'd been placed on the topmost ledge of one of those two new buildings they've decided to build—both higher than the Empire State—somewhere down in the Battery. Where did this suicidal courage come from?—to challenge him with the risk of *my* life?

But after a pause, I had a rare taste of his bedside manner. "What kind of a party would this be then?" As if the physician had abruptly discovered that the patient had a much higher temperature than he'd previously expected.

"It would be a small party. A girl I know—she's no girl, she's a woman—except she's an aging girl—and a little boy. With whom—" As long as I had him solicitous, I would press my advantage like a fiendish invalid. "—I'd expect you to play 'Hidden Billy'!"

" 'Hidden Billy'—?" He remembered, but couldn't understand.

"That game you played with your kids on Thanksgiving. In addition to which—I'd expect you to do whatever else I wanted, for the few hours that you're here. That is, if you want my belt, fist, prick—or love—any time in the future."

I think the thermometer blew up in his hand. "Lad, what are you up to?"

"I have no idea. Will you be here?"

"Yes. I'm going to try to take three weeks, if I can reschedule—"

"The date's not important."

"I'll call you when I get back—"

"Ta ta then!" In my blossoming euphoria I anticipated him. "Be a good lad now!" And hung up.

And came back from the ledge, temporarily—I put back his heart—with my fever metamorphosed into bliss—and wondered how I could get through three weeks, with the thirds of my life all taken away . . .

Perhaps it will be a dress rehearsal of genuine nonentity.

February 8

Terry, lad, you've surpassed yourself in nonsense! "A dress rehearsal of genuine nonentity." As if death was some sort of spectacular production!—preferably at the Metropolitan Opera House. Death is not, my boy, as you'd like to believe, a thrilling Nothingness, accompanied by trumpets and drums. It is simply—

nothingness. Accompanied by nothing. Not even one's self. Which has gone to the same place a candle flame goes when it's been lackadaisically blown out. A black hole.

Does this make me want to live? No. But I'll have to reconcile myself to the sheer banality of nonbeing.

What *can* be rehearsed is the difficult emptiness, the dry friction, of being exactly what one is . . .

For the next few weeks—while all three thirds of my life are gone—I will give myself freedom. That's what everybody pretends to want: the leisure to—BE YOURSELF!

It's a perilous undertaking. You had better be careful, George Meany, when you fight for off-time for the workers. Watch out, you ladies like Edith Willington, who chatter about the deadliness of the simple daily necessities. When the minimum wage is twenty-five dollars an hour and there's no work week at all, you workers too will know the fear and the anguish of absolute leisure: the panics of freedom. And you also will begin to play with your lives in the sterile games of arbitrary experience. And ladies, beware the belief that you'll find your own soul when you've stripped away chores. Beneath the diapers, beneath the vacuum cleaner, there may just be a vacuum. It's the shape of the coming world, however: the housewives will manufacture important social problems to solve, the garbage men will take classes in modern dance, and all the cleaning women will read *Scientific American* . . . And the thought of that world makes my blood run funny and cold.

Nonetheless—these next weeks I'll force freedom upon myself and become an experiment in the utterly unnecessary.

February 8: Later: in the afternoon

A bad day to begin. I went to the gym—vanity, I'm sure to find, will be one of the few remaining forces when all real demands have been removed—and only the Beaver and Dead-dead were there: a rich kid who *has* no necessities, and a pleasant nut whose favorite pastime is collecting dead actors.

And it's February too: the cemetery of the year: a bad time to start to be free. The sky this afternoon was like lead, like an adverse judgment, like visible living death. The air had that penetrating cold that no clothes are proof against. All the senses registered something endless and inevitable. The perpetual twilight became a state of mind.

"Oh was there ever once a sun
Above this frigid city?"
                    "No."
"Was there once warmth, souls animate?"
"No. Just immortal ice and snow."
"Did lovers kiss, did children run,
Did old folks sit in Central Park?"
"No. This has always been its fate:
Cold air, dead sky, eternal dark.
Believe that if you can. You'll find
If not—"
            "I know. I'll lose my mind.
But was no promise made of light?—
A promise living things would grow?"
"There was. Yes. Ages past. You're right.
But for some reason we don't know
The Covenant is broken now."
"Oh Lord, that surely can't be true!"
"Yes. God *is* dead. Or gone away.
Just bored with us. And Nature too.
They've left us though—don't try to pray—
This endless freezing final night."

Sorry, folks, but something did become necessary: I had to write that sad song down.

February 10

I cracked. The strain of my tripartite dismemberment became too much, and I called my friend Sam—yes, he of the tints and hair curlers—in hopes that the Balling Couples might be abroad last night. They weren't, but I got invited instead to—whoopee!—*Rumpelstiltskin and the Tattoo Party!* All fags, of course. Most straight guys don't feel compelled to demonstrate their masculinity by having pictures etched into their skin.

And why not a gay night? It's been a long time since I did any homosexual socializing. Every now and then a trip to Giddyville can be very entertaining. And I felt like being completely queer yesterday. I don't ordinarily swish or mince, but last night—Mary Dugan!—the mood was upon me! (I once knew a delicious little freak whose only curse words were "Mary Dugan!" He uttered them just as solemnly as any of you might say "Jesus Christ!" And who knows, perhaps he did think of the Deity as being some kind of vast omnipotent drag queen.) These fits of total homosexuality overtake me very rarely, but when they do, I usually enjoy them. I like the psychological set, the certainty, the trustworthiness of the spell. And the mannerisms too. It isn't that one becomes effeminate—Mary Dugan, no!—but say that if one was a paper doll—and perhaps I am—one has been cut out a little too neatly along the lines.

Delightful! But who would I be last night? Ravishing, luscious, gorgeous I felt. And I had it! I would be a female Mae West!

At eight, in a tasteful but understated outfit—that featured black boots, fatigue pants, and a garrison belt, climaxed by a leather jacket—and after my usual look in the mirror—"My dear, you're divine!"—I set out, disguised as Springtime Mae.

But *he* recognized me, of course—"Woof!"—my arch enemy! "Don't woof at me, you beast! I'll slap your furry face."

"Woof!" And he pushed his snout further under the window.

"Oh woof, for heaven's sake! Go on and woof! Who cares what you think of me anyway? I'm ravishing, luscious, and gorgeous—and a star!" (I don't hate you, Mae. On the contrary: when I was a child, I fell in love with you. And Jeanette MacDonald too. And Cary Grant and Nelson Eddy!) "Bye-bye, Bow Wow!" I gave him a disdainful lift of my wrist and tripped on down to Hudson Street.

Because, on Hudson Street, once upon a time—yesterday— lived one of the craziest cats of the last half-century: a soul whose insanity—a blessing really: you can see it and consequently deal with it—is depicted upon his skin: Billy Barnstable. He is old, over seventy, and from the collar up—a high collar it is—from the cuffs to the ends of his fingertips, you would think he was the executive of a fairly successful, a bit too conservative, middle-class bank. (In point of fact, he sells insurance.) But clothes off, revealed, you behold his madness presented in the most audacious visibility that I've ever witnessed in a human being. With the sole exceptions of his hands and head—preserved for his working hours and the other small times he must spend in the so-called world—he is a mass of living tattoos. Feet too! There's a rattlesnake writhing out of his asshole, there's a Gila monster on one of his calves; the Archangel Michael—sword too, uplifted— on half of his chest—well, I won't, and can't, do his whole epidermis, because I don't have that much time. Since he started back in the nineteen-twenties, there are tattoos on top of tattoos, and the whole effect—if you don't pass out—is altogether dazzling. Your first thought is—a nineteenth-century sideshow freak. Your second—this is the brilliant pictorial witness of one man's sexual fantasies.

I envy him: I have seen him come. He will stand before a mirror, caressing snakes, lizards, angels, Turkish dancing girls, and at a certain intensity of self-absorption, when every inch of fictionalized skin has been eroticized, he will shudder—his prick will spill—and his tattoos become alive, for an instant of blessedness. And isn't it truly enviable—when your dreams vibrate along your flesh, and your smallest capillaries pulsate with the cosmos that you've become?

He throws a tattoo party three or four times a year. Knowing all the tattoo craftsmen from Coney Island and the other workshops of anatomical artistry—and them being outlawed, now, poor lads—he hires a couple of blokes, with the sputtering needle machine, and invites anybody—everybody! and their friends— who might want a free tattoo. I had been once before, and didn't want a tattoo—the world outside of me is my skin, and the pictures there have to live, be real—but I was allowed to return last night because I'd appreciated the host so audibly and articulately, like an art historian in the Louvre.

Sam told me that splash-down was at twenty-one hundred— "Right in the middle of Swan Lake, sweetie!"—so at twenty-two hundred, several Scotches and my—Mary Dugan!—madcap mood inside me, I reported in to the loft on Hudson Street.

The party consisted of:

One quiche queen from Kips Bay Plaza (I shouldn't make fun of that place: when I was alive, a good friend of mine, perhaps my best, lives there) who was trying to decide which tattoo "was *me!*"

One spade faggot hairdresser—sorry, my husky Militant, but he *was* a flibbity-jibbit thing—a friend of Sam's who was still, on Sunday, trying to come down from the total hysteria of spending nine hours a day attempting to straighten out kinky locks in the Medusa Beauty Parlor in Harlem. But they don't do that any more, do they? Nowadays it's all Afro coiffure—and let the kinks twinkle! And better so. (I only wish I had the guts to let my kinks twinkle.)

One hustler: a sad, superannuated thing, in a costume much like mine, who knew that his whoring days were done. But who'd come to have one last hopeful tiger tattooed on anyway.

Sam: drunk, and playing with himself in a corner. Since the handsome tattooer he liked was straight. He kept saying, "Mercy! My roots are showing." And they were: his hair isn't Mediterranean black—it's North Dakota nondescript mouse.

Me: *half* drunk. And half Mae West. And half dead. (Not quite enough.)

And a hook-nosed Jew: one of those depressing Semites—and God, there's no one who can say "yid" or "kike" with the same emphasis as an anti-Semitic Jew.

And off in one corner a sad, hairy young ugly, who gave the impression of someone who'd just flunked out of a charm school for hermaphrodites.

And our host: stripped already—the full-length mirror out—and beginning to groove on his own multicolored cells.

And the two tattooers: one straight, one gay—and the gay one trying to pass, with flourishes of nonchalance, as simply the friend of the one who was simply his friend.

"I *honestly* can't make up my mind!" said the quiche queen from Kips Bay Plaza. (And how do I know he cooks quiche? Because there's an aura about a gay gourmet.) "I want something butch to bulge out of my biceps."

"How about a bar or two from *Pelléas et Mélisande*?" (That was me. I was entering into the spirit of things. And talk about auras—mine too was as bright as the northern lights: good body, cruel wit, and affectionately sadistic in bed.) (But I'm *not* your typical fun-loving toe-tapping sadist!)

"And look, afterwards let's go to the Sty!" chirped the

anti-Semitic neo-goy, with a glass in his hand. "Auschwitz! Otherwise known as Funsville East." And he waltzed by himself and sang, "Oh I used to be Jewish, but I may be a Nazi tonight. I feel *mean!*"

La Quiche, who proved in the course of the evening to be a Mad. Ave. fashion designer, eventually settled on "a classic dragon. Scales, flames—the whole bit!" While the rest of us sat around boozing and watching, he got "Didi Dragon," as he christened her, put on—with frequent impetuous trips to the mirror to ask frantically, "Do you think it'll make *Vogue? I* think it will!"

"Let's have some music!" the hysterical spade demanded. "I can't stand the sound of that needle! Too much like my black mama's sewin' machine."

"*A Night on Bald Mountain,*" the Jew-hating kike proposed. (Sorry, folks, but the only Jews I really loathe are the anti-Semitic ones. Like this Levantine sociologist—and Karl Marx.)

"Shirley Temple singing 'On the Good Ship, Lollipop' would be more like it." (That was me again. I was tasting the sweet cyanide that a camp like last night always makes me salivate.)

"Charming, Terry," said Sam. "You're such a cunt."

"True, true," I sighed. "You've hit the clitoris on the head."

"But you're also a prick. So we forgive you."

I gave him my calculated lip-curl. (Even more effective in faggotry.)

"You need to fall in love!" Sam diagnosed my malady. "That's all you need."

"I *am* in love!" I answered abruptly, the truth unexpectedly breaking through my cast-iron camp.

"Who with, you secretive motherfucker?"

"With—oh, the motht wonderful man in the world!" I recovered myself.

"*Who?*"

"Spiro Agnew."

We began a game of one-line fantasies: the best single sentences we'd ever heard—and they had to be the truth. The dragon-cum-quiche—a clever fellow, and likable once one had penetrated the glossy fleece—came up with a great one: a Marine sergeant, in the throes of belief, had pushed his head away and said, "Don't eat me tonight, dear—I'm menstruating." My own was pretty good, but far from the best. I know a failed Trappist, and a couple of years ago he jumped up, snatched the sheet off the bed, and swathed and cowled himself in it, with these words: "I'm a white-robed monk and you're my abbot, master!" The spade's entry was a single word: he'd been blowing a biochemist who suddenly burst out, *"Permerect! I'm going to invent Permerect!"* But we gave the prize to Sam: a trick of his stood up regally, extended his right hand, like the Olympia Apollo, and announced, "I'm a charioteer returning to Thebes, and you're a handmaiden laboring in the fields!" . . . Which one would you have voted for? . . . I *adore* recording this!

And all this time, oblivious, the Man of Tattoos was swaying in front of his mirror: a living course in zoology, angelology, demonology: Walt Disney autism.

At ten-fifteen, two new arrivals. "Now no one say *anything!*" ordered Sam. "This is a tragedy."

"A faggot tragedy is a faggedy. Just as a popper hangover is a popover."

"Oh *will* you shut up, Terry! We all know you're a writer!"

"Sorry, boss, sorry, boss."

The faggedy, in this case, was a couple who were breaking up. Ten months of eternal fidelity. The younger of the two, it seems, had fallen in love with a handsome truck driver who liked Mahler. But to prove their still undying devotion, they were going to have each other's initials—H.I., S.T.—tattooed on one another's arms. And we, drunk creeps, were to witness this solemn ceremony. (Henry Ives, Stan Trachman: those *were* the initials—not my acrostic, God's.) Which we did, all boozing sentimentally, while the painful needle buzzed . . .

Sad lovers, sad lovers—you make Harold sigh and shake his head. And need to write—"Harold's Lament for Two Likable Young Men Who Misjudged Their Love"—

> A glinting nothing thinks it is all:
> A homosexual love affair.
> Part joy, part sorrow, and part mere fashion,
> It flickers and flitters—its wings brightly beat;
> It feeds on dreams, on the empty air—

And has no notion what fate it will meet.
For it grows in the spring, but must die in the fall,
Then, dead, decay in the failing heat.
The quick insect life has spent its passion.

Tattoos completed—the classic dragon was madly acclaimed—
we offed to the Sty: so called because the pigs raid it so often it
was more their turf than the sadomasochistic clientele's.

The leather black-star bars are all alike. Indeed they are the
same place: same people, same costumes—leather jackets, the
Honda honeys, who wear leather all year round, like ladies
showing off their minks—and dullest of all, exactly the same
propensities. This latest, the Sty—having been okayed by the
Mafia, the fuzz, and one pivotal masochist who brings the two
together. (If only he was in government! The country would be in
much better shape.) The Sty is on the waterfront. But it might as
well be on Fifth Avenue, Broadway, or Wall. There are certain
monuments completely immune to the ravages—and also the
creativity—of time. "Hi, Frank!" "Hi, Joe!" "Hi, Hank!" "Hi,
Moe!"—it's like a goddam fraternity. The occasional weekend
stranger is devoured instantly and digested into the exotic
familiarity of stylized clothes, conversational S-M clichés, and the
infinite wishing for new sensations. I show up in these bars about
twice a year—or at least I used to, when years were real—reaffirm
my abhorrence, leave in despair—and show up again in six
months.

Not that there aren't some beauties there. Last night, for
example: there was a clutch of comely cocks midway at the bar.
And they always know who they are, the aristocrats of flesh. They
coagulate, gravitate toward one another in reciprocal admiration:
eyes calculated above the rejected admirer's head, always hovering over some other horizon, exiles among the ugly—the princes
of perversion, in their melancholy splendor.

"Hi, Terry!" "Hi, John!" "Hi, Mary!" "Hi, Fran!"

What is never lacking moreover is hatred: of oneself, one's
friends, one's country—the world.

Sam went up to one, in his great Samlike honest way, and
asked, "Whose masturbation fantasy are *you?*"

I usually get blotto as fast as I can.

And I did last night. By eleven-thirty I was drunk, stoned, *blind!*—just a-floppin' around like the young Helen Keller. A pity, because I might have scored the way I'd wanted to—if I hadn't been so slobbering.

There was this humpy out-of-towner off in one corner. And obviously an out-of-towner: the perplexed expression—"Do I really want to be here?"—that always turns me on. He was younger than I—but *I'll* never tell, Gerontion, never!—yet my years in this case might have an advantage. I think he was probably only twenty—

Oh be of good cheer, all ye aging homosexuals! When fathers fail, as they do, repeatedly, in our time, their image becomes a sexual object. So perk up, all you gray-beard Marys—even now your young lovers are worrying their painful way to you all!

—twenty-five at most, but I fucked it up abominably. I staggered up in front of him, with a shit-eating grin, convinced I couldn't score—and of course I couldn't because I was convinced I couldn't—and drunkenly shlurped, "Well, whose masturbation fantasy are *you?*" (I shouldn't have listened to Sam: he carried it off with the right disbelief—but I couldn't.) He gave me a look—which may or may not have been disappointment: that my clumsiness had prevented it all—and moved off. And pretty he was. Like a graduate student—he must have been—who was studying some docile subject—geology, or botany, somewhere.

Oh Ralph O'Toole—if that's your name—forgive me!
If I'd been sober, we'd have grooved—believe me!

Pride bloody but unbowed, I lurched on to the next rejection. Which must have been Slavic, two or three generations back: he had the high cheekbones and the trace of immemorial Asia in the eyes. But the soul had been hatched in arrogant America, in a Polish enclave in Chicago perhaps. He was well aware, in his lower-class cockiness, of the power good looks can give a poor boy: the sort of boy you might find for a week or so behind the counter of a Howard Johnson's—and then you might find him in a chic Upper East Side apartment—but don't call after five o'clock, because that's when Francis gets home from the bank!

I commit a special kind of psychological suicide with this type. Since I'm fluent when I'm relaxed, I become tongue-tied; since

I'm educated, I project an artificial ignorance; since I'm fairly presentable, my features rearrange themselves—and I feel them doing it—into a nondescript homeliness.

"Hi." How's that for an opener? Brilliant, what?

"Hi." A genuine bastard can condescend in a monosyllable.

"Are you Polish?"

And he can evince contempt in a casual glance. "Half."

"You've got those great bones in your face. A friend of mine's Polish—" (That's true. A stereo nut whom I love. But Teddy isn't nearly as pretty as you, you prick, although he's at least twenty times the man.) "—but his bones don't work quite as well as yours!"—with a girlish giggle of admiration. (Forgive me, Teddy. A single short hair from your crew-cut head is worth all the blond fleece on this shit's whole body!)

His silence was acceptance of appreciation he felt was due.

"You speak Polish?"

"No."

"Teddy does. He's that friend." I stumbled—as I've always stumbled—over the obstacle of small talk. But my idiot breath staggered on. "He says I should learn to speak it."

"Why don't you find him—" The turn of his shoulders away from me was the glacial movement of utter boredom. "—and start to learn to speak Polish."

> Mike Shimkus, you're a prideful prick—and screw you!
> If I'd been—no, I never could undo you.

The last phase of a night in a gay bar, for me, is the cultivation of a smirking, aloof expression, which I carry rigidly, like a fragile mask, off into a corner, where I brood on life Satanically: a skeptic, a scoffer—one of those who reign from the thrones of scorn. If you manifest enough disdain, you sometimes attract, in the last few hours, something servile and serviceable.

But what I attracted yesterday was neither. It was my fate—a *memento mori: "Hodie mihi, cras tibi,"* as the skeleton said, with its hand resting coyly across its chest. This omen was dressed exactly like me—boots, jacket, belt—in a mirrored image, but twenty years older, that jarred my sullen reverie. On his face there was a knowing, smug, and unsatisfied smile: the burnt, healed scar of cynicism.

"Hi."

"Hi." I repeated his intonation.

"I've seen you around for years," said the grim and expectant destiny.

"No you haven't. I don't go to bars that much."

He must have sensed my defensiveness—getting bald, getting gray, getting fat, getting *old*—him! him! not me, you vicious watching witnesses—for his certainty held me like a hand. I felt like a big uncircumcised dick that he casually skinned. "I know. You drop out of sight for months and months. But then you come back. You always do." His smile lengthened lifelessly. "I've wanted you for ten years."

"I'm flattered," I stuttered. He made me afraid.

"You weren't the first time I made a pass."

"When was that?"

"Way back in the days of the Hula-Hoop. Remember?—on Eighth Avenue? You've been working out since then."

"And a good thing too! Back in the days of the Hula-Hoop—" I tried self-directed irony, to defend myself against compliments. "—I looked like a dehydrated fetus."

"Don't knock a dehydrated fetus. You add the right amount of water, and it turns into a weight lifter." He had my own sense of humor too, this devil's reflection. My face said "Touché!" "I've been wondering when you'd show up again."

"Been waiting?"—superciliously.

"Yes."

He was one of those people—like Danny Reilly—who enslave me by their naked needs. "Well, don't hold your breath. I'm taking off." I finished my drink with a flourish.

"I'll be here." In need he may have been, and perhaps in despair, but beyond these similarities he was unlike myself in his stillness. And his certainty. "I've waited ten years already—I can wait ten more, if necessary."

Apart from a dip in an ice-cold pool at dawn, there's nothing like truth to sober you up: if I had lived, this soul *would* have collected me. I don't know what he wanted in bed—sadistic? masochistic?—I sensed that he simply wanted to possess me in any way he could: to turn me into what he was. And indeed I could have become this man. In an adolescent's leather jacket, face wrinkled like cuneiform, with a fixed grin that seemed to be imitating a stone head in the desert—here I was!

"We'll see each other again," he said. "Either here, or in the next bar that opens up."

Here I was. And between bars, where was I? At sixty years old—he must have been sixty at least—sixty-five—I was cruising the men's room of a YMCA, singing, "I'll Take Romance" at the top of a high falsetto voice.

I haven't panicked very often. But I panicked last night. And fled that living mirror. Fled that bar like Lot from the city expecting to be pelted by fire. And the fire has nothing to do with guilt. It has nothing whatsoever to do with sin. The physical love of men for men can be a thrilling, and overpowering satisfying thing—when it's been divorced from gay bars, tattoo parties, and baroque leather clothing. The fire is simply boredom, monotony: the endless consciousness of one's self.

> Old self, be gone!
> Let me alone!
> Young self would rather die—and so be free—
> Than share your joyless immortality.

My panic, and also the revulsion I felt at the homosexual Puritanism—the strict inverted morality of a room full of only one sex—was transformed into lust, as I walked through the cold night home. And it had to be a woman. Not simply to get the taste of the Sty out of my mouth. For me men are a destination, and women a threshold. Last night I felt circumscribed. There are times when one wants to reach a goal and other times when one wants to go beyond a boundary. Especially a woman's dark wet limits.

I called Connie. "Can you talk?"

"Who's this?"

"Guess."

"Tehwy—?"

"Is Max there?"

"No. He's out playin' poka."

"I want to see you."

"Now?"

"Yes. I need to see you. Now."

"I can't, Tehwy—"

"Look, your kids are asleep, aren't they—?"

"Yes."

"—and they're safe. Just come over here for a half an hour. I'll pay for the taxi. I'll meet you downstairs. Max won't get back—but if he should you can leave a note and tell him that one of your girl friends called. You had to go see her. You'll be back in a half an hour. I'll *pay* for the taxi—both ways! I'll put twenty bucks between your legs—but, Connie, I've got to fuck you. I've got to chew the clothes off you. I want hair from your crotch stuck between my teeth."

"Jesus, Tehwy—!"

"Now I'm going downstairs and wait for you. It's cold too, but I'm going to wait in the street. If you want me to be on my knees, I will. I'll wait for you on my knees."

"Tehwy!"

"Hanging up now. I'll be down in the street."

And I did hang up, in absolute conviction that Connie would come to me.

And she did: unmade up, bedraggled, harried—and absolutely necessary. I had turned her on on the phone. And when I began to nibble her fingers, lick her thighs, devour her toes, she lost control completely.

"Not yet—not yet. We're going into the bathroom first. I want to see you in the tub." (Ah toothbrushes! You're necessary too.)

"Wha' fa'?"

"I'm going to piss on you."

"No!"

"Oh yes! Oh yes. And then you're going to piss on me. And don't fret it, sweet Connie. There's nothing dirty until you think it is."

Do you turn away?

Don't!—my pits of witnesses. Myself.

"Tua res agitur! . . . " It's *you* who are discussed here!

There's no safety for me apart from you.
Either *I* die—no, all of you die too!

February 13

They are gone. They're all gone. To confirm their absence I've made three telephone calls. Anne's phone, and Edith's, just rang and rang. There's no emptiness like an unanswered telephone. Jim's secretary—a gruff lass he's described to me—said that the doctor was taking a little vacation—would I leave my name? No: a personal call—I'll call back. All scattered. Vanished. San Diego, Denver, the Caribbean . . .

And the ocean of time beats aimlessly against the cliffs of consciousness. But the wearing away of the soul is too slow.

To distract the waiting—articulate it, even if meaninglessly— I've invented this game: I will make love every day, but one day will be Ladies' Day, and the next for the men. And desire will have to be disciplined strictly by law: I'll alternate rigorously: any inclination, preference, so far as gender is concerned, will be ruthlessly ignored.

Great idea! I'll retrace the steps of my history!

When I was at college I used to come down to New York and do a little nervous cruising at the Biltmore Bar. So much superior to the tacky and now defunct Astor! . . . I'll into a suit, I'll into a cab, and up to the Biltmore—right *now!*

February 14

So far so good. Not good. But at least I'm on schedule: I scored last night.

But sad, sad, sad: a young soldier on his way to Vietnam today. Just twenty. My God, such children do really exist!

He wasn't attractive. Thin, pimpled—but as soon as he opened his fear to me, I fell in love with the poor doomed kid. In love with him bodily: I wanted his scrawniness in my arms. When the terror appeared: a dull terror, accepted hopelessness. "It's the ambushes I think about. You don't even get to see who's shooting at you!" His drunk laughter was the friction of fate on despair. "It doesn't make any difference in the end, but I want to *see* who's shooting at me."

He had a room in the Biltmore—"I thought, my only night in

New York, I'd stay in a nice hotel." I got him upstairs by proposing that we go out to dinner—but I'd like to wash up first. Yeah, he would too. (The proximity of the bar's men's room was blissfully ignored.)

He got much more than he bargained for. I decided that it should be all for him, and I blew him and rimmed him and licked his fingers and ate his feet, and I don't think anyone had before: he seemed dazed by the maddened gifts I gave him. The immanent death in his flesh turned me into a selfless maniac. A rotten cocksucker—and he couldn't get fucked—at one point he insisted on jacking me off: "So you can have fun too."

Sweet boy. Good lad. Pvt. William Tarbell. At this minute he's flying to California. And then off to that arbitrary abyss of useless misery.

> Vietnam! Vietnam!
> Was. And always will be. Am . . .
> Was there a time you were at peace?
> I can't remember—or see how.
> Will this sad nonsense ever cease?
> Too late: I'm used to dying now . . .

He may well be dead before I am . . . I love him.

February 18

On schedule, folks! I haven't bothered to send you daily bulletins because most of the ass has been so goddam dreary. The baths, the bars on lower Third Avenue—

Oh but *she* was delicious! I must tell you about—The Hooker With The Heart Of—not gold, perhaps, but something at least more valuable than brass. Picked her up on—Sunday was Ladies' Day—at Gallagher's, a drinking and eating establishment frequented by many young ladies who are gainfully unemployed. Got her back to my apartment. A drink. And the ditsy little twit insisted on "making conversation." The subject of vacations came up. (How? God knows! Out of some hooker manual on keeping your partner amused, as well as aroused and satisfied.) My dippy Marge says to me piquantly, "I like to get away, hon'—don' you?"

And Sister Stiltskin, whose pubic hairs were curling with boredom—he only wanted to complete the rite and send her on her way—said, "No! I like to stay in one place. And stay and stay: in one place, in one chair. Until every square inch of the walls of your room, every millimeter and every molecule of those walls, has been drilled into your head and become your brain! And the chair too has become your brain! And then, after the madness has come and passed, you attain a kind of peace."

"Ooo, my Gawd—!"

I am laughing so hard that my hand can't write! If you all could have heard the bleak horror with which she said, "Ooo, my Gawd—!" "This guy's *crazy!*" her bird mind was chirping at her. So I added lightheartedly, "But sometimes I go to Coney Islan' too!"

And we made—rather nervous love on her part, rather pixyish on mine.

That all is a postscript. The delightful thing happened today.

> Oh stupid masculinity!—
> You always miss the point.
> One flatters femininity.
> It's never just your joint.

Now remember: I only said sex on alternating days. I didn't promise that I had to take my clothes off, get a hard-on, or have an orgasm. The vow was Sex. And those of you who don't recognize it when it happens outside the flesh can leave the room right now. (Oh no you can't! Stay right where you are! I need company.) (Jim, Barney, and Anne—I feel them like nails at the ends of my extended limbs.)

There's this woman—frowzy and blowsy and bosomy—who lives in my neighborhood. We've nodded to each other for years. And a head of lettuce finally brought us together. Out it tumbled from a paper bag—I rescued it—and she asked me up for a beer—a platonic beer, I knew it would be—"After all these years." And we spent two absolutely delightful hours! In the first of which she praised the joys of domesticity—husband, children—in the second of which she damned them to hell.

She said, "There's some days when a woman just wants to—"

"Wants to what?"

"Express her rebellion! *I* don't know—!"

"How?"

She looked at me and began to laugh. I sensed exactly what she meant, and I laughed too. It was *not* by committing adultery!

As fast as I was out of her door, Harold ran home and wrote "Harold's Lament for the Harried Housewife":

> Oh ladies, ladies, when you're trapped at home,
> When hubby's out grubbing and you're left all alone,
> When you're horribly harried
> And wish you weren't married,
> And your stomach's distressed,
> And the children aren't dressed,
> And your hair's awfully messed—
> When life's *too much for you!*—
> Do you fart out loud? . . .
> (I'll bet you do.)

February 20

God, I must put out some kind of aroma. Or—how you say?—a stink!

To the baths last night, it being Boys' Town—and what do I find but *another* young married man who wants to get his ass strapped! There may actually be some elusive kind of subliminal odor that one emits: a chemical that only the self-chosen quarry reacts to. Not as handsome as Jim—but that was his charm: a slightly potbellied mediocrity. A podiocrity! Who bent over forward to make sure that I enjoyed myself. Brian Roark. The ocular lock: and before you could say "Jack Masochist," I had scooped him up and taken him home and plied him with poppers, and shown him, as Our Gal Stella Armstrong well knew, that life can be beautiful. Especially with a belt across your ass. And no—no marks! . . . And the fool wants to be friends!

(But today—for the ladies—I went up to Emma's Friendly West Side Brothel and got a blow job from that gifted little colored gal whose tongue flickers—wet wings—at the end of your prick and feels like the epidermal equivalent of the fabulous Sutherland trill.)

But my heart wasn't in it—sorry, Alice!—although Louie finally did his duty. I only went there to keep my promise as quickly as possible. In my groin, not my brain, I was still turned on to Brian's behind. He can't compare to Jim, of course—in looks or hauteur or insolence—but a good, fast lad who openly shows his appreciation. And I like that.

Naive too: wants to take me home to meet his wife and kids. (You'd think I *liked* husbands, wives, and children, the way people urge me to come home and meet theirs!) Said Brian ingenuously, "After all, Ter', we could've *met* somewhere, couldn't we?"

Indeed we could, Bri'! And did.

And what would you have thought, his wife? Would you guess or suspect anything? I hope you would, for the sake of your next forty years. In fact, I hope you would so much that—"Harold's Song for All You Unwary Wives Out There"—

> Oh ladies, ladies, be careful, please!
> Your marriages are breakable.
> Bri' Roark, Tom Schwartz, and Norman Pease—
> Unwary wives, they're makable!

> Beware the new buddy who comes for brunch!
> Beware the camaraderie!
> They *may* just be friends—but I've got a strong hunch
> That they're making it, Bri' and he.

> Don't trust that young man in the Brooks Brothers shorts!
> All that locker-room horseplay—for kicks.
> You may think that it's just about college and sports,
> But Tom knows that it's all about pricks.

> Above all—Best Men are all dangerous queers!
> Your Norman's old roommate—alas!
> Who would have believed, after all of these years,
> Ol' Norm' still takes him straight up the—

Dammit! The telephone . . .

Him! It was Brian! . . . E.S.P. does exist!

"I'm around the corner. And hot as hell. I told my wife that I had to go back to the office—"

"Get it up here, man!"

"Yes, sir."

And I do *not* promise not to leave any black and blue stars on his tail! He and his wife can make love in the dark. (Unwary wife—does your husband make love in the dark?)

Come, Brian! come, Brian—oh Jesus, if only it could be Jim—

> —but hurry! hurry! I'm hot with despair!
> There's thunder and lightning in my living room air!
> Rumpelstiltskin is clawing and tearing my hair!
> *Devils! Diamonds! Disease!* I don't care! . . .
> The buzzer!—and one lovely husband is there!

February 21

I won't see him again. He was good, but as a substitute, not good enough. Not cruel: too vulnerable. His feelings got very pulpy last night: too malleable. I felt the challenge and aversion of a sculptor for marble.

No. No . . . Good-bye, Brian.

The excuse will be—now what would a middle-class jerk believe?—that I've gotten engaged? To a marvelous girl! He might. But *I* couldn't stomach saying that . . . I'll think of something. My closet is full of skeletons, but also tender lies.

February 23: Late. Eleven

The sequence is broken. So sweetly! Listen closely now, my hopeful Hobbits.

At three o'clock, the telephone, on this grisly, chilly winter afternoon: a tentative high voice said, "Mr. Andrews—?"

"Yes—"

Self-confidence streamed into his tone. "This is Ben!"

Jim's Ben, Ben Whittaker. I instantly felt the fragile sensation of Jim's hand, arm, upon my shoulder: he has a way of resting them there as delicately as a woman's, and even when I'm in the labor of selfish consummation, the gentleness of it drives me wild.

"We're asking you to Sunday night supper!" Ben was speaking, manfully, as the delegate of himself and his negligible sisters, and against the impressive better judgment of Mary Wicks: "She said you'd be busy, but I said, then he can *tell* us so!" That darkened little boy. (I loathe my own eyes at this moment!) He'll never enjoy the most rich sense, but he's got such balls! Mawkish I felt, on the telephone. And sentimental. I wanted to kiss him and stroke his head. The way Jim had, when he'd hurt himself Thanksgiving Day.

"Well you tell Mary Wicks to get out the waffle iron—"

"*Pancakes,* it was going to be! How did you know?"

"The pancake platter then. Because what else do you have for Sunday night supper?" (Are pancakes becoming another of my devils, I wonder?)

"French toast!" he rebutted me elegantly. The gorgeous little motherfucker! So much brighter and more alive than my Barney.

I was to come—"quick! Come right away!"—but we settled for six o'clock. I insisted upon that hour so that I could appear at ease, in control, not frantic—as I was—to whip on a coat and come rushing up, pell-mell, to Riverdale right away.

Which is just what I did: after two or three of my own maple syrup, I took a shower, changed clothes, and hopped on the subway, craftily planning to walk from the station to the Whittaker house, and so get there a little after six. As the cars rattled on, I was millionaired in anticipation: those six children of his! (And why not? I, who sit in the warmth of other people, on subways, on buses—did I not have a right to feel rich?)

Grim February was charmed by my mood, relaxed, and began, not too coldly, to snow, not too thickly, with a wonderful freedom of flakes: these random crystals came drifting down benevolently, self-given gifts.

And a blessing stood over Riverdale: a suburban city's winter twilight: the houses a little inhibited by caked ice and the night, the dark—but comforted with interior lights.

"At *last!*" Ben opened the door. "We're all *starving!*"

"Well, it's just a little bit after six."

"In winter, on Sundays, we get hungry at five," a little girl midway in the brood piped up.

Beyond the big molecule of quivering children loomed a familiar eminence. "Hi, Mary."

"Mista Andrews. If you want to hang your coat up there and go into the living room. I'll bring in some ice."

All psychiatrists should be elderly, somewhat overweight colored ladies! "Thank you, Mary."

"But maybe instead, why don't you come into the butla's pantry? That's where Docta' locks the liquor up."

"He locks it up—?"

"When he goes on vacation. Then when he comes back, we all have a big opening out again. Kind of silly, since I've had the key all the time. You children go in and sit awhile—"

"Oh Mary—!"

"Oh *Mary*—!"

"—and let Mista Andrews enjoy himself."

"I'll be right in in a minute."

That wonderful grudging children's "Oh all *right*."

"How do you handle them all by yourself?" I asked Mary Wicks in the butler's pantry.

"I handle," she answered magisterially, and deigned to hand me a bottle of Scotch. And I wouldn't have dreamed of probing the matter any farther.

"Whose idea was it, Mary, having me up here?"

"Ben's. But it didn't take much to get the girls convinced."

I sipped the fairly strong drink I'd made. "Well—here I go, Mary!"

"Don't be afraid, Mista Andrews." Her eyes were like two amused microscopes. "They're good kids. They won't bite you."

And those colored lady psychiatrists should wear plain blue domestic dresses with sparkling white aprons tied over them.

If I'd been afraid of silences, awkward pauses, while all of us waited for Mary Wicks to cook pancakes—forget it! The youngest kept offering me her milk bottle, in responding to which—"Why thank you very much! Gug gug gug!"—I imitated Jim, while the others speculated about what presents their parents would bring them from the Caribbean. "It'll just be *beach* hats!" the girl who got hungry at five in the winter opined. Ben felt his way through the crowded darkness and stood beside my chair. His constant,

307

yet tentative presence—in the dark one always is tentative—energized my left side, where he stood. I wanted very much to drop my arm, with tremendous nonchalance, around his shoulder, but didn't dare. Then the postcards were shown. There was one for each child, so far. Thank God!—not the all inclusive "you." But of course Jim and Carol were smart enough to recognize identities.

Ben, at his own insistence, got more ice for my drink from the kitchen. "Are you writing more Harold stories?" he asked, as he lifted the glass and waited for my hand to take it.

"You're just like your mother!" I grumped. "That's not bad."

"Well *are* you?"

"I haven't been writing any. But I've been telling some."

"Who to?"

"A little boy I know. He's younger than you."

"Oh that's all right!" The delicious egotism of kids! Their best, and worst, and most abiding attribute.

"What's all right?" I feigned.

"If he's younger than me. We still want to hear one. He *can't* be any younger than Liz!"

Mary Wicks came in and announced, authoritatively, but after a delay, "All right—supper."

Oh shit, my Militant! I apologize in advance, but I can't stop from coming—"Harold's Song for All Black People Like Mary Wicks"—with her arm resting protectively across the back of the Galactic Throne—

> You colored servants, soon you'll go,
> And will not be replaced. (Nor ought you all to be.)
> Your beauty comes from—I don't know—
> A kind of hard-won grace. (That most of us don't see.)
>
> It's not the fact you're servants, slaves—
> That's crap that Snow White sells.
> But you have qualities that save.
> It's that you are yourselves.
>
> We've mocked and we've degraded you,
> And judgment waits above.
> *You* plead for us—we've no right to . . .
> From Harold. And with love.

Boy! Talk about the wads of damp wool of our dismal liberalism—but I do love you, Mary!

Four batches of pancakes—and very much better than Edith's had been—were gone through without any trouble at all. Uncle Remus here, Hans Grimm-Tolkien, sitting at the head of the table and well aware he was in Jim's seat, downed about six, and then feasted on watching those six children gobble up dozens more.

In anticipation of impotence—"What do I do for them *now?*"—I'd concocted a big date back in the city. (Kids nowadays are old enough.) But during the postpancake lull, while the littlest were still slurping up syrup—and I was on the point of a glance at my watch and a faked mature apology—Ben said, "*Will* you tell us a Harold story?"

"I don't honestly have one ready—" I used my fake voice in a different way.

"Oh, he doesn't want to hear one anyway!" said the tallest girl. I think she's Nancy.

"*Yes* I do—"

"He only wants to play blind man's buff."

In an airplane once I heard a sound that made me think we were going to crash: a net of apprehension and fear grew tight around my head. And I felt that way now. "Blind man's buff—?"

"Yes. He always wins," editorialized that midway little wit: Lucinda, I believe: the character of the crew. (Watch out, Streisand!)

"Well, if Ben wants to play for a while—" The airplane that I had become dipped out of its nose dive. "—I don't have to get back right away."

"Oh all right. But you better know, Mr. Andrews, when we play blind man's buff out here, we play it for *real!*" (You've just lost, Barbra.)

"For *real!*" turned out to be the kind of eyeshade insomniacs wear, held strict to the face by a rubber band around the head. I wondered through what strange accommodations—hells, heavens, realities—this family had learned to play this game.

"You're not as big as Daddy—" Ben groped and tested my head. "—but his ought to fit on you."

"Now I'm not too certain—" He fitted the shades around my

eyes. They were snug, and did black out all light. I was frightened.
"—blind man's buff is—"

"It's nothing!" Lucinda pronounced ruthlessly. "It's everybody just running around falling into things. Except Ben. Because *he* knows where everything is!"

"It is *not!*" Ben protested vehemently. "It's playing tag in the dark. And it's fun."

It may have been that Mary Wicks had spiked the pancakes—but my slowly swelling inebriation turned into a dread that raced straight out. The fear I'd felt when Ben settled Jim's shades across my eyes became deadly and inexorable. It wasn't that I identified with Ben's darkness which, infinite though it was, he had adjusted to; it was the horror, perhaps something physical left in the eye-shades themselves, that Jim must feel when he puts them on: that his son would never see. Whatever it was, for the first time in my life, I dreadfully feared the dark. The black. I never did, as a child.

Not the star-blackened dark that was left when someone had kissed you and said good night and closed the door behind her. Nor even the deeper, total darkness, when you woke up later and found that the night light had been turned off. I could cope with darkness—then, at least. But not yesterday. I began to sweat.

"And no going under the couch, Liz!" Ben was enumerating the rules. "Just 'cause you're the only one little enough to fit there! And we have to stay downstairs. Mr. Andrews hasn't been in our bedrooms."

"And out of the kitchen?" Nancy offered.

"No, we can go *into* the kitchen tonight!" Ben declared. "Mary's in a very good mood. She won't badchildren us tonight."

"That's what *you* think!" the embryo skeptic, Lucinda, chorused.

"I'll start—"

"You always start!"

"—and Mr. Andrews, you have to run away somewhere—but walk! Unless you remember where the chairs all are. And I try to find you. And the one I tag is the next It. Oh, and also I have to stay out in the hall and block my ears—and I *do* block my ears—so I won't hear where everyone's hiding. All ready?" His voice went high with excitement: a child's modulation into adventure that ordinarily takes me with it.

But that terror of the spangled nothingness that my eyes were seeing—and I knew absolutely that this was Jim's deepest and innermost nightmare—had overcome me, and my voice jiggled as I said, "All ready."

I, naturally, was his quarry. He shouted his counting—"*One—two-three-four*"—up to a hundred, to prove that he wasn't listening; the girls evaporated in different directions, soft footfalls and shivers of vanishing laughter; and I felt my way into the sun porch. Released from the numbers that had held him bound, Ben flew through the living room—I heard him—like a night bird set free. It was his world now: he was master of it. One girl squeaked, as a hint—she wanted to be It—but the vivid boy would have none of her. It was me he wanted. And me he found.

I thought I had hidden myself pretty well, behind a chair, hunched under a table, and I thought my breath was under control, but his radar picked me out instantly. I could hear him hovering closer and closer, enjoying the finding of what he sought; he paused just before me, and lengthened a moment, demonstrating his dark authority. And then both his hands were upon my face—God, how beautiful!—a little boy's hands, with those lovely unfinished fingers—and he kept them there as he whispered softly, "I've got you, Mr. Andrews." As if it was some kind of secret between just the two of us.

Then he shouted his conquest out loud: "*I've found Mr. Andrews!* Now *you* have to count and I hide." He wheeled off in his medium. Disappeared.

"*One-two-three-four—*"

My quest began. But I knew right away it was futile: I would never find that child.

I staggered through the living room, heard flaunted giggles—poor kid, she did so want her turn—and hoped that I wouldn't, by accident, stumble upon a little girl. It was Ben I was seeking, hopelessly: a little boy hidden away somewhere in a Dutch colonial house. In Riverdale.

For the children's sake I knew that I had to prolong the game, despite the hellish—I was going to write "despair." And despair was a part of it. And rage: the rage of those in Hell who hate themselves even more than God. That newfound fear of the dark: a horror of pure black emptiness. And—oh, an abyss of other regrets and dreads all boiled together within my brain. But I had to take it for the children's sake—I'd give up the search for Ben, find a little girl, and—and I couldn't. I felt a chair and toppled over it purposefully. *"Ow!"*

"What happened?" came his voice.

"I just about broke my back, is all."

"You shouldn't *run!"* The sound neared from the dining room.

"Great game you've got here. Can I take my eyeshade off and see how many bones are broken?"

"Go ahead."

Light re-created the ordinary living room.

"How many?" Lucinda asked curiously.

"Well, what do you know—not a one!" I couldn't face that outer and inner blindness again. "Would anyone rather hear a story?"

"Yes!" said Ben.

"The girls might not." I pouted maturely, hoping that I could intimidate them. "They haven't had a chance to be It."

"No, a story—" "A story—" "We can play this dopey game any day!"

"Okay, here we go." But I couldn't quite muster the nerve to send a kid into the kitchen to hustle me some booze. *"Harold and the—"* I didn't know what yet. *"—Harold and the I-Don't-Know-What-Yet.* We'll make this up as we go along."

Ben felt his way to the arm of my chair and stood leaning against it, his jittering eyes, in their darkness, fixed only upon listening.

"Harold woke up one morning, and—sure enough!—something wrong! 'Has a corgi puppy—' Hey, where *is* Harold?"

"The vet," said Lucinda. And diagnosed gloomily, "Worms."

> Has a corgi puppy come down with the worms?
> Yes.

" 'Well that's not so bad,' Harold thought.

> The vet cures each and every worm
> That inside corgi puppies squirm.

"So he guessed again:

> Is doomsday getting really that near?
> No.

312

It was though, I added. (In parentheses.) (To myself.)

Then is it—hey wait! There's somebody here!

"Harold jumped up from the pile of laundry he was sleeping on. This laundry happened to be in the corner of an apartment on West Seventeenth Street, and Harold had chosen to stay there because he just couldn't imagine how an apartment and a neighborhood could be so *nowhere!* Well, Harold leaped off the laundry because he heard a kind of 'shoosh' in the corner. 'Who's that?' he said.

" 'Oh—it's just me,' said a small voice, being apologetic.

" 'And who, in this particular case, is *me?*' demanded Harold. He wasn't at all used to waking up and finding strange people where he was sleeping.

" 'I'm just—' The voice faltered. '—I'm just a little Fragment of Dark.'

" 'A Fragment of Dark? Come out here!' said Harold. He had never met any darkness before. He didn't even think it could talk. So he was getting pretty interested. 'Let's see what you look like.'

"Out from one corner sort of drifted, sort of shooshed, a handful of night. About as big as Ben's fist. And a sad small voice came out of it: 'Here I am.'

" 'So you're a Fragment of Dark,' said Harold. 'The first one that I've ever met. Well, I never! Say, what are you doing here? It's daytime now.'

" 'I was looking for you,' said the Fragment of Dark. 'Last night I was part of the night, but I wasn't very happy—'

" 'Why not?' interrupted Harold.

" 'Oh—you know.' The Fragment shifted from side to side. 'I'm not so happy about the night. So black, you know. Scares kids. Hides burglars—with all black stars.' "

"What's 'black stars'?" Lucinda asked.

"Black stars," rationalized yours fictionally, "are stars that have collapsed. They've become so hard and tight and dense—that means that nothing gets out!—even light they drag in—they're black holes in the sky. Do you get it?"

"No!" Lucinda reasoned. "Sounds stupid to me."

"*Anyway!*—'So last night I was riding along on the other side of the earth with the night—I was just a little corner of it, but I got to see dawn—and I was worrying—'

" 'You worry too?' said Harold. 'I worry an awful lot myself!'

" 'I was worrying what to do, all black and gloomy as I was. Really awful, I felt: mad at everything. And then I decided: I'll just detach.' "

"What's 'detach'?" piped a voice.

"Get away from!" said Ben impatiently. I ate—and relished— the pause of his waiting. And he added the immemorial inquiry: "What happened next?"

"Next—Harold said, 'So what happened next?'

" 'So I detached.' The fistful of darkness sort of shrugged. 'And I came to find you.'

" 'Why me?' Harold asked.

" 'This comet had told me about you,' the Fragment of Dark explained. 'I was groaning and grumping, how I really didn't like being part of the night, and this passing comet said, 'Go see Harold.' I looked through ten thousand and eight bedrooms till I found you, too. On that pile of laundry.'

" 'Well here I am!' said Harold jauntily. (He was pretty happy at being looked for.) 'Now what can I do for you?'

" 'I don't know,' said the Dark forlornly."

"What's 'forlorn'?"

"Oh shut up!"

"It's hopeless. The Fragment of Dark had no hope. So anyway—Harold got very unhappy. He was sympathizing with the Dark—"

"What's 'sympathizing'?"

"Shut up!"

"It's, he wanted to help it, but he didn't know how. And also, he hadn't slept well." Ah!—I felt it! Direction: narrative: motivation —all the old-fashioned gestures of storytelling. "There was a bright street light outside the window, and it kept Harold awake for most of the night.

As a matter of fact—very sad, this fact—
Harold was becoming an insomniac!

"That means he couldn't sleep. Lights kept him awake. He'd about decided that he'd have to buy an eyeshade, like the ones we all wore tonight. Except Ben. But he didn't really like the idea of tying something around his head. 'I'm sure I could think of something,' said Harold, 'if I only felt better. And I'd really like to. You're such a friendly Fragment of Dark.'

"Now look: we've found the name of this story. It's—*Harold and the Friendly Fragment of Dark.*

"'What's wrong with you?' asked the Friendly Fragment of Dark. And when Harold had told him—'no sleep, lights bug me, et cetera'—the Dark sort of shrugged its shoulders that weren't even there and said, 'Maybe I could do something. Lie down on that laundry again. Is it clean laundry, by the way?'

"'It's clean enough,' said Harold. 'Let's not be picky! I'd sleep on a pile of old T-shirts—if I could really get some sleep.'

"'That's one thing about Mom Night,' said the Dark. 'She's really clean.'"

Where did that come from? "'Mom Night?' said Harold. 'Where did that come from?'

"'Well it's Pop Night too, of course,' said the Dark.

"'It can't be both!' said Harold.

"'Yes it can, yes it can,' said the Friendly Fragment of Dark irrationally. 'But I don't want to talk about that now.'

"'The Night,' thought Harold to himself, 'Mom Night, Pop Night. I want to go there! And soon, soon, soon.'

"'If you'll just lie down, maybe I can give you a little nap. That's the one thing about the Night I do like: it helps people to sleep.' Harold lay on his back on the laundry, and the dark shooshed and shooshed above his eyes. There was a little leftover too, to spread a veil over his forehead. As to weight, the Friendly Fragment of Dark wasn't nearly as heavy as an eye-shade—or even a face cloth. It was more like the feeling of an easterly breeze, that blows over your face just before you wake up. And it slid back and forth too, rhythmically. 'Now Harold,' said the Dark, 'if you'll just try to relax, and—Harold? *Harold*—?'

"'Zzzzzz,' said Harold . . . For Harold already was fast asleep . . . He slept for two hours: the deepest, soundest, best sleep of his life.

"Then, after two hours, the Dark slid off his face, because it decided he had slept long enough.

"'Where am I?' Harold sat up. The Dark was curled in his lap. 'Oh *there* you are! Friendly Fragment of Dark, how *can* I ever thank you? That was the sweetest sleep I've ever had!'

" 'Oh—that's all right,' said the Dark. It jiggled a little, embarrassedly.

"Harold briskly rubbed his hands together. He was feeling very businesslike now—and he'd had his magic somewhat restored by such a pleasant snooze. 'I think I can help you. If you don't like being a Fragment of Dark—mmmm—' Harold was thinking very hard. '—I've got it!—I'll make you a candle flame! He spread his fingers out like a spell and began to sing—

> First off, I'll give you a special name—
> And then I'll make you a candle—

" 'No!' hollered the Friendly Fragment of Dark. 'I mean, I apologize, Harold, for interrupting, but—but I don't *mind* being dark. It's just, I'd like to be—'

" '—friendly,' Harold understood. He nodded his head and stroked his chin. And flung his arms up and down a few times for good measure. 'If only everybody could feel you the way I felt you, when you lay on my eyes and put me to sleep.'

" 'Look, Harold, I have an idea,' said the Fragment of Dark. 'I'm pretty good at this sort of thing—'

" 'Better even than a grain and a half of Seconal,' nodded Harold. That's a sleeping pill.

" '—so why don't I just stay here with you—I mean, if you wouldn't mind—and I'll put you to sleep whenever you want me to. And in the meantime you can loan me out.'

" 'Great! great!' Harold's arms flashed up and down through the emptiness. 'There's a garbage man I know who can't sleep—actually he's a garbage gorilla, but very nice and gentle and kind—'

" 'I'd *love* to help him!' interrupted the Dark.

" '—and Mrs. Throttlebottom's retired cook, an arthritic St. Bernard, named Heidi—'

" 'Oh Harold, this makes me so *happy!*' said the Fragment of Dark. 'I was scared I'd become a piece of pure chaos. I've felt such rage recently.' Chaos is bad. It's what happens when everything jumbles together. 'But now I won't,' the Dark sighed happily.

" '—and Danny Reilly—he'd like to be a Bowery bum—'

"Well, there's no point in telling you everybody that Harold planned to have the Dark put to sleep. There were many, and many more. Between times, when the Dark comes back to Harold, he stays—guess where?"

An absolute stillness: I refuse to speak.

"Under the couch!"—a middle-sized daughter's voice.

"In the cellar!"—an older one. (Lucinda!)

"Ben?" I invite. He adjusts his face toward my voice. "Where *do* people keep little things that they like?"

"In your pocket—?"

"Right! That very first day—and that was about a week ago—they decided that the Friendly Fragment of Dark should stay in Harold's pocket. Harold pulled the opening of his pocket wide and said, 'Just shoosh in there, Joe, and see how you like it. You don't mind if I call you Joe, do you?'

" 'Not at all,' said Joe Dark.

"He shooshed in. And from the bottom of Harold's pocket a voice said, 'Who's that?'

" 'It's a Friendly Fragment of Dark, George,' Harold called in his pocket. 'Name's Joe. That's my rabbit's foot George, Joe. Say hello to each other.'

" 'Hi, Joe!'

" 'Hi, George!'

"Fortunately, George Rabbitfoot was also very friendly and didn't mind having a pocketmate at all. They got on together famously. In fact, they got on so well together, and Harold is so happy to be sleeping well these days, that he made up this song, which he sings all the time—

> A little Friendly Fragment of Dark
> Is living now in my pocket.
> I much prefer to keep it there.
> Than around my neck in a locket.
>
> It's name is Joe, and it and George—
> George Rabbitfoot, that is—
> Get on together famously,
> And me—I sleep in bliss!
>
> They're my best buddies. They never leave me.
> I talk to them all the time.
> They answer back. And usually—

"Now Joe and George pipe up from the pocket together:

We answer back in rhyme! *Har! har!*

Gratifying murmurs: the bubbling of fulfilled listeners.

My arm didn't know where it was going, but before I could stop it, it had circled Ben's head and my hand lay over his empty eyes: Jim's gesture: disappointment, hate—and above all, love . . . Presumptuous of me to have done it.

"And now—I'm going home."

"No! More!"

"No more." I stood up. "It's getting late. And I have to get back."

"It isn't *that* late. Only Liz and Lucinda and Jane have to go to bed."

"Like hell I do!"

"Lucinda—!" the oldest, Nancy, warned—already in Carol's husky voice.

"Good-bye!"—"Come again!"—"Good night, Mary"—"Mista Andrews"—and into the Riverdale night.

The snow was stopping, withdrawing itself—"Good-bye now," "Good night"—with an almost conscious calculation. There had just been enough to gently blanket the suburban bed; then, not too tightly, to tuck it in. Through the last flakes that came ambling down I could see stars and in the south a partial moon: on its way to the full, I hope.

I believe that on that walk to the station I was happier than ever before in my life.

Very happy that I'd made those children happy.

And most happy of all that I would die!

"No!" . . . Did one of you say "No!"? . . . You're wrong. And you don't understand. I know: the fact that there is a single lighted home—in Riverdale—with six children in it, and one of them blind, and all of them happy, should be enough to make a person want to live. But human beings are like that moon. We have our bright side turned toward the earth: warm seas, and mountains, the builded cities where people live—an inhabited planet. But the other side of us faces the black interstellar stars.

It is not just Jim, or Anne, or Dan. Not enough of the light from the idea of life has reached me. So I've walked around, to the other, dark side. And from the ores I've discovered there, the minerals of Night, I have forged this intricate winter, my timepiece. Fate—an infallible apparatus. And to feel it ticking to its end in bliss—the happiness of children—is a far better reason to die than despair.

God, that snow yesterday! . . . How it entered me like cold sparks of white light . . .

> You clean Impossible New York snow,
> Though soon you'll be in black banks drifted
> You come down like the pure white essence
> Of some good God who can't exist.
> He can't. My intellect says so.
> But still—oh absolute white snow!—
> Since one void soul you've made feel blest,
> Its void dark into whiteness sifted,
> The emptiness is filled with Presence.

There!

February 26

My dream meadows have gone fertilely berserk. This whole week I've been harvesting the wheat of night, one crop after another. And it's always Jim or Anne. Wet dreams. You'd think at my age—but I'll never tell! oh the hell with that! forty-one—I'd have done with such adolescent extravagances. But night after night. And even when I've had to masturbate, to put myself to sleep.

The thing is, they're both so fucking beautiful!

God damn them both! I loathe them! In their beauty—I'd like to kill them!

> Yes! Let this be a genuine curse!
> God damn my Jim! And God damn my Anne!
> God damn the man that they think I am—

I think, the next time I jerk off, I will fantasize Jim and Anne making love with one another.

(R.S. and Harold—twins! Oh well—God damn you both—and what the hell!)

This ditty: HATE! I truly execrate
Those whom I love. And there are only two.
Be it a male or female—Jim or Anne—
There's something in my heart that never can
Be free from rage. I'm hopelessly in hate
With those who wake humanity in me.
Why do you plague me, kindly, both of you?
Tell me to die! And that will set me free . . .

It's no go friendship. No go family.
No go a father, son, a mother, brother.
It's just—no sweat—but it's too late for me.
There comes a time when it's not worth the bother
To stay alive. I simply choose oblivion.
My idiot living friends can—chin up!—*carry on.*

God damn them, I hope listlessly . . . Why isn't it night now?
So that I can sleep. It's only eleven o'clock in the morning . . .
Come back, please, both of you! . . . Soon, soon, soon.

March 1

Don't *criticize* me, my figments! I'm in a fit of killing rage! Since
you don't exist, I can't destroy *you!* (But don't press that
advantage too hard.) And don't *judge* me, all of you! . . . But of
course you must. (More soft now: growling, but with no teeth
bared.) That's why I created you in the first place.

I *shall* go out there; I shall go in an hour; he's coming in to pick
me up. *I've promised him!*

Oh God, that bitch! How could she have—no, how couldn't she
have, poor pitiful bitch. Grabbing at happiness while she still has a
chance . . .

I'll bet he does get the hash, too. I loved the innocent way he
said, "Sure I can, Terry. One of my welfare people's a pusher."

March first. An agonizing month. The hinge on which winter
swings into spring. In days of yore it used to be one of my favorite
seasons. My street is canted towards the east in such a way—

The March sun down my street, so bright
In those raw, glorious afternoons—

> It used to challenge me with light
> Like candles, hearths, and crescent moons.

I do have to admit, he was pretty thrilled when he got my call. And even more when I stated flatly he was driving *here* to pick me up!

> They're weird, those fires. The cosmos is
> Devoid of life. But they're a symbol
> That harps the human heart with bliss.
> One trusts in the Impossible.

And it was a lovely touch that he has a dentist appointment first. You *can* call up a human being and make a date to commit experiments—and if he or she is unavailable—if he has an appointment for lunch at Schrafft's, or the dentist—why you can postpone the Impossible to a more convenient time.

A few more minutes of pacing, waiting, writing—avoiding all of you! . . . He'll be on time. He always is—precisely: it's part of the ritual . . .

The curious thing is, how automatic the process was. After Edith's call my hand never left the receiver. I waited a moment and dialed Danny instinctively.

Her ebullient tone so early in the morning ought to have warned me that something was wrong—"Terry?—Edith!"

"Hi."

"Congratulations are in order."

"Congratulations. For what?"

"We've done it! Frank and I. We're married!"

Before thought, dread raced to a conclusion. "That's great—" Then thought caught up with it. "Is—"

"*Ber*-nard was our best man!"

"Well. Well well well." What *do* people say on a pyre or in the electric chair?

"You've been so sweet this winter. I wanted to tell you right away."

"Thank you."

"We'll be staying a little longer, of course. And when we get back, it'll be one week of furious packing—"

"Packing—?"

"—and then straight out here again!"

"But what about—*Ber*-nard's school?"

"Who *cares* about school? He's finally got a real father now! Of course he wants to see you. And I want to see you too! We'll be able to see you, won't we?"

"Oh yes."

"Frank wants to meet you very much."

"I had this thing planned—"

"What?"

"A kind of a party. For *Ber*-nard."

"Oh—fun!"

Great fun: the three thirds of my life being brought together. Could I kill them *all*, I wonder? All at once? "Is he there?"

"He's upstairs."

"Say hello."

"I will. And we'll see you in a week or so. Then it's good-bye, New York—hello, Denver!"

March 2

I don't think that I'll ever—ridiculous delusion: "ever"—I don't think that for the next few weeks I'll be free of the smell of smoke. There are moments when it almost chokes me—I gag—but others when I seek the acrid odor out and inhale it like oxygen, in exhilarating gulps.

The empty air itself now feels like me: a complex, programmed, predestined machine.

I buzzed him in. He still couldn't believe it. "Here's the hash—sir."

"Why didn't you leave it in the car?" His strange good looks—massive features and *black,* thick black hair—worked on me exactly as I wished, suggesting the abandon with which he is in love with death. "I'm going to smoke it out at your place."

"You *are* coming—?"

"Yes! And by the way, have you got any sleeping pills? Like Seconal?"

"No—sir."

"Can you get some? Is there a druggist out there who knows you and will give you some?"

"Yes—sir."

"I ran out of mine." My little boy almost gobbled them up. "And I want some more. Today."

"Yes—sir. We'll stop on the way." In the armor of his obedience, the helmet of servility, his eyes flashed alive for an instant. "Can't you sleep?"

"No. It's a very sad fact. I'm afraid I'm becoming an insomniac."

Sorry—

March 2: A couple of hours later

The smell of smoke was bad just then. I threw up. Pretty melodramatic, ay wot? Smoke tastes bad too. No it doesn't. It all depends what's on the fire.

Friends, let me tell you something: Hempstead is the ideal community in which to commit a crime. The banality, the ordinariness, of all the houses there is the perfect mask for a murder. Why else were these facades constructed—if not to disguise insanity.

I was high by the time we got to Danny's. And I hadn't started to smoke yet, or had a single drink. But the certainty of termination is a real turn-on. And Dan's house was the climax. Dull, indistinguishable, it seemed already to be on fire—though the flames were still invisible—burning, burning, burning, in white-hot anonymity. Inside—the same: the pathos of ugliness. The whole place was full of the seeds—or the fossils—of what could have been a human life: furniture—"I bought that Barca lounger five years ago. Most comfortable chair I've ever sat in!"—and objects—oh, objects that crushed the heart!—with which he tried, and failed, to demonstrate something: himself—an existence. One in particular did me in. He showed me a trophy: a diver mounted on a circular stand.

"You remember me telling you about that foster father I had? The one I liked. Who was the truck starter—"

"I remember very well."

"He gave me this. It's his."

First Prize. High Dive. ROLAND JAMES. *1917 Norfolk, Va.*

He was tentative and nervous, almost a little womanish, as he showed me around his home, wondering whether I'd like it or not, and seemed nearly alive in his frightened embarrassment.

"Do you want to eat early?"

"Yes."

"Do you want to turn on first?"

"No."

"It's just steak and baked potatoes. And salad."

"Fine."

An all-American meal. Cooked by an all-American masochist. For an all-American murderer.

And I enjoyed it! The meat was prime, I'd had a couple of double Scotches by then, and he made sure that it was medium rare. Of course. I prefer steak charcoal-broiled, but he didn't have a grill. (Not a kitchen article, that is.)

"Okay: *now.* I want to turn on."

"Yes—sir." There it came: his rhythm of obedience.

"Got a pipe?"

"Yes—sir."

A choice detail: Dan Reilly smokes a pipe. I made him puff it awhile, in front of me, ordinary tobacco, sitting in his Barca Lounger. He didn't know, but—this was what got me hot—he was a perfect counterfeit of a man.

I told him to get some tin foil and doctored his pipe to suit the hash. "It's Lebanon Red, they call it. And supposed to be awfully good."

I made him take some. He didn't want to—I didn't know why, then—and said—another turn-on—"I don't think it's right—for someone in my position."

"Light me up, lad. Shaggy, handsome—manlike—*welfare worker!*"

"Yes—sir." (Words! When will you stop cursing me?)

And I smoked almost a whole bowlful—"Nothing's happening. This stuff is oregano"—and then realized that I could see the invisible air: it was a universe of ordered and transparent atoms, impressed upon my retina.

"How long have I been here?"

"We got out about five o'clock, sir—"

"No. Here. In this chair." A strange place. East o' the sun and west o' the moon. "With this pipe."

"A couple of minutes—"

I could see the invisible universe. Beyond his living room windows the night was being generated: I felt it come into being, dark fragment by fragment.

"Is it working?"

"Don't be a stupid fool!" I felt superior—*was* superior: a skeptic, a scoffer, one of those who reign from the thrones of scorn, because totality had become apparent.

"I'm sorry—sir."

"You want to take off your clothes, don't you?"—with insolence, wine on the tongue, in the invitation.

"Yes—sir."

"Then do it! But first—for no reason at all—for not any reason at all—" Except the air, the darkness, the night, which all had become imperative. "—go over to that corner of rug, and take that corner of this rug in your mouth." He did. And the sight of his hulk, on his knees, with a corner of living room rug between his teeth unleashed a beast of furious love. "*Now*—take off your clothes!"

"Yes—sir."

"You're very handsome tonight, lad."

"Thank you—sir." (His accent too was a questioning anchor on me.)

And he was—unanswerable! The sag in his guts was masculine, and the cross of black wool on his chest, with a track leading down to his crotch, was virile and thrilling. His nakedness stunned me with desire. I felt like a bell made out of lust, struck, that was now reverberating.

"Let's go to your bedroom—"

"Yes—sir."

"Where you sleep. Where you dream. Do you dream there—?"

"Yes—sir."

"Count the stairs!"

"One. Two. Three. Four—"

A wood railing beside the staircase—a worn thin rug—wallpaper, with a hunting scene, to my right: a galaxy had condensed on this town, on this house, on this utterly nondescript and unendurably beautiful man. I followed him up—through what felt like the levels of Dante's Heaven—and into his bedroom, on the right.

"Now look—" As I stripped. "—it's completely unimportant to me if I beat your ass or not. And I've got a hard-on. But that too doesn't matter a single bit." The voice of a jurist: objective, calm, methodical. "What matters to me *very* much is that I hold a belt in my hand, and lift my right hand up and down. Slow up, fast down. And now look—if you want to put your tail under it—okay. But if you don't—then okay too. Put a pillow down there on the bed. The important thing—look! *look* at my right hand!—is just that my hand goes very slowly up, and comes down again very fast. Okay?"

"Yes—sir."

"You want to put your butt under it?"

"Yes—sir."

I would guess that during the time that I flogged him eight whole new species were evolved.

The incredible thing about a high like that is—you know exactly what you're doing. I was hallucinating: he was a dog, a god, a man. But I also knew perfectly well I was somewhere in Hempstead, a dull, dreary little city, in a vulgar nothing house, whipping the ass of a damned and uninteresting man. But the margin of consciousness—yes, *here* is the lovely point!—did not detract from the pleasure. The opposite! Imagination kindled, blazed—burned up the believable.

"Is there someplace else you'd like to show me?"

"Yes—sir."

"Is it here—in this house?"

"Yes—sir. It's the cellar."

"Oh—" Feigned weariness can be as taut as a violin string about to break. "—all right." And the simply expected—a willingness to see a cellar—the simply accepted—can be an accommodation to kill. "Let's have a look. You're really pretty tonight. You turn me on. It's not just the hash. You seem so—you seem so—" (The hash stole my weapon—words.)

"Thank you—sir."

"Before we go down, lie next to me here. Put your arms around me. Now kiss my mouth." He hesitated. In all our sessions, I have never kissed him once. "Go on—"

"Yes—sir."

A girl's kiss from a grizzly bear. "Was it all that awful?"

"No, Terry. Sir."

"Lie quietly. Let me love you awhile." One of the great experiences is to feel the contradictions of weakness and strength —to hold them in your arms.

"You want to get fisted?" Don't giggle now. It was asked in the sweetest, most loving of tones. For a person like Dan, whose body aspires to be a pillaged city, an offer of a good fist-fucking is sheer romance. And generosity on my part. After manipulating Jim's elegant guts—yes, children, some intestines *are* more high-strung and aristocratic than others—Dan's innards felt sloppily common-place.

"Downstairs, sir. Please."

"Why downstairs?"

He rolled his head off my shoulder, and hesitated again, and said, "I can't tell you."

"You tell me, within the next five seconds, or before God I will put on my clothes and make you drive me back to New York." And I would have: one phase of a hash high is absolute resolution.

He began to sweat. In an instant his forehead was bubbling. "So that—while it's happening—I can look at the pipes and the wood."

The proof that God does not exist is that his desperate honesty didn't drive me screaming from that house right then. But instead of running, "All right," I slowly sang. "Let's go."

I disbelieved, as I walked down the stairs to the first floor, and then the cellar stairs. I knew it, of course—the fact was there, in my mind—but I couldn't lend it any credence. And even the sight of it—a pyre constructed around an innocent water pipe—did not convince me. But about this time I believe I too began to sweat.

Oh, how many of you have your pyres all built?—in your cellars, or in your minds? . . .

He had brought down a jar of cold cream and some towels, and I fisted him, as he lay across a pile of logs: his idea.

"Don't make me come, please."

"I won't," my voice lured melodically. The second self of a human being is either the best—

And after several centuries—"I want you to come now, sir."

"Why?"

"I want you to. Can you fuck me while I'm down here?"

"I suppose so."

"May I be on my back?"

"Why?"

"I want to watch you."

"Okay." Pipes, wood, and me he wanted to watch: his equipment.

He gave me a glorious consummation—the imminent was the essence of it—and almost came himself, but saved his fullness for something later . . .

(Indeed, it *was* absurd. You're right. On a pile of logs, protected from splinters by towels, in a cellar in Hempstead, this nearly human beast and I made love. The pits of his eyes never left me. I would hazard the guess that my bottomless pits also never left his.)

"Was that good?"

"Yes, Danny. That was good."

"Will you do me a favor?"

"Yes, Dan."

"Just put on your clothes."

"All right."

"No—let me put them on you."

"Okay."

We went up to his bedroom, and Danny dressed me: tied my shoelaces, insisted I put my jacket on. Although we were inside a heated house.

A drugged slave, I obeyed him as he waited on me.

"I put the sleeping pills in your jacket."

"Thanks."

"There's something else in there too. But don't look till you're on the train."

"Okay."

"Will you come back down to the cellar now?"

"Yes."

"I know nothing's going to happen—"

"No."

"But come down. And please—lock me up. I've got a pair of handcuffs—"

"Do you?" I inquired dreamily.

"I just want to feel what it feels like to be strung up, and know you can't get away."

"Oh. I see."

"You want some more hash? There's some left."

We were in his tinder living room. Every object I saw seemed like something that might be—and longed to be—burned. "That might be a good idea."

He gave me another pipe of hash, and held me in his arms as I smoked it. Held me with strength! My second self stood several light-years away. And watched.

There was a gathering of nonbeings: the Three-Legged Nothing, the Rat, Rumpelstiltskin, Harold, Dan Reilly, myself—all watching ourselves with suspended breath.

"Can we go downstairs now?"

"Yes."

The steps were the rocks that lead down to the caves at Lascaux.

"I seem to recall this place," I smirked.

No good: he was far beyond irony. "What I'd like is—I'd like to be tied up. But I have to do something first."

Like a stevedore—which he does look like—like an ant, like a Pavloved animal, he neatly and swiftly consolidated his pyre around that pipe.

"You'll just have to push those logs and that kindling wood in right there," he explained. And explained his explanation: "I mean—so I can feel what it feels like to be completely helpless."

"I see."

It had all been planned, and of course rehearsed: every log, board, stick fitted into place.

(In the Middle Ages did they build broad wood platforms, I wonder? Or just little sufficient bonfires?)

"Now push those in. Please—sir."

I did.

"The handcuffs are over there." He was crotch-high in wood,

and standing against the pipe—what?—stake. "You just have to click them—no, *I'll* put this one on my wrist!—behind my back. If I may, sir! Put this one on my wrist myself—"

"Why are you talking so rapidly?"

"I'm not—sir! Honestly I'm not! There's one thing more too—"

"Is there? What?" I saw him at last, in this final position, the one he'd dreamed into reality—hopelessly bound, and rearing above what was still unlit—with an eyesight that tingled back and forth between disbelief and—yet, there he was. He *was!*

"You see that little trail of shingles—over there? Over *there!*"

"Don't shout at me."

"I'm sorry—sir."

"And don't talk so fast. One would think—" A wave of hallucination—no, I didn't hallucinate. It was more a surge of intensity: one of those rushes that hash can give you. I fell in love with the hair on his body. It seemed—yes, seemed—I could almost smell it—fragile and inflammable.

"It's—if you lit that shingle out there—it would take a while for the—" He didn't say "fire." He sensed my horror of the word and went on, with taut normality. "—for anything to get going here."

"That seems quite reasonable," I affirmed.

Time froze us both: glacial seconds.

"I *would* like to see it lit," he admitted offhandedly.

"What lit?"

"That shingle over there."

"Oh. That shingle over there?"

"Yes—sir." His eyes, in their pretense, failed him then, and he looked down at all that passionate wood that was piled around his waist, and pleaded, "Please!—sir. Just let me see it lit."

"Well I'd like to, lad—" I reached for any posture of voice—cynicism, indifference, cruelty, contempt—but came up with nothing except mere words. "—but I don't have any matches."

"They're behind me." He did not dare look up. "Behind this pipe."

"Oh. I see." I found them. "Of course it's hard to light a shingle—even a thin one like this one is—with only a match."

"The first one's been soaked in gasoline." With his head hanging down, came the little confession that he hoped wouldn't turn me off.

"Oh. I see." Now pure time—hash time, or the time of the giddy quick electrons that whirl around an atomic nucleus, or the time that a glacier inches along—is something that we don't understand. I don't have any idea how long it was before I said, "I suppose you just strike one—and hold it under a corner."

"Yes—sir."

"I mean—would it be like this?"

"*Yes*—sir!"

I put the flaming shingle down at the start of the endless trail.

And time again—*time*—overwhelmed me: the endless centuries that it can take for a single flame to flicker upward, and disappear, and be replaced by more burning of the wood beneath.

I became aware that someone was shouting at me. "*Go away now, Terry! Go away! You can't watch. I know you couldn't take it! Go away!* When you get outside, you go two blocks to the right, and then three blocks to the left—" He was giving me directions, as the flames ate toward him, on how to get to the local train station.

Dearest but too permissive God—surely on some other planet You must be conducting a more successful experiment than man!

It was in some year here that I smelled the smoke. But it too failed to convince me: neither sight, nor smell, nor the sound of him praying me away could make me believe this world was real. In a philosophical interlude I speculated that there were five senses.

Five senses?

Yes, five. And I named them to myself: sight, smell, hearing, taste, and touch. There's also that sixth, the kinesthetic sense, but I've always been vague about that.

Now if the first three didn't work, I logically postulated, and the last two also failed to convince me that what I witnessed was happening—why then it could not be real. Simple?

Simple!

And beautiful. Aristotelian logic. Or Platonic. Or something.

Well, I wasn't about to taste Dan—or the flames—but touch I could. And did. I stroked the dark, matted hair on his stomach. And then stroked his hair below. "You know—I really dig your hair, Danny—"

"For Christ's sake, Terry, *go away!* You won't be able to take it—"

"—why didn't I dig it before? I mean—really dig it, Dan?" I leaned across the piled wood and buried my face in his nest.

"Terry—*please!*"

"One thing though, Dan—" I stood up. "—I think your hair is—but all human hair is—it's what they call inflammable." His eyes jerked into focus on mine. "Isn't it?"

"Yes—*sir!*" He had read my tone correctly: for the writhing desire it was. (The marketplaces were full, remember, all during the Middle Ages. Yes full! . . . Were *you* there too?)

"Of course yours might *not* be inflammable. I wonder, I wonder—"

"Sir—"

"Shall we conduct an experiment?"

"Yes!"

To my pure and beguiled amazement the flames had only reached the third shingle in Dan's demure little trail. There must have been six or seven altogether: enough for me to get well away. I lit the fourth and carried the burning third back to the stake. "Now—I'm holding this thing—"

"Yes, sir—!" I believe he swallowed . . . No, I did.

"And if I should put it down there—"

And *that* is the odor—burning human hair—of which I shall never—for a couple of weeks more—be free.

His moaning increased in intensity, and I'd guess that his screams were just seconds away, when I started to beat his fire out—

"No, *don't,* Terry!"—whimpering pleafully.

—and burned my hands, for which I'm glad—

"Don't please!"

—and kicked that simpering, flickering trail apart.

"I *knew* you couldn't—"

"You *fool!*"

And you too—all of you are fools! So relieved that sweet humanity triumphed at last! . . .

It did not.

What I found, and what I made Dan believe, and what I finally believed myself, as the crawling train took me back to New

York—and discovered, in my jacket pocket, an envelope containing five one-hundred-dollar bills, with a penciled note: "Thank you, sir"—is that with enough hash and Scotch, and madness, a person—I—you!—*tua res agitur!*—can burn a human being to death—*and relish it!*

"Rumpelstiltskin's Song to His Friend the Fire Freak"—

> Dear Danny, it's a frightful fate you want:
> To die in flames, flesh melting raw, on fire:
> A modest holocaust for one, that's all.
> You ask, "Give me a light, please." But you can't
> Find anyone who will. "No major blaze,"
> You say. "A frightened neighbor's sudden call
> Will bring the fire trucks to put me out."
> What's left: black skin, black blood, and black eyes glazed.
> "Please help me, someone. Please. I've got my pyre
> All ready in the cellar. Just one match
> Is all it takes. I'll try to wait, not shout.
> Won't someone burn me—?"
>   Yes! I'm finally here!
> So trust me. Trust me! Soon.
>   And Danny dear,
> I *will* stay there a little while. And watch . . .

But I have to have a party first.

March 5

Have you been to the wedding of King Valium and Queen Dexadrine?. . . No?. . . Oh yes you have! I am it! Between these two poles of up and down, in and out, our soul is suspended like a speck of dust in a microscopic magnetic field. Or perhaps that microscopic magnetic field is the boundless universe itself. Or perhaps a molecular amusement park.

It's the queen's day today. I understand that with some harried graduate students who are struggling to finish a dissertation she's the essence of sobriety. But with me Dexy Baby cavorts, kicks up her heels, lifts her skirts—and occasionally, having solved the problem of his name, having rid herself of the grisly little brute at last, she amuses herself by reading the documents found in a safe made out of spider webs in Rumpelstiltskin's hut. One of which is—"His Tender Adieux to His Well-Loathed Victuals"—

> Oh TV dinners—now farewell!
> I'm 'fraid it's time for me to die.
> You packaged foods—gee, you were swell!
> Carnation Instant Breakfast—bye!
>
> You phony stuff all did your best.
> It's not your fault I won't survive.
> The sustenance of angels blest
> Could not keep our dead soul—

March 7

King Valium rules a dark realm indeed; he wields an extraordinary scepter. If we swallow enough of him—but saving Danny's Seconal, like vintage wine, for a special occasion—and drink enough Scotch, he wands us asleep and into his kingdom, but the dreams I have there—fuck this "we"! who do I think I am? Marian Anderson? or some other self-conscious monument?—yes I *do* think that's who I am!—the dreams I have there are not personal. I haven't seen Jim or Anne, at night, all week. And the queen keeps their apparitions gay in the daytime. But asleep I go—well, to Heaven and Hell as a matter of fact. And the void.

Can *anyone* comprehend the richness and intricacy of the void? The steady state theorists hold that between the stars matter is constantly being created, and even the big bang proponents—who agree it'll all end in one big black hole—admit that unoccupied space is complex, but no one—not Einstein—can guess at the wonder and diversity of thrilling nothingness . . . One thing I do humbly offer, however—because I felt them working through me: there are far more dimensions than four . . . Oh Einstein, if we could have only extracted your brain, like ambergris from a dead whale!

I tried to capture between the tips of my fingers a single speck of the cosmic dust that drifts between the galaxies. The wish to hold one, if only for an instant, was based upon an old intuition. If one held—and *knew*—a grain of sand—I mean, knew it totally: every detail—one would know the details of the universe, and every single one of them. Anyone would: the dimmest, most retarded child would know the whole if he understood a single thing completely. So last night—or two nights ago—one night I was trying to catch a single speck of dust—when I had to stop.

Because I was there. I lived in that dust.

A dreadful disappointment. I was in that dull suburb you live in, gentle whoever-you-are. No, it was a ravishing forest glade. No, it was—Goddamn it!—a gas station. Asphalt. Pumps. In Toledo, Ohio, at that.

It took me quite a while to realize that this was Hellheaven: the Hell aspects had reached me first. The dimensions of Heaven occurred when I found myself in a run-down section of East St. Louis, and—

No it wasn't! It wasn't East St. Louis at all! I recognize those dilapidated structures now: I was in the ruins of the Washington Market, alone among buildings being torn down. And I thought, this is one hell of a place to have died into! I travel through space, circulating like a welcome guest at a party of stars, and arrive at—the change took place—bliss! This destination, half-eaten warehouses and cobbled streets that were being torn up—I laughed at my stupidity—was nothing but Paradise. I touched a beam that had fallen from some derelict roof. And sensations from my hand went into the rotting fibers of it, and into the molecules, into the atoms, until I touched the absolute truth of that piece of worthless wood: ecstasy! A discarded beer can too—I held it in my hands as tenderly as a newborn son—was another of Heaven's gestures. Then suddenly I was elsewhere—

On a high plateau, surrounded by mountains: space cupped in aeons of undiscovered beauty: streams, meadows, forests—and no one had ever seen them before. Except the tame wild animals. Who were waiting for me. I thought—good God, if the Washington Market was Paradise, then *this* must be—

It was one of the phases of Hell. Eohippus came cantering up and lifted his head beneath my hand. I stroked his fuzzy hair a while, until he became—

—an old-fashioned set of venetian blinds that fell clattering into the meadow's green—

—water. I had to swim in it a long time. Then it was—

—an ugly orange shag rug. Which revealed itself, abruptly, to be—

—a sheet of the finest aluminum. And here Heaven reasserted itself again: it *was* aluminum! Every cell of my body melted into the exquisite precious metal.

And on and on, as the coin, Heavenhell, was flipped this way and that.

I understood, after a couple of Kalpas more—

> You see, Hell is only the transient: the unreliable.
> And Heaven is permanence, understood: the held Impossible.

As soon as the truth was in me, I saw God, and also the Other One. There were two masks constantly hovering in the air above me: not full face masks, just the elegant dominoes that conceal the eyes: one red, one blue: one God, and one His Antagonist. But Which is Which?—as They drift above us all. And watch.

> Yes, this the dead can plainly see:
> The One Mask rules Heaven, and the Other Hell.
> But the final vile mystery—
> They are Both absolutely identical.

March 10

They begin to return! The thirds of my life are reassembling themselves. And for the last time, the Red or the Blue Mask willing. (Which One? Which *One?*)

But that bastard!—you might know that *he* wouldn't call!

"Terry—?" The phone, at ten this morning. "This is Carol Whittaker—"

"Well hello! When did you get back?"

"Last week." My silence—an amalgam of anger: why *didn't* he call me? and curiosity: why did she?—intimidated her. "You said I could give you a ring sometime. On New Year's Eve."

"What's taken you so long?"

"Just—" She reached to describe the domestic plethora.

"—the exigencies of housewifery."

"That's it."

"In an overstated nutshell."

"I was wondering—could I take you to lunch?"

"No. But I can take you."

"Terry, *I* called—"

"I ain't gonna come, except on my terms! Where are you?"

"In the city. I've got to go to Bloomingdale's."

"Mmm." I hummed a logistic mystery. "Would the Metropolitan Museum of Art be too far uptown?"

"No—"

"They've got this cafeteria, beside a pool. The food's not so hot, but the water's great."

"I'd love to!"

"Twelve-thirty at the big main entrance? Or one?"

"Twelve-thirty. More time!"

I have always enjoyed the telegraphic ending of making a date. "See you then."

"Good-bye."

And most especially with another man's wife.

I balanced the king and queen, the royal mod robes, on the seesaw of a semihigh, and took the subway up to Central Park West. The last snow had almost melted, and I wanted to walk through the park. In some article or other in *Scientific American*—which I gave up reading six months ago, but the sad rejected thing shows up every month in my mailbox nonetheless—I read that there are certain dumb buds that begin to germinate even under a blanket of snow, if enough light reaches them. Stupid automatic nature! But I like the park when that raw March pain—earth aching upward through patches of ice, trees groaning as they are shaken awake—begins to hurt. Hurt visibly.

She was waiting for me. "Hi, Carol! You want to see some of my favorite paintings?"

"Yes."

I conducted her up that aristocratic staircase—you're a duke by the time you reach the top—and led her to the Vermeers. "Now that—" Queen Dexadrine was about to launch into a very poetic rhapsody, when King Valium put his hand on her shoulder and whispered, "Listen, love, she came to have lunch, not endure a high tirade on your personal aesthetics."

"That what?"

"That's sanity. That's all. Let's eat."

"No, wait. How is that painting sanity?"

"It's not just that one painting—it's Vermeer. The integration he always achieves. The art historians say it's the way he paints light. But they're wrong. No, they're right—but they're not right enough. In a painting by Vermeer the molecules all fit together. Even the atoms bow politely and ask one another to dance. You see—there are all kinds of sanities. The simplest one is, 'Jack Sprat could eat no fat—' That's an obvious matching of terms. But it works. And it's how most people get by. So God bless it! But at the far other end of the scale there's—Vermeer. There's the Dante of the *Paradiso*. And God!—above all—there's the music of Bach. Those guys somehow managed to make apparent the vast, complex, well-intregrated sanity of man. And believe me, my dear, *they're* where it's at. If 'it' is anything, and 'at' is anywhere. Now we *are* going to eat!"

We didn't talk as we went through the line and began our lunch. The royal pair had again reestablished a royal equilibrium and the need for SMALL TALK, which sometimes occurs in the necessity of capital letters, became imperative.

"Well—how was the Caribbean?"

"Just wonderful." (*Small talk* can occur in italics too.) "Jim needed to get away."

"Oh? How so?" My sweet-and-sour voice had been dipped in a double vat of dye. There was true disinterested curiosity in it—because I do like to go backstage in the theater of the heart—but also the cyanide taste of hopeful animosity. Rumpel S. delights in tracing the cracks in damaged china, and he also gleefully busies himself in finding the hidden flaws in a marriage. He has a passion for imperfections and thinks of them as precious gems. If he could, he would wear all the faults of his friends—and flaunt them!—the jewelry of human inadequacy. If he could. But alas, one can only wear one's own failures. "Nothing wrong," I hoped.

"Just marital necessities." She smiled out of the rich, weary wisdom of men and women—husbands and wives—who have somehow managed to come to terms with their lives. Then glanced away from my single ignorance. Served me right. (Ms. Stiltskin, beware when you probe for living wounds!) "We talked about you often."

"Me—?"

"Yes. There was this great bay we saw, in Jamaica, and Jim said, 'I wish the lad could see this—' "

" 'The lad'—" R.S., beware, beware! You probe for something, and you don't even know if it's pleasure or pain.

"Yes. That's you. In our house—even with the children— they've picked it up from Jim—whenever anyone says 'the lad,' it has to be Terry Andrews." You see, R. darling, you always discover the wrong sensation. "But this bay—in the shape of a crescent moon—Jim said, 'That lad could describe this to Ben much better than we can.' Whatever he sees, you know, he wants to remember and tell to Ben."

She dipped into her salad. And I dipped into about as complex a combination as I have ever felt: Jim, Ben—this woman—his wanting me to see what he saw, so that I could reveal it to his blind son.

Her eyes flashed up from lettuce, ham, radishes. "What *do* you think of Jim?"

My face prepared a bland compliment, but the words I heard, to my own amazement, were "I think he's a cold, insensitive, egocentric prick!"

To Carol's amazement too. She shone suddenly in disbelief. Then delight. And began to laugh. "That's perfectly true! You're right—he is." She stilled her jiggling fork on her plate. "At last someone's said it!" Her mezzo voice collected itself, behind her lifted hand, and released a pent-up solo of mirth. " 'A cold—' What was it?"

" 'Insensitive, egocentric prick.' "

"Oh my God—that's beautiful—"

"You're going to choke, if you don't watch out."

"It's worth it!" Gesture by feminine gesture, she began to reassemble composure. "I needed to hear that." She wiped her eyes, and wiped her mouth, and inhaled a long-delayed pleasure. "Oh, God—"

"You agree with me, I take it."

"Of course I agree! Who knows better than I? I'm married—" Her moment of explosive joy crystallized in a glance of apprehension. "—I'm married to him."

"You're having second thoughts? About my description?"

"No. But that's not all he is though."

"What else is he?"

She worked through a decision. And resolved to go ahead. "Well, he's more than an egocentric prick."

My question was merely journalistic. "What more is he?" Apart from a whore. And a handsome man. And someone whom I hate and love.

"He lives for the children."

Oh Rumpelstiltskin, you pitiful fool—*never* seek the faults of others out! "And for you too," I editorialized.

"Oh yes—he's very fond of me—"

" 'Fond'—?"

"The person that he loves most in the world is Ben."

"That's natural—"

"Yes. I love him most too." But she cast her lot for honesty, and said quickly, self-consciously contradicting herself, "No I don't. I love Jim most."

"So you should."

"It includes a risk."

"Does it?"

"He's like a great big bird!"

I knew instinctively, and immediately, exactly what she meant. "Yes, and you're the falconer. He launches off your wrist—"

"—and goes for other birds—"

Ah, communication! How slyly you sometimes take place. "—his prey. But aren't you used to it by now?"

"No." She became a housewife, a married woman—

"Jim's the kind of a bird who's got to fly off and spread his wings, and preen, and feel himself preen. And catch another bird now and then."

—and worried, and middle-aged. "Some of his prey are bigger than others." For a moment she seemed to be losing—her eyes—and acknowledged it hopelessly. "You know him much better than I do."

"No I don't. But you undervalue yourself." A woman at a loss commands such powers of sympathy. "Coffee?"

"Yes, please."

Dawdling is an art: cream, sugar, spoons stirring, eyes gazing around a room, a pool—avoiding each other.

She said, "There's something else about Jim—"

"What?"

"Apart from being an egocentric prick, and a marvelous father—"

"Did we decide that?"

"Yes. Ben. And he dotes on the girls. He's also—solitary."

"Solitary—?" My dear, he's been fucked, sucked, whipped, kissed, loved, and despaired of by every fag in New York! Each and every orifice in his body has been penetrated by whole populations. "How so?"

"Oh I know he knows a million people." Communication, I prayed, be discreet now: don't let her intuit what I'm thinking. "He's the most gregarious person alive. But still, he's basically solitary. It's because of his father, I think. He was sullen and stupid and a brute of a man. Very handsome though. It's as if there was Jim before there was Jim. Do you know what I mean—?"

"Exactly. Go on."

"And his mother is a timid little woman—fat, and too good a cook—but who didn't know how to keep Jim from learning not to trust. I watch him at parties—he loves to go to parties too—"

"If I was the social lion he is, I would too."

"Yes but—" Frustration twirled her spoon. "—there's something not right. I mean, of course he's always a huge success, and a center of attention—and I'm horribly jealous most of the time—" Her spoon stood rigid with jealousy, then collapsed in laughter at herself and rattled on the table top. "You'd think I'd have learned not to be by now! But I am. But jealous, suspicious as I am, I stand off sometimes and watch him: charming, charming. He's like an atomic reactor. Women and men are energized by him." She swung that articulate spoon in small vague arcs of something like helplessness. "But I feel—"

"—sorry for him?"

"That sounds patronizing, doesn't it?"

"Not if you feel it."

"Oh, not that he doesn't thrive on attention, admiration. But even when he *is* surrounded—by a circle of giggling student nurses—" And interns too, love. "—to me he still looks solitary."

"Well, at least he isn't solitary when he's with you—" That was Mr. Stiltskin's vulgar and obvious invitation for further confession.

But she did need to talk. "Oh sometimes he is. I get left quite alone, fairly often."

"Fairly often," I understood, meant when they were making love. Yes, Carol, I know: the same thing has happened to me. There have been times when I've been inside your husband, or when he's happened to fall asleep and I've ventured to gather him into my arms, when I too have felt alone.

"The only real times when he's *never* solitary—"

"—are when he's with your kids."

"Yes."

"I could see that. He's at his most—" I was about to say "beautiful," but tripped up the precipitous tongue in time. "—his best then."

"I think—"

"What?"

Her spoon was now hesitating; it held reserve. "I think Jim's very fond of you. Cold egocentric prick that he is—"

"I guess I shouldn't have said that."

"—he doesn't have very many friends. Hordes of acquaintances, yes—but I think he thinks of you as being a very good friend."

There are all kinds of knives, folks, all kinds: meat cleavers, broadswords—direct insults—but one of the most needle-like and fine—long, thin, and very sharp—is to be told you're a *good* friend of someone with whom you're in love.

"It comes out in strange ways," she went on. "In Jamaica we finally saw *Doctor Strangelove*—"

"A marvelous picture!"

"Yes, marvelous. We've been missing it for years. But when we came out of the theater Jim said, out of nowhere, 'I bet that's a picture that Terry likes.'"

"Why me?"

"Exactly. That's what I asked. And he said, 'It's farcical, and pessimistic, and Terry's one of the few people I know who does believe in Doomsday—' "

"He's right: I do."

"Well, the fact that he saw that movie through *your* eyes—I don't know what friendship really is, I guess—but that must be a very strong part of it." Her own eyes eluded, and alluded to, a final inquiry. "Don't you think of Jim as a good friend of yours?"

Carol Whittaker—with her oversized hips and ox-eyed Juno eyes! Was she putting me, gently and quite properly, in my place? "Remember, lad, you *are* just a friend." Was she giving me some kind of wild permission? Was she even forgiving me for loving her husband? All three? I have no idea. I only know that I envy those human beings—and they're not writers, I'll tell you that!—who can deal with the unspoken. My silence was tight with everything I needed to speak, and hers was simple, honest, and open.

"Yes, I do think of him as a good friend of mine."

(Communication! You are at your best, and most full, most complex, when an absolute stillness reigns.)

"I have to get back to Riverdale."

"All right."

"The children are planning—oh God, the children! That's why *I* wanted to take *you* to lunch! They were so excited by having you come out to Sunday night supper."

"It was fun. I enjoyed it."

The great hall of the Metropolitan Museum was made to be passed through: space steadies you and shows you off the way platinum steadies and shows off a gem.

"Then when will you come up again?"

"Soon." Soon! Soon! Since going out to Dan's, the word steadies me like a threat. Or a promise.

"I hope I didn't take you away from anything important—"

"You didn't."

"As a matter of fact, I was hoping that I *did* take you away from something important. Like a new children's book."

"Oh for God's sake, Carol—"

"All right, all right. All I know is, if *I* had written *The Story of Harold*—"

"The *hell* with *The Story of Harold*! I'm sick to death of that God damned thing!" Her wincing communicated hurt. "I'm sorry, Carol. I apologize. And Harold does too. He wrote you a poem a few months ago—"

"What?"

"Would you like to hear it?"

"Yes."

> My dear, don't regret for a single second
> The fact that you cannot create.
> If the arts, in their privacy, never beckoned,
> That does not mean you've been left behind.
> For when human capacities finally are reckoned,
> I know no one who's famous or gifted or great
> Who could cope with a child, her own child, who is blind.

"You wrote that for me?"

"Harold wrote that for you. Do you have a scratch pad and a pencil in that purse of yours?"

"Yes."

I wrote out the jingle, propping the pad on the granite shoulder of a cold Assyrian god. "There."

"May I show this to Jim?"

"You may show it to Jim—or show it to anyone you like—or keep it entirely for yourself."

The fingers of her right hand grazed my chin. "I just wish that I could do something for you."

Do you snicker? . . . You pricks! (You flittery, fluttering love bugs!)

She wasn't offering me herself. Although I believe if I'd wanted her badly—hopefully—enough, I could have had that too.

"Now if you promise not to get angry—"

"I don't."

"I say 'if,' not when, but *if* you write another *Harold* book, let him wake up one morning and *not* say 'Something wrong, something wrong—' "

"You mean more like, 'Something right, something right! Been having pleasant dreams all night!' "

"Okay—I'm no author. But why *is* he so frantic all of the time?"

"Just his nature, that's all."

"Well anyway," she wrote it off, "I guess we're all lucky that whatever devils are driving him are driving him in the right direction."

Yes. Like out to Hempstead . . .

Then she went down those grand exterior steps. And for a few minutes she'd given me the greatest pleasure that any man can ever have: to be held in the glance, in the vague all-inclusive understanding, of a generous—yes, of a *loving* woman. (And *damn* all—)

March 13

They are all back now! Anne the day before yesterday, and Barney today. And it's set for a week from—right now! A week from tonight they'll be here. I disbelieve it, this party, but I know that like death, or the end of the world, it is there. It is waiting, ordained.

Jim did busy-ness on the telephone: just got back—patients, needing care. But not so busy that he didn't want to come down that same night and hear "our record." But I don't want to see him until next week—I don't want to see a single living human being whom I know—and made up a date, a dinner with my editor, that I had to keep. He was hot—I could tell that from his voice—and I'm certain went off to the baths or somewhere, but counterbalancing jealousy, the vise-like tightening in my chest, was this absolute need to be alone. He agreed on next Thursday, however. And I know he'll keep his word.

Anne was all breathless enthusiasm, at being back. "San Diego—really! Thank God for filthy, polluted New York!" For her I invented a cold: sore throat, running nose—"feel downright miserable!" But got her promise for the twentieth. "My goodness, yes! When *you* give a party, I'd have to be dead not to come!" And she promised to bring some food.

Edith, newly wed and ecstatic, was ridiculous and quite likable. "Yes! Just got in today." Could *Ber*-nard come to my house next Thursday—? Of course he could—"but we're leaving on Friday—"

So am I, I pray!

"—he does want to see you so much, once more."

Thursday then.

"Yes! He'll love it!"

"I'd like to see him before next week—but I've got this awful cold. I'm sure I'd just leave him with a suitcaseful of bacteria—" Not even that boy can I stand to see. "—so tell him hello, and I'll see him next week."

For the next seven days—which I need for myself—I will visit, revisit all the sites in New York where the steps toward extinction were trippingly, all-unknowingly taken.

March 18

Here they are! (One must collect all one's experience before one throws it all away.)

Pennsylvania Station to begin with.

I was nine when they brought me to New York for the first time, and the wonder, the thrilling undignified mystery of this city, struck me first in Pennsylvania Station. I remember stopping as Mom and Pop rushed on ahead for a taxi—"Come on!" "Well, what are you waiting for?"—paralyzed by the revelation that I never could live anywhere but New York.

And of course later on there were stops in the men's room—

Queen Dexadrine, I need you now! . . . The sad vulgarity of cruising a john . . .

It doesn't take very long . . . The exciting risk—life lived out of the corner of the eye—of standing next to a handsome man, at the enamel shrine of a urinal, and showing him what you've got.

Good-bye, Penn Station! Alas, they've destroyed your great space . . .

37 West Eighty-sixth Street.

Folks, you'll have to excuse me. I know it's cornball, but I've got to hymn the apartment house where I first made love with a woman. (And with men? you ask. There was someone that I grew up with—a dimwit neighborhood kid—an' we played wid each udder! Until, at the ripe old age of fourteen, I was fucking him.) Her name was—my God, I've forgotten! . . . Estelle!—that was it. In my freshman year at Harvard a guy from my Latin class—unlikely pander, wot?—arranged a double date in New

York. And dull, dreary Estelle was mine. Three years older than I, and obviously she'd been being banged for years. I took her home. Her parents had gone away for the weekend. A little perfunctory necking—which I enjoyed, but she seemed pretty bored by—and I suddenly realized, this is just preliminary ritual: she's expecting me to screw her!

Panic!

But after panic—a sense of expansion—the universe does expand—a sense of pure possibility. I touched her thigh, a much-fingered thigh I'm sure, and felt—well I thought I felt the galaxy in Andromeda.

Now Estelle wasn't very attractive. I've forgotten her face: a bad sign. And she wasn't intelligent, and God knows not gifted. She was, however, a woman. When I entered her, and passed that threshold—the vivid hot wet feminine dark—I entered the other half of my life. If infinity is ever felt, it's felt when you're inside a woman's thighs. And even the most sophomoric of broads can communicate the unknown to you.

And gentle heeders, remember this: be it sex, politics, or philosophy, in the great punctuation which we all are, the question mark is far more noble and deserving of praise than the exclamation mark or the placid period.

238 West Eighteenth Street. Roy O'Brien's apartment. And you harps have got a lot to answer for! Namely, the fact that I didn't get a good piece of ass off that poor perplexed Catholic lad. (They're either Danny, or him.)

It's curious, the ghosts one leaves where one has lived. They stay there, in Pennsylvania Station, on Eighty-sixth Street, in a shoddy and nondescript brownstone just north of Greenwich Village. And they wait for you. I felt all over again the dry, stretched frustration of not being able to make love to Roy, a separateness made bittersweet by the knowledge that he wanted it too.

(Where *is* that handsome bastard now? The last I heard—four years ago—he'd accepted a job teaching English and history in a prep school in the Midwest somewhere.)

Well, fast Hells are the best. It only went on for a couple of months.

480 East Seventy-seventh Street.

This ghost is sensual and satisfied—at least as it lounges in bed. Tina Farr was a little overweight. But I've always preferred Rubens' women to Modigliani's.

The sensation was, simply, adultery. The fact of her being married was the essence of the pleasure as well as the pain: the nasty simplicity of making love all afternoon, and then having to leave before Mike got back. And the even more viciously titillating ironies of going home to shower and change, and then coming back to a dinner party there: "Hey Teen—it's our author!"—"Oh *hi*, Terry! How are you?" . . . I managed to keep that Hell going for almost a year . . . But she beat me at last: she played the game of cheating by iron rules of easiness that I never could master or understand.

The Turkish baths. This afternoon. With no intent whatsoever to come. But simply to pay my last respects. To the ghosts of myself who, God knows, will prowl those dirty halls forever. And when the building has been torn down, and a selfless skyscraper put up in its place, that spirit that looks like me will still be searching through corridors—that now are ghosts themselves—for something that it's not likely to find.

White robes that lack identity. Acts passionate, but without consequence. At night—a businesslike frenzy of seeking . . . But in the daytime—something softer, more moody, and unanswerable. Yes, go on a weekday at three o'clock to some sunny, dusty Turkish bath. You will find them, the baffled adolescents and the old men trapped in endless afternoons—experimenting, searching for the sources of desire.

But at times the discoveries are quick and overwhelming, and unbelievably complete. And—

> Here's one for New York's Turkish baths—
> Taut places of joy, frustration, pity.
> They have distinct advantages:
> Pure lust, variety, anonymity.
>
> But they're strange, those crowded corridors,
> So bereft of whatever the heart dreams of.
> You sometimes discover a person there
> Who instantly drains you of all your love.

(I met Jim there once. So drunk that he didn't recognize me.)

March 19

Three locations today. And I know that I ran a risk of being seen—but I *was* careful, honestly!

To Riverdale this morning. I didn't go too close, but it seemed necessary to see his house from all four quarters. Like a burglar in the vulnerable suburbs I skirted, stalked, edged cannily around street corners—the sun was suspicious, in the midst of its tender ministry upon all those houses, but no one else was—until I'd consumed that home in my sight. Dutch colonial. It exists now within my brain. And in all its dimensions . . . Yes.

Then early this afternoon—to Murray Hill. And the same thing with Anne's apartment house. I looked at her windows from the street, counting up the floors several times, to make sure, and then walked around the block. And I *know* I saw her kitchen window. It faces west. Yes, that had to be it. So critical it feels, to build these buildings accurately. Inside the mind.

And Edith's—no, his—in the late afternoon.

Damned brute sun—getting stronger and stronger. Prolonging the day.

But why build a Dutch colonial home and two nondescript apartment houses inside your own head?

The reason is obvious, you fools! The people who live in them are imprisoned within your own skull too. Molecularly, they become yourself.

March 20: About 10:30 in the morning

Iris is coming. I got her to change her day from Wednesday. But I didn't tell her why. She promised to be out by six. Unreliable though. She's always late . . . No, I don't mean that. I love you, Iris.

March 20: Almost time!

I'll sing a song
About a single speck of dust.

I'll sing it all day long—
Not that I want to, but I must.

To this one flake
Of space, of time—the world inverse—
All souls must shrink. Or make
Themselves the boundless universe.

March 20: Three thirty—God, I'm fearful!

I'd rather far have been Vermeer—

No.

I'd far prefer
To be Vermeer—

No. *No!* . . .

I'd like to have been Bach—

No use. Language too has abandoned me. My best friend since
the first word I read.

I've got to get out of here. Before Iris comes. And walk. And
then pick up Barney and bring him back . . .

It *is* time, finally.

March 20

No, March 21. It's past midnight.
As it happened:
Black bitch!—pardon, Iris—she hasn't yet gone when Barney
and I get back.
Unavoidable introductions: "How do you *do*, Mr. Barney!" she
says, and elaborately shakes hands.
Unavoidable explanations: "Barney's having dinner down here
tonight."
Eyes wide with pleasure and disbelief: "The two of you—?"
"No. Two more."

"Who?" At the same time that it angers me I delight in her honest demand to know.

"Miss Anne—"

"Miss Anne—!"

"—and a friend of mine named Jim Whittaker."

"Mr. Andrews is giving a party!" She pranced around the living room, knees high, filly-like at sixty-eight. Then had second thoughts. "Mr. Andrews, I'm *mad* at you! Why didn't you *tell* me that company's coming? Is that why you asked me to come today?"

"Yes."

"I could have done something special!"

She has won me by now: her performance of injured dignity, the craftsman deprived of his chance to show talent, is irresistible. "Like what?"

"Well—washed those filthy windows, for one thing! You tell Miss Anne—"

"I will. The filthy windows are all my fault."

"You can *also* tell her that the mess in the closets is due to you too! When a gentleman goes socializing—" Her dancing hand, which is elegant in its morality, cuts capers in the crowded human air. "—he ought to—" Inspiration! "We could wash 'em right now!"

"No, Iris, there isn't time."

Hand drops from beauty down into the commonplace. "All right." She goes into my bedroom, to change out of her work clothes—I hear mutters of mingled disapprobation and joy, as she fantasizes about the evening—and comes back looking like a buyer for Bergdorf's: black skirt, gray and blue striped silk blouse, and a string of what should have been genuine pearls. "At least pull the shades down! So no one can see them."

"I will, Iris." Good taste has nothing to do with class, race, or anything but taste. "Good night, Iris. Thank you."

" 'Night. Have a good time now. Pleased to meet you, Mr. Barney."

And the instant that she is gone, and I'm left alone with him, a dread begins to compress my chest.

But before I live that dread again, I must finish with Iris. Five minutes after she's left, the buzzer—and it's she, with two big jars of macadamia nuts. "Iris!—what are you doing? It isn't Christmas—" We have this ritual: every Christmas I give her a box of hard candy from Schrafft's, which she loves, and she gives me a jar of macadamia nuts. "And two of them! These things are expensive. That's almost your whole—"

She looks at me with sad, angry impatience and love. "Mr. Andrews—you're *socializing!*" And waltzes down the stairs: an example. "Now enjoy the macademy nuts."

Again, I'm alone with Barney, waiting for Jim and Anne. That dread which had started as simple pressure, now tightens around my whole body, python-like.

"You want a macademy nut, Barn'?"

"All right." He munches one methodically.

I'm in panic because I suddenly realize I have nothing planned: I don't know what's going to happen tonight. It somehow seems imperative to bring these three people together, but now—what? The vacancy, emptiness—nothing to do: the sheer incompetence of being such an inadequate host, in addition a feeling of endless helplessness—becomes overwhelming. I have got to fill the void with words. "Well?—so?—Barney—you haven't yet told me: how was the wedding?" Edith was vivid when I picked him up. It's the second time around that a bride really shines. "Did your mother look pretty?"

"She had a green dress."

"I like that color!"

"My favorite is red."

"So is mine. But green is nice too."

This child's silences! I don't know whether they're as deep as the Pacific Ocean, or as thin and quick as a razor blade. It's occurred to me that he may be retarded. Like me. But no, I don't think so. Just drastically withdrawn. And I've reached him—nowhere.

But have to keep trying, tentatively: "How did Mr. Henderson look?"

"All right."

"Did he show you all around Denver?"

"Yes."

"It's a very nice city, isn't it?"

"I guess so."

The buzzer—and the vacuum is suddenly webbed with nerves. "That'll be Mrs. Black. She's usually prompt. Dr. Whittaker is always late."

At the door—"Here! Take this! It's hot. There's more in the cab"—she hands me a round something wrapped up in aluminum foil and cloth.

"Take it into the kitchen. I'll get the rest." I escape—for a second—but am forced to come back.

"Don't turn the big white box upside down. There's a caramel cake inside. The bowl with Saran wrap around it has salad. You can spill that if you want. I don't think it turned out very well." She merries on.

There are also, in refrigerator bags, two pints of ice cream: "Vanilla and chocolate," Anne explains. "Tastes being what they are."

"You didn't meet Barney—"

"Yes I did. While you were lugging things upstairs."

"Anyway, Barney, this is *the* Mrs. Black, who—"

" '*Mrs.—Black?*' " she ridicules incredulously. "Who is she? Come *on,* Terry! This isn't 1610. *You* can call me Mrs. Black if you want to—he's calling me Anne."

I enjoy—and most likely begin to flush—my being mocked by her. And relax. Start to, at any rate. I should have known that I could depend on her quick, kind intuition: an area in her where feelings and speed and reason meet.

"I've put the casserole on the stove—that's a casserole, that is: a meat and tomato casserole—and *very* good: I've been eating it all the way down in the taxi!"

"Can I get you a drink? I *can* get you a drink, Anne. I bought you a bottle of that flimsy Dubonnet you like."

"I'd love a Dubonnet. Without any put-down!—if you don't mind."

The door to my kitchen isn't solid wood: its upper half is a screen you can see through. I linger over Anne's drink, so that I can watch the two of them.

"Where do *you* live, Barney? I live in Murray Hill."

"On East Sixty-eighth Street. But I'm moving to Denver tomorrow."

"You are—!" Her voice doesn't condescend to a child. As these written words make her sound. She's excited and inquisitive. "How come?"

"My mother got married."

She flashes a glance toward the kitchen—where she sees that I'm watching: a look to share her amusement at Barney's artless remark, and also her deepened curiosity. "And that's where your new father lives?"

"Yes."

"That's very exciting! Just last week my plane back to New York stopped at Denver. I was out in California, and flying back, I saw all these mountains—"

"You made the Rat's Christmas tree."

I'd been focused on Anne, observing her work to contact him, but his solemn pronouncement recenters attention for both of us. Denver—later maybe; mother's marriage—better never; the present for Barney is that this is the lady who made the Rat's Christmas tree.

"I made whose—"

I come out of the kitchen. "Here you go. Don't get loaded now."

"Who, may I ask, is the Rat?"

"He's a friend of Barney's and mine. I've been telling stories behind your back."

"You must introduce *me* sometime!"

The buzzer again. A tight sense of fulfillment takes hold.

"Hi, lad!"

"Anne Black, Jim Whittaker." Thus do you blandly introduce two hemispheres. "And this is Barney Willington." And crown the meeting with a child's belief: he is dazzled by the sight of him, by the sight of the two of them, shaking hands. There's the small social hubub of strangers testing each other, and meshing.

"Sorry I'm late."

"When weren't you?" Me, furthering.

"No cabs, lad."

"I had an awful time myself."

He has brought two huge tear-shaped bottles of Almaden wine. "I didn't know which was in order, red or white."

"Just like me. I brought chocolate and vanilla ice cream."

He chuckles and grins: his Sexy Devil mask; it's been turned on
e a few times too. "We were made for each other!"

Good: he's begun to dally already. That will occupy the two of
em for a while.

And Barney, like myself, is preoccupied with a child's meta-
ysics. He doesn't say, out loud, "You're the one who made the
at's Thanksgiving." But that's whom his gaze is brooding on. He
inks these two myths of mine, who are sitting before him,
atting and flirting. And he savors, as a seven-year-old can savor,
e Impossible: their sheer reality.

I demand to be busy, and out of their reach; I supervise the
ating of the casserole; I serve; I pass plates around. Anne wants
help, but I insist. As I putter, create activities, that feeling of
ing complete, fulfilled, begins to assume the dimensions of
ving died. A good death.

Barney's silence is linked to mine, in the kitchen: he incarnates
-and I think, unknowing, he knows he incarnates—the child that
would like to be. In the presence of those whom I love.

After sketchy exchanged biographies, which Jim plays like a
rtatious flute—"Six children! My Lord! I only have one, and
e's more than I can manage." "Well, it's never too late!"—as we
art to eat, the artificiality of the manufactured situation,
arney's being there with three "grown-ups," affects the atmos-
here. They include him as best they can. I am useless to the two
f them, held mute and intense, like a jewel in the setting of their
resence.

Jim talks about his kids: the presents that he and Carol brought
ack from the Caribbean—"hats and crazy kinds of clothes. If I'd
nown I was going to meet _you,_ Barney, I'd have brought
omething for you too."

"Did the clothes go over?" Anne asks. "My Helen _hates_ to be
ven clothes. She's at the age when she wants to choose."

"They went over with the girls. For Ben we bought a maraca.
hat's a hollow gourd, with a stick attached, Barney. And seeds
side. You shake it and it makes music. Too damn much music!"
e masculinely mourns to Anne. "He's driving us crazy now."

"Ben's the boy who is blind," Barney witnesses, and accepts.

"Yes." Jim's face quizzes me swiftly. "You should come up to

Riverdale and meet him. He's a little bit older than you, but think that you both would get along. I'm afraid everybody else a girls—"

"I can't. I'm moving to Denver tomorrow."

And quizzes me again: what *is* the meaning of this limboed La Supper? And *how* does he know about Ben?

I do not meet his eyes.

Anne steps into the breach: "I think it's time that *I* move to—"

I partner and challenge her: "Don't you dare! I love tha apartment of yours!"

"But it's fun to move! Especially to another city."

There is talk about schools—"We're lucky though: there're tw good schools for blind kids in New York." "Oh I didn't kno that!" and "Helen and I went to see five or six before we finall decided on Porter's. And lucky to get in!—the way things ar today." And then there's dessert. I take away the saucers streake with melted ice cream.

"Hey, Barney, did you know there's a grasshopper loose in th room?"

"Jim—let me get you another drink—"

"Okay."

"Anne—?"

"Yes."

"And the name of this grasshopper is Hidden Billy. Because h hides in people's clothes."

"I know. You played this game with the Rat."

"The Rat—?"

"There *he* is again! He's someone that we've got to meet, Jim.

I've gone into the kitchen. And shut the door. I must watch this but not be part of it. I make a stir with bottles, their glasses, as Jin explains the game.

"However!—it has to be played on the floor."

"Barney—that's us. On the rug."

"And of course Hidden Billy has to be looked for." He is sittin, cross-legged, and laughing, eager. Anne's preparing herself fo some rough-and-tumble. Barney's baffled, and frightened, a little and hopeful. "It involves a little tickling. Okay—" Jim flops dow on his back. "—*he's in me!*" and the two of them go after him.

And in the kitchen, fulfilled, I would like, right now, to die.

"*He's in me!*" Anne gets her turn.

And I can. Since going to Danny's, I've kept his sleeping pills, in a little plastic jar, in my pocket. I could say I was feeling upset. Yes. Thirty-five Seconal, in addition to the amount of Scotch I've drunk, would probably make you feel upset. And do the trick. Poor Dan will just have to keep on his quest.

"Now you, Barney!" Jim says. "Say it! You have to say, 'He's in me!' "

"He's in me—" the child weakly offers.

Jim and Anne—their hands, laughter—gobble him up. And he too begins to laugh. Being tickled. Being happy. In the presence—under the very hands—of those whom he loves.

If I could die now, but linger a while, and watch—not long: only minutes, but truly be dead—yet see the three of them playing together—and then absent myself—forever—negate—I sense an overwhelming readiness for the blessing of—

Barney's turn chuckles into a halt. Through the screen of the door I see Jim lean over and whisper to him. He sits up and gropes with the idea for a moment. Then stands, and shuffles toward the kitchen. He opens the door, delays for a moment—and timidly pokes me in my side. And retreats.

"Hey, where're our drinks?" Jim calls.

"Right here."

I hand Anne her glass, Jim his, and stand above them.

"Well okay, Barney," Jim prompts, "where is he?"

He points at me sheepishly. "He's in him."

Jim's forearm locks around my knees—jerks—and I topple down on all of them. They instantly rearrange the geometry of their bodies to include me as their base. I am under their fingers. And they laugh. I will an emptiness into my chest. And wait for it to be filled. It is not . . . I *am* hollow, after all. And the deadly richness I felt in the kitchen—that too begins to drain away. As if, on a beach, the tide goes out in one long receding wave.

"Sorry to disappoint you folks," I comment editorially, "but it happens I'm not ticklish."

"Spoilsport!" grumbles Anne.

"Leave it to the lad." Jim untangles himself from the human knot we've been and relaxes on his back, hands under his head.

Barney stares at me, mystified, disappointed.

The game is over.

I can't even remember the trivia we talk, to get us through that last drink. Jim and Anne concoct whatever of it there is. I try to contain my hollowness, a vacuum that I feel is spreading, making everyone nervous. Poor innocent Barney too. He'll blame himself that the evening has failed and is incomplete . . . No, no—it is I, with this swelling emptiness, into which all your efforts have fallen!

I want the two of them out of here as quickly as possible. As they sip their last, I glance at my watch. "Getting on toward bedtime, Barney." Obvious, but it frees them both to go. "Barney's staying over the night. His mother's apartment is a mess, what with packing and everything."

The conclusive setting down of glasses. The saying of good nights. They make a last effort to realize tangibly, for Barney's sake, their affection for him: "When you get back to New York you've got to come up to Riverdale"—"Yes, and come and see me too! And Helen. She's pretty nice. Though a girl."

"Your pajamas are in that bundle we brought down from your mother's. It's in the bedroom."

He mumbles something beginning with "good" and ending with neither "night" nor "bye"—miserable and incompetent at leave-taking too. And that also, tonight, I have done to him.

"You've got your car, Jim, don't you?"

"Uh-huh."

"Would you mind dropping Anne off? It's East Thirty-eighth Street."

"Be glad to. On the way there perhaps she can tell me what *she* was doing here tonight."

"Got invited to a party," she shrugs.

He turns his question—sympathetic and also a weapon—on me: "Perhaps someday you will tell us both."

"Perhaps I will. Good night." I will *not*. God damn them!

In their absence despair breathes easier: it feels almost like relief.

Barney shuffles in from the bedroom, pajama-clad, in his usual doldrums. He sits beside me on the couch.

"Did you have a good time tonight?"

"Yes."

"Get enough to eat?"

"Yes."

"And Jim and Anne—did you like them?"

"Yes."

"Can you say anything besides 'yes'?"

He can say nothing, and he does.

"It *is* getting late, Barney. Wasn't your toothbrush in that undle too?"

He looks as much reproach as he can.

"Well—?"

"Aren't you going to tell me a story?"

"Oh Barney!" My irritation, unhidden, is real. The greedy little end! "I've been telling you stories all winter long! Do you want nother now?"

"Yes."

"You *are* a hungry, empty little boy," I complain. "Well all ght, but—"

"And make it have the Rat in it too! Please. And Harold."

"Yes—sir. The Rat, and Harold, and—the little boy." Why not? he last. "That's the name of this story: *Harold—and the Little oy.*

"Well, the Rat was asleep one morning, bewilderedly dreaming f Heaven and Hell, because he'd taken a good strong dose of alium the night before—that's something that made the Rat eep and dream—when there came a knocking, a very urgent nocking, on his door. The Rat shuffled up into consciousness, out f his weird dreams of Heaven and Hell, and angrily called, Who's that?'

" 'It's me!' came Harold's voice. 'Let me in!'

" 'Oh God,' the Rat grumped. He swung his lower claws out of ed, stood up, and pulled on a pair of dungarees. 'Now what? As I didn't have enough trouble already!' He opened the door, and 1 rushed Harold, carrying something. The something was vrapped up in an enormous handkerchief. (The handkerchief was eally just one of Harold's little ones, but by magic he'd made it ight times bigger than it should have been.) 'What's that?' asked the Rat suspiciously.

"'Just look!' said Harold. He folded back the top of the handkerchief—"

"Wasn't Harold going to go away?"

"Yes he was. And he is. Next day, as a matter of fact."

"Where?"

"You asked me that before. And I told you—anywhere! Queens! The Bronx. Harold had this longing to explore the Night over Queens. Now don't ask anything more! This is where the story gets interesting. 'Just look!' said Harold. He folded back the top of the handkerchief—and there was the head of a tiny baby.

"'Get it out of here!' shouted the Rat.

"'Now Rat, look—' Harold began.

"'I have nothing to do with children,' the Rat said furiously.

"'You're my best friend,' Harold appealed.

"'Since when? Since *when*—!'

"'Since forever, Rat. Oh I know, you're mean and nasty, and cruel and sadistic'—that means, watch out!—if he loves you, he'll hit you! it's the only way he knows how—'and old-fashioned and behind the times—'

"'Well for God's sake—!' grumped button nose.

"'—but Rat, you're still my best friend. And there's nothing that we can do about it. We're just trapped, that's all.'

"'That doesn't mean you can bring brats into my apartment!' declared the Rat.

"'There's nobody else I could turn to,' said Harold.

"'Oh—turn to your *magic!*' the Rat commented contemptuously. That means, the hell with it! 'You're so proud of it, that magic.'

"And then Harold looked hurt. 'You know that it's almost gone,' he said. His right arm—the left was holding the baby—lifted and fell in helplessness. 'I had to turn to someone who'd better be a friend.'

"'Oh all right! Come on in,' grumped the Rat.

"'Can I put the little boy on the couch?' said Harold.

"'How do you know it's a little boy?'

"'Look—' Harold folded back the bottom of the handkerchief.

"'Hmm!' The Rat made a philosophical sound. 'He's a little boy, all right.'

" 'Can I lay him on the couch?' asked Harold. 'I mean—he *is* a baby and he might—'

" 'Oh put him on the couch already! On *that* couch what does it matter?'

"Harold gently set the baby down. He looked at it for a minute. Then he softly sang:

> Lie down there. And try not to pee.
> Just stay still. That's a good baby.

"He found, somewhat to his surprise—after all the shock and everything—that he was becoming quite fond of this little boy.

" 'Where'd you find it?' said the Rat.

" 'Biggest shock of my life!' said Harold. 'I was over in the Bowery—I sometimes spend a night over there, in a hardware store—but last night the hardware store was closed. So I found this livable ash can, and I emptied out all the trash and cleaned it by magic and conjured up a few blankets—it really was quite comfortable too, this trash can, by the time that I got through with it—and I fell asleep. Then, just about an hour ago, I woke up with a start. And right away—

> Something wrong, something wrong—

" 'Oh for God's sake, skip that!' grumped the Rat. 'I've heard enough of it.' He chuckled in a Ratlike way. 'I thought you threw out all the trash.'

" 'Anyhow,' Harold went on—he refused to be made angry— 'There *was* something wrong!

> Is it a broken expensive toy?
> No.
> Then is it—Good Lord! It's a little boy!

" 'I jumped up inside the ash can—and knocked the top off with my head—and there he was, lying on the sidewalk outside. With a note attached to his chest by Scotch tape. The note said, "Okay, Harold, here he is! You better take care of him now!" '

" 'How was the note signed?' asked the Rat.

" ' "Never-mind-who"! But there was an R.S. I mean, a P.S.: "He really *is* yours too!" '

" 'Very strange.' The Rat stroked his whiskers awhile. 'Well— what are you going to do with it?'

" 'That's why I came here,' Harold said. 'To ask your advice. What should I do?'

" 'Put it back in the street.'

" 'Oh *Rat*—'

" 'So take care of it then.' The Rat shrugged. 'How the hell should I know? Me. The little I know about kids.' He looked at Harold in a queer way. 'But you better do something fast. Don't you have a trip planned?'

" 'Yes,' said Harold. 'For tomorrow. I'm going to explore the Night above Riverdale—' "

"You said Queens!"

Retentive little bugger! "The Night above Queens—the Night above Riverdale, the Night above anywhere—it makes no difference, Barnacle. When a person sets out to explore the Night, he has to explore the whole of it. So—'That's why it's urgent!' said Harold. 'I've got to decide what to do right now. Rat—do me a favor, will you?'

" 'What?' grumped the Rat suspiciously.

" 'Get *everybody* together! Go collect everybody—will you? I need all the advice I can get.'

"The Rat was going to say something Ratlike—but instead he decided to do what Harold asked. He had never seen his friend with such a squinched-up expression before.

"Harold had to wait for hours. He kept pacing up and down the Rat's living room, but stopping every now and then to look down at the baby on the couch.

"Then he heard a muffled tapping on the Rat's door. He opened it, and there, flapping this way and that in the air, was Jake Moth. 'I been bangin' here for ten minut'sh, Harolharol!'

" 'Sorry, Jake, I didn't hear you.'

" 'Well, shay, man—' Jake Moth flew in. '—jush how loud do you think a Moth'sh wingsh shound?'

"After Jake everybody arrived pretty quickly. There was—Ted Bear—he's the one who went berserk—and his friends Art Panda, Anita Peacock, Dick Pig, and Isaac Owl. And there were Minkcoat and Bluesuit, and Hanky and Necktie were riding in Bluesuit's pocket. Oh, and Big Bob Bat."

In the pause while I'm trying to think who else I've invented,

Barney hopefully asks, "Did Dr. Whittaker and Mrs. Black come?"

"No. They had visited the Rat a few days earlier—been down to dinner, as a matter of fact—but now they were out of New York. Dr. Whittaker had taken his wife for a vacation in the Caribbean, and Mrs. Black was visiting a sister in California. It's too bad they weren't there too. Harold had an idea he was going to need them—there was lots of worry in the air that day—but he didn't begin to suspect how much." Who else then? . . . Ah—him! "One human being did come though: Dan Reilly. Do you remember him?"

"The man who had the scream."

"That's right. He arrived last of all, with that lifeless expression of his. And he didn't say a word; just went off in a corner and sat by himself, and watched all that was happening. So—Harold explained to everyone about the little boy. And everybody had different ideas. Ted Bear and the other toy animals looked wistfully at the baby. They wanted to take him home to replace their boy, who was growing up. 'But the parents would never allow it.' Ted Bear shook his head. 'I'm sorry, Harold, I don't know what to suggest.'

" 'Start him working out,' said Big Bob Bat. 'He could grow up to be a weight lifter!' But Harold told him to shut the hell up! He just wanted to make it to being a little boy.

" 'He certainly can't stay here,' said Minkcoat. 'Really, Rat, this apartment!—it's simply a mess.'

" 'Oh shut up!' the Rat shouted. 'You phony bitch!'

"From Minkcoat's pocket came a glittering giggling. She had brought down the Jewels, and the Jewels just *loved* the idea of anyone calling Minkcoat a phony bitch!

"But Bluesuit didn't much like it. 'Now just a minute, Rat—'

" 'Oh for heaven's sake,' shouted Harold, 'will all of you stop this bickering! We've got to decide what to do with this little boy! The toys can't take him, the Clothes—well—'

" 'We'd just *love* to!' said Minkcoat effusively—that means she really didn't mean it, but felt obliged to pretend a lot. 'But darling Harold, you know how messy babies are, and—'

" 'All right, I know,' interrupted Harold. He hadn't held out much hope for the Clothes anyway. Off in his corner, all by himself, sat Dan Reilly. 'No! no!' thought Harold. 'Anything would be better than being raised by a scream.' And Jake Moth was no help either. Jake had a good heart, but he wouldn't be any good at bringing up a little boy. 'Rat, there's only you,' Harold pleaded.

" 'I can't,' said the Rat, kind of shamefaced and a little apologetically. 'I just can't, Harold. I don't know how.'

"Now right here—a little apologetically—the Friendly Fragment of Dark peered out of Harold's pocket, and tried to soothe everybody down. Oh my God—" I remembered frantically, "you don't know who he is—"

"He's from a *story!*" Barney hungered.

"Yes! And he's *real!*"

" 'If only the little boy was older,' Harold groaned. 'He could find his way by himself.'

" 'That's it!' exclaimed the Rat. 'You'll have to grow him up! Tonight!'

" 'I think that's an absolutely *divine* suggestion!' said Minkcoat. 'Just make him eighteen, and we'll send him to Princeton.' That's a college where Minkcoats like to send their sons.

" 'You don't do it like that!' said Harold. 'Children grow up year by year. You can't skip the first seventeen and expect a kid to live!'

" 'Then do it year by year,' said Ted Bear.

" 'But it takes too much magic!' moaned Harold. 'You know I don't have that much left.'

" '*Try!*' said the Rat. 'We'll help. We'll think and we'll wish and we'll concentrate.'

" 'I might up to—' Harold looked at the baby. '—seven. I think if I got him up to seven, he could find his way by himself.' He paused a moment—then flung his arms up and down. 'Okay! I'll try.' And took off his coat and vest: it was going to be very hard work. 'Everybody sit down now, in a circle on the floor.' Harold took the baby in his arms and went into the center of the circle. 'I guess he's, maybe, one year old—but what do you do with a one-year-old baby?' he asked in confusion.

" 'You kish him!' said Jake Moth. 'Kish him, Harolharol! Go on an' kish him!'

"Harold decided that Jake Moth might not make a bad father after all. But only for a little moth. He kissed the little boy on the cheek and sang softly to him—

> I guess you're, maybe, one year old.
> And that will never do.
> Before this kiss grows dead and cold,
> I wish you would be two.

"Immediately the baby grew heavier in Harold's arms. 'It's working!' he breathed.

"Everybody applauded. And Jake Moth, who was treading the air above their heads, so he would have a better view, said, 'Groovy! Groovy, Harolharol! Keep goin', man!'

"With a corner of the big handkerchief that he wrapped the baby in Harold wiped some perspiration off his forehead. 'Just a minute. This is going to be even harder work than I thought.' He rested a little and jiggled the little boy in his arms, to hear him laugh, and then sang—

> The twos—they say they're terrible!
> They very well may be.
> So why not try—it's possible—
> Why not? Yes! You are three.

"'*Groovy!*' shouted Jake Moth.

"'Oh for God's sake,' grumped the Rat, 'can't you think of something to say besides "groovy"?'

"'Let him be, Rat,' said Harold. 'Jake's working hard to make this work. And I'm going to need all the help I can get. I'm exhausted already—and he's only three.'

"'Why don't you rest, Harold darling?' said Minkcoat. 'And while you are, I think we ought to get the little boy some clothes. He's outgrowing that handkerchief.'

"'Oh, clothes are no problem,' said Harold. 'The physical things don't use up much magic. It's growing him up that really takes it out of you.' He snapped his fingers and ordered—

> Pants and shirt and socks and shoes!
> Hair—comb, face—wash! The childhood dues.

"And instantly the little boy was dressed.

" 'Say, Harold,' said the Rat, 'if he's three now, shouldn't he be able to talk?'

" 'Oh my God,' Harold exclaimed, 'I forgot about that! Er—um—' He looked at the little boy in his lap nervously. '—you *can* talk can't you? I hope!'

"The little boy looked back at him for an anxiously long while. And then said, 'Yes.'

"Everybody applauded again. And a few—Art Panda and Necktie, I think it was—cheered. Jake Moth was about to shout his favorite word, but he saw Rat glowering at him, so he just said, 'That kid'sh a winner!'

"Big Bob Bat said, 'He'll be a great weight lifter!'

" 'Can you say anything besides "yes"?' Harold asked the little boy hopefully.

" 'Yes.'

" 'Well—say it!' He wasn't too talkative, this child, but Harold had confidence in him. 'Please say it.'

"A minute longer than most minutes passed. 'I can say, "Yes—sir," ' said the little boy.

" 'It isn't much—' Harold shook his head. '—but it's a beginning, I guess.'

" 'Harold,' Ted Bear ventured timidly, 'I mean—three *is* the heyday for toy animals—do you think he'd like to play with me?'

" 'Ask him,' said Harold.

"Ted waddled over to the little boy and tugged him by his right hand. 'Hey—you want to play with me?'

" 'Yes.'

"Ted clambered up into his lap and said, 'Okay. So play!' The little boy snuggled him comfortably.

"Not to be outdone, Isaac Owl strutted out in front of everybody and said, 'Would he like to hear the national anthem?' Before anybody could answer, he had pressed the button in his belly button. And the music box inside him began to play 'God Bless America.' 'Damn that Kate Smith!' said Isaac Owl, and punched himself in the stomach.

" 'Come on, we've got to keep going,' said Harold. 'There isn't that much time left, and we're only up to three.' He took the little boy back in his lap and sang, rather wearily—

Did you like three? I do hope so.
But you can't stop. There's more.

> More toys, more clothes, and tales, and woes—
> In fact, my lad, there's four.

"No one clapped after the child reached four years old. Because they could all see how tired Harold was getting. In fact, a certain amount of worry began to ripple around the Rat's living room: eyes avoided eyes, and voices went low—sometimes into whispers. Rat dabbed Harold's forehead.

" 'I wish I had one of Miss Amanda's strawberry and apple pies,' sighed Harold. 'I bet that would fill a whole year for him.'

" 'I got no piesh,' said Jake Moth, 'but you want a joint, Harolharol?' He reached behind his ear, where he always kept one of his kooky little cigarettes.

" 'No, thank you, Jake.' Harold shook his head. 'It wouldn't work in this case. It's magic, or nothing.'

" 'Well how about the kid?' said Jake. 'Would he like to turn on?'

" 'Really!' said Minkcoat, in a minklike way.

" 'I don't think so, Jake,' said Harold, who understood that the offer was meant sincerely.

" 'Oh. Okay. I jush' thought I'd ashk. Doesh anyone min' if I turn on?' No one minded, so Jake lit up one of his kooky little cigarettes, and before very long he was so turned on—that means he was happy and wanted to share it with everyone else—that he was doing the bugaloo in the air. That's a dance done by a turned-on moth.

> You sort of dig it by now—don't you?
> This groovy thing: to be alive.
> So you will help me too now—won't you?
> You're sick of four—
> You must explore.
> And look—now you've found five!

" 'I'd skip the fancy stuff, Harold, if I were you,' the Rat said gently—in a very un-Ratlike voice. 'Just stick to the simple spells. They'll take less out of you.'

" 'I know,' said Harold wheezingly, 'but when a person gets to be five, he has a right to expect something special. You *want* something special,' he asked the little boy, 'don't you?'

" 'Yes.'

" 'We're almosh' there, Harolharol!' Jake Moth had stopped doing the bugaloo in the air and was trying to help by concentrating. 'Jush' two more yearsh.'

" 'They get harder as he gets older,' said Harold. 'Oh, but I know who can help! The thought of her always helps.' He sang, with a kind of tired joy—

> Now here's a spell from Iris Brife—
> And also from black Mary Wicks.

"You met Iris tonight, and Mary Wicks is another colored lady whom Harold loves.

> They revel in the throes of life!
> Get ready, Barney—you are six!

"Nobody said a word, at first. There are times when even encouragement can be a burden. But after a minute or two the Rat said, 'Harold, I'm going to get you a glass of wine. There's some left over from that little party I had with Jim Whittaker and Anne Black the other day. Do you want red or white?'

" 'Red, please,' said Harold weakly, 'and thank you, Rat.' He lay on the floor and rested, as the Rat went into his little kitchen and got him a glass of red wine. 'That feels better.' Harold drank off the last of it. 'I think I can make it now, if—'

"But just then there was a pounding of footsteps on the stairs in the hall. Someone started to beat on Rat's door, and a shrill voice screamed, 'Let me in! Let me in!'

" 'Don't!' Harold said to the Rat. 'Don't let him in!'

"But the shrill voice outside the door was heard singing a creaky incantation:

> Come on, little lock! *I* have magic too.
> Come on, little bolt! Turn! I command you!

"And the door swung wide open.

"Rumpelstiltskin's eyes were blazing with fury and envy. He ran through the circle of everybody—and everybody fell back. They all hated him. Except for Dan Reilly. Off where he sat in his corner with his lifeless expression turned into a smile—but it was a smile that was far worse than lifeless. With bony fingers Rumpelstiltskin seized the little boy's arm. 'He's mine!' he screamed. 'And I claim him.'

" 'He isn't yours!' said Harold. 'You've done nothing to earn him. And if you got him, you'd—'

" 'If I got him,' sneered Rumpelstiltskin, 'what I did with him would be none of your business! But I have plans, I do, I do, for this little boy and me!'

" 'You haven't spun any straw into gold—'

" 'Oh haven't I just—!'

" 'You don't have any claim—'

" 'Oh don't I? Well listen, my dear, I've been spinning all winter! I've spun with Jim and I've spun with Anne and I've spun with everybody else. And I've made him miserable! And you know it. His misery is my gold—and you know it! I've worked—and sweetie, I enjoy my work!' Rumpelstiltskin gave Harold a horrible wink. 'And now I've come to claim the prize. This child is mine!' He put his arms around him and sang—

> Come on, little hopeless, lonely boy!
> You have no home, and you have no toy—

"But Harold lifted *his* arms and shouted—

> You want him, Stiltskin—but I say no!
> The hell with you and your damned ho! ho!

"Rumpelstiltskin went rigid. Except that his eyes continued to be on fire.

" 'Now grab him!' commanded Harold. 'Rat, hold his right arm! Minkcoat, take his left! Ted Bear, lock his legs together! Big Bob, grab his shoulders! You claim to be so strong. And Jake, fly up on his head! Do the bugaloo there. And keep on saying "Groovy!" I only need time enough to say one more spell.'

" 'You fool!' Rumpelstiltskin's voice was far away and small, but still fierce and ringing with rage. 'You wretch! You *coward*! What God damned difference does it make to you anyway? You're going off to explore the Night tomorrow. You don't give a damn what happens to him!' "

"Why *does* Harold have to go—?"

"Barney, don't interrupt." I interrupt my precipitous talking. "Don't you like this story? We're getting to the most exciting part—"

"Yes, I like it, but *why* does he have to?"

"He has one spell left—and that's all. That's the last of his magic. And remember, he's only three feet tall. Sometimes he's only two. So for God's sake—you damn brat!—I don't mean that—" He hasn't heard. "—what *can* he do?"

"He can be a little person."

"What—?"

"He can be a little man. If he's only three feet tall."

A wave is collecting. A wave of nausea. And elation.

"Are *you* going to tell the story now?"

"Oh no—" He cowers before any such ambition.

"Do you want to hear what happened next?"

"Yes."

"Harold ignored what Rumpelstiltskin said. He summoned up all that was left and sang—

> And here at last, from Jim and Anne,
> There comes both Hell and Heaven.
> Accept it, without plot or plan.
> It's here, my son—you're seven!

"A huge sigh, which sounded in some cases like a groan, went up from everybody.

" 'Let him go,' said Harold peacefully. Rat, Minkcoat, Jake, Ted Bear, and Big Bob Bat let go of Rumpelstiltskin. 'He can't hurt anyone now.'

" 'Oh can't I?' said Rumpel. 'Can't I just!'

" 'He's seven now. He can find his way.' Harold frowned. 'But I guess, to make sure he keeps on growing, I better say those words I made you say, Ted.'

" 'Listen, Harold,' the Teddy Bear warned, 'unless it's absolutely necessary—don't!'

" 'Well—I guess it's absolutely necessary.' Harold flattened his voice and said as fast as he could—

> Let-him-grow—let-him-grow—let-him-outgrow-me.
> Let-him-even-forget-me-if-need-be!

" 'There! It's all finished.'

" 'Finished?' croaked Rumpelstiltskin. 'You think it's finished? It isn't, Harold! If I can't have that little boy, no one will!' He lifted two fingers into his mouth—like this—and blew a terrific whistle.

"And instantly, from the street below, like an echo, only ten times louder—and terrible!—there came a dreadful sound: a scream. A pounding of feet—three feet—was heard on the stairs—the door was burst open, broken in splinters—and there stamped and slavered the Three-Legged Nothing, waving its four arms and roaring with its two heads. Everybody was petrified! Harold too. They all fell back against the wall. Jake Moth tried to keep his courage up by saying 'Groovy!' a couple of times. But then he couldn't say any more. He covered his eyes with his wings and began to cry. Because the Three-Legged Nothing is a very bad trip—the worst trip in the world, in fact—for a turned-on Moth, and for everyone else too.

"None of anybody—not even Harold—had seen it this close before. And it was simply *horrible!* The worst thing about it, Harold realized, as he stared at it in terror, was that one of its heads looked like a man's head, a well-groomed man's ordinary head, and the other, with a little makeup on, looked like an ordinary woman's. And the heads cackled and laughed and roared at each other—and sometimes kissed each other too—in the most appalling way.

" '*Now*,' said Rumpelstiltskin gleefully, 'we'll find out what's all finished! You see, ol' pal Harold, what you didn't know is, some people have a pet cat named Sally, and some have a little corgi puppy, and some have a cobra snake named Moe—but for *my* pet *I* have the Three-Legged Nothing! Don't I, my dearest?'

" 'Oh yes!' said the man's head, and 'Yes! yes! yes!' said the woman's head too. Then 'Give us a kiss, Mom!' the man's head said—'Delighted to, Pop!'—and they kissedkissedkissed.

" 'My pet!' With one hand Rumpelstiltskin stroked the man's head, while he gave the palm of the other for the woman's head to lick and kiss. 'My beautiful pet. My rare pet.'

" 'Yes! yes!'—'Oh yes! yes! yes! yes! yes! yes!'

" 'And tell me what you've been doing tonight.'

" 'We had supper!'—'Supper! supper! supper! supper!'

" 'And what did you have for supper?'

" 'We had forty-eight left shoulders!'—'With *green* sauce!' They giggled and kissed one another again. 'And we liked them very much!'—'Oh yes!'

" 'But you're still hungry, aren't you?' Rumpelstiltskin asked slyly, and smiled an unpleasant smile at Harold.

" 'Oh yes! Always hungry!'—'Always always hungry!'

" *Then eat this little boy!*'

" 'Delighted to, love!'—'Oh yummy-yum-yum!'

" 'Harold can't stop you,' Rumpelstiltskin gloated. 'His magic is finished. *That's* what's all finished! So eat him—eat him, and let me watch. And after that—' He pointed a bony finger at Danny Reilly. '—you can take him! And do what you want with him. You can—oh, I'll leave it to both of you.' He fingered his cigarettes.

" 'We have ideas!'—'Oh yes! We have plans!'

" 'Fast ideas, and slow ideas!'—'Hot ideas, and cold ideas!'

" 'I don't care what you do with him!' said Rumpelstiltskin impatiently. 'I just want to watch you gobble up that little boy. He's seven, you know—a delectable age! A child is very sweet at seven. At eight a certain toughness sets in—in the chest especially —but seven!—mmmm!'

" *'Mmmm!'*—*'Mmmm!'*

" 'We'll each take half!'—'Take half! Take half!'

" 'Shall we rip him apart first?'—'No! No, no!'

" 'Shall we start at each hand and eat toward the center?'— 'That's it, love! We meet at the center! The very best part, the center is!'

" 'Give us a kiss, Mom!'—'Delighted to, Pop!' The heads kissed one another again and slobbered ecstatically at the thought of the coming feast."

The gathering sickness is building within me. I've got to get Barney to bed. But the spindrift of the wave is joy.

" 'Start now!' commanded Rumpelstiltskin. 'And make Harold watch too. You know what he's thinking—the idiot! He's thinking, "If the Three-Legged Nothing would only eat me, it might not gobble that little boy up." Too late, Harold darling. What kind of a Nothing do you think would eat a wrinkled three-foot-tall *little man,* when it could have *this* tasty morsel?' "

I stood up. Because that wave was about to break. An error: you don't breast the great Atlantic surf standing up.

"Barney, I'm sorry, but you do have to go to bed now—"

"What *happened?*" His eyes have been flashing fearfully.

And I haven't even been looking at him. But his face is a mask of abject terror.

" 'You *can't* help him any more, can you, Harold?' Rumpelstiltskin demanded to know and laughed.

" 'No,' Harold whimpered. He closed his eyes."

I've got myself here—about to puke—but I've got to save Barney's belief somehow.

"And then, from nowhere, to everyone's great surprise, the little boy spoke up himself. He said, very reasonably, to the Three-Legged Nothing, 'Wouldn't you rather have food than me?'

" 'Food?'—'*Food—*?'

" 'We never eat food!'—'If we can't eat people, we eat ourselves!'

" 'Why not try a little food?' said the boy. To everyone's great surprise: he had been so quiet up till now.

" '*Human* food?'—'We never eat human food!'

" 'The Rat said that there was some left over' . . . All right now, Barney, you tell me: what did the little boy offer the Nothing? . . . Come on—you're telling stories tonight."

"Casserole?" he ventures.

"Yes. And—?"

"Red wine—"

"Right."

"And macademy nuts."

"There you are . . . Now you do have to go to bed. I'll finish the story tomorrow, I promise. Your plane doesn't leave until evening. I'll come up and tell you what happened. Promise! But quick now—into bed."

He scuttles away, flounders into the bedroom: his own clumsy version of hurrying.

And the wave crashed at last.

How long has this wave been gathering? Weeks? Days? Perhaps minutes? Yet it is a drowning wave. I feel its death when it still is a long way out, when only the barest pressure is pushing against my chest. Now, almost visibly, it towers above me. Sensations that contradict each other: I take a pure pleasure in something so huge: that it simply can be: unbelievable! But at the same time I am terrified, whirled round and round in my living room: I know that this wave will obliterate me—I cannot possibly swim through it. An awareness of swelling, lifting, ending—being tossed from hand to hand—its thundering march began a continent away.

I go into the bathroom—throw up—then feel the cool comfort of the toilet bowl's sweating white marble against my forehead . . .

Absurd Three-Legged Impossible God—is this the story You have to tell: it is not possible not to live?

March 21: About three

The sensation of physical illness has passed. I have a shipwrecked feeling now, a Gulliver, Robinson Crusoe feeling: stretched out on some beach, exhausted to still be alive. And a little bemused by the whole thing too . . . Is this land inhabited?

March 21: Five o'clock

Wherever I am, I can stand up now. I begin to trust this shore: it is endless, extending infinitely in either direction. The experience of the wave, the memory of it, still breaks within me . . . Oh I hope it never goes away—to be spun, and dissolved, and then come together—

March 21: Six forty-five

Called Dan. These two things at least must be finished. I'll call Jim's office at nine o'clock.

He was dumbly astonished to hear me: "What—?"

"Yes, it's Terry. You working in New York today?"

"Yes."

"Come and see me first. Come at eight o'clock. Or between eight and nine." His baffled silence. "And don't ask questions! Just *be* here."

"Yes—sir."

Totalitarianism dies hard. I will never be free of it completely. His obedience still bows all my nerves with a self-affirming chord . . .

The boy is asleep. I'll give him another half-hour.

March 21: Eight o'clock

Woke Barney up.
"Now don't ask what happened!

> Teeth—brush, hair—comb: the childhood dues.
> Put on your clothes! Put on socks and shoes!
> Later on today—there may be news.

"I'll see you before you leave."
He looks at me with puzzled impatience.
"Quick! Into the bathroom! No questions! No answers!"
And then into a taxi.
I called his mother, to tell her that *Ber*-nard was on the way up, and ask her if I could come up around five.
Yes!—"And Terry, the most fabulous thing has happened! *Frank's* flying east today! And *just* so that he can fly back with us. How about that?—for a husband."
"Great."
"I'm so anxious for you two to meet."
"Well I guess we will. This afternoon. Your place."

March 21: Nine o'clock

"Have I done something wrong?" His essence—intimidation craving nonbeing—despairs in his face as I open the door.
"No you haven't. Come in. Sit down. Do you want some coffee?"
"No, thank you—sir."
"We'll skip that this morning."
He sits on the couch, as nervous as a virgin, and waits.
"I just have to tell you, Dan—it's all finished." One feels ridiculous, telling another human being that you're not going to be his murderer. The thrust and force of the wave still spins a part of me giddily, but the pity I feel for this man, despite its speed, is also slow and sad. "I just can't. That's all."

"You could—" He tries to recall a crazy strength, drained out to sea.

"I know I could. But I can't anymore."

"I could get—"

"No. Sorry. The hash won't work. I've gotten beyond the possibility."

"What happened—sir?"

"Say my name."

"—Terry."

"A lot. But the simplest way to put it is—I want you to live."

His face crumples, and within that hulk the tiny creature he really is begins to cry. "You could have done it, Terry. You're the only one who—"

"If that's true, I'm glad. Because now I can't either. It's just not possible not to live. Oh Danny, come here!" I tug the top of him, shoulders and head, down into my lap, and mother the beast. He begins to speak, but his voice gets swallowed. "Make no mistake, lad. I have no more hope for my own future than I have for yours. However, the future is all there is." His sobbing against my thighs excites me. "And don't get the idea that because I—because I won't burn you to death—I've turned into Saint Francis."

"Can I see you again?"

"Sure." I lift him up. "How about this weekend?"

"Is that too soon?"

"If it was, I wouldn't suggest it. Dope! You're a good-looking man. A little thick in the gut perhaps—" I whack his stomach: his flattered smile glints, vanishes. "—but you have possibilities. Saturday. Would you like to have lunch? There's a lot of good restaurants in the Village."

"Lunch—?" His eyes doubt, disbelieve for a minute: the idea of eating food together—you would think it more fearful than the stake. But then maybe. "I'd like that."

"Come early. Around twelve o'clock. We'll have lunch."

"Yes—"

"Say my *name!*"

"—Terry."

"But now say, 'Yes—sir.' "

"Yes—sir."

"You won't look for another killer—"

"No—sir."

"Okay. Now get out. I've got a lot to do today." He shambles into his overcoat. "Who are your welfare people today?"

"An epileptic man, and an old woman with a broken hip." At the door the timid bear holds me a moment, and says—ah well, what he says is "I love you."

For the rest of my life this dull, small, and invaluable soul will love me.

"That's nice to know."

So be it! I will learn to love him.

March 21: Nine-thirty

Jim's operating this morning—I should call again, around two . . . But how *can* I get through this endless day? . . . (Is this land inhabited?) . . . Oh *there's* someone—!

March 21: Eleven-thirty

Teddy swears at me prodigiously. But then cancels a class in Russian to help me buy a new hi-fi set. And a beauty too. A KLH, model twenty: turntable and two superb speakers. To give it the acid test we also buy the Reiner version of *Also Sprach Zarathustra* . . . And my God, that guy from *2001* was so right to use those opening bars to suggest the birth of a new world.

Teddy had to go back to a seminar. (There are so many hours still ahead!) How I'm going to need him! In fact, need all my living friends. But especially—

Dear Teddy—

Some people are blossoms—just pretty offshoots.
Some people are branches—you're one of my roots.

Well—I can't write love poems to all of my friends . . . Is it possible that even I am beginning to appreciate the diamond value of silence? . . .

No, not diamonds! (Can't afford them anyway.) But—

March 21: One-thirty

"Terry!—they're beautiful!"

"I didn't know whether you like tourmalines." Two earrings, held in her palm. "In the right light this kind flashes blue and green." But semiprecious gems at best.

"I love them. Where did you get them?"

"At Tiffany's."

"*Tiffany's*—! When?"

"A half-hour ago. You were nice to come down to my party last night."

"I enjoyed being there—"

"We enjoyed having you. And next week we go to *Peter Grimes*—right? You'll enjoy the production. It's very good. In the meantime I'll be in touch."

"What's *happening* to you, Terry?"

"I don't know. Nothing very important. See you soon."

I leave her in the doorway, staring at me with perplexed affection . . . The practice of this love is silence.

March 21: Three o'clock

Reached Jim. In grim decision.

"What's so important, lad?"

His cool voice—"Got a pain somewhere? Need an operation?" —is as handsome as that face I visualize.

"I think I do. You've got to be cut out of me."

"You do sound melodramatic, lad. May I ask why this surgery is necessary?"

"I guess the growth has become malignant. Surely this isn't the first time that a case of yours has been diagnosed as hopeless."

"Usually *I* make the diagnosis."

"Well this one time the patient does."

"You want to come up to the office and fuck me? I've never been fucked in the office before. But we couldn't use the belt. Old Fergie, my secretary—"

"God damn you!"

"Am I entitled—" His perfectly feigned obedience, as always,

378

makes the skin of my emotions tingle. "—to know what's happened?"

"No! You are not. You're entitled to listen. And nothing more. Look—there's something I want you to know. You may know it already—but I want you to hear me say it now: it is absolutely impossible for me to love a human being any more than I love you. Or even as much. You're as close as I will ever get to being a human being. But I've got to get rid of you. My life—I mean, my continued existence—it isn't what you'd call a life—depends on it. What—happens inside me is not just one fag's attraction to another and very handsome fag at that. It may come as something of a shock to you, but you're *not* the prettiest ass I've been in."

"Oh?" He questions me coldly, acquisitively. "Who else? I'd like—"

"Shut up! But you got to depths that I wish no one ever had. But it's too late for that: you did. If God had invented a special device to ensnare my life, with every apparatus connected to it specifically designed to trap my love, you would have been that machine."

"What about the scenes we've had?—the kicks."

"They've been the best in my life. And you know it. And you've had some great times too. But don't worry. You'll find a new fist. And with a little bit of looking, you'll probably find a new master to master."

He elaborately doesn't comprehend. "So because you love me as much as you can love anyone—which you just said—and because the sex we've had is the best—and you've taught things to me too—you know that—"

"Yes—"

"—because everything that takes place between us has been wild and exciting and great—you're cutting me out like a tumor."

"Yes!"

His slow intake of breath descends to weary ignorance. "Lad—logic is not your strong point. *Why?*"

"Because it's destroying me. And I don't want to be destroyed any more."

He creates—calculates—a silence. "It seems so stupid. Such a waste. We've known each other for over a year. I don't make that many attachments—"

"Stop that!"

"—at least doctors don't—so that I can let one blow up without trying to understand."

"I've explained. It's malignant love. That's all there is."

In his armor of stillness, guarded and invisible, I do not know what he feels. His voice shows no clue: it is flat as he asks, "And what do I tell Carol?"

"I don't give a damn! You're a very accomplished liar. I'm sure you'll think of something."

"You won't even *see* us—?"

"No!"

"Fine. And what'll I tell the kids?"

"I don't *care!* If it's important—I don't hate your wife and your children, Jim—I'll change my telephone number. I'll get an unlisted number. I'll *move*—if you want me to. I'll get another apartment. You can say that I've gone to Rome! San Francisco!" His silence mocks all my efforts, with quiet self-confidence. "Or better still—why not tell your kids the *truth?* That their daddy's a whore. And one man finally got sick and tired of fucking what must be the most overworked asshole in the city of New York!"

He takes that, within his stillness. Then journalizes again: "All right. That's what I'll tell the girls. Now advise me what I should say to Ben?"

"I don't *give* a goddam! The little blind bastard! He's not my responsibility!"

"I know. He's mine"—understated. "He's Carol's too. But mostly he's mine. And whoever else's I share him with."

"You unutterable motherfucker—"

"When you make this momentous move of yours, you must give me your address—"

"Like hell!"

"There's something that Ben wants to send to you. He's gotten to a point in his class where we buy them typewriters. It's easier than handwriting. Ben's writing out that story you told him. Harold and the patch of darkness—"

"It's a fragment of dark! *The Friendly Fragment of Dark!* You cocksucker! I have my own life too—"

"Sorry. 'Fragment of Dark.' Ben told it to us the day we got back from the Caribbean. As soon as we got inside the door, he

380

sat us down and demanded we listen. Then he wanted to know what presents we'd brought."

"You cur! How *dare* you use that child against—"

"I'll use anything against you I can." Pragmatically—a victor, and he knew it—"Now I have an idea. A week from Thursday is Carol's birthday. Will you buy her a cake from Sutter's and surprise us all at your place?"

"Six kids and two adults? I can't fit you all in—"

"It's time you tried."

"Jim—"

"Yes?"

"You *don't* love me, do you?"

"No. Not in the way that you want me to. But that doesn't mean I'm about to allow you to get out of my life. Besides—who would take care of you?"

"Who *wants* to—!"

"My lad—don't beg for compliments from *me!* Now will you, or won't you, throw Carol a surprise birthday party?"

Defeat. "I will."

"Good! And leave the logistics up to me. I'll arrange, by accident, for us all to be there at six o'clock."

"All right."

"Oh, and Terry—one thing more—"

"*Now* what?"

"Get *milk* for the kids, not some cyclamated shit. My wife and I are trying to keep them out of that habit for as long as we can."

Defeat. "Yes—sir."

"Ta ta!"

But the bliss of this experience has freed me at last to write "Harold's Song—At Last—For Someone Whom He Loves"—

> Dear Jim—no sweat! Now don't get irritable!
> It's not your fault I love you to excess.
> You handsome, fairly ordinary man.
> Despite your wild extravagance you're well.
> Be free then! I remove my curse from you.
> Your children and your wife, you—all I bless.
> Be what you are—but let me be a part.
> (No sweat! No more than what you want me to.)
> Go on, incarnate the Impossible—

The subject of my love, lust, childish art:
The human things I'll never know, unless
You or one like you in his kindness can
Share lives with me, share happiness, share ill,
And show me, in my ignorance, what's true,
What's real, what's right: the man I might be. Am.

Defeat . . . I apologize, my weary witnesses. (But be of good cheer: you are almost free.)

And "Courage," does one of you dare to mumble? . . . But then why should life shame me?

Never mind. It's too late. Shame, humiliation, joy, rage—I accept everything . . .

Among the discoveries I've made today: it seems you cannot feel a single emotion—you have to endure them all.

And also, one can't love a single human being—we have to love every one of us . . .

March 21: Three-thirty

But there's still so much time! Until five o'clock . . .

I've forgotten—there's you!

Go now, my witnesses—you're free!
I know that I've used you ruthlessly.
But despite your unreality,
You've somehow contrived to see me through. . . .
I apologize (sorry!) but I love you too . . .

I'll walk all the way up to Central Park. That will take up a lot of time . . .

A rose chews my heart—a delectable pain!
I can never go back to that old self again—

No . . . I first have to make a call.

March 21: Three-forty

Her voice, as it always is, apprehensive: "Hello—? Are you all right?"

Mine echoing: "Yes. How's Pop?"

His arthritis . . . Her real human miseries . . . My left shoulder? . . . "Well soak it and soak it! You've got a bathtub, don't you?"

Enough! . . . Oh damn them both—

> Damn my mother and father—the Impossible!
> The Three-Legged Nothings. Yes, but well,
> If they are a black, tight, lightless star—
> *I* will reflect the gloomy light we three are!

March 21: Eight o'clock

To no one then, and as it happened:

About four-thirty—I told her I'd be there at five: their plane leaves at seven o'clock—I take down the picture and put it in a brown paper bag: an awkward package. It'll have to do.

Strange season, this . . . Especially in Central Park.

When does it come every year, that day? In the latter part of March—not May? The day of change, as if, all at once—its gray touched suddenly by another color—the entire park has had a green idea.

I walk across the park to Edith's. The sky is clotted and overcast, and looks like the earth—they repeat each other—but the air is threateningly warm.

"Terry—at long last—this is Frank. Frank Henderson, Terry Andrews."

We shake hands. He's a big guy: bland features, but another twist of God's screw might well have defined him handsomely. "I've heard a lot about you." (We haven't all missed. But most of us have.)

"And I about you too." I reciprocate the well-meant drivel. "Up and back in one day."

"I think my time sense is somewhere over Tennessee."

"You can pick it up on the way back."

"We can't even offer you a drink. What was left of the liquor I gave to the elevator man."

"That's all right." I've had enough before coming up.

"It's depressing, isn't it?" Her apartment has been stripped: no pictures, no books: the visible presence of emptiness. A few chairs and the couch are left. "The rest of it all gets shipped tomorrow." And their suitcases, neatly assembled beside the door. "There's nothing worse than a house or an apartment when someone's moved out, before someone else has moved in. I'm so glad that *Ber*-nard was down with you last night. It's even more depressing when you have to go to bed. You had quite a party, I hear."

"A couple of friends of mine. Who like kids."

He is sitting on the couch: vacant waiting, all unfulfilled listening.

"I'm afraid I have to finish a story. I promised I would."

"Can we stay here too?" asks Frank Henderson.

"If you want to—" No! Let them go away. "—but I don't think it will make much sense."

"I'd like to stay," he persists.

"All right." But how can I speak in front of them? "Well—the Three-Legged Something decided to try some human food—"

"The Three-Legged *What?*" Edith interjects, with delicious incomprehension.

"Shh, hon'," her husband silences her. He is looking at me, not my story, with skeptical curiosity. "Let him tell it the way he wants."

"Rumpelstiltskin was furious, of course! He shouted, 'Now listen, you Nothing you—are you my pet? Or aren't you?'

" 'Oh, we are!' said the head that looked like a man.

"And 'Yes indeedy!' said the woman's head.

" 'But we'd like to try some human food. Bring on the casserole!' "

Edith is dramatizing amazement, but her husband's concerned indecision has yielded to a subdued, bemused attention.

"The little boy brought out the meat and tomato casserole, and the red wine, and the macademy nuts.

"And the Three-Legged Something took a taste.

" 'It beats left shoulders!' the man's head said.

" 'It does! Why yes it does!'

"And the Something ate almost everything up!

"Rumpelstiltskin was raging. He jumped up and down and kept saying, 'I won't stand for this!'

"But the Rat put his hand on his shoulder and said, 'Now take it easy, Rumpel S. And don't pull your old tricks. I'll be damned if I'll let you stomp your leg through *this* Rat's living room floor, and then tear yourself in half!' "

"Terry, *really—*"

They are sitting on the couch together. Frank takes her left hand and presses it, with gentle authority, against his right knee. And says—to her, nothing—to me, "Go on."

"Everybody began to relax. Minkcoat unruffled herself, Bluesuit brushed the fear from his sleeves, the Jewels said, 'Well what do you think of *that?*' And the toy animals just sat down and thanked God. Big Bob Bat started doing push-ups. Oh, and Jake Moth stopped crying, and said to himself, 'It'sh a groovy shene after all, I guesh.'

"And in fact—in *fact*—it turned out to be a fairly groovy scene after all. Not the grooviest, but groovy enough. Since the Something wasn't going to eat anybody, and since being that much afraid had given them all an appetite—a party was held! Isaac Owl played all the wrong songs, Jake Moth did the bugaloo, and, naturally, Rumpelstiltskin sulked. He stayed off in a corner with Dan Reilly, and neither one of them said a word. But finally, when Harold decided to offer them both some leftover meat and tomato glop, to his great amazement, they accepted it.

"And that's all there is. Except that I regret to say that the Three-Legged Something got drunk on red wine. The two heads became very sentimental. With their two arms each they began to feed one another: a forkful of casserole, a sip of red wine, a macademy nut popped into one another's mouth. And at one point the head that looked like a man said, 'Happy birthday, Mom.' And the woman's head simpered and giggled, and said, 'Thank you, Pop!' and began to cry.

"That all happened several days ago. Since then the Something went over to the East Village and bought a lot of mod clothes—in case it decided to become a hippie—a hippie is like Jake Moth—but it also went up to Madison Avenue and bought a gray flannel suit. In case it decided on advertising. (Or to write children's books. It could, you know.)

"The Clothes and the toy animals went home. So did Big Bob—up to the gym. Jake Moth is back in Mrs. Throttlebottom's apartment. And Rumpelstiltskin—a curious thing: he's bought himself a lot of straw and decided to take up spinning again. So far all he's spun is more straw. But dumb Rumpel has hopes. Dan Reilly is living quietly—with a TV set—and the Rat is drawing pictures again."

Not ended. Barney won't be deceived. He questions me with conviction: "What happened to Harold?"

"He's rented an apartment in New York. He loves this city after all. And that's where his friends all are. And that's all. Except for this. Too many exceptions?" I ask his parents.

"No."

"Go ahead."

I produce and present my mystery: a brown paper bag. "On that night of the party—since everyone was drunk and happy—and since it was the little boy's birthday too—everybody decided to give him a present. But they couldn't decide what to give ... However, the Rat solved the problem. He suddenly shouted, 'Well of course! It has to be that!'

"And just at that moment, a very peculiar thing happened to Harold: his left shoulder began to tingle. 'Oh my God,' he said, 'my left shoulder's infected. I've been suspecting this. Get hot water, Rat!' So in very hot water, Harold bathed his left shoulder. But much to Harold's surprise—instead of an injury out came this last half-ounce of magic. It dribbled out drearily.

"The Rat held something in front of him. 'Put it in here. We'll make it a surprise.'

"Harold let the one half-ounce of magic drain into the present. 'But careful now! That's powerful.'

" 'I wanted it to be,' said the Rat. He handed the present over. 'Be careful now. That's a really powerful present.' This picture."

"Oh Terry—" Effusive thanks.

"Aren't you going to say 'Thank you,' Barney?"

"Thank you."

"You call him Barney?"

"It's what he calls himself," says Frank Henderson.

On the strength of his shrug—that minimal human understanding—I'll have hope for this child for the rest of my life.

"I have to go. You have to catch your plane."

We all stand: awkward parting.

"If you're ever in Denver—" says Frank Henderson.

Oh damn you! *Damn you!*—all you people in Denver! He'll be there among you! Be decent, please!

"—I'll be sure to look you up. Let me look at that picture again, Barnacle." Harold lifts his admonishing index finger, warning the world of something wrong: something wrong, but reparable. "It's really pretty good. Good-bye."

"Bye." He turns away—mournfully, hopefully—I don't even know which.

And back through the park. To Columbus Circle. Too dark now to see the sky, the earth . . . That day of change is a long way off. A wasted winter.

> No. Barney's heard stories. Ephemeral fun.
> And I have—ephemeral too—had my son . . .

But when will it strike?—the knife wound of his suddenly realized absence . . . I feel it lifting behind my back . . . Don't let it go too high, too deep.

March 21: Midnight. Or maybe the twenty-second.

It's awfully late. . . .

And it has struck . . . I don't care . . . Will it last for weeks, I wonder? Months? Years? For the rest of my life? . . . I don't care . . .

Surely better than nothing—if not a beginning—is the pain of this chaotic and belated love.

> I'd rather have been Vermeer or—best!—Bach
> Than waste my life in this ridiculous way.
> It does no good to promise or to pray.
> The lightning, in its privacy, never struck.
> Nor did the human lightning strike. But look—
> I have felt children when they cry or play,
> And searching in the heart's woods, March or May,
> I'll try to find one more good children's book.
>
> I've got to *write* some more, to stay alive!
> You TV dinners, back! You could be worse.

The bitterest food I ate—not you. A curse.
Dead words, away! Let our words try to live . . .
And as for me, my living friends—all you
Will have to live my life, so I can too.

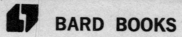

BARD BOOKS

**the classics, poetry, drama and
distinguished modern fiction**

FICTION

ANAIS NIN READER Ed., Philip K. Jason	49890	2.95
THE AWAKENING Kate Chopin	45666	2.25
THE BENEFACTOR Susan Sontag	11221	1.45
BETRAYED BY RITA HAYWORTH Manuel Puig	36020	2.25
BEYOND THE BEDROOM WALL Larry Woiwode	47670	2.95
BILLIARDS AT HALF-PAST NINE Heinrich Böll	47860	2.75
CALL IT SLEEP Henry Roth	49304	2.50
A SINGLE MAN Christopher Isherwood	37689	1.95
CATALOGUE George Milburn	33084	1.95
THE CLOWN Heinrich Böll	37523	2.25
A COOL MILLION and **THE DREAM LIFE OF BALSO SNELL** Nathanael West	15115	1.65
DANGLING MAN Saul Bellow	24463	1.65
EDWIN MULLHOUSE Steven Millhauser	37952	2.50
THE EYE OF THE HEART Barbara Howes, Ed.	47787	2.95
THE FAMILY OF PASCUAL DUARTE Camilo José Cela	11247	1.45
GABRIELA, CLOVE AND CINNAMON Jorge Amado	18275	1.95
THE GALLERY John Horne Burns	33357	2.25
A GENEROUS MAN Reynolds Price	15123	1.65
GOING NOWHERE Alvin Greenberg	15081	1.65
THE GREEN HOUSE Mario Vargas Llosa	15099	1.65
GROUP PORTRAIT WITH LADY Heinrich Böll	48637	2.50
HERMAPHRODEITY Alan Friedman	16865	2.45
HOPSCOTCH Julio Cortázar	36731	2.95
HUNGER Knut Hamsun	42028	2.25
HOUSE OF ALL NATIONS Christina Stead	18895	2.45

SUN CITY Tove Jansson	32318	1.95
THE LANGUAGE OF CATS AND OTHER STORIES Spencer Hoist	14381	1.65
THE LAST DAYS OF LOUISIANA RED Ishmael Reed	35451	2.25
LEAF STORM AND OTHER STORIES Gabriel García Márquez	36816	1.95
LESBIAN BODY Monique Wittig	31062	1.75
LES GUERILLERES Monique Wittig	14373	1.65
THE LITTLE HOTEL Christina Stead	48389	2.50
A LONG AND HAPPY LIFE Reynolds Price	48132	2.25
LUCIFER WITH A BOOK John Horne Burns	33340	2.25
THE MAGNIFICENT AMBERSONS Booth Tarkington	17236	1.50
THE MAN WHO LOVED CHILDREN Christina Stead	40618	2.50
THE MAN WHO WAS NOT WITH IT Herbert Gold	19356	1.65
THE MAZE MAKER Michael Ayrton	23648	1.65
A MEETING BY THE RIVER Christopher Isherwood	37945	1.95
MYSTERIES Knut Hamsun	25221	1.95
NABOKOV'S DOZEN Vladimir Nabokov	15354	1.65
NO ONE WRITES TO THE COLONEL AND OTHER STORIES Gabriel García Márquez	32748	1.75
ONE HUNDRED YEARS OF SOLITUDE Gabriel García Márquez	45278	2.95
TENT OF MIRACLES Jorge Amado	41020	2.75
PNIN Vladimir Nabokov	40600	1.95
PRATER VIOLET Christopher Isherwood	36269	1.95
REAL PEOPLE Alison Lurie	23747	1.65
THE RECOGNITIONS William Gaddis	49544	3.95
SLAVE Isaac Singer	26377	1.95
A SMUGGLER'S BIBLE Joseph McElroy	33589	2.50
STUDS LONIGAN TRILOGY James T. Farrell	31955	2.75
SUMMERING Joanne Greenberg	17798	1.65
SWEET ADVERSITY Donald Newlove	38364	2.95
62: A MODEL KIT Julio Cortázar	17558	1.65
THREE BY HANDKE Peter Handke	32458	2.25

Where better paperbacks are sold, or directly from the publisher. Include 50¢ per copy for postage and handling, allow 4-6 weeks for delivery.

Avon Books, Mail Order Dept.

224 West 57th Street, New York, N.Y. 10019

BD (2) 2-80

BARD BOOKS
DISTINGUISHED DRAMA

THE ALCESTIAD Thornton Wilder	41855	2.25
ARMS AND THE MAN George Bernard Shaw	01628	.60
CANDIDE Lillian Hellman	12211	1.65
THE CHANGING ROOM, HOME, **THE CONTRACTOR: THREE PLAYS** David Storey	22772	2.45
DANTON'S DEATH Georg Büchner	10876	1.25
A DREAM PLAY August Strindberg	18655	.75
EQUUS Peter Shaffer	24828	1.75
THE FANTASTICKS Tom Jones and Harvey Schmidt	22129	1.65
GHOSTS Henrik Ibsen	22152	.95
HEDDA GABLER Henrik Ibsen	24620	.95
THE INSPECTOR GENERAL Nikolai Gogol	28878	.95
THE IMPORTANCE OF BEING EARNEST Oscar Wilde	46771	1.50
THE LOWER DEPTHS Maxim Gorky	18630	.75
MISS JULIE August Strindberg	36855	.95
OUR TOWN Thornton Wilder	45732	1.75
THE PLAYBOY OF THE WESTERN WORLD John Millington Synge	22046	.95
THE CHERRY ORCHARD Anton Chekhov	36848	.95
THE SEA GULL Anton Chekhov	24638	.95
THE SHADOW BOX Michael Cristofer	46839	2.25
THREE PLAYS BY THORNTON WILDER Thornton Wilder	48231	2.25
UNCLE VANYA Anton Chekhov	18663	.75
THE WILD DUCK Henrik Ibsen	23093	.95
WOYZECK Georg Büchner	10751	1.25